SONGKEEPER

Other books by Gillian Bronte Adams

The Songkeeper Chronicles

Orphan's Song

Songkeeper

Out of Darkness Rising

Songkeeper

The Songkeeper Chronicles — Book Two

Gillian Bronte Adams

an imprint of
GILEAD PUBLISHING

Songkeeper by Gillian Bronte Adams
Published by Enclave Publishing
an imprint of GIlead Publishing,
Wheaton, IL 60187
www.enclavepublishing.com

ISBN (paper): 978-1-62184-069-5

Cover Illustration and Design: Darko Tomic

Printed in the United States of America

For my beloved Grandpa Ken
You have a true craftsman's hands,
a heart that overflows with love,
and the strength of a warrior.
And you give the best hugs.
The great Amos McElhenny himself
would doff his feathered cap to you.

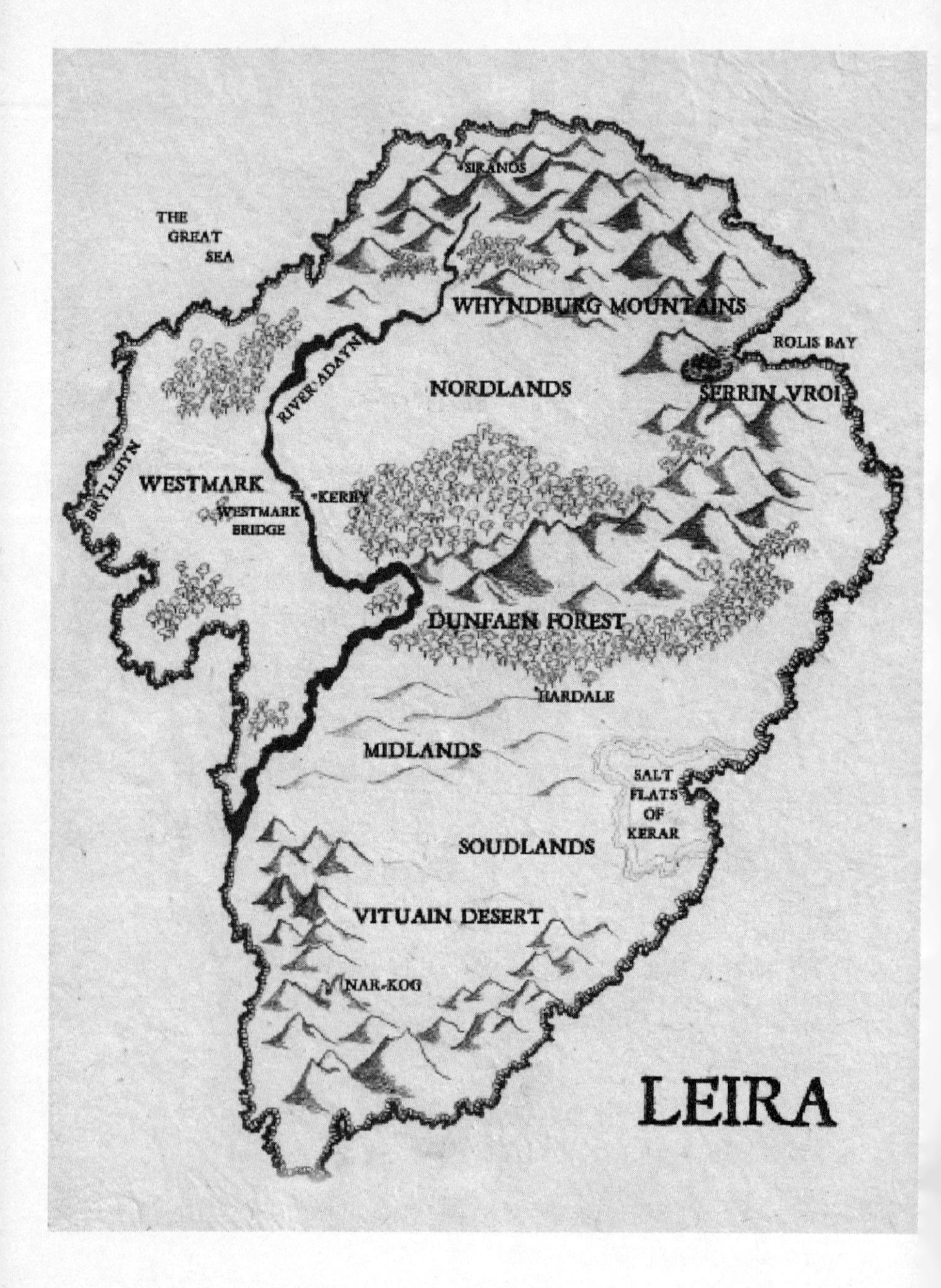
SIRANOS
THE GREAT SEA
WHYNDBURG MOUNTAINS
ROLIS BAY
RIVER ADAYN
NORDLANDS
SERRIN VROI
BRYLLHYN
WESTMARK
KERBY
WESTMARK BRIDGE
DUNFAEN FOREST
HARDALE
MIDLANDS
SALT FLATS OF KERAR
SOUDLANDS
VITUAIN DESERT
NAR-KOG
LEIRA

PART ONE

1

Silence rested on her shoulders like a crushing weight. The thumping of her heart magnified tenfold as Birdie strained her ears for the familiar melody—a cluster of notes that brought warmth and comfort to the soul, piercing despair with a glimmer of hope. Instead, she heard only the groaning timbers, crashing waves, and creaking blocks of the Langorian ship. Within the hold, chains rattled and muffled coughs echoed from the bulkheads, the sounds of the sick and dying.

Yet the Song remained silent.

A hand grazed her arm, and she started back.

"It's all right," Ky grunted. "It's just me."

She peered in the direction of his voice, though she knew she wouldn't be able to see his face through the gloom. A hacking cough came from somewhere to her right, punctuated by wheezing that sounded more like groaning. In the weeks since their capture, it had become a familiar sound. The herald of death.

Somewhere in the hold, a captive was dying. Alone, ignored, abandoned—even by his fellow prisoners. Though their hands were free, chains bound their ankles to the deck, restricting movement to a few feet in either direction, and anything above a whisper drew the wrath of their captors. No one would dare lift a voice in comfort or to call for aid.

She had witnessed it many times, felt it moving in herself, that hopelessness that deadens compassion. They were all made selfish in their fear. Weeks spent shackled in the hold with countless other poor souls, and she didn't even know who they were. Would they all die so in the weeks to come, forgotten?

Another strangled cough. Then silence.

Horrible, dead silence.

Her hands shook. She clutched them to her damp forehead and huddled with her elbows tucked into her body, but she couldn't stop them from shaking. Not even when the hatch flew open a few minutes later, releasing blinding light into the hold, and two pirates stumped down the ladder carrying buckets of stale water and hard bread. Her hands trembled as she choked down food, and as the pirates dragged the dead slave up the ladder and the hatch thudded shut behind them, plunging the hold back into night.

Outside, a loud splash, then something thumped against the side of the ship.

"Ky ..." She broke off with the name scarce spoken.

Even a whisper seemed disrespectful in this floating tomb.

"Yeah?"

The words sounded in her head, but somehow she couldn't muster the courage to get them past her tongue. How could she tell Ky she was sorry he had been dragged into her mess, that he should never have tried to help her, that she knew it was *her* fault he was a prisoner?

Chains clinked to her right, and his voice spoke beside her ear. "What is it?"

The rehearsed speech failed her, so she blurted out the first thing that came to mind—anything to distract from the terrible silence. "Do you ever think . . . What would you be doing right now if you were back in the Underground?"

"Probably running for my life." He snorted. An attempt at a laugh, but a pitiful one. "I tend to do that a lot." His chains clinked, indicating a shift of positions. "I just wish I could know they were all safe. Meli, Paddy, Aliyah, even Cade."

Or Amos.

Birdie couldn't bring herself to say his name out loud, but the thought of the gruff peddler brought a tear to her eyes. For all she knew, Amos McElhenny was dead, lying cold and forsaken on the beach where she had left him when the pirates dragged her away. She shoved her trembling hands into her lap and clenched them beneath her knees.

She might not be able to *will* her hands to stop shaking, but she could force them. This at least was something she could control.

Across the hold, a child gasped for breath.

The five broken notes of the child's melody filled Birdie's head. Weak as a candle quivering before a gust of wind. The sound tore Birdie to the heart.

"Why don't they help us?" Ky muttered. "It doesn't make a lick of sense. You'd think they'd give us a little light, air, fresh water, if only to keep us alive until they can sell us, instead of leaving us here to rot! Dead slaves aren't worth anything. Why do they let us die?"

Birdie knew the answer, but she couldn't bring herself to give it voice. Tales of the Langorian pirates had been a common subject of travelers' tales at the Sylvan Swan. The tales spoke of a brutal people who valued strength above all else. Pity was a thing unknown to them, for pity was weakness, and slaves in a hold were considered little more than cattle, worth only what they could bring on an ever flooded market. With a fast ship, a brisk wind, and a crew of swordsmen, new captives were ever ripe for the taking.

The child's cough faded, replaced by whimpering.

Ky slapped his palms against the deck. "I can't listen to this anymore. Please, Birdie, you have to help them. You did it before, didn't you? Why don't you do it again?"

Heat drained down the back of her neck, leaving her suddenly chilled. There was no need for him to explain what *it* was. For weeks she had been dreading this question.

"*Can't* you do it again? Heal them?"

Even though she couldn't see him, she could feel his gaze fixed on her, and oh, how she longed to say *yes*. But her hand flew to her neck instead, and she gently massaged her throat, fingers trembling over the bruise marks Carhartan's hands had left.

"I . . . I can't."

"But your voice is back now."

She nodded, but could not speak. Her *voice* had returned after Carhartan's attempt to choke her on the beach outside of Bryllhyn. But the Song itself was gone. It had mysteriously abandoned her, just like everything else. She still heard it all around her, five broken notes sung by dozens of different voices in dozens of different keys, tempos, and tones. Some she could trace to the captives near her, others to the pirates. Ky's voice was easily recognizable now. But the complete melody that had torn through the Westmark Bridge and scattered her foes in Bryllhyn, full of beauty and depth beyond anything she could describe, was distant. It hummed in the background, always just beyond reach.

The Song might be powerful, but it was a power she didn't understand and certainly couldn't control. *Little Songkeeper*, they called her—the pirates, Carhartan, even Gundhrold. But she could no more command the melody to her will than she could summon the tide.

The child moaned and the five-noted melody grew even fainter.

"I'm sorry, Ky." A tear slipped down Birdie's cheek. "I . . . I can't sing."

I don't know how.

"Do you fear me, little Songkeeper?"

The slow, heavily-accented voice of the Langorian pirate lord washed over her, and Birdie raised her eyes, still blinking at the daylight, to meet his gaze. It took every ounce of courage she had to endure his scrutiny without looking away. She swallowed to keep the truth from slipping past her lips and forced herself to stand straight though her head barely reached Rhudashka's barrel chest.

Of course she feared the man. How could she not? The deaths she had witnessed in Bryllhyn and the slaves rotting in the hold of his ship painted a vivid image of his character. Even now, the five notes of his melody coiled around her like a noose threatening to choke the life from her lungs, until she couldn't bear it anymore and broke free from his stare.

Overhead, sails strained against their lashings and taut rigging hummed in the wind. The scent of brine hung heavy in the air. Spray dashed over the side of the ship, soaking Birdie's dress and stinging the raw marks on her ankles where the chains had chaffed her skin. When the pirates hauled her above decks, they had released her from the heavy ankle irons that bound her to the ship. But before unlocking her chains, they secured her wrists with a pair of manacles on a length of chain that dangled like a lead on a dog.

"You *do* fear me." A grin spread across Rhudashka's face but failed to reach his eyes. He stood at the base of the foremost of the ship's two masts, an imposing figure shaped like a boulder, clad in a crimson knee-length robe over loose trousers, with gold chains around his neck and rings on his fingers. Dark hair billowed about his face, knotted in tangles by the swift breeze. He balanced with one hand on the rail, his ponderous bulk shifting deceptively easily with the motion of the sea.

With her hands chained, Birdie lurched and stumbled every time the ship swayed. Beside her, Ky didn't seem to be faring much better. But he at least had the "support" of the pirates flanking him on either side. For some reason, her guard stood a good three paces back.

Someone cuffed the side of her head. "Answer the captain, *naishka.*" Fjordair, Rhudashka's second in command, appeared in the corner of her vision: a slight figure in a loose blue tunic, shoulders hunched, fingers fiddling with the hilts of a dozen daggers stowed in the sash at his waist.

"Aw, come on." Ky wrestled with his guards' restraining hands. "What do you want her to say? Sure she's terrified. We both are. You cursed Langorians don't exactly have a shining reputation around—"

One of the pirates slammed his fist into Ky's stomach. He doubled over, groaning.

"Ky!" Birdie broke toward him, but Fjordair grabbed her chain and slung her back toward Rhudashka. She stumbled and fell.

The pirate lord loomed over her, crimson coat filling her vision, and then bent so his head was on a level with hers, his face only inches away. "My men, they fear you." His breath, flushed with brew, washed over her.

She shrank away from the stench and backed into Fjordair's legs. He yanked on the chain, hauling her up and roughly into place. The pirate lord continued. "They fear you will do something . . . terrible . . . to them. That you will *korsa* the sea and the wind with your *naian*—with your magic voice—and kill us all."

Birdie licked the salt from her lips and let her attention flicker to her guards. They *did* seem nervous—standing with weapons half drawn, eyes fixed alternately on her and on the deck planking beneath their feet, taut as a drawn crossbow string. One clutched a beaded scarf to the lower half of his face, as though he feared she carried some sort of infectious disease.

"My men think I take big risk bringing you aboard, but I know better." Rhudashka clucked his tongue at her. "You are but *naishka*, a young one. This thing you cannot do. Otherwise you would be free, and my ship, she would be at the bottom of *zahel*."

Birdie released a heavy breath. "What do you want from me?"

"We must reach an agreement, you and I. In one week, we reach Langoria. Korsakk Haitem is old. He will not live long. With you as my *Naian*—my Songkeeper—the other lords will see my strength, and I will become Korsakk in his stead."

His Songkeeper.

So she would not only be a slave, but a prize to be flaunted. A token of his victory. It wasn't completely unexpected. Even in Hardale, Birdie had heard talk of the Langorians and their fierce and barbaric king, the Korsakk. Still, hearing the words from Rhudashka, Birdie's mouth went dry.

But now was not the time for tame submission. The pirate lord might not fear her reputation as a Songkeeper, but the others did. Perhaps that could gain her something.

"You said this was an agreement?" Birdie tilted her head back and forced herself to stare Rhudashka in the eye. Strong, calm—that was what she needed to appear, even if everything within her trembled at her boldness. "Why should I agree?"

With an exaggerated sigh, Rhudashka flicked a hand as if shooing a troublesome fly.

Fjordair shoved Birdie forward. Unbalanced, she slammed into the rail and nearly pitched onto her face. Behind, a commotion broke out. Boots thudded across the deck. Cursing in a foreign tongue.

Then Ky cried out.

Birdie spun around. The thin pirate held Ky in a death grip, a dagger pressed to his throat. A grin split Fjordair's face as Ky struggled, feet scraping the deck.

"I make it plain," Rhudashka said. "You agree, or I kill little *zabid* . . . your friend, no?"

Birdie clenched her nails into her palms. In the background, she could hear the Song, but it was faint and seemed so very far away. Nothing at all like the times when it had leapt to her rescue. She closed her eyes and reached deep within to summon the melody. Her unspoken plea echoed in her ears, hopeless.

Empty.

Her eyes flew open as Rhudashka's hand settled on her shoulder, and she shrank from his touch. "You will be my *Naian*. You will sing when I say. You will do what I command. You will yield to my wishes, and I will protect you and little *zabid* here. But sing one false note, *Naian*, and Fjordair will go to work. He is a true artist with the blade. He would make great masterpiece out of your *zabid's* face."

Birdie's gaze dropped past her chained hands to her bare feet and the scarred planks of the deck. How could she do what Rhudashka demanded when she couldn't summon the Song or bend it to her will? When whatever power she was supposed to possess as the Songkeeper constantly eluded her?

Worse still, how could she be the *Songkeeper*, if she had no control over the Song?

Rhudashka's phlegmy rumble spoke next to her ear. "Think it over, *Naian*."

2

"Boggswogglin' varmints!" Amos tugged his feathered cap low over his forehead to shield his eyes from the pelting sand, and ducking his chin to his chest, pressed forward into the wind. "D' ye think we lost 'em?" A gust fairly tore the words from his lips, replacing them with a mouthful of grit.

"Perhaps." Gundhrold limped past, broken wing dragging the ground, leaving a trail of dust and torn feathers in his wake. Even wounded, the griffin set a pace that left Amos panting. "But we must hurry all the same."

"Hurry, aye, but hurry *where*?" Amos halted midstride and spread his arms wide to encapsulate the view. The Vituain desert surrounded them, vast in its nothingness. Miles upon miles of sand dunes punctuated by jagged rock spires and ringed by tall, craggy mountains. The nearest line of mountains stabbed up from the earth to their left, still a good half day's journey away.

Four weeks they'd been traveling. Four weeks since the skirmish near Bryllhyn, where Amos's mother was slain, and Birdie—the wee lass that he'd sworn to protect—was carried off by the cursed Langorian pirates. Four weeks on the road, forced to endure the company of the sanctimonious griffin. Journeying through a country gearing up for war, like a cornered beast preparing to turn and rend its attacker.

Amos glanced back over his shoulder. Some attackers deserved a bit of rending. There was still no sign of their shadows, though with all the wind gusting and sand whipping about, five Khelari could be easily missed. The foul slumgullions had been following them since they passed through Caacharen five days past. Apparently his recent exploits had resurrected the name of Hawkness . . . and the bounty on his head.

What with Gundhrold's injuries and his own wound sapping both their strength, he didn't much like the idea of a five on two fight. At least not until he'd made sure Birdie was safe.

With a sigh, he turned back to the griffin. "D' ye have any idea where we're goin'?"

"In truth, peddler?" The look of disgust on the griffin's face might have melted a less hardy man, but Amos McElhenny had walked the secret paths below Mount Eiphyr and witnessed the horrors of the Pit. He was not a man easily dismayed.

So he whispered to himself as the griffin's unblinking stare settled on him.

"Is your ignorance so blatant that you no longer care, or do you crouch behind the excuse of old age and its softening of memory?" Gundhrold's head lowered until his massive beak was only inches away from Amos's nose. "I am a son of the desert. This was once my home—the home of all my kind. I know every crag, every slope, every crick and hollow—"

Amos rolled his eyes. "Every blatherin' speck o' sand?"

"I know where I'm going. Don't interfere." The griffin padded off, broken wing still trailing the ground, leaving Amos racking his brain for a suitable insult for the . . . the . . . insufferable *beast.*

Try as he might, he couldn't find an insult harsh enough to satisfy his ire or sharp enough to truly ruffle the catbird's feathers. Another reason to dislike the griffin. Amos added it to his mental tally. So far the list covered a variety of annoyances from the catbird's repulsive eating habits—critters gulped down raw with much smacking, spattering, and cracking of bones—to his incessant need to *be in control.*

Boggswoggle! Was it so unreasonable to want to know where they were going?

He huffed a sigh and started after the griffin, adjusting the sword belt at his waist as he went. He took care to avoid touching the hilt. The weapon was wrapped in the tattered remnants of his cloak, but Amos had witnessed too many accidents in years past to risk direct contact with the sword.

"We must hasten, Hawkness!" Gundhrold called back. "Pray reserve your dawdling for a more opportune time. The storm is building. It will worsen ere nightfall. We must seek shelter while we may."

With a grunt, Amos jogged after the griffin, clutching a hand to his side. The wound was mostly healed, though it had a tendency to flare at the worst possible times. But right now, the wind did seem to be picking up, and he'd heard enough tales of the desert storms to know that they would not wish to be caught out in the open when it did.

Bilgewater! Why was the beast always right?

"Well done, beastie." Amos spat a glob of sand out of his mouth and brushed at his worn overcoat and trousers. Sand fell away in waves, though the worst of it seemed embedded in the fabric itself and in the skin beneath. "Hundreds o' miles o' desert, an' ye manage t' pick the one section with only a wee rock outcropping t' shelter beneath. Brilliant, aye, just brilliant."

Gundhrold shook like a dog, releasing a cloud of sand into the air.

"Oi!" Amos swung his hands in front of his face, scattering the cloud. "Careful, beast." He set his back to the outcrop, swiped the sand from his eyes, and peered out at the desert stretching endlessly before his feet, quiet and still now that the fury of the sand storm had passed. Almost too quiet.

The griffin sniffed and flapped his good wing, stirring up a final poof of dust. "I am responsible for choosing our path, peddler. The landscape is no fault of mine. None of the other outcroppings were remotely near our route. A route which I believe you insisted be short, swift, and to the point."

Indeed he had.

Given the past four weeks of fair weather and swift winds, the pirates should be nearing the southern tip of Leira on their way to the island of Langoria. In rounding the tip, their vessel would come within a few miles of shore, giving Amos his best hope of *somehow* intercepting the ship and rescuing Birdie. He was still a wee bit fuzzy on the details.

But once the Langorians passed the tip …

"Coming, peddler?" Gundhrold stalked out from beneath the shelter of the outcrop without a backward glance. "I believe the Songkeeper is waiting."

Amos gritted his teeth and strode after him. Once again, he'd been left staring, without the faintest inkling of a cutting response. He must be losing his grip. It was growing downright tiresome.

"Hawkness!"

The griffin's roar startled him out of his pained reverie. He stumbled back and smashed into the rocks behind. Just in time. A spear thwacked into the sand at his feet and stuck there, quivering.

His hand brushed Artair's sword as he reached for his dirk. Out in the sand about fifteen yards away, the griffin faced off with three figures in dark armor—Khelari. Amos's blood boiled at the sight. Seemed their *shadows* had caught up with them at last.

But only three?

Acting on instinct, Amos flung himself to the side, rolled away from the outcropping—straining his wounded side—and came up in a fighting position, dirk drawn. A second spear clattered off the rock face where he had been standing a moment before.

The remaining two Khelari emerged around the side of the outcrop, spears in hand. Bloodwuthering blodknockers! The dirk might be Amos's favorite weapon, but it did have its limitations. No denying that. Limitations that included fully armored men with spears.

"Surrender, Hawkness!" the first soldier called as they inched nearer. "Give it up. You can't escape now."

Up close, they seemed a ragged pair. Rusted mail, tattered leathers, dented helms. Not quite the level of spit and polish Amos expected from the Takhran's everywhere victorious army. Maybe conquering the known world was turning out to be more difficult than the Takhran had anticipated.

The first soldier halted a few paces away and rocked back on his heels, puffing out his chest. "Takhran's got quite the bounty on your head, boyo. Wouldn't care to be standing in your shoes. You see, he didn't exactly specify whether he wanted the rest of you along with the head or not, and the Hawkness's killers, well, they'll go down in history. What do you think, Royd?"

The second Khelari—Royd—scratched his grizzled beard with a gauntleted hand. "I say we save on transportation costs and just bring the head. Less painful for him, less trouble for us, Takhran's happy either way."

Less trouble?

Pair of crook-pated moldwarps.

Amos spun into the attack, slamming his dirk at the open face of Royd's helmet. The man *was* a moldwarp, no doubt about that, but he had been trained for battle. Sudden as the attack came, he flung up his spear and deflected the blow, barely.

Amos allowed the force of the deflection to carry him past Royd to where the first spear still stood upright in the ground. He plucked it up and spun to face the two Khelari, dirk in one hand, spear held in a one-handed thrusting grip in the other.

The soldiers circled warily, alternately jabbing with their spears and shuffling back whenever he responded with a move of his own. Maintaining their distance—a smart move. It proved his reputation was still good for something. But the first soldier kept pressing farther and farther to the right—another smart move.

If the soldier got behind him …

Amos spun and threw his dirk at the soldier's head. A hasty throw and a longshot. It bounced harmlessly off his helm, but the soldier stumbled back. Before he could recover, Amos sprang on him and rammed the spear through a gap in the man's armor.

A scream burst from the soldier's throat, and he collapsed like a felled zoar tree, landing with such force that Amos's spear snapped, leaving him holding the broken haft.

Movement caught the corner of his eye.

Amos twisted around in time to parry Royd's thrust with the

broken spear. He retreated, wielding the haft one handed, as one might a sword. His fingers found the wrappings covering Artair's blade. If ever there was an excuse to handle the weapon, this was it.

But somehow, he couldn't bring himself to do it.

He forced his hand away from the hilt.

The Khelari's spear slammed into the broken haft. It flew out of Amos's hand and clattered against the outcrop. A swipe of the spear knocked his legs out from under him, throwing him to the ground. He struck his head, hard. Darkness blurred the edge of his vision, and cold metal bit into his throat, preventing him from rising.

Royd sneered at him, breath wheezing through clenched teeth. "I expected more from the *great Hawkness*! Growing slow in your old age, pappy? You'd better hope—"

A roar drowned the rest of the Khelari's words. Something huge and tawny rammed into Royd, knocking him out of the way. Screams stabbed Amos's ears and then suddenly cut off, replaced by the heavy, snuffling breaths of the beast.

Crookneedles! Saved by Gundhrold again. The griffin was making quite the unhealthy habit out of this. He'd never hear the end of it now. Stifling a groan, Amos sat up and found himself looking into a pair of dark brown, almond-shaped eyes set in an even darker face.

He groped for his dirk.

One of the Saari, the desert dwellers.

"Steady now, *pappy*. I have no interest in hurting you." The Saari flashed a quick smile and brought the tip of a spear to his forehead in salute. "Don't tax yourself. I will help your friend." In a whirl of flying braids and animal hide, the warrior spun around and dashed away, shouting, "Inali! I swear, if you don't get out here, I will …"

The rest of the warrior's threat lapsed into the strange, guttural language of the desert, leaving Amos in ignorance of the unknown Inali's imminent fate.

He staggered to his feet in time to see his rescuer leap into the fray, mounted on the back of a lion. A *lion*! No mistaking the beast, with that tawny fur and mountainous mane, and teeth as large as daggers. He'd heard tales that the Saari rode such beasts into battle, but never imagined to see it. In truth, it was a tad disappointing. Next to Gundhrold, the beast looked small, though still massive compared to its rider, who nearly disappeared in the thicket of mane.

With a wild cry, the Saari dove from the lion's back and hit the ground running, spear in hand. The lion pounced on the nearest Khelari, driving him to the ground, and the Saari dispatched him with a well-placed blow.

In a few moments, the Saari and Gundhrold had felled the last of the Khelari and stood among the corpses, panting.

"Skilled, isn't she?

Amos nearly dropped his dirk at the unexpected voice. A young Saari warrior stood beside him, skin the dull bronze of the desert. He clutched the upright shaft of his spear in two hands, point buried in the sand, cheek pressed against the haft. Hair the color and consistency of dried earth hung in knotted strands to his shoulders, interwoven with clay beads. A pair of spectacles perched on the bridge of his nose.

Unusual that, in a warrior.

"What d' ye …" Amos's voice trailed away.

A lioness padded over and flopped at the young man's feet to lick her paws. He didn't seem to notice, just pointed toward the distant Saari warrior now speaking to Gundhrold. "Sym. She's quite a fighter."

She …

Amos's brain began to catch up. His rescuer *was* a woman, he could see that now. Young too, like the warrior at his side. She wore her dark hair bound behind her head in intricate braids and was clad in a sleeveless tunic that looked to be made from lion's skin.

"But how …"

Out of the corner of his eye, he saw the young man tuck a roll of parchment into the satchel he wore over one shoulder, then straighten and throw his head back. "I am Dah Inali, brother to Sa Itera, wife of Matlal Quahtli."

From the way he uttered the names, Amos had no doubt they meant *something* important. But he was a wee bit rusty on current desert happenings. He seized the young man's hand and shook it. "I'm . . . Hawkness."

"Hawkness?" Inali blinked. His left eye twitched, revealing a thin scar carved down across his eyebrow. "I have heard of you."

"Figures," Amos muttered and limped over to retrieve his dirk. There were problems with having a reputation like his. Folks either wanted your hide or wanted your help to save theirs. There was never any happy, indifferent middle ground.

"Who *hasn't* heard of the great exploits of Hawkness?" A hoarse, woman's voice spoke behind him. His rescuer stood with Gundhrold at her side and the male lion at her heels. She was even smaller than he'd imagined—her head barely reached his shoulder. But if he'd learned anything from the Creegnan brothers, Jirkar and Nisus—fighting dwarves of the Whyndburg Mountains—it was that size had no bearing on skill.

"And to think I called you pappy!" Still clutching her spear, she crossed her arms over her chest and glanced him up and down. Bilges, but she was a bold one. "I have heard tell no one bandies insults with Hawkness and lives."

Gundhrold sniffed. "Rumors."

Amos grinned at the beast's discomfiture. "Aye, but truth is oft stranger than rumor. Don't worry though, I'll let it slide. Just this once."

"I see." She snapped the spear out to the side in salute. "I am Sym Yandel. The great one tells me you seek the aid of my people in a matter of urgency?"

Amos cocked an eyebrow at Gundhrold, but the griffin merely preened his neck feathers with his beak. *Well then* ...

"Aye, we seek the aid o' yer people."

Inali slowly shook his head. "It is not our way to aid strangers, but these are dangerous times. We may all have need of aid in the near future. And what man who claims to oppose the Takhran could refuse aid to Hawkness?"

Sym whipped her spear back over her shoulder and slid it beside two other spears in a long quiver strapped to her back. "You travel in the company of a lord of the desert. What choice do we have? You are both welcome to the hospitality of my people. The Matlal will hear your plea. I will escort you to him."

3

The acrid scent of danger filled the air, overwhelming the tang of salt water, rotting fish, even stinking pirate. Paused on the top rung of the hatchway ladder, Ky took a long whiff and blinked to allow his eyes to adjust to daylight. During his years in the Underground, he had gotten pretty good at sniffing out trouble.

And this—whatever *this* was—did not bode well.

Fjordair yanked the chain connected to the manacles on his wrists. "*Ahtesh!*"

It didn't take a scholar in the Langorian tongue to understand the pirate's meaning or the significance of the hand straying to his belt full of daggers. With a sigh, Ky scrambled out of the hatchway, giving Birdie room to climb up behind.

Pirates lined the deck, some lounging against the rails, others hanging haphazard from the rigging, all faces turned toward the hatch. They might not possess the rigid discipline of the dark soldiers, but that didn't make them any less dangerous. Ky shifted beneath the weight of so many eyes focused on him and moistened his dry lips with his tongue.

Fjordair jerked him forward and the surrounding pirates shuffled aside, clearing an opening to the raised stern deck where the massive bulk of Lord Rhudashka loomed beside the helmsman. Over his shoulder, Ky caught a glimpse of Birdie's white face.

"Ah, little *Naian!*" Lord Rhudashka stepped forward, jowls stretched in a smile that looked more like a grimace. Maybe he'd gotten a whiff of the stink from the hold on their clothes. "We are . . . honored . . . to have you in our company. You have decided, yes?" The pirate lord rubbed his hands together, rings flashing on his fingers. "You will become my *Naian*, my Songkeeper?"

Birdie did not reply.

Ten seconds . . . then fifteen …

Ky studied the wood grains in the deck planking. Better that than meet Birdie's gaze and see the decision in her eyes—or worse, let her see the fear in his. No matter what she chose, it wasn't likely to end well for him, and he could still feel the cold edge of Fjordair's blade against his cheek.

Slicing into his skin.

He shuddered.

Sure Rhudashka had promised to protect him if she agreed to help, but the way Ky saw it, he was expendable. Birdie didn't need his help with her *magical* song, so the pirates couldn't much care whether he lived or died. He was just in the way.

The feeling was uncomfortably familiar.

"I …" Birdie's voice broke, and he couldn't help peeking over at her. She looked so small and pale standing before the vast crimson girth of the pirate lord. "I . . . I can't."

A knife sliced across Ky's cheek.

He gasped at the pain.

Warm blood dripped down his neck and soaked his collar. Fjordair seized him by the hair and dragged him beneath one arm. He gagged at the stench of unwashed pirate, then caught his breath as the tip of the knife trailed across his right eyelid. A tremor clutched his limbs. Cold panic rooted in his stomach.

He closed his eyes and fought the urge to be sick.

Couldn't she have just agreed?

Birdie shouted something, but her voice seemed to come from far away. He couldn't make out the words. Whatever she said just seemed to rile Fjordair. The pirate jerked and the knife gouged a line across Ky's temple.

He uttered a cry and clamped his teeth around the sound. It couldn't end like this. Not now. Not after promising Meli he would return.

He *would* keep his promise.

"Stop!"

Small hands seized his own. He forced his eyes open. Birdie stood between him and the other pirates, head thrown back, dark hair floating in the cross-breezes of the sea wind. Tears glistened on her cheeks.

She spoke to the pirate lord without turning. "Please, Lord Rhudashka, don't hurt him. It's not that I *won't*. I just can't. I don't know how to do what you want." There were no tears in her voice. She sounded hard, almost brittle. "I'm no true Songkeeper."

The pirate lord's face darkened and a space cleared around him as the other pirates shuffled back. "Ah, little *Naian*, such power hindered by such ignorance. The way of the *Naian* can only be learned through pain. You claim you know not how. You must learn. Suffering will teach you."

Ky found it hard to swallow. He had to do something . . . speak up . . . protect her . . . somehow. But nothing he said would make them heed his demands. Except for the whole carve-his-face-into-bits incident, they'd practically ignored him this entire time.

Not that he was complaining.

Better a pawn than the prize.

"Don't kill him," Rhudashka said. "Not yet."

Wait . . .

Before Ky completely processed the words, Fjordair shoved him. He landed hard on his knees and buckled forward, slamming his forehead into the side of the ship. A booted foot crashed into his side. The air escaped his lungs in a groan.

"What are you doing?" Birdie cried. "Leave him alone!"

Ky pushed up onto his hands and knees and shook his head to clear his blurred vision. The motion felt thick and sluggish, like someone had wrapped a thick cloak around his head.

Something struck his arm. Pain shot through his wrist. He crashed on his face and rolled into a ball, clutching his throbbing wrist to his chest. Blows came hard and fast, and he didn't even try to defend himself. Just stayed in a ball, waiting for it to end.

So this was why he was still breathing.

At least something finally made sense. He was their whipping boy. Leverage. The strings they tugged to force Birdie to become their puppet.

Good luck with that.

"So." Matlal Quahtli, chief of the Saari, drew the word out as if savoring the flavor. His hazel eyes—startlingly light against his dark skin—narrowed at Amos. "You are Hawkness."

Amos scrubbed his sweaty hands on his sand-crusted trousers, painfully aware of Gundhrold's piercing glare also burrowing into the back of his skull. Ever since Sym and Inali agreed to lead them to the Matlal, the griffin had warned him repeatedly not to say anything to offend their host. Probably with good cause. Amos's tongue had a way of running off on its own, and the Saari apparently were a touchy people.

Best not to say anything yet.

He shifted on his heels, boots scraping on the rough stone floor. The sound echoed through the Council Hall, a vast chamber carved into the cliff face of Nar with one side open to the valley below. Matlal Quahtli stood with his back to the opening, presenting an imposing silhouette against the afternoon sun—a warrior's figure clad in a massive lion skin cloak, mane forming a collar about his neck, spear held upright in his hand. Gold beads rattled in his dark braids, and jeweled cuffs gleamed on his wrists.

"Outlaw . . . thief . . . peddler." Quahtli sounded almost amused. "Hero *and* despoiler of Kerby. Sworn enemy of the Takhran. You have worn many guises over the years." He took a step forward, and all humor vanished from his voice. "I wonder . . . which guise do you wear today?"

Amos cleared his throat, racking his brain for a suitable response. One that preferably didn't include any name calling or insultery—a feat in and of itself. Just how *was* one supposed to respond to a question like that?

"A different guise altogether. One I'm not over-fond o' wearin'."

Quahtli raised an eyebrow. "And that would be?"

"I stand before ye as a humble servant t' petition ye for aid, great Matlal. In return, I offer my service in your struggle against the Takhran."

"The great Hawkness offers us his service?" A voice spoke behind him—a deep, mellow woman's voice. "Well then, our fight is as good as won."

Bristling at the implied insult, Amos twisted his neck around to see the speaker. A woman emerged from the shadows of the arched entrance and crossed the Council Hall on sandaled feet. Her scarlet robe stood out against the dull red of the stone like a patch of blood. Tawny hair hung in beaded locks to her waist. A white lioness padded at her heels, two small boys seated on its back.

Quahtli extended a hand to the woman and drew her to his side. "My wife, Sa Itera."

"Hawkness." Itera tilted her head to one side, studying Amos.

He pulled the feathered cap from his head and fought the urge to retreat before the onslaught of yet another scrutiny. Itera was tall, her head level with Quahtli's, leaving Amos wishing for just a few more inches. He resented having to look *up* at anyone.

The white lioness flopped to the ground at his feet, breath expelling from her lungs in an audible huff, and the boys tumbled, giggling, off her back into the space between her forepaws. Purring like a thunderstorm, the lioness licked their heads with her great, pink tongue.

Revealing a set of massive, curved teeth.

Amos started forward, reaching for his dirk, but the lioness looked up at his movement and growled deep in her throat. He halted. "Um . . . is it wise t' let the beastie do that?"

Quahtli's brow furrowed. "We are the Saari."

As if that explained anything at all.

The lioness practically had the lads' heads in her jaws now—jaws that could split their skulls as easily as Amos could snap his fingers. He forced himself to look away, fighting the queasiness in his stomach.

Itera was speaking. ". . . exploits are known even here in the desert. It is wondrous—the stuff of legends."

Gundhrold chuckled, breaking his self-imposed silence for the first time since Sym and Inali had shown them into the Council Hall. "Indeed. Pure legend, most of it, but that is beside the point. Matlal Quahtli, Sa Itera, there is no time to lose. The Songkeeper has been captured by Langorian pirates who sail along the southern coast even as we speak. If we make haste, we can intercept them before they round the tip and should be able to free the Songkeeper, but we will require your assistance if we are to succeed."

Require?

And the beastly catbird had been worried Amos might come across too strong?

Quahtli broke away from Itera and halted on the edge overlooking the valley, lion skin cloak ruffling in the dry desert breeze. "You say you require my aid to rescue your Songkeeper, but you offer no reason why I should give it. My people prepare for a battle we cannot win in a war intended for our destruction." He turned around and folded his arms across his bare chest. "Why should I risk their safety to rescue a legend?"

Amos studied the sun-bleached toes of his boots. This was one question Gundhrold would have to handle. After only recently being forced to admit the existence of the Songkeepers, Amos hardly made the best advocate.

The griffin tossed his head, neck feathers bristling like the lion's mane about Quahtli's neck. "I am a son of the desert and the last of my kind. Believe that I speak true when I say that the safety of the desert children is foremost in my mind. Legend or not, the Songkeeper may be the best hope we have of resisting the Takhran."

Sa Itera placed a gentle hand on Quahtli's arm. "Not just a legend. You know this."

Quahtli turned away. "I will speak with Hawkness. In private."

Without a word, Sa Itera and Gundhrold stepped back into the shadows of the Council Hall. Even the lioness padded after them, dragging the two boys by the back of their fringed trousers, leaving Amos alone with the chief. Quahtli beckoned him to the edge. He paused with the toes of his boots jutting out over a hundred foot drop and surveyed the surrounding city and the valley below.

The city climbed up both sides of the cliffs flanking the valley, buildings simultaneously carved from the sand-blasted rock and built into it. Narrow bridges connected the two halves, Nar and Kog. Rough workmanship all of it. Functional, strong, but with none of the unnecessary embellishments common elsewhere in Leira. Here there was no point to adornments. The desert claimed all sooner or later. Before the force of the sand storms and the endless wearing of the wind, ornaments would crumble. But this city would endure. It was, Amos realized, as much a thing of the desert as the cliffs on which it was built and the Saari warriors who had built it.

"The Khelari are coming."

Quahtli's voice sliced through the silence, recalling Amos to his purpose.

"Daily my warriors skirmish with the Takhran's soldiers on our northern borders. It is only a matter of time before his army marches into this valley. And what then? I must either surrender my people and our freedom to his rule, or see their corpses lie cold and prey to carrion fowl in the sand." Quahtli fingered the tip of his spear. "We are too few to fight him."

"So it has ever been." Amos clasped his wrists behind his back, coaxing the stiff muscles in his wounded side to stretch. "We are always too few."

"But fight we will."

Amos huffed a laugh. "Aye, 'cause that's what we do. Ye and I. We're warriors. It's how we lived an' it's how we'll die, fightin' till the last breath leaves our lungs an' our bodies cling t' the dust whence we came. It's the only thing we know."

He gestured at the balcony of a sand-worn house on the opposite cliff where a Saari woman was just visible, rocking her baby to sleep. "But what about them? Don't they deserve better 'n that? If there's the slightest chance ye might be able t' protect 'em, hadn't ye ought t' take it?"

"The slightest chance. Is that what this is?" Quahtli fell silent a moment, then his stern face relaxed into an expression Amos suspected was meant to be a smile. "Then yes, you are right, I must take it. Options are scarce, and promises of aid are few and far between. Two more warriors are nothing, even if they are Hawkness and the Songkeeper, but hope—that is a rare gift. I shall give what aid I may to rescue the Songkeeper, and in return, you both will help protect my people and inspire their hearts to courage when hope fails. What do you need?"

Bleating bollywags, that had gone quicker—and calmer—than he'd expected.

Amos tugged his feathered cap over his forehead and rattled off the agreed upon list. "Oh the usual. Weapons, supplies, any warriors ye can spare. Oh, an' transportation t' the coast, if ye don't mind."

"Is that it?" Quahtli hefted his spear over one shoulder. "Are you sure there isn't anything *else* I can do for you?"

Was that a trace of sarcasm in the chief's voice? It would appear king stone-face had a sense of humor after all. "That should about cover it, but if I think o' aught else, I'll let ye know."

Amos turned to leave, but Quahtli's voice stopped him midstride.

"It was said that Hawkness stood apart and swore allegiance to no ruler, divine or otherwise. How then do you now seek the Songkeeper? Are you willing to bow to a master's will? Do you believe she can help us?"

Cool bronze met Amos's questing hand. He rubbed a finger along the familiar swoop of the hawk's head pommel of his dirk.

What did he believe?

Birdie was the Songkeeper, no doubt about that. He'd seen far too much to try denying it anymore. But that didn't mean he was ready to acknowledge Emhran's lordship. Not yet at least. The old catbird was the one convinced Birdie could somehow save them all.

All he wanted was to see her safe.

He shifted his weight to the other foot, twisting to meet Quahtli's frown. "Aye, I do."

It was boggswoggling how easily the lie slipped past his tongue.

• • •

The blows continued even after Ky's groans lapsed into silence.

"Stop. Please, please, stop." Birdie's voice was so hoarse from begging, she could scarce hear the words over Fjordair's rasping breath as he pummeled Ky's limp form again.

And again.

"Sing, little *Naian*." Rhudashka's breath fell hot against her ear. His eyes glittered with unfettered desire. "Sing if you wish it to stop. If you wish to save little *zabid*."

"I can't." Birdie clenched her fists until her arms shook with the force, rattling the manacles on her wrists. She stumbled to the ship's rail and leaned forward, breathing in the crisp sea air and letting the spray wash the tears from her face. "I can't."

I must.

Chest heaving with constrained sobs, Birdie clung to the rail and closed her eyes. The dull thud of Fjordair's blows seemed to slow in the background. It scarce surprised her to hear the dark melody skirling in and out among the rhythm of the beating.

But the Song . . . *the Song* . . . where was the Song?

Where are you?

Faint on her ear, she caught a trace of it dancing through the deep throb of the ocean waves. Distant but not absent. Full, powerful, beautiful—just as she remembered it. A burst of sunlight in the midst of a storm. It rose to greet her like an old friend.

She grasped at the thread of melody and pulled with all her strength. She was the Songkeeper. The Song *must* answer her call. But she might as well have tried to pull down the stone walls of Kerby barehanded.

The melody refused to answer her summons.

She tugged harder and it retreated.

Head reeling, Birdie collapsed against the rail, legs too weak and exhausted to support her frame. The sobs she had been trying to hold back ever since her capture spilled at last, and she no longer cared that the pirates witnessed her weakness . . . and her shame.

Rhudashka's heavy voice washed over her. "You are weak, little *Naian*. Your friend suffers, yet you do nothing to help him. You are—"

A babble of Langorian broke out behind, cutting Rhudashka off midsentence.

Birdie slid down to her knees and rested her forehead against the rail. It was no use. No matter how she tried, she couldn't control the Song. Couldn't control anything. The sea breeze swept around her, tugging at her matted hair and lifting it from her shoulders. A cool drop spattered the back of her hand.

She raised her head.

A wall of dark clouds swept across the sky toward the Langorian ship. The breeze increased to a steady wind carrying the scent of rain in its gusts. Waves billowed and grew until they were the size of the hills surrounding the Sylvan Swan, back in faraway Hardale.

It was a storm . . . a storm at sea . . . and it would reach them in a moment.

The deck erupted in a flurry of motion. Pirates hurried this way and that, resetting sails, coiling lines, lashing down any loose cargo on deck. Rhudashka barked a command, and two pirates scooped up Ky and tossed him down into the hold.

Rhudashka turned to her. "We are not finished, little *Naian*. There is much more you still have to learn. The storm, it has given you little . . . reprieve. We will speak again." He motioned with one hand, and Fjordair seized Birdie's manacles and dragged her back to the hold.

She stopped on the top rung and caught Fjordair's arm before he flung her down into the hatch. "I won't let you hurt him again. I *will* stop you."

An empty threat, but she could do no more.

Fjordair simply barked a laugh and shoved her down the ladder. She crashed against the filthy floor of the hold and lay where she had fallen, too weary and sickened to try to move.

The hatch slammed shut.

4

"Please be all right, Ky. You have to be okay." Birdie muttered the words beneath her breath, working feverishly to tear a strip from her skirt. In the chaos of the storm's onset, the pirates had left the manacles on her wrists but forgotten to chain her to the deck. Or perhaps they had simply realized that it didn't matter. Ankle irons or no, there was no escaping from the hold. At least now she had some freedom of movement to tend Ky's injuries. Outside, the storm howled and the ship shuddered before its force. Roaring waves, wind like thunder, and the creak and groan of straining timbers filled her ears. The ship tilted to one side, and she skidded forward, chains digging into her wrists. She caught herself and scrambled backward to press against the side of the ship, bracing her feet on the slick floor.

Her heel struck something soft—Ky. She felt for his limp form and tugged until his head rested in her lap, cradled from the battering fury of the sea. Newly torn rag in hand, she bent over him again. In the darkness of the hold, she could hardly see her own hands, let alone Ky's face. But she could feel the warm stickiness seeping through the cloth and coating her fingers.

Blood . . . on her hands.

She drew in a shuddering breath. It was fitting. Ky had been injured because of her. Because of who she was and what she was supposed to be. Because she had failed. It was starting all over again. Others suffering because of her. *Instead* of her.

Gritting her teeth, Birdie allowed the pain of the thought to wash over her. The ache—she drowned in it. As if the sorrow she felt could somehow atone for her inability to change *anything.*

A hand gripped her arm.

She started and the rag slipped from her fingers.

"What . . . happened?" Ky's groan was barely audible over the raging wind.

"Ky." She gasped in relief and only just managed to steady the quake in her voice before she responded. "Ky . . . are you all right?"

"Dunno." His words slurred together, voice so low she had to tilt her head forward to hear. "Still in . . . one piece?"

"Yes."

He grunted. "Good. Wasn't too keen . . . on old Crazy-knives . . . practicing his artistry."

Birdie felt for the rag and clutched it in her lap. Why *had* Fjordair put aside his knives? He hadn't been bluffing when he threatened to carve Ky's face. So why just the beating and not the knives?

Her stomach churned. She couldn't escape the feeling that this was just a short reprieve, a ploy to set her at ease, before the real danger began. Next time, it would be the knives and not the fists. She had to figure out how to master the Song before then.

"I'm sorry," she whispered. "So sorry."

"Yeah, well, sometimes there's nothing you can do."

Words had never sounded so hollow. She could hear the lie in his tone. He didn't believe it any more than she did.

Ky's head lifted and his shoulder brushed against hers as he sank back against the side of the ship and then scooted away. Silence hung between them, so thick Birdie felt she could reach a hand out and touch it. Behind her, the ocean roared, beating angry fists against the side of the ship. Was it just her imagination, or was it getting louder?

"She probably thinks I'm dead by now, or taken by the dark soldiers. Meli . . . she was waiting for me to come back. I promised."

Birdie's breath caught in her throat and she searched in vain for a reply.

"I *promised.*"

She twisted the rag around her fingers. "I know."

What was it he'd said? *Sometimes there's nothing you can do.* Maybe sometimes promises had to be broken. Maybe sometimes you were doomed to failure from the start, no matter how hard you fought. But acknowledging your own helplessness was no consolation—if anything, it just made you feel worse.

The ship tilted suddenly, sending her skidding to the right. Splinters of coarse wood stabbed into her hands. She slammed into something that yielded to her touch—tattered cloth draped over a thin, bony frame. A slave. He groaned and broke into a hacking cough.

Grimy fingers clutched her shoulder. Birdie scrambled back, hands and feet slipping on the slimy deck. The ship settled, throwing her against the side wall.

The storm was getting worse.

Over the years, she had overheard plenty of sea-faring tales of hurricane winds and endless storms from the sailors and travelers who frequented the Sylvan Swan. But their stories failed to capture the true force and terror of a gale at sea. The ship was tossed about like a child's plaything, utterly at the mercy of the wind and the waves. It had no control. Its rudders and sails were as frail as twigs and cobwebs before the storm.

Birdie set her back to the wall beside Ky and hunkered down with her arms clasped around her knees. How could anything survive such a pounding?

Lion stink clogged the air. Amos's hands reeked of it, and no doubt his clothes did too. It clung to everything with the tenacity of a limpet. Foul beasts. Wouldn't have been his first choice for transportation, but the Saari had offered, and he had gotten the distinct impression that they had accorded him some high honor. That wasn't the sort of offer a desperate man refused. Not when he wished to make allies.

His lion stumbled, and he clutched at the steering collar to keep from falling. "Bilgewater!"

"Easy, there, pappy." Ahead, Sym casually swung her legs so she was sitting turned around in the strange contraption the Saari had the audacity to call a saddle. Propping her heels on the lion's hind-quarters, she leaned back against the raised pommel. Her lion tossed his mane but otherwise didn't seem to mind her unusual position, and somehow she managed to effortlessly keep her seat through the beast's strange, rolling gait.

Backwards.

She grinned at Amos, eyes creased into a smile so tight they almost disappeared behind her high cheekbones. "Best hold on. It would not do to suffer casualties on the road to the battle. I hear that sort of thing is frowned upon in legends."

Amos simply growled in response, too preoccupied with staying in his saddle on *his* lion to manage anything more eloquent. Through the cloud of dust stirred by their passing, he surveyed the company of Saari warriors surrounding him, all mounted on lions of their own. Matlal Quahtli, it would appear, was a man of his word, and his forces mobilized with the quickness of a desert sand storm. Scarce an hour after their meeting, he had informed Amos and Gundhrold that the Saari were ready to depart.

Now mid-way through the third day of their journey from Nar-Kog, Amos almost dared hope they would arrive in time.

If he didn't die first, that was.

With a grunt, his lion lurched up the side of a rise. Amos dropped the steering collar and gripped the beast's shaggy mane with both hands. "Fiddlesticks and roughnash! Steady on there, ye fool beast."

Sym chuckled and dismissed his fears with a wave of her hand, then spun around in the saddle and urged her lion ahead to stroll beside Gundhrold at the front of the line.

Beswoggle and *confound* that lass.

Amos reached for the steering collar again. He had been accustomed to riding the occasional farm-horse in his former line of work—nags really, nothing so grand as a warhorse or battle-trained steed. But even then, he occasionally had the luxury of riding in a saddle, and this *devilish* contraption full of straps and buckles and fringed leather flaps, mounted on the back of a massive lion, was a far cry from anything he had seen before.

As if that weren't enough, the bush-pated beast progressed in an awkward series of leaps and bounds. Sure it might have been graceful to watch, but it was boggswoggling uncomfortable to ride. No wonder the Saari warriors were as much a matter of legend throughout Leira as Hawkness himself. They must have hides made of steel plates.

Amos vented his frustration in a muttered, "Boggswoggle."

"Been talking to Sym, haven't you?" Inali came abreast of Amos, all lanky arms and legs and loose elbows. He bent over his lioness's neck, peering after Sym's retreating figure, and shook his head ruefully. "She has that effect on people."

Was that a trace of wistfulness Amos detected in the young warrior's tone? He cocked an eyebrow and received all the answer he needed when Inali ducked his dark head and avoided his gaze. Amos suppressed a grin.

To all appearances, young Inali was smitten.

The line of Saari ahead slowed and came to a halt. Amos's lion—thankfully—stopped on its own with its nose to the tail of the lion before him. Preoccupied with maintaining balance as he was, stopping and steering were more of an afterthought than anything else.

"What is it?" He glanced at Inali. "Why are we stopping?"

The young warrior simply shrugged and raised a hand to adjust the spectacles on his nose. Overwhelmingly helpful lad.

"Right." Amos gingerly dropped the steering collar on his lion's neck and crawled out of the saddle. He landed flat-footed with an aching thud. "Watch the wee beastie an' be sure he doesn't wander off. I'll be back."

Careful to maintain his distance from the other lions, Amos edged his way to the front of the line where Sym and Gundhrold were engaged in earnest conversation. Sym glanced up as he approached and nodded. Her expression was grim. Even the smile lines around her eyes had all but disappeared. "Good tidings, Hawkness. We're almost there. The coast is but a few miles ahead."

"Then why the delay?"

"Can you not sense it?" The griffin regarded him with eyes of steel, and Amos resisted the urge to retreat, opting instead to indulge in a witty response. Only to find himself tongue-tied a moment later, still searching for said witty response. “You have grown dull indeed. Can you not feel it in the air and smell it on the wind?”

Amos took a sniff then shook his head. “Look, ye great ormahound, unless ye’re referrin’ t’ the stench o’ a hundred unwashed beasties or the foul stink o’ lion’s breath, I can’t smell a blatherin’ thing right now.”

Gunrdhrold opened his mouth to speak, but Sym answered first. “A storm is coming.”

“So what’s a wee rainstorm t’ us?”

Sym pursed her lips. “Not a *wee rainstorm*, I am afraid. Storms that blow off and around the tip of Leira are always incredibly fierce and unpredictable, and if they happen to collide with a desert storm inland, the mountains tremble and rocks split apart. We must find shelter before it strikes.”

Not an option. “There’s shelter on the coast, right?’

“Some, yes.”

“All right, then we keep goin’. We have t’ get t’ the coast before the Langorians round the tip an’ split away. ’Tis our only hope. I won’t turn back. I can’t.”

Gundhrold nodded, and Amos thought he detected a trace of respect—begrudging, though it was—in the griffin’s yellow eyes. “And what of the storm?”

“Not my concern.” Amos shrugged, still grasping for a witty response. “Ye’re the one who claims t’ be a follower o’ Emhran, catbird. Reckon ye should take the matter up with him.”

“You know not of what you speak. Do not jest in ignorance, peddler.” With a haughty sniff and a flick of his tail, Gundhrold padded away, while Sym signaled commands to the rest of the Saari.

Amos stepped aside to allow the line of warriors passage on their trek through the swirling dust toward the coast and the coming storm, to say nothing of the attack he *still* had to plan. When Inali reached him, he reluctantly took control of his lion’s steering collar once more and climbed back up into the saddle. The blathering beast grumbled deep in its throat and turned a baleful glare toward him.

"Aye, stinkhead, from the sound o' it, ye missed me just as much as I missed ye."

He shifted into a more comfortable position, slipped his dirk from its sheath and flipped it with one hand, allowing his mind to wander to the upcoming fight. The odds were stacked against him. It was a million to one that he would never be able to reach the coast before the Langorian ship rounded the tip of Leira. Or if he did, what chance did he then have of commandeering a vessel, overtaking the pirates, sneaking aboard, and rescuing Birdie . . . all without getting her killed?

Faced with such overwhelming impossibilities, the *old* Hawkness would have simply blustered his way through. But there was too much of Amos McElhenny, the traveling peddler, in him now. He knew his limitations. Better than anyone else.

And he had rarely felt so helpless.

All things considered, maybe petitioning Emhran for aid wasn't such a bad idea. It was doubtful his request would garner a better response than Gundhrold's, but it couldn't hurt to ask, could it?

Before he could settle his mind, they crested a bluff and Amos saw the coastline—still several miles away—stretching out below. The sea was a tumult of white flecked waves, and a mound of dark storm clouds, flickering with lightning and belching torrents of rain, loomed over the shoreline. And somewhere out there—if Amos's rusty navigational skills were not sorely lacking—foundering in that swirling mass of wind and rain, would be the Langorian ship.

And Birdie.

"Oh Emhran." The plea slipped out before Amos could stop it. "Keep my wee lass safe."

• • •

There was fear in Ky's eyes.

Even half-blinded by the torrential rain, Birdie could see it. Unmistakable, heart-wrenching fear. Hands chained before him, Ky balanced on the rail, teetering with every sickening plunge of the ship. Rain plastered his hair to his skull and ran down his bruised face in streaming rivulets.

The ship pitched sideways and a wave crashed over the rail.

"Ky!" Birdie lurched forward, but Rhudashka's meaty hand dug into her shoulder, holding her back. She watched, helpless, as Ky wobbled on the brink of falling. At the last moment, the chain connected to his wrists jerked taut and Fjordair hauled him upright again. A fiendish grin knifed across the thin pirate's face.

"You see, little *Naian*?" From the looks of it, Rhudashka was shouting, but Birdie could hardly hear him over the roar of the gale. "We will save little *zabid*. But you must save us first. Sing and stop this storm before we all perish at the bottom of *zahel*."

Birdie blinked the water from her eyes and allowed the full weight of Rhudashka's words to sink in. For a moment, the thunder of the storm stilled and the roar softened to a low growl.

Sing to stop the storm?

She couldn't do that . . . could she?

A gust struck the ship. Something snapped high above. Shards of wood, snapped lines, and bits of tackle showered the deck. Pirates scattered before the falling debris. Fjordair dodged a chunk of wood. His sudden movement jerked the chain, bringing Ky crashing to his back on the deck. He lay there, groaning.

"You see?" Rhusdashka gripped her shoulders and wrenched her around to face him. "We are all in danger. We will all die . . . unless you act."

Fear flecked the pirate lord's eyes and creased his brow with rigid lines. His hands . . . they trembled. She turned and took in the white-cheeked terror painted across the faces of the pirates clinging to the life-lines crisscrossing the deck, the massive waves billowing on all sides, and the heaviness of the ship as it wallowed between one trough and the next, and slowly it dawned on her.

This was no longer a game of pawns. Rhudashka wasn't just trying to manipulate her. He was really and truly desperate.

For once in their "bargaining," she had the upper hand.

She shook her head, flinging her streaming hair back from her face. "Why should I care what happens to you or your ship? I'm your captive. Isn't death at sea better than a slow death in slavery?"

"But we are not alone on this ship, are we, little *Naian*?" He loomed over her, so near she could see the rainwater spraying from his lips as he spoke. "What of your fellow captives perishing in the hold? Little *zabid* over there? Would you let them die when you have the power to save them?"

Birdie shook her head, suddenly dizzy at the implications of his words. No . . . of course not. But she couldn't do what he claimed. The Song had healed the injured Underground runners, caused the River Adayn to rise, and broken the bonds of the Waveryder captives. But this . . . this supposed ability to command the sea and its gales . . . surely *this* was too much.

A roar filled her ears, though whether it was the clamor of her own thoughts or the thunder of the storm, she could not tell. She clutched her aching head in her chained hands. Behind her, someone shouted something in Langorian. She couldn't understand the words, but it sounded like a warning. A wave slammed into her, knocking her off her feet, and swept over her head. She gasped for air and choked on saltwater. Splinters tore into her fingers as she scrabbled for a handhold on the slick deck, but the sea seized her limbs with all its vast, irresistible strength and dragged her toward the rail.

Above and behind, she could hear bellowing and splashing, but the sounds were muffled by the rush of water in her ears.

Something seized her by the hair, and pain shot through her scalp. But the wave receded without her, leaving her breathless and choking, lying with her back pressed to the firm planks of the deck. Rhudashka towered over her, water dripping from his tangled beard and hair, sodden coat clinging to his bulbous frame.

"Would you sacrifice all to destroy me, little *Naian*?" He spat onto the deck beside her face, and little droplets of spittle struck her cheek. "Perhaps I was wrong. Perhaps suffering has taught you more than I thought. But know this, little *Naian*, power without control is useless, and that is what you are." He stepped back, lip curling in disgust. "Useless."

Birdie didn't deign reply. She coughed out a mouthful of brackish water and pushed up onto her hands and knees. Her limbs felt as shaky as a petra trapped in the sunlight. When she did not rise immediately, Rhudashka seized her elbow and hauled her upright. She shook free of his grasp, stumbled to the rail beside Ky and collapsed against it.

A swirling mass of angry greens, grays, and blues churned before her eyes. So fierce. So terrible. The sea could swallow her in a single gulp. Consume the ship and never even notice. Rage on, hunger unsated, even after devouring them.

The melody thundered in her ears. She closed her eyes and focused on the music. Raw. Fierce. Unimaginably strong. She was a fool to think she could control this. How could one command such power?

But she had to try . . . didn't she?

She stretched as far as the chain linking her manacles would reach and trailed her fingers in the surging water. The sea tugged at her hand, coaxing it deeper until the water swallowed her forearm, but she gripped the rail with her free hand and held tight to the ship.

"Birdie ..." Ky's voice was just a croak.

She refused to look at him. Just stared out at the sea with the taste of salt on her tongue and the scent of new rain in her nostrils, nerving herself to try it. It was going to be all right. She whispered the words to herself.

Somehow.

It reminded her of the time several years ago when she had dropped one of Madame's prized crocks. Terrified, she had scooped the broken pieces into her skirt and carried them out to the barn to see if she couldn't find some way to mend it before the innkeeper's wife found out and her wrath descended. In the end, she couldn't repair it and Madame *did* find out. But just as she had known then that all the broken pieces must fit together even if she couldn't see how, she knew now.

The pieces lay at her fingertips . . . if she could only grasp them.

"Birdie . . . don't . . . it's all right."

Birdie blocked out Ky's voice and the rumble of the pirate lord and the shouting of the pirates clinging to the life-lines on deck, until all she could hear was the fury of the storm and the melody so deep, deep in the distance. She reached for it, and it evaded her. Gone, just like that. Slipped from her grasp.

Tears clogged her throat, reducing her voice to a whisper. "No …"

Shouting broke out, just loud enough to be heard over the crashing waves. She couldn't decipher most of it, but one phrase stuck in her ears and turned her limbs to ice.

"The shore . . . the shore!"

She lifted her eyes, and through the sheeting rain, caught a glimpse of a dark headland visible for a moment when the ship's bow fell into the trough between waves. Then the ship rose to ride over the mountainous crests, and all was rain and spray and wind again—deadly wind driving them toward the shore and ruin.

Birdie dropped her gaze to the sea where it seemed the mysterious melody lurked just beyond reach. "Please …" she whispered. "Please help me."

Emhran.

The name drifted to her on the breath of the wind, and she breathed it back, putting all her fear and sorrow and hope into the word. "Emhran."

The storm swallowed her voice, but the Song rose from the depths in answer. Strong. Rich. Powerful. It swept over her, and for once, it did not draw back. She raised her chained hands as the music welled within her chest and then burst from her open mouth.

The released melody swirled around her, and she felt its touch like that of a friend long missed. Thicker than amassing storm clouds, it gathered at her fingertips and grew. Building. Summoning force. She felt the strain in her chest and at the back of her head as though she sought to lift something far beyond her strength.

The ship shuddered beneath her feet, and every timber groaned. Birdie dropped her hands and clung to the rail.

The sea erupted. Walls of water surged into the air on all sides with a deafening roar. The ship shot forward into a whirlwind of blinding spray and crashing water, all consumed in a wild, rushing cataclysm.

Ky's shout barely reached her ears. "What are you doing?"

She swallowed back the fear, steeled herself to doubt, and kept singing. Though her vision blurred and she dropped to her knees, head reeling, still she sang. And somehow, beneath the deep, throbbing rhythm and heart-breaking notes, she discerned the Song's intent. Just a tendril of thought that drifted through her mind, but she latched onto it, as the only solid thing in a world swallowed by the raging sea.

Shipwreck . . . beached on the shore.

But somehow . . . *somehow* . . . the ship and all aboard would be safe.

She clung to the promise, just as she clung to the rail, while the world dissolved into a blur of blue and gray, and all that had seemed solid quaked beneath her feet. The ship hurtled forward, gathering speed and momentum.

All would be safe.

The ship struck, and the impact threw her from her feet, jarring all the bones in her body. She skidded several paces on her hands and knees.

The roar of the sea faded. The wind died. Her own gasping breath sounded loud to her ears—ears that still rang from the echo of the ocean's voice. Dazed, she sat with her head hanging, struggling to clear her mind from the onslaught of fear and power-thrill that sought sway over her still.

Her breathing calmed, and she could once more hear the throb of the Song in the waves receding from the shore, but it dimmed before the sharp splintering of broken wood settling beneath the ship's weight and the groans of the captives in the hold and the pirates on deck.

A voice swore repeatedly in Langorian.

Birdie lifted her head to behold the ship broken in two and keeled over on its side. Pirates and captives spilled out of the split in the deck and staggered out onto the sand below. To her left, on the same half of the ship, Rhudashka struggled to lift his waterlogged bulk from the deck. Beyond the shattered masts, a fierce orange landscape stretched to the horizon.

Birdie needed no map to tell her where she was. This place, with its stacked sand dunes and craggy, wind-worn rocks, could only be the desert she had heard travelers speak of in awestruck whispers. But whatever perils might await them here were bound to be a thousand times better than a life of slavery in Langoria.

"I don't believe it." Ky's voice rasped in his throat. He pushed himself up with his chained hands and stared wildly in all directions. "We're alive?"

She nodded and found that little action all she could manage. Words escaped her. She had not the courage to look Ky in the face. Strength gone, she sagged against the splintered rail and allowed her head to sink into her trembling hands. She dug her fingers into her scalp and willed the shaking to stop.

A rough hand seized her arm, and the heavy scent of brew steeped in salt water swept over her. Rhudashka hauled her close so that she looked straight up into his wrath-contorted face. "You think to destroy my ship and survive, little *Naian*? To stir *zahel* against me and live?"

He shook her, fingers digging into her arms until Birdie gasped at the pain. Ky shouted something she couldn't quite make out, and his chains rattled as he struggled to rise.

"Bloodwuthering blodknockers!"

The familiar voice and phrase dashed against Birdie's ears, and the life drained from her limbs, freezing her in place. She couldn't turn to look and she didn't dare believe.

Didn't dare *hope*...

"Unhand her ye slobgollomly lump o' charbottle!"

Rhudashka released her and spun around, groping for his sword. A meaty thud sounded out, and the pirate lord reeled backwards, revealing the sturdy frame, defiant stance, raised fists, and wild red hair of Amos McElhenny.

Alive.

Gundhrold appeared behind Amos and pounced on the pirate lord, bringing him down to the deck with an earth-shaking thud. The griffin snarled with his beak scarce inches away from Rhudashka's nose, then let out a roar. The deck was suddenly crowded with people Birdie had never seen before, armed with spears, clad in various skins and leathers, and mounted on massive, hairy beasts. They swarmed across the wreckage of the ship and down the split into the hold, and the sounds of battle and of triumph rang out, followed by the cries of the pirates as one by one they were slain.

But Birdie had eyes for Amos alone.

The peddler swaggered forward, massaging his fist, and grinned at her, a wild, desperate, exhilarated grin. "Ahoy there, lass! Were ye responsible for this mess? I think 'tis safe t' say sailin' may not be the best path for ye. If ye ask me—"

But Birdie didn't wait to hear what he had to say. She scrambled to her feet and flung herself at the peddler. A sob welled in her throat and threatened to choke her. His arms settled about her battered and bruised shoulders and held her tight.

"There now, lass," he muttered. "It's all goin' t' be all right. Ye're safe now. Safe."

PART TWO

5

"Here we are, lass." Amos tilted to one side in the saddle so Birdie could see past him from her seat on the lion's rump. "The city o' Nar-Kog, refuge o' the Saari."

Birdie's eyes widened at the sight of the city crawling up both cliffs on either side of the narrow defile. Flat roofed buildings carved from orange, sand-worn rock were stacked above and beside narrow crisscrossing paths, while a network of bridges arched the gap, connecting the two halves of the city.

The lion started off again, trotting in an effort to catch up with the line of Saari warriors and freed captives, and Birdie hugged Amos's waist to keep from losing her balance. Around his elbow, she caught a glimpse of Ky riding farther up the line behind one of the Saari. The woman warrior—Sym—rode at the front, leading them along the defile until they reached the center of the city where she turned to the right and mounted a wide, paved road to an imposing building lodged halfway up the cliff face, with a courtyard, thick columns, and narrow arches that flared at the top marking the entrance.

"The chieftain's palace." Amos muttered over his shoulder. "Matlal Quahtli's his name—ye'll meet him soon enough."

There was an undercurrent in his tone that Birdie couldn't quite identify. It sounded like he was worried or concealing something from her. But after the events of the last few months, she was far too weary to care. It was enough that Amos was alive, and that at least for the moment, they were all safe. With an effort, she ignored the voice in the back of her mind whispering of danger not fully realized and relentless pursuit.

The Saari halted their lions in the courtyard and dismounted. Amos lowered Birdie to the ground but had scarce alighted himself when Sym drew her from his side and led her into the palace. The warrior's swift footfalls fell with uncanny quiet down the length of the torch-lit halls, and the sound of Birdie's feet as she jogged to keep up seemed loud in comparison. It was a moment before she found her voice. "Where are you taking me? What about Amos and Ky?"

Sym halted before an arched doorway covered by a crimson curtain and turned to face her, lounging against the frame with her arms crossed over her chest. "Worried, are you? You should not be—not if you are as powerful as the legends say."

Birdie fought the urge to shrink from Sym's searching gaze. It was challenging but not threatening—not like Rhudashka. She had withstood the pirate lord; she would not be cowed by a lone Saari warrior. "And what are the legends?"

"The usual fanciful tales—no doubt you have heard them. The Songkeeper can summon a storm with his or her voice, command the waters to battle in her defense, and comprehend the hidden thoughts of the hearts of men." Sym quirked an eyebrow at her, but her expression remained stern. "I heard your voice upon the storm winds, little one, before the ship crashed—yet even I can scarce believe it. The legends did not speak of one so young. You must forgive us if we are doubtful."

Before Birdie could craft a reply, the Saari warrior flung the curtain aside and ushered her into a low-ceilinged room made homey by the light of half a dozen flickering torches. "You will be reunited with your friends soon, but in the meantime, Sa Itera wishes that you be shown the hospitality of the Saari. It would not do to enter the mahtems' council covered in the reek of slavery."

Birdie made it two steps across the threshold and then stopped with her heart hammering in her throat. An enormous white lioness sprawled in her path with two small boys crawling across its back and tumbling down to wrestle between its massive paws. The lioness's head swung toward her, and she was taken captive by the beast's huge yellow eyes.

A menacing growl rumbled in its throat. "Beware your step, two-legs. Don't much care for the smell of you. Dare touch a hair of my cubs' heads and you'll face my wrath."

Instinctively, Birdie raised her hands palms out, hoping to appease the lioness with evidence that she was not a threat. She couldn't tell if it worked or not, but the lioness's growl softened and five distinct melodies fell on her ear—all harmonious—of varying tones and rhythms, filled with unique layers of emotions she could not begin to differentiate.

She shook her head to clear her mind.

The beast's eyes narrowed in suspicion. Somehow, in that moment, Birdie knew that the lioness understood her ability and that she could comprehend its speech as no ordinary "two-legs" could.

"Silence, Quoth."

At the stern command, the lioness fell silent and shuffled its bulk around to face the far side of the room where the speaker, a tall woman, rose from a low bench. Long hair hung in tawny braids to her waist and the train of her crimson robe brushed the stone floor with each step as she crossed toward Birdie.

Dark eyes lowered, Sym dropped to one knee and snapped a hand to her chest in a warrior's salute. "Sa Itera, I did not expect—"

"You may leave us." The woman inclined her head and motioned a hand toward the doorway. Birdie watched, utterly entranced by the regal grace of her every movement. "I will see to the Songkeeper myself."

Without a word, Sym exited, drawing the curtain closed behind her. The torches flickered with the rush of air, and the walls seemed to creep closer as if the room were made smaller by its occupants and the presence of the massive beast. Birdie turned to the woman Sym had called Sa Itera, but found that she had already scooped up the two boys and moved back to the low bench.

With a grunt, the lioness shoved to its feet, shadowed the woman's retreat, and flopped at the base of the seat. A deep purr vibrated in its chest, but Birdie's eyes were drawn to the fierce claws advancing and retracting as its paws kneaded the floor.

Settling one child on her knees, Itera placed the other beside the lioness who immediately seized the boy and began licking his head, mumbling words of feline affection.

"Do you know who I am, child?" The woman's imperious voice drew Birdie's attention from the lioness, and she shook her head. "I am Sa Itera, wife of Matlal Quahtli who sits enthroned beneath the Star of the Desert, and Mahtem of the Sigzal tribe in my own right."

Birdie did not need the impressive list of unfamiliar names and titles to recognize that this was someone of great importance. She sank to one knee in imitation of Sym's posture and bowed her head in respect.

The lioness growled. "Stop fawning, two-legs." Birdie could have sworn that the beast rolled its eyes—to be sure, its lips curled in disgust, revealing a set of yellowed teeth. "Rise if you would be seen as a lion and not a mouse. Rise and stand firm as the cliffs of Nar-Kog. You are not her inferior. To those who call the desert home, strength is second only to courage. Have you courage, two-legs? Or has it too abandoned you?"

Goaded by the words, Birdie rose and met the penetrating gaze of the Matlal's wife.

"Now you know who I am," Sa Itera said. "But what of you, little one? Who . . . and *what* . . . are you?"

Birdie took a deep breath, let it fill her throat, and formed it into words. "I am the Songkeeper." And with that simple pronouncement, the tension eased from her shoulders and back. With the release came the sudden awareness of countless aches and pains from her time in captivity and the harried race on a lion's back from the coast to the desert city.

"Are you?" Itera fondled the child in her lap, and the tenderness in her expression tugged at Birdie's heart. "I do not think you are sure. And if even you doubt, you cannot expect us to trust your word on the matter. There is too much at stake."

"I don't understand. What do you want from me?"

"Proof." Itera's eyes flickered up, and all hint of motherly affection had vanished from those dark orbs—hard, they seemed, and unforgiving as the cliffs themselves.

"I . . ." Birdie looked to the lioness for aid, but the beast closed its eyes and turned away, evidently bored with or unconcerned by her predicament. Taking a deep breath, she sought to summon the Song pulsing in the background, but it did not answer her call—again.

She nearly cried out in frustration, and it took every ounce of composure she had to hold it in. Strength and courage—that was what the Saari respected.

So the lioness said.

Birdie seized the thought. "I can understand the speech of creatures." She gestured toward the lioness. "If you've heard the legends, then you must know that this is said to be one of the skills of a Songkeeper. When I came in, the lioness warned me to stand clear of her cubs—your sons."

Itera was silent a moment, then shook her head and rose to her full, impressive height. Faint lines of disappointment marred the otherwise flawless poise of her expression. "Nay, little one, I am afraid we require better proof than that. You are clever, to be sure, but one does not need to understand the tongues of beasts to read Quoth's protectiveness toward my sons."

She snapped her fingers and the lioness rose. With gentle efficiency, she positioned both boys on the beast's back and strode to the doorway with the lioness at her heels. "There is water in a basin and clean garb at the rear of the room where you may refresh yourself from your travels. The mahtems' council will meet in a quarter of an hour—Sym will summon you. Be forewarned, little one, they will demand proof of your claim, and you must be prepared to answer them."

Birdie nodded, unsure what else to say. In the end, did it really matter whether they believed her or not? Given the rushed pace of their return from the coast, she and Amos had not yet discussed their plans following Nar-Kog, but she did not expect them to be here for long—though now that Amos's mother had fallen, she doubted he would want to return to Bryllhyn.

Rather than being daunted by the uncertainty of the future, Birdie found herself growing excited. The whole of Leira lay before them, and there was no Madame to gainsay her desires, no Carhartan cursing at her heels. For once in her life, she could go anywhere, be anything, live and see that freedom was good.

Sa Itera paused on the threshold with the curtain lifted in one hand, the shadow obscuring her face. "You have not yet convinced me, and the council will prove even more difficult to satisfy. And they have just cause to be wary, little one. There are many who exhibit signs of possessing the abilities of a Songkeeper and yet never come into their full gifting." Itera's gaze bored into Birdie. "Which one, I wonder, are you?"

The curtain fell, leaving Birdie alone in the torch-lit room. Itera's final words ran through her head, blending with the soft tread of the woman's sandaled feet down the passage and the four variations of the melody retreating with her, the lioness, and the boys.

Once again, Birdie was left with more questions than answers. Perhaps she was not a true Songkeeper and that was why she was unable to command the Song. But if there were *many* who appeared to possess the same abilities, then why had she never heard of them?

It was time for a talk with Amos and Gundhrold. Willing or not, after everything that had happened, they must speak with her.

They *had* to.

Careful to blend with the shadows, Ky peered around the pillar at the chiefs gathered in the Council Hall. With his back to a railing-less balcony overlooking the valley and his wife to his right, Matlal Quahtli sat on a carved throne that formed a jagged double peak above his head resembling the cliffs of Nar-Kog. Between the peaks, a crystal the size of Ky's fist blazed in the light of the afternoon sun. The Star of the Desert, the Saari called it. Ky had to tear his eyes away from it. Pocketing such a gem could have kept the Underground in supplies for years . . .

If lifting it didn't get them killed first.

Twenty one broad-shouldered figures with bronze skin and dark hair, clad in flowing tunics, fringed leggings, and lion-skin capes sat on low stools in a semi-circle before Quahtli. Garbed in similar clothes, Birdie and Hawkness sat at the midpoint with Gundhrold at their side—though of the three, only the griffin seemed at ease with his surroundings.

All in all, it was a right impressive sight. Ky had never seen anything like it before. Here were warriors—*real warriors*—the sort of fighters who could hope to stand against the dark soldiers, survive, and win.

What Cade would've given to be in his place. Though Cade would have taken the stool set out for him in the circle instead of crouching behind a pillar. But this cavernous room reminded him of the Underground, and after several weeks of close scrutiny in captivity, he was ready for a chance to disappear.

"You misled us, Hawkness." Matlal Quahtli rose to his full height and slammed the butt of his spear against the ground. "You promised us aid and *this* is what you bring us?"

Ky peeked over at Birdie. She sat beside Hawkness, hands clasped in her lap, looking down at the ground. Surrounded by so many warriors, she looked a bit like a karnoth fledgling Ky had once found fluttering on the cobblestones of Kerby, tumbled too soon from its nest. Her hair hung over her face, concealing her expression. He was half tempted to creep over and invite her to join him in his hidey-hole.

Hawkness snorted, assuming a defiant posture with his arms crossed over his broad chest. "Ye misled yerselves. This *is* the Songkeeper. If ye expected somethin' different 'twas no fault o' mine. We had an agreement, an' I intend t' hold t' my end o' the bargain an' offer ye our aid. Take it or leave it. Makes no difference t' me."

One of the mahtems rose on creaking limbs and spoke with a voice that carried slow, heavy dignity. "And what aid can you offer us? The one, a dying legend. The other, a myth not yet full grown. We are hard pressed on all sides, yet we sent nigh two companies of Saari warriors with you—warriors we needed to defend our borders from the oncoming scourge. How many have died that should have lived because we aided you, hoping for aid in return?"

"Now, see here—" Hawkness began, but Gundhrold interrupted him.

"How many have died, you asked?" The griffin paced the length of the semi-circle, injured wingtip trailing behind him. As he passed, each lion bowed its head and sank to the ground. It startled Ky to realize how much larger the griffin was than his earth-bound cousins. "Who can say? But I guarantee that it is but a speck of sand compared to the numbers that shall yet perish if the Takhran is not stopped. Even now, his armies are bent on the conquest of the Midlands, and when they have fallen and his full attention sweeps to the desert, what hope have you then?"

Matlal Quahtli gathered his cloak around him and resumed his seat. Torchlight fell on his bronze face, throwing the bones beneath his skin in sharp relief. "That is the question, is it not? What hope can your *little* Songkeeper offer us?"

Silence followed his words, and Ky did not need to see the mahtems' faces to know that all eyes had shifted to Birdie. She raised her head at last and seemed to realize that the focus rested on her.

"I . . . I can fight . . . if those are the terms of the agreement." She faltered over the words, so it wasn't exactly the most convincing speech Ky had ever heard, and the look on her face as she turned to Amos was accusatory at best. Still, there was a strength and firmness to her tone that made *him* want to believe her.

But the mahtems seemed a hard lot to convince. An uneasy rustle of movement and whispers passed around the semi-circle before one rose. He had a sharp, triangular face that reminded Ky of a petra. "We have spoken many words this evening and dallied over concerns and doubts as numerous as the sands, and yet we have sidled 'round the most important question of all."

"An' what is that?" Hawkness rested his elbows on his knees, shoulders hunched forward, massaging his throwing hand.

"Whether the child is indeed the Songkeeper."

The griffin's neck feathers rose, and his voice deepened to a growl. "You have the word of Hawkness, the promise of a lord of the desert, and the witness of your own people who testify to hearing the child's voice on the winds of the storm when the Langorian ship crashed. What other assurance do you need?"

"I desire not assurance, but *proof.* Clear, undeniable evidence. This council has been deceived before. Let her be tested before we acknowledge her gifting."

"An' how d' ye propose doin' that? It's not a beswogglin' magic trick."

"There is *one* way." The Matlal's wife, Sa Itera, spoke up. "We can—"

She broke off as Sym pushed her way into the semi-circle in a flurry of flapping skins and flying braids. She dropped to one knee before Quahtli, one hand resting on a quiver of light spears strapped to her back, and delivered a message in a swift, harsh whisper that Ky was too far away to overhear. Just as quickly as she had come, she was gone.

For a moment, Matlal Quahtli regarded the spear in his hand in silence, then he lifted his voice to fill the Council Hall. "A messenger has just arrived from the border. It would seem our list of allies grows thinner still. As of two days past, the Nordlands, the Midlands and the entire west coast have fallen to the Khelari. He brings bitter tidings of cold-blooded slaughter and deaths beyond count."

Hawkness started forward in his seat. "I thought King Earnhult signed a treaty with the Takhran grantin' his army free passage through the Midlands."

Quahtli nodded. "A treaty, yes. King Earnhult allowed the Khelari to pass, but instead of responding in kind, they demanded a blood price from every Midlands town. They must have been close upon your heels as you traveled hence from Bryllhyn, Hawkness. The Takhran's forces march on the desert even as we speak. War is upon us."

The hall erupted in a clamor of speech, but Ky's heartbeat thrummed in his ears, drowning out the noise. The Nordlands—Kerby.

He reached for his sling, only to recall that it was gone, taken by the pirates. The Matlal's words haunted him. *Cold-blooded slaughter. Deaths beyond count.* Kerby had been under occupation for the past five years, and in the Underground, they'd been convinced that they had seen the worst the dark soldiers had to offer.

But they'd never experienced anything like this.

Even without closing his eyes, he could see them all, frozen like a painting in the back of his mind: Meli, Paddy, Aliyah, all the Underground runners as they had looked after the dark soldiers' attack just before he raced down the tunnel and their faces vanished behind him.

If he could just know they were safe …

"Take courage, my lords." Sa Itera's clear voice cut across the commotion. "We are the Mahtems of the Saari nation. War is no stranger to us, nor should we be surprised to hear that battle draws nigh. Still, we would be foolish to deny any aid that is offered. The name of Hawkness is renowned among those who stand against the Takhran, and there is none that the Takhran fears so much as the Songkeepers of legend. Knowing that Hawkness and the little Songkeeper stand on our side should be enough to strengthen the heart of any warrior and strike fear into our enemies."

The petra-faced mahtem pursed his lips and shook his head. "Such knowledge may bring hope, but it rarely lasts beyond the moment—and once gone, it oft proves impossible to revive." A murmur of approval met his words, and the mahtem turned in a slow circle to address each member of the council individually. "How can we know she *is* the Songkeeper? You say we have need of aid, but I ask you: should we trust in help unproven? Should our hopes prove vain yet again?"

"No, we should not." Itera rose, towering over the mahtem so he had to tilt his head back to look at her face. "Let her be tested. Let her prove her gifting. Let my brother, Dah Inali, take her to the Hollow Cave."

6

The Midlands were gone.

Gone. Gone. Gone. The word hardly held any meaning for Birdie anymore. It had become a part of living, like breathing in and out. Things came and things went, people lived and people died, and somehow, she was always left behind to mourn the passing.

Dimly, in some far corner of her mind, she knew that the council had drawn to a close, that the mahtems were rising, that they had decided something—something to do with her.

But it hardly seemed important now.

For a few short days, she had felt safe. Secure. She had almost dared believe that here in the craggy mountains of the desert was a strength that rivaled the Takhran's, a force that could stand against the tide of his soldiers. But the mahtems were afraid—deeply afraid. She could see the terror lurking in their eyes, hear the falseness in their voices, perceive it in the pitch of their melodies. And in their fear, they wanted *her* to prove her abilities in the hopes that she could somehow save them? She couldn't fault them for desiring proof.

Not when she doubted herself.

But now even Amos wanted her to fight, and *that* alone was enough to set her reeling. It was as if in her weeks of captivity, the world had shattered beyond repair . . . and for some mad reason, they wanted to hand her the pieces.

"Come, little one." Sa Itera stood before her, and though the woman's posture remained as rigid and regal as a zoar tree, there was the faintest hint of softening in her voice.

Of kindness.

Birdie grasped at the thought and somehow managed to find her feet and blindly follow the Matlal's wife through the gathered mahtems and out of the Council Hall. She could feel Gundhrold's stern presence at her back, hear Amos's heavy footfalls somewhere to her right, but of Ky she found no sign.

In the corridor outside the Council Hall, Sa Itera halted and motioned to two Saari warriors stationed at the entrance to draw the hangings closed. At the end of the corridor, a young man sat cross-legged on a low bench, hunched over a parchment, a piece of charcoal in his smudged fingers and an open satchel at his feet. Knotted strands of dusky hair hung to his shoulders. He wore fringed trousers and an open vest, and a clay bead hung from a gold chain about his neck. Intent upon his work, he did not look up as they approached, simply kept scattering charcoal across the parchment in broad, sweeping lines.

"Dah Inali, brother-mine." Sa Itera laid a gentle hand on his arm. "The Matlal has need of your service. There is an important task you must do for these, our guests."

He shrugged her hand aside, added a few more strokes to the parchment, then slipped the charcoal into his satchel and dusted his hands on his vest. "Sister-mine, Hawkness, Gundhrold . . . and the little Songkeeper." With a flick of his hand, he adjusted the spectacles perching on the bridge of his nose and turned back to Sa Itera. "What does the Mahtem of the Sigzal tribe require of her disinherited brother?"

The smoothness of his tone was not enough to conceal the bite of his words, but Sa Itera simply clasped her hands and held them at her waist. Her voice assumed an air of enduring patience. "The council of mahtems have ruled to test the little one's gifting as a Songkeeper. You understand why your help is required. You are to show our guests to the Hollow Cave, accompany the child inside, and bring a report."

Inali unknotted his limbs and shoved to his feet, suddenly as taut as a vine stretched to the breaking point. With a shaking hand, he removed his spectacles and rubbed the lenses on his vest. "Sister-mine, I beg you. You cannot ask this of me."

"I do not ask." Sa Itera lifted her chin. "The Matlal rules."

• • •

"Come along, little Songkeeper." Dah Inali beckoned to Birdie from the base of a narrow path that retreated into a cleft in the side of the mountain. He settled the strap of his satchel over one shoulder, steadied his spectacles, and hefted a spear in his free hand. "We must hurry." Impatience bled into his tone and shuffling feet.

Birdie released her grip on the lion's mane and only half heard the beast's gruff rumble of gratitude. She flexed her hand to work the blood back into her fingers, nerving herself to face whatever trial lay before her. Inali had proven himself skilled at ignoring her questions, and the two mahtems who accompanied them had spent the hour-long trek arguing with one another in their own tongue. Neither Amos nor Gundhrold had been able to provide any insight into the mysterious testing, and she had not seen Ky since the meeting in Matlal Quahtli's Council Hall.

"The day wanes," Inali urged. "We are running out of light."

Already Tauros hovered on the western horizon, bathing the path with fire-glow and casting monstrous shadows to Birdie's left.

Still she hesitated.

"It's all right, lass," Amos whispered, propping one elbow on the lion's neck and offering the other hand to help her dismount.

She gripped it—more for comfort than for aid—and slipped to the ground, landing beside Gundhrold. The griffin's face was turned to the cleft, one eye in shadow and the other blazing with the glory of the setting sun, feathers ruffling in the breeze. He spoke without turning. "This is a hallowed place, little Songkeeper. Had the mahtems not insisted that you come, I intended to bring you here myself."

That was some comfort, at least.

"But what is this place, Gundhrold?" She was pleased that her voice was steady and bore no hint of the turmoil she felt inside. "What am I supposed to do?"

"You cannot know." Inali broke in. "It is part of the testing."

"Boggswoggling foolish, if ye ask me. But I s'pose there's nothin' for it now."

No, there really wasn't.

That understanding drove Birdie up the narrow track at Inali's heels. There was nothing for it but to keep moving, onwards and upwards, following the path charted before her, even if it felt like the earth was spinning beneath her feet. What choice did she have? Now that Amos had promised her aid to these strange desert warriors . . . now that she had sung the Song and seen the waters rise . . . now that she had a chance to discover if she was a true Songkeeper or not.

At the entrance to the cleft, Inali gestured for the others to stop and motioned Birdie forward. "As the desert lord has spoken, this is a hallowed place, little Songkeeper. Only you and I may enter. Our companions shall await our return here."

"By Turning, we shall not!" Amos's face took on a livid hue that vied with the sunset for brilliance. "Of all the seaswogglin' addlebrained ideas! Have ye gone soft in the head, lad? If ye think for one second that I'm goin' t' let my wee lass out o' my sight, ye're madder 'n a night moth."

"It must be done." To Birdie's surprise, Inali met Amos's glare without shriveling. There was more strength in him than he let on. "She shall be safe, you have my word."

The peddler could not be relied upon to think objectively when her safety was threatened, so Birdie sought confirmation from the griffin instead. She had no cause to distrust Inali, but George's betrayal and the weeks chained in the hold of the pirate ship left her uneasy.

Gundhrold shook his head. "Nay, Dah Inali. This may be hallowed ground, but I shall enter with you and the little Songkeeper." Amos started to bristle, but the griffin cut him off. "It is my right as her Protector."

Inali's face fell, but he did not argue. "Very well. Do as you will." He squeezed through the crack and was gone.

Birdie moved to follow, and Gundhrold's whisper fell soft on her ear. "Take peace, little one."

Peace. She turned the word over and over in her mind as she slipped through the cleft and the path immediately began to descend before her feet. Peace seemed a foreign concept, something that belonged to the realm of myths and fireside tales. Try as she might, she couldn't recall the last time she had known anything but this terrible restlessness that churned within her soul like the storm at sea.

She did not know peace.

With an effort, she concentrated on Inali's footsteps ahead and the heavier thud of the griffin's padded paws behind. Before they had traveled a hundred feet, the light of the entrance had dimmed, and when the passage took a sudden curve to the left, Birdie toiled in the dark, feeling her way by running both hands against the opposing walls.

A hum grew in the back of her mind—deep as though it sprang from the heart of the earth, hollow sounding as if carried on the breath of the wind. It grew in breadth and volume until it overpowered the steady crunch of their footsteps.

The passage lightened ahead.

The glow grew stronger and took on the pinkish hue of evening, while the hum swelled even louder, until the cleft widened into a circular cave larger than the hold of the Langorian ship. High above, a shaft in the ceiling opened to the darkening sky.

Inali halted beneath the shaft and turned to face her. Caught between light and shadow, his bronze skin appeared pale. "This is the Hollow Cave." He spoke in a whisper, but his voice magnified off the walls so Birdie could hear it even over the humming. "This is your testing, little Songkeeper."

She turned in a slow circle, taking in her surroundings. "But what do I do?"

"*Listen.*"

Listen . . . Listen . . . Listen.

The word danced around the room, rebounding from every nook and cranny, teasing her with its challenge. She closed her eyes and hearkened to the humming. The noise of her own breathing faded. The rustle of Gundhrold's feathers quieted. The whisper of Inali's movements as he paced back and forth dwindled.

The humming radiated until it filled the entire cave, until it seeped beneath her skin and reached inside her bones and lodged somewhere in her chest.

She did not know her legs had crumpled beneath her until her knees struck rock. A gasp of pain parted her lips. Instantly, she felt the comforting warmth of Gundhrold's wings enveloping her, but he could not shield her from the force of the Song. It blazed through her like a raging fire. It shook the earth beneath her feet until the very stones seemed to crumble. It gusted around her like the winds of the gale that had beleaguered the Langorian ship.

A voice thundered in her ear, and in her mind, words materialized from the melody and became images painted across her closed eyelids.

It was all so confused. So rushed.

A glimpse of a river, rippling with the notes of the Song—*Tal Ethel*, the voice said.

Herself standing in a dark hollow with bodies strewn all around, blood staining the rocks beneath her feet, and the blue-white sword—Artair's sword—in her hand.

A flash of a bone-dry riverbed, sullied with corpses.

A country ravaged by war. Cities burning. Crops untended and withering.

Two men—alike as twins—kneeling side by side on a riverbank.

Then the images honed in on a vast fortress built into the side of a mountain with a gate that yawned open beneath a massive portcullis and walls bristling with soldiers. She did not need the voice to speak and declare this to be Serrin Vroi, the Takhran's stronghold. Somehow she knew.

Reeling, she tried to pull back, to force the melody to slow its pace and yield its secrets one by one. "I *am* the Songkeeper," she ground between gritted teeth. "Listen to me."

The images faded, and the melody fell silent, but not before it uttered one final sentence, *Seek Tal Ethel, little Songkeeper.*

Birdie came to herself, held in Gundhrold's wings, kneeling on the cold, stone ground with her face buried in her hands and tears running down her chilled cheeks. The weight of the griffin's wings was suddenly confining. She managed to extricate herself and stumble away from his concerned queries, coming to a halt beneath the shaft of light with her hands on her knees, gasping for breath.

Inali bent over her, his face a puzzling blend of eagerness and anxiety. "What did you hear? Did he *speak* to you?"

Somehow she could not bring herself to try to put words to the incorporeal images and thoughts and voice that had inhabited the notes of the Song of the Hollow Cave. Not yet. It felt wrong. Like slapping clay on a stick figure and proclaiming it a living person.

She shook her head, but Inali would not be dissuaded.

"By Sigurd's mane." The words hissed across his lips and he seized her by the shoulders. His grip was surprisingly strong. "You heard something, I can see it in your eyes."

Gundhrold roared, and Inali's hands tore from her arms as he lurched toward the far side of the cave, propelled by a blow from the griffin's good wing. "Unhand the Songkeeper, earthling! Dare lay hands upon her again, and I will leave your bones to the dust whence you came."

"It is the testing." Inali fumbled on the ground for his fallen spectacles, settled them over his ears, and drew to his full height. "Mandated by the will of the Matlal and the council of the mahtems of the Saari. She must tell me what she heard. They expect a full report."

The air drained from Birdie's lungs as both pairs of eyes settled on her.

"What did you hear?" Inali pressed.

"I thought . . . only a voice. Nothing more."

"A voice—what did it *say*?"

She shrugged and hoped it would convince the strange Saari warrior. "I don't *know*. It was too confusing, too jumbled. I have to sort it out before I can explain. You must give me time."

"We shall be on our way then. You can speak later." Gundhrold silenced Inali's protests with a glare and beckoned her with a wing tip. She moved toward him on legs that were suddenly shaky. His yellow eyes pierced her through and through, and she knew there would be no fooling the griffin with vague or shadowed answers.

He would have the truth.

She glanced at Inali as she passed. His brow was furrowed and his shoulders slumped, though whether it was from relief or disappointment she could not say. In any case, unless she could provide him with answers, she doubted he would bring a favorable report of her abilities to the mahtems.

Perhaps that too was for the best.

She was suddenly weary of it all. It did not matter if they accepted her as the Songkeeper or not—she should not care.

She *should* not, but she did.

7

Ky stalked Sym through the torch-lit corridors of the Matlal's palace, utilizing every trick Dizzier had ever pummeled into him—embracing the shadows, becoming one with his surroundings, studying and imitating his mark's gait so the sound of his footsteps blended with hers. Sym moved with a swiftness and agility that could put any lion to shame, pausing now and then to take a report from a guard or deliver a message. Still Ky followed her meandering path, driven by the question burning at the back of his mind.

Consumed by his own thoughts, he realized too late that Sym had stopped in the middle of the corridor. Her back was toward him, but he had strayed too near to simply turn aside without seeming suspicious. He eased his pace, stuck his hands in his trouser pockets, and sidled past with his eyes on the ground.

A spear struck the passageway floor, directly in his path.

He jumped back, groping for his sling—his hand came back empty, of course. "What was that for? You trying to kill me?"

Sym's dark eyes flickered with amusement, and she ran a hand along the shaft of one of the spears strapped to her back. "You are fortunate that I make a habit of looking before I strike, Nordlander. Why are you shadowing me?"

Maybe trailing a mark was something he needed to practice more often, but Ky preferred to chalk it up to the uncanny senses of a Saari warrior and leave it at that. "Look, I got to meet that messenger you were talking about earlier. Couldn't take me to him, could you? I need to find out what he knows about my home town."

Her eyes narrowed, and he thought he read his own disappointment in the hardening of her pupils, but to his surprise, she motioned for him to follow. "Keep up, Nordlander."

Keeping up should have been easy for someone so accustomed to tunnels and back alleys. But Sym moved at a whirlwind pace that left Ky scrambling to regain his sense of direction, until they emerged at last in the courtyard where they had dismounted upon their arrival from the coast. Groups of Saari warriors clustered around saddled lions, sparred in pairs with the rapidity and ferocity of a desert wind, took turns throwing spears at distant targets, or sat on low benches honing their spear heads.

Sym paused at an open bench and threw a leg over the seat, nodding toward a short figure clad in a loose, sand colored robe standing on the throwing line. "There is your messenger. Goes by the name of Migdon. Do try and be polite. He can be a mite touchy."

At the mention of his name, the short figure glanced up and stomped toward them, allowing his weapon—a sling—to dangle from one hand. Ky could scarce tear his eyes from it. His fingers twitched of their own accord, longing for the familiar feel of the leather straps and the weight of the stone and that perfect moment when his hand somehow knew to release.

The stranger stopped at Ky's elbow, rocked back on his heels, and ran a thick-fingered hand through the curly hair sprouting atop his head—a head that stood no higher than Ky's shoulder. Dwarves were not entirely uncommon in Kerby but Ky had never seen one face to face before. For once in his life, he felt tall, and he couldn't help standing just a bit straighter to accentuate the difference.

The dwarf snorted. "That's rich. Rub it in, why don't you?"

Touchy—right.

"Sorry." He let his shoulders fall back into their natural slouch. "Look, I heard you'd been traveling north of the desert, and I just had to know if you—"

"Hold on there," the dwarf growled and shoved a finger in Ky's chest with such force that he nearly stumbled backward. "Manners, bucko. Names first. Information later. *Maybe.* If I like you." He thumped a brawny fist against his forehead. "I am Migdon Hipicarious Listarchus Noonan, advance scout of the Third Cohort of the Adulnae. Among other things."

He paused, eyebrows lifted, obviously waiting.

"Ky—Ky Huntyr." Ky scuffed his bare feet in the dirt, trying to rid himself of the unsettled feeling in his stomach. Names weren't meant to be bandied around like apples after a bobbing run. The *less* folks who knew who you were the better. "Do you have any news of Kerby?"

Migdon pursed his lips, and for a moment, Ky was afraid he was going to ignore the question. "Don't like to beat around the bush, do you, bucko? Me neither. It's what sets us men of action apart from the thinkers and plotters with their sweet talking ways and forked-tongues. But you know what they say, 'Honeyed words ease the tang of bitter news.' Or something to that effect." The dwarf snapped the sling between his hands, and the noise reminded Ky of the crack of lightning. There was a finality to the sound that set his heart thumping.

"Kerby?" he whispered.

With a heavy sigh, Migdon dropped into a seat on the bench, sling hanging limp between his fingers. "They say the Midlands had it easy in comparison—and I agree with them. Sure the Khelari left a string of bodies and burned villages in their wake, but once they passed through, it was over. But for Kerby, the Takhran decreed the slow death. Blockaded. Trade at a standstill. Supplies running short once the soldiers ransacked the market. No one allowed in or out. The city is under siege until the people starve and the dead rot in piles in the street." The dwarf shrugged. "Said you liked it straight, bucko, and that's as plain as I can tell it."

Dead in the streets . . .

Not too long ago, Ky had been running down those streets, bobbing apples and picking pockets with scarce a care to weigh him down. As he struggled to comprehend the full meaning of the dwarf's words, his gaze roamed across the palace courtyard, over the Saari warriors training for battle and the lions standing sentinel at the head of the path, but instead of fringed leggings and bared weapons and shaggy manes, he saw the runners—his brothers and sisters—wasting away in the damp cold of a fireless Underground.

It had become their tomb, and he their grave digger.

He had taken the sword from Kerby to draw the Takhran's wrath away from the Underground, and the plan had seemed to be working. The Khelari had trailed them all the way across the Westmark, hadn't they?

But there was no telling what had become of the blade in the aftermath of the battle of Bryllhyn, so for all he knew, it was just as likely to have wound up in the hold of the pirate ship as lost in the ocean or back in the hands of the Khelari. But of all the places it undoubtedly wasn't, Kerby certainly ranked tops.

So what led the Takhran to focus on destroying his city?

He caught the dwarf's gaze. "Why …"

"Broad question, bucko. Could have a whole slew of answers depending on how you interpret it, but I reckon I got the gist of it. The why's not hard to figure out. You know what they say, 'The battle fought soonest oft results in a dozen battles avoided.'" Migdon scratched at his beard. "Or was it a *score* of battles avoided?"

"What does that even mean?"

There was pity in the dwarf's face, and somehow that made Ky more uncomfortable than apathy. "It *means* the Takhran is making an example of Kerby to deter anyone from standing against him. Just like he did at Drengreth. It's a picture of what will happen to those who interfere with his plans."

Ky gritted his teeth to keep from venting his growing wrath.

He had no intention of merely *interfering.*

Sand blasted Birdie in the face as she neared the end of the tunnel. She squinted her eyes shut against the tiny granules pricking her skin and ducked out of the Hollow Cave into a world obscured by dusk and wind.

"It's about time." The peddler's gruff voice greeted her, and his rough hands gripped her arms. He was shouting, but Birdie could scarce hear him over the wind. "What in blazes took so long? We've been waitin' out here almost two hours an' there's a foul storm brewin'."

"Where do we go now?" Sand flew into her mouth when she spoke and threatened to choke her. As if he could sense her discomfort, Gundhrold's wing instantly lifted to shield her, and she sought shelter behind his feathers. "Do we return to Nar-Kog?"

"In this blustery madness? Not even the pathfinding skills o' the great Saari warriors could ensure our safe arrival. No, we must find shelter, an' soon afore the storm worsens."

"There is no shelter for miles." Inali's dry voice came from somewhere to Birdie's left, but she could not see him through the night and sand. "There is nothing but the cliffs and the sand."

"There is the cave."

Beneath the griffin's wing, Birdie felt the deep rumble of his voice even more than she heard it. There was strength in it and assurance, no hint of the fear and doubt that seemed to reside in her chest like a trapped animal waiting to claw its way out.

"For once I agree with the catbird—back into the cave, an' this time we're all goin' in."

"But the cave is sacred!" Inali's voice rose in pitch, and somewhere in the storm, the two mahtems voiced their disagreement.

"Beswoggle an' confound it all!" Amos tugged her toward the entrance, lurching against the force of the wind. "Sacred or not, it's where we're goin'."

Buried once more beneath mounds of rock, Birdie set her back to the wall and tried to shake the layer of sand from the clothes Sa Itera had given her while the others stumbled past. She identified them by the sound of their footsteps rather than trying to unravel their tangled melodies. Amos, Gundhrold, Inali, their lions, and the two mahtems—despite their misgivings, they too sought refuge, here in this sacred place.

"This is far enough," the griffin rasped. "We are protected, and there is no need to venture further and disturb the solemnity of the Hollow Cave."

"Indeed." Inali's voice snapped like a bowstring. "Though it is late to be thinking of that now."

Amos blew a long breath across his lips. "Right. What about a little light? Anyone got a tinderbox on 'em?"

"In my satchel—and a torch, too." Inali heaved a sigh. "I will fetch them."

Birdie slowly slid down the wall until she sat with her knees pulled up to her chin. Outside, the angry voice of the wind still raged, but within all was muted—heavy and yet not silent. A soft moaning crept through the tunnel on the caveward side. Heartrending, sorrowful, yet strong—it called to her. She closed her eyes and let the melody fill her mind.

Once again, she saw herself.

Standing in the heart of the earth, bathed in the glow of torches, the blue-white sword—Artair's sword—in her hand.

Bodies all around.

The sharp *tck tck* of flint striking steel called her back to the present just as Amos managed to catch a spark to Inali's torch. He handed it off to the two mahtems and they clustered around it with their lions at their sides, like night moths drawn to the light. Inali joined them and soon all three heads were bobbing in earnest conversation. The low, flickering light made them all look like corpses.

With a grunt, Amos dropped at her side and stretched his legs out across the width of the tunnel. A rustle of feathers heralded Gundhrold's approach, then he too sat back on his haunches beside her. His eyes glinted in the torchlight, and Birdie had no trouble reading the message written in the stern lines of his face.

He was waiting for her to speak.

But she would not speak first. Stubbornness did not guide her decision so much as a sense of fairness. It was up to *them* to break the silence for once. It was up to *them* to provide the answers that were wanting. But she had scarce resolved to maintain her silence, when the words slipped from her tongue. "I heard a voice in the Song."

Silence followed her declaration, until Amos broke it with a cough. "Did ye now? An' what did the voice say?"

Sometimes it was difficult to tell when Amos was mocking and when he was serious, especially when she couldn't read his expression. But this was no matter for jesting—not anymore.

"I didn't *just* hear it tonight in the Hollow Cave. I've heard it before . . . several times." Now that she had begun to speak, all the vague responses, excuses, and emptiness of the past months drifted to the forefront. She didn't try to keep the desperation from her voice. Perhaps it would convince Amos where her pleas had failed so many times before. "I need answers, Amos. You promised to give them to me. Now that we are here, now that I have proven myself a Songkeeper, now that you have promised my aid to the Saari in battle, I *must* know."

"Now, lass?"

"Yes, Amos, *now*. Please."

"Fine. Ye do it, griffin." The peddler's voice was edged and rougher than the rock behind Birdie's back. "Ye can explain it better 'n I."

Gundhrold chuckled softly. "Now *that* should be recorded for posterity's sake. Even the great Hawkness is willing to admit ignorance when it suits him."

Amos blustered some sort of a response, but the griffin's gaze was fixed on Birdie and hers on him, and as she stared into his massive, golden eyes, everything else—both sights and sounds—seemed to fade.

His voice dropped to a husky whisper, almost frightening in its soft intensity. "I will tell you what I know, little Songkeeper, but I fear you will be sorely disappointed in what I have to say. Even I, a Protector, do not know much. The secrets of the Songkeepers were meant to be passed down from one to the next. Never before have we had to endure such a gap of years on our own."

He broke off, and Birdie used the silence to breathe a question. "Who was the last?"

"The last Songkeeper was *your* grandmother. She entrusted you to me moments before she was slain by the Khelari on Carhartan's orders. Moments before I was wounded. Moments before I lost you."

The words—so unexpected—fell with a dead weight on her ears. Hugging her knees to her chest, she searched the griffin's eyes and saw the truth reflected there. The unbelievable, impossible, staggering truth. Somehow he had been acquainted with her family, tied to her life since the beginning . . .

And now, finally, the pieces were beginning to shift into place.

It felt as though the tunnel floor had suddenly dropped out from beneath her, and she was tumbling head over heels into the unknown.

"I . . . I had a *grandmother*?"

"She fell protecting you. She knew you were our only hope. Our little Songkeeper."

"Songkeeper." Birdie let all the bitterness, fear, and anger of the past months imbue her words. "I don't even know what that means. How can I not know what I am?"

"Through no fault of your own, little one. How could you know, when there was no one to tell you?" His eyes closed and his voice assumed a rhythmic cadence until Birdie could scarce tell if he were speaking or singing. "It is said that long ago, before the stars burned or the sun awakened, the Master Singer wove the fabric of the world through the threads of a Song and bound the melody within a river that flowed throughout the entire land of Leira. It became a source of life and of healing to all the people and creatures who lived here, and the music sang in every fiber of their being."

Drawn beyond herself, Birdie leaned forward to catch each word that fell from his tongue. "It sounds ..." She sought for the right word. "Beautiful. What happened?"

Amos barked a harsh laugh. "What d' ye suppose happened, lass? Folk revealed their true nature. They sought t' control access t' the river, keep its power for themselves. Blind, mudgrubbing slumgullions. Leastways that's how Artair told us the story. Back in the old days, gathered around the fire, hiding from the Takhran's forces ..." His voice trailed off.

Gundhrold continued. "As one familiar with the tale, Hawkness, you must know that one day the river was simply gone—vanished. Scholars have debated the cause for centuries. Some say that it was the natural course of things, the power was used up, like a well run dry. Others say it was bottled up by one man to save the power for himself. Still others claim it happened when the first man was slain in the struggle and the spring ran red with his blood. No one truly knows, but as the Song faded from the hearts and minds of the people and creatures of Leira, the first Songkeeper appeared, tasked with keeping the memory alive."

The echoes of the griffin's voice skittered down the tunnel leaving the weight of his words to hang like a heavy mantle over Birdie's shoulders. Tension creased her forehead. "But how do *I* do that, Gundhrold?"

He clacked his beak softly. "I wish I knew the answer, and I do wish to help you as I may." Will you not now tell me what you heard in the Hollow Cave?"

What she had heard? Yes, that she could tell and gladly. But as for what she had seen, somehow that was still too raw and near and terrifying for her to muster the courage to utter the words. "The voice, it told me to seek out someone or something called Tal Ethel. Do you know what that is?"

"Never heard o' it. What about ye, griffin?"

"I have heard it before, I know it. Somewhere." A growl rumbled in the back of the griffin's throat. "The thought is as near as a breath of wind across my feathers and yet I cannot grasp it. *Tal Ethel . . . Ethel.*" He mumbled to himself.

"Did you say Tal Ethel?" Inali suddenly loomed over them, spectacles magnified and face elongated by the light of the torch in his hand. "Tal Ethel?" He spun toward Birdie so quickly the beads in his braids clacked together. "I *knew* you heard him in the Cave. What did he say? What did you see?"

She longed to retreat from the intensity of his interrogation, to fade into shadow and obscurity, but she was weary of backing down. The time had come to stand. "The voice said to seek out Tal Ethel, and in my mind, I saw the city of Serrin Vroi."

Without warning, Inali shoved the torch into Amos's hand, plucked the spectacles from his face with unsteady hands, and wiped the lenses on the hem of his vest. "Tal Ethel . . . I cannot believe it."

"Well, get on with it, laddie. Don't just sit there like a blushin' fireflower. D' ye know the seaswogglin' name or not."

"Know it?" Inali swiped the back of his hand across his mouth and gave way to a shaky laugh. "How could I not? I once sought it in vain. Wandered many dark paths and endured many perils, only to fail at the last. It is the spring that fed the river that once carried the Song throughout Leira."

Amos snorted. He had that pinched, skeptical look on his face that he got whenever he was about to unleash a tide of Amos-logic. "Utter podboggle. How could a single river run through the entire country? Ye'd think folk would take notice o' something so large as an interconnected web o' dried streambeds."

"It is a legend." Inali shrugged. "That does not mean there is not truth in it. The legends also claim that one day the voice of a Songkeeper will release Tal Ethel, and the rising river will wash away the stain of the Takhran's rule. Now that the little Songkeeper has been told to find it, perhaps that day is here ..."

Birdie started to her knees. "Do you know where it is?"

"Indeed I do. As do you, if I read your vision aright. Tal Ethel is buried beneath Serrin Vroi, in the heart of Mount Eiphyr."

"Nonsense." Amos slapped his fists against the tunnel floor, but it was his eyes that captured Birdie's attention—huge, red rimmed, haunted by a fear that rivaled her own. "This is all a bit farfetched, don't ye think? Lass, ye've never even been t' Serrin Vroi. How in the name o' all things fair an' foul d' ye think ye could possibly recognize it? An' if somehow this place did exist in Serrin Vroi, 'tis beyond foolishness t' talk o' goin' there. Ye'll find naught behind those foul walls but darkness an' terror an' . . . an' death. Help me, griffin? Ye know I speak the truth."

The griffin reared his head back and flared his wings with the creaking and cracking of ancient bones. "There is another matter of greater concern to me at the moment, peddler. You say you sought the spring, Dah Inali. Why?"

Inali shrugged, but his apathetic air was surpassed by the dullness of his voice. "It was thought I was to be a Songkeeper . . . once."

8

Amos McElhenny rocked back on his heels, studying the drawn face of the young Saari before him, and for once found himself at a complete loss for words. It was mind boggling, that's what it was, to think that Inali, brother-in-law to the Matlal, had almost been a Songkeeper. What did that even mean? How was one *almost* a Songkeeper? Had the lad failed some unknown test in some strange, inexplicable way, or had it all been a misunderstanding?

Truth be told, the more he thought he understood about this mysterious world of melodies and Songkeepers and magic, the more he was forced to admit his own cursed ignorance.

And it wasn't a confession he enjoyed making.

Still, if naught else, Inali's claim explained the council's hesitancy to accept Birdie as the Songkeeper without proof. Mayhap this testing in the Hollow Cave was where Inali had failed.

"I understand it might come as a shock." With painstaking care, Inali replaced the spectacles on the bridge of his nose. "But it was long ago and means nothing now, save that I may vouch for the little Songkeeper's abilities. We accomplished what we set out to do. And yet …"

"Yet *what*?"

"The voice told her to seek Tal Ethel." Inali squared his shoulders and met his glare head on. It appeared the lad was made of sterner stuff than Amos would have guessed. "It spoke to her, Hawkness. You cannot simply ignore that. I may not be the Songkeeper, but I know a little of the legends. More than most. And I know that one day, a Songkeeper will appear who will stand against the Takhran and free the Song so it may flow once more through the souls of all Leirans. This *must* be that day."

"Ye're out o' yer crook-pated mind if ye think I'm allowin' my wee lass t' dredge the bowels o' the Pit below Mount Eiphyr." Amos massaged his aching forehead and couldn't help wishing it were possible to somehow erase the painful memories seared forever in the back of his mind. "Venturin' into Serrin Vroi will only see all o' us killed, an' then where'd Leira be without a Songkeeper once again?"

"It is a conundrum, Hawkness." Gundhrold shook his head. "Yet like Inali, I do not believe we can in good conscience ignore the significance of this night. Who are we to reject the dictates of the Song of the Master Singer?"

Amos opened his mouth to disagree, but a light touch settled on his arm, stifling the rapid flow of indignation before it could rip from his tongue.

"What if he's right, Amos? I have to believe this all happened for a reason. It cannot simply be chance. This is who I am, and I'm so tired of being hunted. Of running, running, *running*, knowing that I will never find anywhere safe so long as the Takhran knows I'm alive. I would rather fight than be caught on the run, and if that means taking the fight to him for a change, who am I to argue?"

"Lass, knowing ye'll never be completely safe an' running headlong into danger are two mighty different beasts."

Birdie stared at him. "You're the one who signed me up for a war."

"Aye." Amos bowed his head, the sudden image of his lass standing before a horde of Khelari with Artair's cursed blade in her hands seared across his vision. He'd promised the Saari their own fighting Songkeeper, but still kept the blade hidden in his chambers in Nar-Kog. Hadn't even told her that he had it. Soon, he would have to summon the courage to give it to her, and if she had but half the strength and power he suspected, in time, she would become truly formidable. The Saari would not willingly consent to her departure.

It was beginning to seem more and more a devil's bargain.

But even a devil's bargain was preferable to the horrors below Mount Eiphyr. Here, even in battle, he could promise her some sort of protection. Fighting a war was one thing, but infiltrating Serrin Vroi, that was madness.

Birdie's hand settled on his forearm. "What if there's a better way to fight?"

"Lass, what ye're suggesting is not a fight. It's a suicide mission." He would have done anything to stamp out the disappointment that flared in her eyes and soothe the lines of worry that creased her brow. She was but a wee lass, too gentle for this world of nightmares. What right had Emhran to lay such a burden upon her?

The griffin cleared his throat. "Yet it *is* a mission. Let us be honest here, Hawkness. Neither you nor I are equipped to guide the Songkeeper in her duties or train her into what she must become. I am but a Protector, and you are but an outlaw. Who are we to tell her what to do or where to go?"

"Ye forget, I've *been* there." Amos jabbed a finger toward the griffin's face. His whole body was quaking now with restrained fury, but there was naught he could do to control it. "I've walked the lightless paths. I've seen the horrors. Horrors ye cannot even begin t' imagine. We cannot take the Songkeeper there."

"*You* forget, Hawkness, that I have been there too." Inali's mild voice cut through the cloud of images accumulating on the edges of Amos's vision and shredded them like mist. "I may have failed my task"—his voice fell to a whisper—"but I survived."

"Ye said it yerself, Gundhrold, 'tis our duty t' protect her."

"Indeed. But we have crossed the line from protection to hindrance if in our desire to keep her safe, we refuse her the means to accomplish what she is meant to do."

The griffin's head lowered until Amos found his gaze seized by those fierce yellow eyes and felt himself quailing before the beast's certainty. Why did the sand-blasted catbird have to be so seaswoggling logical? It was downright infuriating.

"I don't like the sound o' it. Pure, utter, boggswogglin' foolishness, if ye ask me. An' I can guarantee the mahtems aren't goin' t' be pleased t' discover we've gone back on our word." He jerked his chin toward the two mahtems seated stoically beside their lions at the far end of the tunnel and dropped his voice to a whisper. "I promised them aid in battle—yer idea, as I recall."

Gundhrold sniffed. "We are not reneging on our promise, simply fulfilling it in a different, better way. There are bigger things at stake here. It is no longer a matter of just winning one battle. If we succeed, we could bring about the ending of this war."

Amos sighed and recognized it as the sound of his own capitulation. He might not be convinced, but he was clearly outmaneuvered, outmatched, and outwitted. Sometimes, surrender was the only option. "Oh, it sounds very grand when ye put it that way. Ye should say it just like that when ye explain t' the mahtems why Hawkness an' the Songkeeper won't be stickin' around for the fight."

"When I explain?"

"Aye, I seem t' recall someone somewhere sayin' somethin' about Hawkness not bein' known for tact or diplomacy." Amos clapped a heavy hand on the griffin's shoulder. "Best ye do all the talkin'."

With a swoosh of beaded fabric, the curtain to the Matlal's council chamber fell at the heels of her companions, leaving Birdie standing in the middle of the hallway with the ache of loneliness clawing within and the peddler's muttered excuse ringing in her ears.

He'd rushed through the words as if afraid to give her a chance to speak. "Mightn't it be best, lass, if ye waited outside and left the matter t' Gundhrold t' settle? Ye agree don't ye? Reckon the old catbird can handle it best."

Then he simply patted her on the head, as one would an obedient hound and hurried inside after Gundhrold, Dah Inali, and the two mahtems.

Her cheeks burned at the memory.

Somewhere within the chamber, the griffin's deep voice rumbled, and for a moment, it was the only sound. Then an uproar of voices broke out in answer and Birdie shifted uneasily, rocking back on her heels. She did not need to hear clearly to understand the cause of their outrage. Perhaps Amos had been wise to leave her behind after all.

Spears in hand, two Saari warriors fell into position on either side of the entrance, and Birdie backed away, unwilling to be relegated to the role of the troublesome child caught eavesdropping while the movers and shakers strategized within. Propelled by the unyielding stances of the guards, she turned from the hall and caught sight of the carved bench where Sa Itera had introduced them to Dah Inali. It was as good a place as any to await the outcome. Better than retreating to her chambers.

She dropped into the seat and leaned back against the wall. A torch rustled in a bracket over her head, and when she closed her eyes, the cavorting flames scattered threads of shadow and light across her eyelids. There had been little opportunity for rest in the Hollow Cave before the sandstorm abated midmorning and the mahtems insisted they return to Nar-Kog. Now she felt her body sinking, drawn toward sleep.

But something within her would not be stilled, a restlessness and a fury that set her chest burning at inaction and started her fingers tapping against the bench frame. This decision had more to do with her than with anyone else. Yet here she was, forced to wait while others determined her fate.

A soft step drew her focus.

"There you are." Ky halted before her with his arms folded across his chest and his forehead wrinkled with an expression that made him look twice his age. The borrowed clothes were no help. In the too-large fringed trousers and jacket, he looked like a child wearing the garb and face of a man. "Been lookin' for you all morning. Where've you been?"

"Sandstorm." She hunched over, resting her elbows on her knees and her forehead in her hands. A layer of grit coated her skin. It was probably embedded in her hair and clothes too. She ran a finger along the beadwork lining the hem and bodice of her loose red tunic, and tried to dust some of the sand from her fringed leggings. "We couldn't find you when we left."

He shrugged. "Something I had to do. Doesn't matter now. But this does." His gaze dropped to his hands, and somehow, in that moment of hesitation, she knew what he was going to say before he said it. "I'm leaving, Birdie. Headed back to the Underground. I got to, you see. They need me. I left them in a right konker of a mess, and I got to help sort it out."

Leaving …

The word stole the breath from Birdie's lungs. "When are you going?"

Ky blinked, most likely surprised that she hadn't tried to dissuade him. But she had no right. He had only stumbled into the chaos of her life by accident. The Underground was his true home, and the boys and girls of Kerby were his family. Because of her, he'd had to leave them behind, only to be captured, beaten, and tortured.

Was it any wonder that he wanted to leave?

"The messenger who brought the news about the Midlands, he's headed back that way. I mean to tag along. Just as soon as I can borrow some supplies."

"Borrow. You mean steal."

"Harvest." He gave a soft chuckle. "That's what we called it in the Underground. Not like it'll be the first time." He fiddled with the fringe on his borrowed hide jacket. "Harder without the pockets though. We put special pockets inside, made apple bobbing and bread nicking easier—a tip in case you ever wind up out on the streets of Kerby."

"I'll be sure to drop by if I ever do."

A grin eased across his face, and Birdie forced a smile in return.

"Confound it all, ye boggswogglin', sand-blasted, rock-pated lubbers! I've had about enough o' this. I demand ye unhand me!"

Amos's shout brought Birdie to her feet in time to see the heavy hanging covering the entrance to the council chamber wrenched from its rod as five Saari warriors burst through dragging the wild-eyed peddler. "Unhand me, ye lolloping ormahounds! I'll not stand for it. Where's my lass? Birdie . . . Birdie, where are ye?"

"Amos?" She started toward him at a run, but the griffin's wing blocked her path.

"Lass!" Amos's roving gaze fixed on her and held fast as the Saari warriors hauled him down the hallway at a half run. "Don't worry. It'll all work out. It's naught but a wee misunderstandin'."

Gundhrold sighed. "That, I'm afraid, is a *wee* understatement."

She broke free from the shackle of his wing and watched until the struggling peddler disappeared around the next bend. "What happened?"

"I warned Hawkness to guard his tongue." The griffin clacked his beak softly. "Yet no sooner had they refused our request, than that stubborn fool insulted the Maltal on his throne, in the presence of his wife and mahtems. It is a unique method of gaining allies."

"I must agree with you there, my lord." Dah Inali emerged from the council hall with Sym at his side. "The Saari are a proud people, and my brother-in-law, the Matlal, no less than the rest. He cannot ignore a slight to his name. The tribes would not stand for it."

"We must speak with them." Birdie started forward but Sym stood in her path.

"I fear that will not be possible." Sym held her spear low, but did not ground it—that, and the faint edge to her voice, seemed a ripple of warning amidst her calm exterior. "We are tasked with escorting you both back to the little Songkeeper's chambers and seeing that you remain there under watch until matters have settled. Sa Itera wishes to ensure your safety until the Khelari arrive and your skills are required in battle."

"Our safety?" The griffin's dignified air only served to heighten the bite of sarcasm in his voice. "It is needless, but we shall, of course, acquiesce to the Matlal's wishes." He swept a graceful wing toward the hallway. "After you."

Sym smiled with all the warmth and emotion of stone. "No, my lord, after *you*."

As they marched down the hallway, Birdie glanced at the alcove in search of Ky, but he had somehow managed to disappear again. Probably meant to use Amos's outburst as an opportunity to *harvest* a few items from the storeroom. Back in her torch-lit chamber, she dropped onto the low bench with Gundhrold at her side, while Sym took up position just inside the curtain. Distant enough to grant some semblance of privacy, yet near enough to warrant speaking in a whisper when Birdie finally summoned the courage to break the silence.

"Back in the cave, you spoke of my grandmother. Would you tell me about her?"

With a sigh that sounded as though it came from the depths of the earth, the griffin sank back on his haunches and regarded her with deep, sad eyes. "Auna. Her name was Auna. It means 'dear heart,' and never was a name more befitting. She was a dedicated Songkeeper—perhaps not as powerful as some, but strong in so many other ways. Selfless to the end ..."

Enthralled by the spell of his words, Birdie tried to conjure up some recollection of the woman who had been her grandmother, but no image came. "What of my parents—did you know them too?"

"Nay, not I. Your father was Auna's son—the eldest of two—but beyond that I know little of him, or of your mother."

"But you know what became of them?"

"Only rumors, little one, so I cannot speak with certainty. It was said that your mother, father, and his brother were captured by the Khelari and taken to Serrin Vroi when you were but a month old. But they are dead—they must be—Carhartan as much as said so long ago."

The crackle of the torch flames in their wall brackets seemed to magnify tenfold, filling Birdie's ears like the whisper of the ghosts of all she had once dreamed. Her family was dead, and it should not come as a surprise. Not after all these years. Still, hearing it from the griffin's tongue awakened a sore she did not know had been festering in her heart.

"The Takhran . . . did he kill them?"

It surprised her to find that her voice was steady even when faced with the end of all her hopes. She could not change the past. She could barely influence her future course. But this moment lay wholly in her control, and she would weather it with the strength of the cliffs of Nar-Kog.

"Would that I knew. I am sorry, little Songkeeper." The griffin's voice rasped like a blade drawn from its sheath. "Beyond the words Carhartan spoke—whether true or otherwise—there is no way to know their ultimate fate. No secrets to chase. No rocks to turn. No paths to follow."

There was *one* path, but Birdie dared not utter it to the griffin. She hardly dared think it. But if she had needed extra incentive to travel to Serrin Vroi and brave the perils below Mount Eiphyr, she had it now. For there, in the Takhran's keeping, lay the secrets of her past.

9

A fist thudded against the wall outside the curtained doorway, and Birdie started up in her seat on the bench. Evening hung heavy over the room. Though there were no windows through which she could track the course of the sun and the shadows, Birdie could feel it in the ache in her bones, the stiffness of her limbs, and the dull throb of exhaustion behind her eyes.

For hours she had sat in silence, trying to comprehend all she had learned, and the griffin had not disturbed her. So many questions tumbled about inside her head, and yet after all this time of desiring nothing more than the chance to ask and be answered, she discovered she could not find the words.

The fist hammered again. Louder. More determined.

Sym shoved away from the wall where she had been leaning and brought her spear up to bar the entrance. "Who is there? Speak."

"Dah Inali, here to relieve you."

Sym relaxed and righted her spear, setting the butt against the ground with a distinct rap. "You may enter."

The curtain slid partway open, then a burly, flame-headed figure barged into the room, swept the spear from Sym's hand, and flung her back against the wall. Her flailing arm swept a torch from its bracket as she fell.

"Amos?" Birdie started forward.

But Sym was up again, quick as an adder strike. She dodged the peddler's next stroke with ease, one hand reaching for the quiver of throwing spears strapped to her back. Out of the corner of her eye, Birdie saw a second figure duck into the room—Inali. He raised a black tube to his mouth, squinting through his spectacles.

Before Birdie could shout warning, Sym swayed and fell, as if someone had cut away the earth beneath her feet.

The peddler spun around and flung his hands up. "What in the name o' all things shrouded an' secretive d' ye think ye're doin'?"

"Pardon me for saving you." Inali stuck the tube through his belt like a sword and knelt at Sym's side. Grabbing her wrists in one hand and her ankles in another, he slung her over his shoulder. "I've freed you once tonight, and I would rather not do it again. I prefer to commit treason as few times as possible."

"She was but a wee thing. I had it under control."

"Indeed." Inali jerked his head toward the doorway. "Shall we go?"

Muttering under his breath, Amos yanked a torch from a wall bracket and motioned toward Birdie and Gundhrold. "I had it under control."

"Undoubtedly." Gundhrold's nose lifted almost imperceptibly into the air. "But quick and quiet aren't really Hawkness's way, now are they?"

Ignoring Amos's stifled indignation, Birdie followed the griffin out into the hallway and stumbled over an abandoned spear. She caught herself against the doorframe and stared, transfixed by the sight of two Saari warriors crumpled in a heap against the opposite wall.

"Excuse me, lass." Amos slid past her, grabbed one set of ankles with his free hand, and dragged the unconscious warrior into the chamber with much huffing and puffing, then returned for the second. Once both were inside, he drew the curtain closed and spun on his heels to face the griffin. The action revealed the hawk headed dirk attached to his belt and a long, thin knapsack strapped to his back.

"Ye were sayin'?"

Gundhrold rolled his eyes, and a grin split Amos's face. From the base of the wall, he retrieved the fallen throwing spear Birdie had tripped over and thrust it into her hands.

"Here ye go, lass. Look fierce an' act like ye know how t' use it. We might need t' bluff our way out." Without another word, he spun and took off down the hallway.

Birdie hurried after him, clutching the weapon with both hands. It was light enough that she should be able to wield it . . . if spear fighting was anything like broom wielding. "But where are we going, Amos?"

"High time we left this seaswoggled place behind, don't ye think? These sun-addled people are as inflexible as steel an' unbending as their sand-blasted cliffs. It's gettin' right tiresome."

Without slacking pace, they rounded a corner and came face to face with Dah Inali crouching beside a bench with Sym's limp form still dangling over one shoulder. He staggered to his feet, cheeks flushed and breath short. "I feared you decided it was safer to stay in captivity."

Gundhrold's chuckle sounded like snapping twigs. "That would depend on your definition of safe."

"My definition? How about anywhere but here? Do try to keep up."

"Hold up there." Amos seized Inali's shoulder, and from the Saari's grimace, he was none too gentle about it. "What are ye doin' with the lass? No need t' bring her. Best ye stash her somewhere safe an' quiet."

"And leave her to sound the alarm?" Inali shrugged free. "I think not." Despite the burden he was carrying, Inali set a swift pace through the dizzying network of tunnels and passageways inside the cliff. They had not gone far before a sound like muffled thunder came from somewhere behind them, and a cloud of smoke bearing the sweet scent of steaming apples and cinnamon rolled down the passage.

Birdie clutched her spear until her knuckles whitened, catapulted back in memory to another tunnel where Underground runners had fought and died to hold off the Khelari she had led to them. She choked down the surge of guilt. "Ryree powder?"

"Aye, 'twould appear dwarf messengers are good for more 'n deliverin' ill tidings."

Inali whirled to face him. "Are you trying to make enemies of my people? They will not forgive an attack upon their own. If anyone was injured—"

"Look, lad, I'm no fool. I took care when I set the fuse."

"But I've been with you ever since ..." He broke off, brow furrowed. "Save when I slipped into the council chamber."

"It's naught but a wee diversion t' hide our disappearance. Besides it's time yer mahtems learned that when Hawkness sets his mind t' somethin', 'tisn't healthy t' stand in his way." His voice dropped to a growl. "Ye'd do well t' learn it too. Shall we be off then?"

With a grudging nod, Inali resumed his trek, moving with the utmost caution along an ever changing course and ducking frequently into empty chambers to avoid Saari men and women strolling through the halls. They met no warriors, but whether that was due to Inali's skill as a guide or Amos's fiery diversion, Birdie could not say.

At last, the passage ended abruptly at a stone door.

Inali jerked his head at Amos. The beads rattled in his hair and his spectacles teetered dangerously close to falling from the bridge of his nose. "Open it."

The peddler passed the torch to Birdie, squeezed past Inali, and seizing the door with both hands, managed to swing the block of stone just wide enough for the griffin to fit through without ruffling his feathers too much. Holding the torch before her like a sword, Birdie followed Gundhrold onto one of the high arching stone bridges that spanned the valley between the two halves of the city.

Torches and fire pots peppered the opposite cliff, marking the road at regular intervals as it wound through the stacked rows of dimly lit houses. Above and below, the surrounding bridges were bathed in light as well, making the torch in her hand seem weak and feeble in comparison. It was barely strong enough to reveal the narrow walkway before her and throw into even greater relief the vast, impenetrable darkness on either side. But the torch *was* bright enough that she could see how the rocks underfoot were pitted and twisted by sand and wind, and in places had fallen away, leaving gaping holes through which the valley leered so far below.

Gundhrold's wing brushed her shoulder and he whispered in her ear. "Never fear, little Songkeeper. I will not let you fall."

The height didn't worry her. *Much.*

"Dim moon." Inali's face crinkled as he peered up at the sky. "That is good. It will give us the advantage when it comes to passing through Kog, and in three days when we have arrived at the border, it will have waned completely. That should aid us in moving undetected past the Khelari."

"What about the Saari?" At the breath of her words, the torch flickered, and she hastily shielded it with her free hand. "Won't the Matlal send them after us?"

"It doesn't sound like the alarm has spread yet." Amos nudged Inali with his elbow. "Perhaps my diversion worked better 'n ye thought it would."

"Oh the alarm has spread, have no doubt about that. But they will keep the news quiet for now, contained within the palace. Extend the search to the rest of the city of Nar when no sign turns up. But they will refrain from alarming all the citizens of Nar-Kog with word that the Songkeeper has abandoned them and Hawkness has gone rogue. Now that the Khelari are so close, Quahtli will not want to diminish morale."

"Hawkness is an outlaw. Don't know how much more rogue ye can go 'n that."

Inali grunted. "In any case, the lack of moonlight would do little to aid us in evading skilled trackers once they are on our trail. It is well that we have taken the finest tracker with us." He tilted his head to indicate Sym's unconscious form still slung over his shoulder. "And I think it unlikely they will attempt to follow us, once it has become clear that we are no longer within the city. Quahtli knows his forces will be better spent preparing to defend Nar-Kog against the Khelari, perhaps even launching a preemptive strike. We, on the other hand, shall go across the bridge and then down through the city of Kog. I have mounts—saddled and supplied—waiting for us at the base of the cliff. We will be miles away before Quahtli and my sister realize we have gone."

"Mounts?" Amos heaved the door shut. "Ye mean lions, don't ye? That's grand. Just . . . grand."

10

Trust the Saari—mighty hunters, trackers, and warriors that they were—to keep their storerooms well stocked. Ky cast an appreciative eye over the crammed shelves and overflowing barrels that filled the fourth storeroom he had visited so far. All locked, of course, but unguarded, and when had locks ever posed a problem for a trained Underground runner?

It was Paddy who'd first taught him the art of lock-picking. Dizzier's skill lay more in the area of brute force than any task requiring fine finger work. He'd sooner burst through a door and deal with the consequences of raising the alarm later.

Silent as a shadow, Ky crept from shelf to shelf, ignoring the ache of battered muscles and bruises deep as bone, a lingering reminder of his imprisonment on the Langorian ship, as he removed a few select items and stashed them in a borrowed sack. Cade always said a good runner took care not to harvest too much from the same patch. One apple could have been misplaced. Half a barrel could not.

So Ky filched a few rounds of flat bread from one storeroom, two chains of sausage links and a hunk of dried meat from another, several knobby, oval-shaped fruits from the third, and here in the fourth storeroom, a pouch of beans and a fist-sized chunk of cheese.

He nicked a piece of twine from the storeroom shelf and knotted it around the mouth of the sack. It was a bulky bundle. Not the sort he could conceal beneath his jacket. But he would need every mouthful of it before the journey was over, if the dwarf's tales of a country in chaos were to be believed. Once he set his back to the cliffs of Nar-Kog, he didn't plan on stopping for supplies until he could see the chimneys and rooftops of Kerby in the distance.

A muffled boom sounded somewhere deep in the palace. Ky

dropped his sack. It landed beside his bare feet, spilled open, and one of the knobby fruits bounced over his toes. He scrambled for his supplies as a commotion broke out in the surrounding rooms and corridors—people shouting in the harsh language of the desert, running feet, cursing.

Ky slung his sack over one shoulder, crept to the door, and eased it open. Just a crack.

A group of Saari warriors—ten strong—raced past his hiding place with spears flashing in their hands and lions pacing at their heels. Less than a minute later, another ten quick-marched in the opposite direction. Ky had spent the past two days familiarizing himself with the ins and outs and secret byways of the palace. From the looks of things, something big had gone down back by the Matlal's council chamber.

It was time to disappear.

He inched the door shut behind him, locked it with a flick of his wrist, and ducked out of the door-well, only to slam full force into a short, burly figure.

"Whoa there." The dwarf caught him with both hands to the chest and shoved him back against the wall. "Watch where you're going, Shorty."

"Don't call me that."

The words snapped out faster than a stone from his sling, and Migdon's eyebrows scrunched together. "Touchy, touchy, bucko my boyo." He craned his thick neck to peer down the hall. "You the cause of all this hullabaloo?"

"Don't think so."

"Pity. Thought maybe you were showing some real promise. Must have been that ryree powder I sold Hawkness. Wish I'd thought of it. The man has a talent for flair." Migdon scowled and Ky found himself squirming beneath a scrutiny as fierce as any griffin's. "You do still want to go through with this, right? I can help get you free of this lion's den, but you can bet your tattered britches there'll be worse dangers to come once I do. Once I land on a clear road north, you're on your own."

"Right."

"You're determined, bucko—I'll give you that. Well then, let's be off." He turned to leave, and Ky noticed the bulging knapsack on his back for the first time. It had more pockets than the jacket of an Underground runner, a thin coil of rope strapped to one side, and the haft of a hatchet sticking out of the top.

The dwarf had come prepared to travel.

"But something's happened. The Saari are on the alert. And my friends ..." Ky shrugged in a gesture of helplessness, unable to say more. He had told Birdie he was leaving, but after all they had been through, to simply disappear without any sort of a good-bye felt wrong.

"Your friends have already cut and run. Why do you think the Saari are on the alert? Trust me, they're long gone by now, and it's past time we moved on too. Oh, almost forgot." Migdon reached a hand into one of the pockets of his knapsack, pulled out a folded strip of leather, and dropped it in Ky's hand.

Ky unfolded it to reveal a sling, identical to the one the dwarf had been using and not so very different from his own—save that it was far better crafted. Decorative stitching ran along the edges of the straps, and the symbol of a three-headed mountain was carved into the pouch. He let the strands slip through his fingers, relishing the oiled suppleness of the leather.

"Saw you looking at old Tildy here." Migdon patted the sling tucked through his belt. "Knew you for a sling man since first I set eyes on you. Hope you're good. You might need to be." He rummaged in his pack a moment more, then pulled out a pouch that clacked and clattered when he tossed it into Ky's outstretched hand.

Ky nearly dropped it.

Migdon grinned. "Lead sling-bullets. Best projectiles there are. Make them count."

The dwarf took off without a backward glance, and Ky hurried to keep up. Without slackening pace, he looped the sling around his waist like a belt and tied the pouch in place. It felt good to have a weapon close to hand once more. He would not allow himself to be captured and disarmed again.

A fierce part of him ached to stand before the pirate lord Rhudashka and that wretch Fjordair, and give them a taste of the suffering the slaves had endured. But the Saari had beaten him to it and left the mangled corpses to rot on the beach until they washed into the seas they had terrorized. The vengeance of the desert was swift and brutal.

To Kerby then and the Underground. He shoved aside his nagging doubts, determined to fall upon the Khelari blockade and drive the dark soldiers away, cursing and cringing like dogs from the sting of his stones.

Bold as a lion in its den, Migdon jabbered away as he strode the palace hallways past stern-faced Saari who scarce noticed his passing. Ky fought the urge to fall into the familiar patterns of invisibility and instead marched along at Migdon's side, shoulders erect, eyes fixed straight ahead.

"Don't look so stiff and concerned, bucko. Word from the wise, sometimes there's no better place to hide than in the open, and no better way to disappear than to stand out."

"That doesn't make any sense."

"Sure it does. Hogan wrote it years and years ago—you do know who Hogan is right? Hogan Micthineous Cadronitus Roardin? No? Oh well, don't worry about it." Molasses dripped no smoother than the sarcasm rolling off the dwarf's tongue. "He's only the finest philosopher, teacher, and strategist we of the Whyndburg Mountains have ever had."

Ky hiked his sack higher up on his shoulder. His battered body was beginning to protest the dwarf's prolonged rapid pace. The breath came short in his throat, and his attention drifted from the dwarf's words to their route. It was starting to look familiar. "Where are we headed?"

Migdon scowled over his shoulder. "They say 'Chaos is the ally of the desperate man,' and I reckon it applies to dwarves and snot-nosed boys too. Let's test it at the front gate, shall we?"

• • •

Tauros's fingers had scarce cleared the tips of the mountains to the east when Amos called a halt beneath the shelter of a stone outcropping surrounded by drifts of sand. Birdie slipped from the saddle and landed on numb feet. She caught the high crested pommel just in time to keep from falling and leaned her weary head against the lioness's muscled shoulder.

A whiskered muzzle nudged her ear. "There now, little cub, are you so weary you cannot wait to set camp?" A hint of amusement crept into the lioness's voice. "I did not know two-legs slept on their feet like livestock."

"Not asleep, Ryn," Birdie mumbled into the lioness's fur. "I'm awake. Truly."

The past three nights of travel had given Birdie more than a passing acquaintance with the lioness she rode. Whispered conversation helped pass the long hours of darkness. Amos's fear of pursuit or stumbling across a Khelari patrol prohibited speech between the mounted pairs, but so long as she whispered in Ryn's ear, no one was any the wiser.

No doubt it was best that way. To anyone else, it would have sounded like she was talking to herself while the lioness simply purred or rumbled deep in its throat, and she knew from experience how utterly mad that looked.

"Right." Amos dropped from his saddle. "Looks as good a place t' rest as any. Decent shelter—" he nodded at the outcropping "—but there's still a fair view in all directions so we can keep an eye out for pursuit."

"Is it really wise to stop so early?" Inali leaned forward, elbows resting on the pommel, bringing his head closer to Amos's level. "Should we not keep going and try to cover as much ground as we may?" He spoke quietly, but in the silence of the night Birdie had no trouble hearing him.

Nor, it appeared, did the others.

Sym's tuneless laugh jerked Inali back to an upright position.

"And why would you suggest that, Inali?" Though her hands were bound at the wrists and a guide rope ran from her lion's steering collar to Inali's saddle, when she spoke, she seemed the captor and he the captive. "Do you fear that your sister will not allow you to disappear? That she will convince the Matlal to send men in pursuit to drag you back to Nar-Kog in disgrace, again?"

"I am *not* afraid of my sister," Inali snarled. "Our mission is important, and I do not wish to delay. That is all."

"Are you so desperate to prove yourself that you would risk leaving our people vulnerable before the Khelari attack? You are a thoughtless fool and a simpering cowar—"

"Enough!"

Inali's scream agitated his lioness, and the beast hunkered down to pounce. Sym looked ready to pounce too, bound hands and all, and one glance at the fury in her eyes was enough to clear any doubts as to who would rise victorious.

"Belay that!" Amos stepped between the two, hands raised. "We're drawin' nigh the border, an' I don't need t' tell ye what sort o' fools ye'll *both* be if ye attract the attention o' the Khelari. I'll kill ye myself an' save ye both the trouble. Inali, I allowed ye t' bring Sym along because ye claimed her skills as a tracker would endanger us if she were free. But as soon as we reach the end o' the desert, I intend t' set her loose, an' ye might as well know it now."

"But—"

"Now," Amos cut him off. "I said we're stoppin' for the day, an' I meant it. If Inali's navigational skills aren't entirely awry—"

"They're not." Gundhrold looked up from preening his wing feathers. "The boy seems to be leading us true."

"*If* that's the case, an' *if* we leave at dusk, we should cross into the Soudlands before midnight. I've no intention o' tryin' t' attempt such a thing in broad daylight when the Takhran's cursed spies could spot us movin' from miles away. Are we clear?"

The griffin nodded assent, and both Inali and Sym muttered agreement.

"Right then, let's get settled."

Birdie searched through the packs slung behind her saddle and removed only the necessary supplies. There would be no fire—they had not risked building one since leaving Nar-Kog—but Inali had packed food aplenty for weeks to come, as well as spare skins and blankets to ward off the winter chill that crept over the desert sands with the sinking of the sun.

Ryn chuckled, a deep hacking noise that Birdie might have mistaken for a cough had she not become accustomed to the sound. "Yon peddler has a most efficient roar. For a two-legs, he would make a decent lion, I think."

A rumble of agreement drifted through the other lions. As Birdie set out her bedroll and curled beneath the layer of skins and blankets with the rock outcropping shielding her from the rising sun and unfriendly eyes, she pondered the lion's statement and Amos's warnings of the dangers they would face in the days to come.

She recalled the words Quoth, Itera's lioness, had spoken on her first day in Nar-Kog. "Stand if you would be seen as a lion and not as a mouse."

Should she go through with this mission, there was no telling what would become of her or Amos or any of her companions. To brave the perils beneath Mount Eiphyr in search of a legend, to venture beneath the Takhran's nose on nothing more than the whispered hints of a mysterious voice interpreted by a stranger, was there any greater madness than this?

Ryn had paid Amos a deep compliment. She gathered that much from her time among the Saari. But if Amos was a lion, then what was she?

A lion or a mouse?

11

The sounds of battle awakened Birdie from slumber: hoarse cries, drumming hooves, and the singing of arrows loosed from the string. Like a roll of thunder, the notes of the dark melody crashed into her with such force that it left her breathless. She tore free of her blankets and reached for the throwing spear Amos had given her when they snuck from Nar-Kog. Her fingers brushed wood and she caught it up, wheeling to crouch on hands and knees to take stock of her surroundings.

"Shh, lass. Stay down." Amos's hand pressed against the back of her head. Sand rustled beneath his shifting weight, and he wormed past her, dirk between his teeth, to peer out through the gap between the outcropping and the sand drifts. Sym, Inali, and Gundhrold were already there, bodies pressed flat against the sand. Gundhrold's tawny wings were spread wide, shielding the two Saari from view. The lions waited in the hollow, growling in agitation.

Clutching the unwieldy length of the spear in one hand, Birdie inched her way up beside Amos and tilted her head to see over the edge. A scarce two hundred yards away, dark figures on armored steeds filled her vision—Khelari. Her grip tightened on the spear until the muscles in her arm trembled. Five . . . ten . . . almost a score of them, wheeling in battle formation to surround two Saari in a circle of ringing hooves and flashing steel.

One of the Saari, still mounted on a lion, paced a slow circle within the ring of death with his spear extended as if daring the Khelari to venture within range of his arm. The other knelt beside his fallen lion, but he seemed to be struggling to rise. Distance could not hide the bright splash of blood on the sand and on his clothes.

"Untie me, Inali." Sym's voice bore a harder edge than the tips of her spears. She gripped his forearm with her bound hands. "They are our scouts! They cannot stand alone. We *must* go to their aid."

"Don't be a fool, Sym." Inali shrugged free of her grip. "What can we do against twenty? They are already dead, and we would simply join them."

An arrow struck the downed Saari, and he collapsed onto the body of his steed. Intent upon the cacophony of music that warred within her skull, Birdie thought she heard a tenor voice break off, mid-note, into a strangled cry that faded away.

"The Songkeeper then!" Sym ground her fists into the sand, and the steel in her voice snapped. "We must do *something*."

Birdie shivered beneath the gazes that settled upon her and felt the prickle of sweat forming on her forehead. She *had* promised to fight for the Saari if that was what it came to in the end, but that didn't change the fact that she did not know how to use the melody against their foes, or how to get the Song to cooperate if she did. Charging out there with no plan and no Song seemed senseless.

"Venturing out there would be madness. We cannot risk the Songkeeper." Gundhrold's raspy voice flowed like cool water over her fears, extinguishing them—if only for the moment—and filling her with relief.

The thought instantly sickened her. When had she become heartless enough to feel *relieved* that she did not have to intervene while two men were slaughtered within sight of her hiding place? She cowered willingly behind Gundhrold's excuse, buying another day to fumble through her role as the vaunted Songkeeper, before they saw her for the fraud she feared she was.

The griffin sighed, even as the death scream of the Saari's lion reverberated through the rocks at their backs. "There is nothing we can do. Not if we would complete our mission."

"He's right. Curse him, but he is," Amos hissed. "Those Khelari are advance scouts, but the main army will not be far behind, an' there's no tellin' what spies were sent on ahead. If we go out now, we'll be spotted sure an' certain, an' it's only a wee step from there t' execution. We'd arrive at Mount Eiphyr sure enough, be taken into the Pit no doubt, but ye can bet yer life we wouldn't be comin' out again."

Sym struggled to rise but Gundhrold's wing held her flat. "What do I care for your mission? Those are my people dying down there—my brothers. I cannot watch this. Unhand me!" She wrenched free of the griffin's grasp and scrambled to the top of the drift.

Whatever she intended to do, bound and weaponless as she was, she never made it. Inali caught her by the ankle before she could descend and hauled her bodily back, sending a fountain of sand cascading over the side.

On the plain below, the Saari scout fell beneath the blade of a mounted Khelari. With a cry, he staggered to his feet and stumbled on a few steps, like a drunken man, straight into the path of a swinging sword. Birdie buried a cry in her hand. The warrior's head flipped backwards, severed at the neck, and dropped to the ground at his feet, followed a moment later by his body. The note of his passing rippled through Birdie's mind, and she clenched both hands to her ears in an attempt to quiet it.

Directly overhead, the shrill scream of a raven sounded out. As one, the Khelari pulled their steeds to a stamping halt and cast about in all directions. A second cry rang out, and the Khelari urged their horses toward the rock outcropping at a determined lope.

Amos dragged her to her feet. "Mount up, lass. We've got t' run for it!"

Forsaking her cumbersome weapon, Birdie scrambled beneath the shelter of the outcropping and flung her saddle and bundle of supplies on Ryn's back. Her hands were shaking so, she could not get the unfamiliar straps through the buckles. Even Sym, hampered though she was by the bindings on her wrists, managed to finish before Birdie. Inali shoved her out of the way, and in a matter of moments, his deft hands accomplished what hers could not. Swallowing her shame, she scrambled up into the saddle and seized the steering collar with both hands, forcing them to be steady.

Amos landed in his saddle with all the grace of a falling boulder, and the lion sagged beneath his sudden weight. Pulling the dirk from between his teeth, he nodded at Gundhrold. "Get us out o' here, beastie."

Before the words were fully spoken, Gundhrold was already moving. But he paused at the top of the sand drift, causing the rest of the company to bunch together in a jostling mass behind him. "Hawkness, we have a problem."

"Can it wait? I prefer dealin' with one problem at a time."

"See for yourself."

The griffin bounded out of the way, allowing Birdie to press up beside Amos and survey the path before them. From the west, the Khelari scouts advanced, settling into a faster pace now that their quarry was visible. They were far too near for her liking, but the griffin's attention was directed toward the northeast.

Birdie tracked his sightline to a dark mass boiling on the northern horizon. Even as she watched, it twisted and grew, approaching at an increasingly quick rate.

"Is that—"

"A sandstorm," Inali whispered. "By Sigurd's beard, we are done for."

"Belay that fool talk!" Amos barked over his shoulder and snapped straight in the saddle. "Sandstorm or not, it's time we moved." He set his back to the scouts and urged his lion into a run. In a moment, they were all flying across the sand.

"Hawkness, this is madness!" Inali pressed forward until his lion was even with Amos's. "We must seek shelter. If the storm strikes while we are in the open, we will be unable to find our way. We could blunder into the path of the Khelari army before realizing it."

"The path?" Amos snorted. "We could blunder into the middle o' their ranks, lad, an' march in step with 'em, an' neither o' us would know it until the sky cleared. If ye've got a better idea, by all means, enlighten me. If not, then save yer breath for speed."

Balanced in the stirrups, Birdie leaned over the lioness's neck, gripping the steering collar with all her might, as if by the force of her hold she could impart strength. The cries of the Khelari were so close now that she did not dare look back. There was no room left in her mind for fear, no room even for thought.

She gave herself up to the repetitive motion of the running lioness, to the wind in her eyes and the cold tears that slid down her cheeks, to the creak of the saddle, the grunting of Ryn's breath in her throat, and the faint scrap of music that danced ahead of them like a wisp of cloud.

Just beyond reach.

"Keep going. Don't slacken pace." Gundhrold gasped. He raced at Birdie's side with his heavy wings folded across his back. "It is working."

She ventured a backward glance and saw that the griffin spoke true. In these heavy, blanketing sands, the Khelari horses could not outrun lions Saari born and bred. But although a few stragglers had fallen behind, the rest remained bunched in a knot, holding their position, and in the lead, a dark-haired Khelari soldier rode a wiry bay horse that easily outstripped its larger companions.

It had become a matter of endurance now . . . and the first to falter would die.

Gritting her teeth against the sand kicked up by the heels of Amos's lion, Birdie set her face forward. The peddler had aimed their course at an angle so as to pass in between the sandstorm and the scouts. But with the swirling clouds roaring down upon them from the left and the thunder of hooves approaching from the right, Birdie felt a little like lamb herded to slaughter across the hills of home.

"Another three have fallen behind." Sym's shout registered in Birdie's ears, but it took a moment before the meaning of the words actually sank in.

"Three more?" A trace of hope crept into Inali's voice. "Then we shall outlast them."

"Only to be taken by the storm."

Birdie half expected Amos to pull some colorful response out of his seeming inexhaustible supply and rebuke Sym for such "fool talk," but the peddler simply goaded his lion on with a thunderous kick to the ribs and the slap of his feathered cap on its rump.

Up a steep incline they bounded, lions lurching forward with their heads down, shoulders hunched, and hind legs slipping out in the deep sand. Over Ryn's pinned ears, Birdie caught glimpses of the horizon, then Ryn skidded to a halt at the top of the dune, nearly catapulting Birdie out of the saddle. She slammed into the high pommel and slumped there, grasping for breath.

"Bilgewater."

For once, the peddler didn't erupt in a flurry of blistering indignation. He didn't even shout. That single, half-whispered word was more powerful . . . and more frightening than anything else Birdie had heard slip past his lips.

She turned to see what Amos had seen and instantly sank back in the saddle, the strength gone from her limbs.

Planted in rows across the barren ground below stood hundreds of little brown tents topped with silver pennants that rippled violently before the oncoming storm winds. Each penant was adorned with a blazing crimson teardrop at its center. In the far corner of the camp, a large herd of horses were staked to picket lines, alongside teams of oxen and draft horses hitched to carts bearing several strange enormous wooden contraptions.

It was the Khelari army, already miles inside the border.

Only a few soldiers milled about in the open. Most seemed to have retreated to their tents to avoid the sandstorm. But when the harsh cry of a raven sounded overhead, Birdie knew it would not be long before new soldiers—fresh soldiers—joined in the chase.

"For the last time, Inali, will you not untie me?"

At Sym's plea, Birdie glanced over her shoulder. The Saari warrior sat with her head flung back, braids escaped from their binding and flying every which way about her face, expression sad but determined. Without a word, Inali slipped a knife from his satchel, stood in his stirrups to lean over his lioness's neck, and sliced through her restraints. From beneath the fender of his saddle, he produced her quiver of throwing spears. She snatched it from his hand and slung it over one shoulder.

"Hawkness." Gundhrold growled, and the sound was so near and deep and threatening that it caught everyone's attention. "We cannot delay. The alarm is spreading. What must we do?"

Amos blinked, like a man awakened from deep slumber. "Run. Always run."

12

Straight for the heart of the sandstorm, Amos headed, and not even Inali dared argue against their course now. It was pure madness to stay and pure madness to run, but what choice was left when fate tossed you aside? It wasn't enough that they had a company of scouts on their tail and a raging sandstorm bearing down on them. They had to stumble across the invading army too. Bad luck, plain and simple. The desert covered the entire southern quarter of Leira with a border that stretched from coast to coast. In this, at least, the odds should have been on their side.

Fooling with us, Emhran?

Amos might not have made a habit of conversing with the Master Singer, but he wasn't above lodging a complaint or two as the situation demanded. The delay caused by the sighting of the army had enabled their pursuers to close the distance. He didn't need to look back to know that. Mayhap it was a lingering sense from his outlawing days, when a man had to watch his back or find his neighbor's knife in it, but Amos could almost feel them on his heels. A sort of spine-tingling, hair-raising *knowing* that summoned his hand to the hilt of his dirk.

And here he'd hoped charging blindly into a sandstorm would discourage them.

An arrow whipped past so close to his cheek that his head jerked back automatically as if he'd been stung. Moments later, Sym cried out, and Amos twisted his neck to see her clasp her fist to a bleeding cut on her thigh. Naught but a graze. Managing a steed and bow would be no easy task in this footing with the winds picking up. It would take a master archer to make a killing shot—that or one with impeccable luck.

Their best hope still lay in reaching the storm. It had seemed so near and terrible when they were trying to outrun it, but now that they sought refuge in its fury, it seemed to crawl across the desert, leaving Amos begging for just a little more speed, a little more time, before the pursuit caught up.

But beggars wound up dead on the battlefield.

Fighters survived.

He caught the griffin's slanted eye and received a nod in return. "On my word," he raised his voice just enough to be heard, "wheel and charge them."

It bore the element of surprise, if naught else. Surprise and the strength of madness. He waited another dozen heartbeats, until his spine was practically burning from the nearness of the threat, then with a bellow, he hauled back on the steering collar and forced his lion into a sharper turn than any horse could make at full speed.

The lion dove straight into the Khelari without waiting for a cue. Amos should have been expecting it, given what he'd witnessed of Saari battle tactics. As it was, the shock of the beast slamming into one of the horses and dragging its rider down nearly threw him from the saddle.

He caught himself just in time and severed the horse's girth with a slash of his dirk—left a decent gouge in its side too and sent the beast into a frenzied spin to rid itself of the lopsided saddle—while the Khelari struggled to rise and draw his sword. The lion roared, rattling Amos's teeth, and pounced on the hapless soldier. Amos clutched the high pommel to keep from losing his balance as his steed worried its prey. He considered himself a hardened man, but bile rose in his throat at the sounds. Killing a man in battle was one thing, but watching your mount tear one to shreds before your eyes was another.

A glint of light on steel caught his eye, and Amos jabbed a heel into his lion's side, forcing the beast to swing left just in time to avoid a downward cut from a second Khelari that would've lopped off his arm—if not his head—if he hadn't been watching.

The Khelari swung back to the attack. Amos evaded again, hesitant to match his dirk against the soldier's sword. The dirk was a *per-*

fectly good weapon—he'd argued its merits more than once around a common room fire with the tavern keeper and his tap on hand—but there was a reason mounted warriors carried weapons with a longer reach.

Throwing traditional technique to the blistering storm winds, Amos kicked one leg back behind him and dropped to the ground. He hit rolling, and the momentum was enough to absorb some of the shock, but his knees still felt as if they were on fire. Up beneath the belly of his opponent's horse he crawled, dodging the stamping hooves, slashed at the back of its legs, and was out of the way before beast and rider collapsed.

Breathing hard, he turned to find his lion waiting for him. He sheltered behind the beast to take stock of the fight. Four Khelari were down—the two he had dispatched with the aid of his lion, one slain by Gundhrold, and another by Sym—four were left.

Inali rode behind Sym, spear-pipe in hand, but from what Amos had seen of the lad, he wasn't much in the way of a fighter. Capable, just not aggressive enough. To his left, Birdie's lion darted through the fray, bearing her from one clear pocket to another. Somehow she'd managed to get hold of a sword—a massive, unwieldy blade that must have weighed nearly as much as she did, but that didn't stop her from trying to steer her mount into the thick of the fighting.

Fool girl.

The words raged in his head, denouncing her stubbornness, but Amos couldn't deny feeling a faint twinge of pride. He hauled himself back into the saddle and caught hold of the steering collar—just in time to keep from being flung off as the lion darted out of the way of a charging horse. With one bound, the lion cleared a fallen Khelari, and Amos plucked the spear out of the man's chest in passing.

Next he knew, he was engaged in a furious game of dodge and attack, trading blow after blow with a grizzled soldier mounted on a horse that more resembled a boulder than a living beast. Out of the corner of his eye, he caught a glimpse of Birdie and Inali faced off against one of the Khelari. She seemed to be holding her own just fine—

A dark bay horse barreled into Birdie's lion. The force of the collision snapped her into the air and knocked the beast to the ground.

Her borrowed sword fell useless to the sand.

Slowly, she began to rise to her hands and knees, head down, gasping for breath. Even in the midst of the skirmish, with weapons clanging, horses shrilling, and lions growling and rending their prey, he could see her shaking as she tried to get her lungs working again.

"Lass!" The cry tore from his lips. He slammed his heels into his lion's sides, but his blaggardly opponent was in the way, smirking at him beneath the visor of his helm. Moving on instinct rather than sight, he blocked the Khelari's strike with the haft of his spear, still watching Birdie.

The bay horse skirted around Birdie until it was opposite Amos with her in between, then the rider dismounted, sword in hand. She scrambled to her feet and backed away, but he stood between her and her weapon, and her lion was still down.

Amos jabbed out one-handed with the spear, trying to force his opponent back, but the grizzled man refused to budge. "Get out o' my way, ye seaswoggled, addlepated slumgullion."

His free hand closed around the flap of the long, narrow knapsack strapped to his back, and with one swift move, he tore open the straps and hauled the cursed blade out into the open. His hand burned at the touch, and an ache ran all the way up his arm into his shoulder.

The old soldier's eyes bulged.

But the blade wasn't meant for him. Amos drew his arm back and flung it with all his strength. "Lass, catch!"

• • •

In one breath, Birdie saw her own death stalking toward her with a light, easy step and a sneer on his face, while she stood, unarmed and defenseless, to meet him. The next, the blue-white sword landed in the sand at her feet, just short of her outstretched arm.

Darkness . . . a cavern . . . bodies . . .

She drove the image from her mind, leapt for the weapon, and felt her fingers close around the hilt. She whirled into motion just in time to guard against the stroke of the bay horse's rider, responded with a slash of her own, and fell back to await his attack. The movements felt both oddly familiar and strange at the same time, as if her limbs somehow knew what to do, but her brain didn't quite recall the commands.

A chill seized her sword-hand, binding her palm to the hilt of the sword before slowly working its way up her limbs. She suppressed a shudder. Beneath the clamor of the fight and the roar of the approaching sandstorm, a thin tremor of music floated, so faint she wondered if she'd imagined it. She seized hold of it, desperate, and allowed the melody to draw her back to the fight.

The rider rushed her, sliced from right to left, and followed up with a backhand slash that jarred the bones in her sword-hand when she blocked. Fast *and* strong, those were his advantages—her brain registered those facts as important bits of information, even as she was on the constant move to evade his attack. But she was small and she was faster, and it gave her an advantage, because he would not expect her to take the offensive.

None of them would. One look at her and they'd all expected her to run. She could see it in their eyes—the flecks of surprise—and hear it in the notes of their songs—the tones of disdain, of laughter. *This was the Songkeeper*? She gritted her teeth against the bitterness of the thought and used it to supply strength to her sword-arm.

It was not hard to feign exhaustion. She was weary of being hunted, of forever running, like a fox with the hounds at its heels. But when the fox discovers its teeth, then let the hounds beware. She allowed her sword arm to droop and stumbled a little with each step she took.

A thin-lipped grin cracked the Khelari's expression, and he relaxed his guard. "Hand over your weapon, little one." He jerked his chin up. "Surrender now and no harm will come to you."

Birdie sprang at him while he was still speaking. He managed to bat aside her lunge, but the tip still tore through the leather of his jerkin and rang against chain mail. She slipped under his blade and sliced across the back of his legs—one of the few unprotected areas in armor meant for horseback.

He fell, cursing, and she drew her arm back for the slaying stroke. His head tipped back, and their eyes met. The heated strains of his melody bombarded her, leaving her battered and struggling to breathe. It sounded dark and terrible, yes, but it also sounded sad.

The notes spoke of a longing insatiable, of life unfulfilled and purposeless.

Her hand trembled.

Summoning all her strength of will, she sought to still it, only to realize that her veins pulsed in time to the melody coursing through the blade, as if the sword had a voice of its own and was calling out. Calling . . . calling . . . and the Song rose in answer.

There was no force behind it. No burst of brilliant light. No rush of unearthly power. It simply crept over her, gentle as a spring breeze.

Softly, she began to sing, staring all the while into the soldier's fear-flecked eyes. Until she could see nothing else. Until they seemed as vast as the cavern beneath Mount Eiphyr, and the fear unraveled and became images and thoughts and moments—those tiny inconsequential moments—of a life that had once been not so very different from hers.

"Lass!" Amos's voice seemed to come from a great distance away, and his words were disjointed and meaningless compared to the song that filled her soul and the soul she beheld in the Song. "Behind you!"

The urgency in his voice blazed through her and she reeled around. A blur leapt in front of her, knocking her to the ground, breaking her grip on the sword.

She scrambled to her feet, blinking against a tide of sand and wind sweeping against her.

Inali crumpled, blood pouring from a gaping wound in his left shoulder, revealing a tall, battered Khelari soldier standing behind him. The man grinned through swollen lips and staggered toward her, blood dripping from the broadsword in his hands.

Birdie dashed toward her fallen sword, but the dark-haired soldier reached it first. Still on hands and knees, he grasped the hilt and instantly dropped it, cursing. Steam rose from his skin, and his hand seized into a claw that spoke of great pain.

She froze, unable to tear her eyes away.

A cry, halfway between a scream and a roar, rang in her ears. The griffin slammed into the big Khelari and brought him crashing to the ground. Gundhrold struck at the man's throat with his beak, but the Khelari seized the griffin's bad wing with one fist and pummeled his skull with the other. Then Amos waded into the fray and brought his dirk down with all the force of a lightning bolt, and the Khelari lay still.

Birdie forced her limbs to move. She scrambled past the dark-haired soldier and reached down to gingerly tap the pommel of Artair's sword. The familiar chill answered her touch, but nothing that warranted the soldier's response or threatened harm to her. She seized her blade and that of the dark-haired soldier and ran back to the others, leaving him huddled and bleeding on the ground.

Sym knelt beside Inali, his head in her lap, hands pressed to the wound in his shoulder while Amos struggled to wrap an unwieldy bandage around his arm and side. The fabric soaked through as fast as he could lay it against the wound, and declarations of wrath and vengeance flowed just as quickly from the peddler's tongue.

Tears glistened in Sym's dark eyes, and she seemed to be whispering something to Inali.

Birdie halted a few feet away, hesitant to draw nearer. "Will he be all right?"

A wing brushed her back, and Gundhrold's breath warmed her neck as he peered over her shoulder. "By Emhran's grace, may it be so. Gather the lions, little Songkeeper. We must ride. The storm is upon us."

Tucking both weapons under one arm, Birdie hurried off into the gloom. A gust of wind barreled into her and sent her stumbling to regain her balance. She could no longer see the storm approaching or guess which direction would carry them backwards or forwards on their journey. The world was lost in a cloud of orange.

She wandered the battle ground, sidestepping the still forms of dead or unconscious soldiers. The horses had scattered. Two lions were down. One with its throat slashed. Another with a gaping wound in its side.

Ryn's throaty voice spoke suddenly next to her ear. "Mount up, little Songkeeper. We must ride with the wind or be torn by it."

"Inali is wounded." Birdie turned to face the lioness. Wounded and perhaps dead . . . but she could not say that. Could not yield hope. He had been trying to save her, hadn't he?

"I, too, have lost my own. But there is no time for grief." The lioness stamped an impatient paw. Another lion—Sym's mount—stood beside Ryn. Dried blood matted its mane, but it did not appear seriously injured. "Quickly. We are true children of the desert, little one. We can find our way through wind and sand. We will bring you safely to the border, beyond the reach of those foul trespassers from the north. But we must leave now."

Birdie mounted, and the two lions bore her to Inali's side.

Amos's head snapped up at their approach. He and Sym were still huddled over Inali, trying in vain to staunch the flow of blood. "We'll have t' ride double." He gathered Inali in his arms and staggered to his feet. Sym's lion crouched and allowed Amos to arrange the wounded Saari warrior on its back before rising. With one hand, Amos supported Inali's limp frame; with the other, he gripped Sym's arm, stopping her before she could mount. The wind was howling now, and Birdie could barely make out the words. ". . . must not return t' the army with tale o' our passin'."

Sym plucked a spear from her quiver. "The Saari do not leave survivors."

In the gusting sand, she faded within a few paces into nothing more than a shadowy figure roaming across the battle ground leaving death in her wake. A soldier's dying groan assailed Birdie's ears. Another begged for his life, but his voice was cut off swiftly and no further sound came.

"One is missing." Sym reappeared beside her lion. She sheathed her spear in the quiver on her back and swung up behind Inali, wrapping an arm around his chest to keep him from falling.

"Why am I not surprised?" Amos beckoned Birdie to ride over and climbed up behind her. The saddle shifted under his weight, and Ryn grunted at the strain. "Haven't seen hide nor hair o' the griffin, either."

"I am here, Hawkness." Gundhrold materialized out of the storm. "There was a small matter of an escaped Khelari that needed to be handled."

"An' have ye dealt with it?"

"It is done."

"We must hurry, Amos." Shielding her face against the flying sand with one hand, Birdie twisted around in the saddle. "The lions can find their way to the border, even in the storm, but we have to leave now before it worsens."

Amos urged Ryn forward with a hefty rap of his heels against her sides. Birdie could feel him fumbling in his pocket with his free hand, then he pulled a kerchief out and shoved it in her hands. "Here, lass, cover yer mouth an' nose. Ye won't be able to breathe otherwise."

As they forged ahead into the whirling maelstrom of grit and wind, she glanced back over her shoulder at the battle ground now shrouded by a fresh blanket of sand. She was stunned by the ease and silence with which a life could be extinguished. Gone as if it had never existed, ended as if it didn't matter at all.

She fought the urge to be sick. But nothing—not death nor disease nor rumors of torture—could force her to be sick in front of the others. They were just doing what must be done to escape.

To survive and defeat the Takhran.

13

Tremors racked Inali's body. He lay on a bedroll beside the tiny fire Amos had built. In the wavering light, his shivering seemed exaggerated, almost grotesque. The color had leeched from his skin, leaving it the pasty gray of the frost that flecked the ground, and the dim firelight only accentuated the hollows behind his eyes and in his cheeks, like caverns.

Caverns. The sword.

Standing in the dark with bodies all around.

Birdie blinked the images away. She sat with a skin thrown around her shoulders for warmth. Hesitant to steal the fire's heat from Inali, she sat several paces away with her knees tucked beneath her chin, back to Gundhrold's side. Or perhaps she was simply reluctant to sit near him. To the man who had thrown himself between her and a blade.

To the man who might die in her stead.

On the opposite side of the fire, Amos's silhouette paced back and forth, and every now and then, she caught the glint of his dirk rotating above his outstretched hand. It had been two days since they left the desert. Two days of bone-aching travel and a fear and tension so tight she could almost sense it like a physical cord binding them together while threatening to tear them apart. They had slipped past the army, it was true. But it could not be long before the Khelari were once more on their trail. Not if past experience held true.

The Takhran's spies were everywhere.

Sym carried a blanket to Inali's side and began tearing it into strips. The noise of the ripping cloth seemed dangerously loud and unnatural. Amos had chosen a small grove of stunted trees for their campsite, but Birdie still felt exposed and vulnerable with nowhere to shelter or hide and no mounts to carry them to safety. When they left the desert behind, they had released the lions and continued on foot. Lions would only draw unwanted attention north of the border.

Amos halted his pacing and squatted beside the fire. "Will he survive?"

"It is too soon to say." Sym's words were clipped, short, her movements quick and efficient, as she removed the previous set of bandages and set them to boiling in a pot over the fire. "If he does, he will almost certainly lose the use of this arm. The blade damaged bone as well as flesh. Infection is setting in. He needs quiet and rest. Not *this*." She gestured at their campsite.

"Aye, an' I'd like nothing better 'n t' give it t' him, but for now, this'll have t' do. Lightin' a fire is a risk in an' o' itself that I'd much prefer not t' take if it could be avoided."

Sym's voice lowered. "Can the little Songkeeper not—"

"Nay, I'm sorry."

For a moment, there was no sound but the crackle of the flames and the squelch of the wet rag in Sym's hand as she cleaned Inali's wound. Birdie pulled the skin tighter around her shoulders. After they had emerged from the sandstorm—battered, exhausted, and crusted with sand—she had tried to summon the Song to heal Inali. *Tried.* The melody had not responded, and in the back of her mind, a voice so soft she wondered if she had imagined it whispered "*No.*"

A shudder ran through her. The fear was still there, caged up inside, cowering like a hunted animal. At her side, Artair's sword gleamed pale gold in the fire-glow. She lowered one hand and brushed her fingers along the grooved ridge that ran down the center of the blade. It was like touching an icicle.

Gundhrold lifted his head and crooked it around to look at her, blinking bleary eyes. "Are you well, little Songkeeper?"

Something about his use of the title irked her. It felt wrong, somehow. Out of place. "I have a name." The declaration slipped out before she could stop it.

He squinted one eye at her. "You have many names, little one.

Birdie is one of them. Songkeeper is another."

"Is it?" She huffed a humorless laugh. "Sometimes I wonder ..."

"Little one—"

Leaves crunched to their left beneath heavy footfalls. An animal, Birdie thought it. Something four footed, at least. The cadence was wrong for a human. Amos sprang into action, scooping a handful of earth over the fire to smother the flames. With the calculated grace of a cat on the prowl, Sym stood and eased a spear from the quiver on her back. Hand clenched around the hilt of her sword, Birdie started to rise, but Gundhrold's wing tapped her shoulder, warning her to stay where she was.

The crackling stopped, replaced by the *swish-swish* of a tail and a deep animal-ish sigh followed by a snort. Buried within that hint of the beast's voice, Birdie caught a trace of the five-noted melody sung in deep, hearty, droning tones.

Like the hum of a dragonfly's wings ...

She stood, ignoring Gundhrold's warning hiss. "Balaam? Is that you?"

No response. Nothing but the constant sighing of the wind in the trees and the distant chittering of a petra to its kit, then the footsteps started again, plodding slowly toward them.

Amos swept her behind him with one motion of his arm. "Stay back, lass."

A stocky, four-legged figure pushed through the low branches of a hallorm tree and halted only a few feet from Amos. The peddler stood stock still, dirk drawn and ready in his hand. There was just enough moonlight filtering through the trees to see the beast's whiskered gray muzzle and brown eyes. It stretched its neck out and sniffed Amos's hand then let out a throaty snort that sounded a bit like air escaping a bellows.

"Well, I'll be ..."

"Balaam?" Amos sheathed his dirk but kept a protective hand on Birdie's shoulder. "Is it really ye? Blitherin' barnacles, but I thought sure ye'd been eaten by wolves long before now."

The donkey blinked at him. Once. Twice. "Daft man, of course it's me. Who did you reckon it was—one of them black armored slumgullions from the north?"

Birdie stifled a breath of laughter. It did not surprise her to discover that the donkey's thoughts ran a lap slower than most creatures she had encountered, or that he spoke in a deep, drawling voice that rivaled a swamp for sluggishness, but hearing phrases she had only ever before heard Amos use—now that was something unexpected.

Balaam's head lolled around to look at her. "Well, if it isn't the little Songkeeper." A corner of his mouth curved upward in a sly, fox-like grin that looked woefully out of place on his sweet, donkey face. "I knew you, I did, from the first moment I heard you speak, but I reckoned you were too young then to risk you knowing it too."

"So you didn't speak to me?"

"Couldn't, now could I?" The donkey's forehead wrinkled with confusion. "Not if I wanted to keep you safe."

"G'on, lass. Ask him how he's been, where he's been stayin', an' all that."

"Hold on, just a minute," Sym shoved her way in between the donkey and Amos. "We have a sick man who needs rest, and the last thing we need is for all this jabbering to bring a Khelari patrol down on us."

Amos dismissed her concerns with a wave of his hand. "We won't take long, an' it could be o' use t' us, maybe even procure us that shelter ye were hopin' for not half an hour ago. Go ahead, lass, ask him."

Birdie squirmed out from under the hand on her shoulder. "He's already heard you, but I can tell you what he says."

"Shelter, aye." Balaam nodded sagely. "I been staying with Brog. He's got a nice little shelter for himself an' a few of the lads who stop by for brew. Don't reckon he would mind sharing with you lot too." Nodding to himself, the donkey turned on his heel and started back into the woods. "Almost time for chow too."

"Wait, don't leave yet."

Her shout brought the donkey to a halt, but he stamped a hoof and fixed her with a look of longsuffering patience. She hastily repeated the donkey's words to Amos.

"Brog, *here*, in the Soudlands?" The peddler slapped his knee. "That's grand news." He sobered a moment later. "Hardale must have fallen. The Brog I knew would never have left the Whistlin' Waterfly behind unless he was driven from it."

"Aye," Balaam muttered in a sad singsong voice. "No more Hardale. No more Sylvan Swan. No more straw or barn or chickens in the yard. It's all gone, gone, gone."

The donkey's words held no surprise for Birdie. Somehow, she had known it to be true since word of the Midlands's fall first reached Nar-Kog. But expecting it did nothing to ease the ache of hearing the news so casually proclaimed.

The peddler nudged her with his elbow. "Ask him if he can take us t' Brog's shelter. 'Twould be good for the lad if we could get him somewhere warm an' sheltered, an' Brog has some experience with the healin' arts."

The donkey simply nodded and moseyed off without waiting for them to follow. Birdie scrambled for her pack, while Amos and Sym eased Inali up onto Gundhrold's back and stamped out the last traces of the fire. Then they were off through the trees, into the night, hurrying to catch up with the plodding beast.

And all the while, the donkey's singsong voice repeated over and over in her ears.

Gone. Gone. Gone.

How long before the same fate befell the rest of them?

"Well, I'll be . . . if it isn't Amos McElhenny!" Brog's welcome boomed out like a Waveryder fog horn. The former tavern-keeper stood silhouetted against firelight in the doorway of a low hut half-buried in the side of a hill. "Truth be told, I never thought I'd see your ugly face again." He held out his massive, craggy hand, and Amos shook it with enthusiasm.

"Nor I ye, Brog, but there'll be time for pleasantries later. We've a wounded man—can we bring him in?"

"Sure, sure." Still holding the door open with one hand, Brog shuffled aside and beckoned for them to enter. "Set your man by the fire."

Amos motioned for Birdie and Sym to enter, then turned to lower Inali from Gundhrold's back. The griffin crouched to make the task easier, but Amos still grunted as the limp Saari warrior fell into his arms. He ducked through the low doorway and in two long strides made it past a battered table and chairs to the hearth where Sym had already arranged a bedroll. He settled the lad and knelt at his side out of Sym's way. The Saari warrior moved through Brog's kitchen like a sandstorm, commandeering supplies with reckless abandon. Within moments, she had a pot of water boiling over the fire and Birdie tearing fresh bandages from a scrap of cloth that might have been one of Brog's shirts.

Brog cleared his throat, reclaiming Amos's attention. "Well then . . . I'll see what I have by way of herbs and medicinals. Stock's a bit depleted, I'm afraid, what with rough times and all." Still chunnering away, he started to swing the door shut, but the griffin's wing stopped him. "Saints alive!"

Amos never would have dreamed the big man could jump so high. Brog landed with a thud and stumbled back, knocking over one of the chairs and slamming into the table. It sagged beneath his weight and skidded with a screech across the floor until he regained his balance. He surged back toward the door, reaching for a broad-bladed woodsman's axe hanging on the wall beside it.

"Wouldn't try it, if I were ye." Amos couldn't help chuckling at the terror on the tavern keeper's face. "The old catbird's been known t' lop off hands for less."

Brog sidestepped away from the axe. "Is *that* what I think it is?"

"Chances are *yes*, if ye've still got at least one good eye in yer head."

Gundhrold sighed, and it was that conceited, enduringly patient sort of sigh that never failed to raise Amos's hackles. "Have no fear good innkeeper, I shall remain outside. I do not think your hovel has room for another."

With a faint dip of his head that could *almost* pass for a bow, the griffin retreated from the entrance. Brog instantly slammed the door shut and slid a heavy bolt into place, then spun around and set his broad back to the door. "Did he just call me *innkeeper*? Now that's an insult, if I've ever heard one. I'll have you know there's miles of difference between a paltry innkeeper and a respectable tavern keeper."

Sym gave a dry chuckle. "But you don't object to him calling this place a hovel?"

"Of course not. It *is* a hovel." Brog's hand trembled as he lifted a jug from the table and sloshed brew into a mug. He raised it as if in toast. "One gets by."

Amos shrugged his pack aside and started rolling up his sleeves. "Brog—herbs?"

"Right." The tavern keeper plunked his mug down and turned to a floor-to-ceiling set of shelves. After a minute of muttering and the sound of glass bottles clinking, he held up a small, browned bottle and a packet of sinew and needles. "Here we are. Distilled from the seed of the corrin tree. Just the thing for staving off infection and promoting heal—"

Sym plucked it from his hand and spun back to Inali.

"—ling." Brog dusted the front of his quilted tunic. "Well, you seem to have it well in hand. I'll just see that Balaam's bedded down for the night." He paused in the doorway. "Your beast won't harm me, will he?"

"He's not *our* beast." Birdie lifted her head from the bandages she was tearing, face as stern and fierce as a thundercloud. "Gundhrold is his own master."

Whoo-hee. Amos stifled a chuckle at the surprise on Brog's face. Sometimes his lass could be quite the fireflower. "He won't harm ye, Brog. Just be polite."

The door creaked shut, and Amos turned to assist Sym, but it was clear she had dealt with her fair share of wounds and considered him more of a hindrance than a help. She moved with confident precision as she bound, stitched, and even cauterized as needed with the heated tip of Amos's dirk. Age had made his hands thicker and tougher and less steady than in his younger days, so he was more than content to leave such delicate tasks to her.

At the beginning, Birdie rooted out supplies and passed them to Sym as they were called for, but by the time Sym tied off the last bandage and pronounced it done, his lass was curled beneath an animal skin, asleep on the packed earth floor. Sym scrubbed the blood from her hands on a scrap of bandage, then settled down beside Inali with her back to the hearth and her legs stretched out before her.

With a sigh, Amos rose on creaking limbs and dropped into one of the chairs at the table. He kicked off his boots and leaned back, studying his hands. Inali's blood had seeped into the cracks and scars of his skin. He knew from experience that it would take a good deal of scrubbing before it fully washed away, but the stain of it would remain engraved on his memory.

One life saved could not reverse the stain of lives lost.

They were headed to the place of his complete and utter failure, to the place that haunted his dreams at night and brought him shivering from slumber. And he—more fool that he was—had not only agreed to it, but he was willingly taking his wee lass into a world of horrors.

The chair opposite him scraped back and then groaned beneath the weight of the tavern keeper. Brog crooked an eyebrow at him, hefted the jug, and poured out two mugs with deliberate slowness. With practiced aim, he slid one into Amos's outstretched hand, and they both drank in silence.

Now that he had a moment to study the tavern keeper, Amos was surprised by the change in his appearance. Though still a big, rawboned man, he was thinner than Amos had ever seen him, and there was a new sense of *smallness* about him. Almost as if he had shrunk in on himself beneath the pressure of the trials he had faced.

His dark beard bristled about his jaw like the mane of a lion, and he was garbed in the rough wrap-around tunic and loose leggings of the Soudlands, instead of the respectable white shirt-sleeves and vest of a tavern keeper.

Times had been hard on the keeper of the Whistlin' Waterfly.

At last, Brog set his mug down, swiped a hand across his mouth, then rested both hands on his stomach. "Well, do you care to tell me what this is all about? How on earth did you find me here?"

Amos eased his chair back. "Wasn't looking actually, more coincidence than aught else. Stumbled across old Balaam in the woods, an' I know that fool beast well enough t' know he'd have found himself a right comfortable set up somewhere. Followed him back here. Long an' short o' it."

"You didn't seem surprised to see me."

That stumped Amos for a moment. It was boggswoggling how easy (and woefully mistaken) it was to write off tavern keepers as less than savvy, when in truth, most were more likely to hone in on the unusual. He mulled over the best response, and in the end gave the one that was the closest to truth. "I've seen far too much in the past months t' be surprised by aught, old friend."

"I reckon we all have." Brog nodded slowly, nursing his empty mug. "It's good that you found me. The Soudlands can be a dangerous place. Especially now with so many fighting bands running about claiming to oppose the Takhran but robbing everyone else. If the Khelari don't get you, I reckon they will. It isn't safe." His brow furrowed, casting his eyes in shadow. "Though I expect you can say the same about most of Leira at the moment."

"What happened in Hardale?"

"You'd be better off asking what *didn't* happen in Hardale." Brog snorted. "Official word of the truce came from Earnhult's fortress not long after you left. That was the start of it. Then the posters showed up overnight, plastered all over town with your face on them and that wee girl's. By the time the dark soldiers finished building their cursed road and marched down through the mountain pass, I knew we were in for it once they reached Hardale, but I couldn't bear to leave the Waterfly. Not yet. More fool I. And I let Ma stay too."

Unshed tears glimmered in Brog's eyes. Amos glanced quickly away, down at his stained hands and the scarred wood of the tabletop.

"They left bloodstained footprints when they marched out of town, but there wasn't any town left by then. You could see the smoke of the burning for miles."

Amos's blood boiled at the thought of it. He'd thought the massacre of Drengreth horror enough, but this was a widespread march of terror and death meant to assert the Takhran's authority once and for all and annihilate any who might stand in his path.

He'd predicted it.

The knowledge that he'd been right brought no pleasure.

"That's when I came here." Brog reached for the jug and poured another mugful. He peered into the swirling brown liquid. "Always figured the Soudlands was the dregs of Leira. It's desolate and wild enough that decent folk don't settle here, and remote enough to lure those who want to disappear or have been chased away from everywhere else. I figured it was insignificant enough that the Khelari would leave it alone. What's the point of conquering no-man's land? Guess I was wrong about that."

"Guess we've all been wrong about a lot o' things." Amos glanced over at his lass, sleeping beside the fire. "There's something I have t' tell ye."

All things considered, Brog took the news that the wee lass sleeping on the floor of his hovel was the next Songkeeper of legend rather well. Until he passed out and spent the remaining hours of the night snoring with his head on the table and an empty mug clutched in his hand. It had been right to tell him. In granting them shelter, the man shared their danger. It was only right that he knew why.

Yet secrets had never spilled easily from Amos's tongue.

He fiddled with the hilt of his dirk and watched the shifting firelight advance and retreat across the tavern keeper's sleeping face, until he felt sleep claiming him too.

He awoke to the sounds of someone moving about. Instinctively his grip tightened on his dirk until the sleep cleared from his eyes. Dawn light filtered through the cracks around the door and cast a hazy light over Birdie as she rummaged through their packs and pulled out several rounds of flatbread and a handful of dried fruit and smoked meat and set it on the table.

She caught him watching and smiled. "Morning! Breakfast?"

"Right." Wincing at aching muscles and a stiff neck—should have boggswoggling known better than to fall asleep in a chair—Amos hauled himself to his feet and shook Brog. But Sym was already up and helping herself to food by the time the big tavern keeper raised his head from the table and blinked bleary eyes.

"Up an' at 'em, Brog. First we eat, then we've plans t' make."

"Plans?" Brog swiped both hands across his face and then skewered Amos with a confused look while he scratched his beard. "Not so fast. Hold on a second while I get my head on straight. Was I just dreamin' or do I recall you making a certain revelation last night about a certain member of your company? You know . . . *her*." His gaze darted to Birdie, and he jerked his chin in her direction.

Subtle, wasn't he?

"Aye, I did."

"Saints alive." Brog sat back in his chair with a thump.

"An' now, there's important work t' be done t' plot our route northward, so eat up."

A feeble cough came from the hearth. "Map . . . in my satchel." Propped up on one elbow, Inali gestured with a languid hand toward the packs. "My satchel."

The lad was awake sooner than Amos had expected and already struggling to rise. Sym forced him to settle back with all the motherly instinct and gentleness of a lioness reprimanding her cub, while Birdie retrieved his satchel. Inali reached a quivering hand inside to withdraw a folded rectangle of parchment. He handed it to Birdie and she spread it out on the table, using Brog's empty mug and jug to hold down the upper corners.

Stroking his chin, Amos bent over the map to gather his bearings, judging by landmarks rather than labels since those were penned in the coarse script of the desert. Like most maps, it was drawn from the artist's perspective—here, that of the Saari. As such, the desert seemed disproportionately large compared to the rest of Leira, and the Nordlands—especially the dunes and mountains surrounding Serrin Vroi—were squished and shapeless.

Dark hair spilled across the lower corner of the map. He glanced over to find Birdie hunched at his side, gazing at the parchment with an expression of intense wonder. Come to think of it, she'd probably never seen such a thing before.

He tapped a finger against the narrow sliver of land just north of the desert and explained for her benefit. "Here's where we are now, lass, the Soudlands. There's no established ruler, no government. Just drifters an' outlaws. It's considered a no-man's land, the home o' the outcast an' abandoned."

Her serious blue eyes turned up to him. "People like us?"

"Sure," Brog chuckled. "And some not so pleasant."

Amos cleared his throat and turned back to the map. "We know the Midlands are crawling with Khelari. I imagine they'll be headquartered out o' King Earnhult's fortress."

Brog nodded. "Last word we received was that Earnhult was dead and they'd placed his son—a lad of seven—on the throne. An easy puppet."

Sym slid a spear from her quiver and reached it across the table to use the tip to indicate an area on the east coast. "The Salt Flats of Kerar—the Khelari have been amassing forces there in secret to march on the desert while the army that took the Midlands is still dealing with . . . local problems. You'll recall we received word of them in the council last week. No doubt it was a portion of that army we encountered on the border."

She dragged the tip of her spear across the map, carving a shallow line in the parchment. "If you figure in supply and messenger routes, you get a nice little triangle from the Salt Flats to the army on the border to King Earnhult's fortress, and we are currently at the center of it. In short, gentlemen," she stood straight and tossed her head, dark braids cascading around her shoulders, "there's not a *good* route north."

Amos caught himself before a thoughtless remark questioning her courage and the strength of her spear arm could spring from his lips, and forced himself to actually consider her words. "No *good* route?"

"Well, of course there's always a way. You would know that better than any, Hawkness. With a good dose of caution, days spent studying the troop movements, restricting our travel to the dead of night to avoid the Takhran's spies . . . there's a chance we can make it through."

"*We.*" Birdie spoke up. "Do you plan to go with us then?"

Sym sheathed her spear. "I intend to see Inali well. My decision can wait until after that. I had no part in this plan at the beginning." Her eyes flashed toward the hearth. "Dah Inali dragged me into it. If it were up to me, I would see the Songkeeper and Hawkness safely returned to the desert to honor their word and fight alongside our forces. But as there is no good route north, there is no safe route south." Her voice softened. "And perhaps there are other ways to fight . . . perhaps there is a part of me that at least half believes your mission could work."

"I, on the other hand, have no faith that your mission—whatever it is—can succeed. I'm content to bide my time here in this tiny, damp, worm-infested hovel and wait for the world to end. Cheers." Brog tipped his mug toward his mouth, but not a drop came out. He plunked it down again with a sigh, and his head drooped into his hands.

Amos motioned for silence. "I'd say our best bet would be t' make our way t' one o' the small coastal towns—big enough t' warrant fair sized shipping—an' borrow a boat t' beat up round the coast t' Rolis Bay an' approach Serrin Vroi from the east."

"Serrin Vroi?" Brog's bloodshot gaze swung around to Amos. "Are you mad? You didn't say anything about journeying to Serrin Vroi."

"Oh, aye. Did I forget t' mention that? Sym, how long before Inali can travel?"

"Give me a week and I'll be fine." The lad's voice was so faint it could scarce be heard over the crackling of the fire.

Sym rolled her eyes. "Give him three."

"Well then." Amos plucked the map from the table and folded it up. "Looks like we'll have t' impose on yer hospitality a wee bit longer, Brog."

"No bother, no bother at all." Brog's voice was muffled by his hands. "Your griffin is welcome to stay in the stable with the donkey—it's more of a shed really—but at least it would keep him hidden from prying eyes."

It took all of Amos's willpower to maintain a straight face at that. "How about I let ye suggest that t' him?" And how he hoped he was around—but a safe distance away—to witness the exchange. "In the meantime, we've scoutin' t' do."

PART THREE

14

If there was one word Ky could have used to describe his escape from Nar-Kog and subsequent journey across the desert, it would be brazen. Downright brazen. Not to mention cheeky, and a little hairy, and on the very rare occasion enlightening. Migdon had a way of doing things that left Ky about a mile behind and doubtful he would ever catch up.

Take the coffin, for instance.

Migdon had declared it a stroke of luck when they stumbled across the plain board box half buried beneath the rubble of a farmhouse just inside the Soudlands border. Once it was divested of its proper owner—and he was given a decent burial at Ky's insistence, along with the other bodies they found in the ruin—Migdon declared it just the "right size" for what he had in mind and lugged it out to the side of the nearest cart track.

Of course he hadn't thought fit to share just what he was planning, just pointed at the box and insisted Ky climb inside. And he, more fool that he was, had obliged.

Now almost an hour later, he was seriously regretting that decision. He chipped at a knot in the wood with his fingernail and shuffled around as much as the space allowed, to relieve the tingly sensation slowly creeping along his cramped limbs.

"Stop thumping." Something thudded into the side of the box. Migdon's boot by the sound of it. "You sound like a rabbit in a barrel."

"What are we doing?"

"Waiting, bucko, waiting."

Before Ky could demand to know what they were waiting for, the rattle of cart wheels caught his attention. The coffin shook as something heavy fell across the top. Migdon's raucous sobs echoed through the wood and raised Ky's hackles.

"My poor, poor son. Didn't I warn you to stay home? Didn't I tell you it wasn't safe, what with them marauding armies about and poor folk—decent folk—getting slaughtered in their fields?"

This type of trickery was well beyond Ky's area of expertise. He preferred to blend in, to disappear so completely into the crowd that no one could recall that you had been there. But Migdon heralded the complete opposite, claiming that if you were loud enough and obvious enough, folks figured you couldn't have anything to hide.

Still, wasn't he spreading it on a bit thick?

The cart's brakes locked on the wheels and the horses came to a stop. "Your son is it?" It was an old, thin voice that quavered like a fiddle in need of new strings.

Naw, not an old man.

Ky bit his tongue to keep from shouting for Migdon to stop. Tricking a harmless old man was lower than low. Even in the Underground, they'd restricted their harvesting to folk who could afford it or were asking for it, like the Khelari.

"Shame that, real shame." The old man sighed. "I seen more fathers burying their youngsters over the past weeks than I thought to see in a lifetime. Didn't know there were any dwarves living in these parts, though." A hint of suspicion crept into his tone.

Maybe not so harmless at that.

Migdon shuffled his weight off the coffin lid. "Not from these parts. That's what I kept telling my son. We're Nordlands folk, I said, he had no right sticking his nose into Soudlands squabbles. Haven't we trouble enough of our own at home without borrowing it from our neighbors? But he insisted on joining one of them fighting bands, said he had to stand against the cursed dark soldiers or he couldn't live with himself. And now he's dead, and I've come to fetch his body and bring it home to his mother. Poor woman—she's sick, don't know how she'll handle the news…"

On and on he rattled, spinning a tale of such complexity with such conviction and real honest-to-goodness sorrow, that Ky would have been tempted to believe him, if he hadn't been playing the uncomfortable role of the dead son in question.

The old man cleared his throat at last, cutting Migdon off in the middle of a detailed explanation of how the Khelari had stolen the cart and donkey he had planned to use to carry the coffin home. "Nordlands, did you say? That's a long way. I'm only going as far as the next Midlands border town, but I daresay I could give you a lift." The cart's axle squeaked, and the old man dropped to the ground. "Let's get loaded up, shall we? It's tempting fate, we are, standing around here. I've no desire to lose my cart too."

Ky heard the crunch of footsteps approaching both the head and foot of the coffin, and then it pitched first one way and then the other before settling with a thud in the back of the cart. A moment later, the old man clicked his tongue and the cart lurched forward.

By the time they came to a halt hours later, Ky ached from the cart's motion and his cramped position. His ears rang from the thud of the box each time it jostled and the clatter of the wheels just beneath him, and his nose itched with an intensity that would have been enough to drive any man mad.

Now that they were still, he could hear Migdon and the old man chattering away up front, and the hubbub of voices in the street—dogs barking, children shouting, sellers hawking their wares. A deadly invasion had come and gone through the Midlands, leaving countless bodies in its wake, and yet here, it seemed, they had escaped the worst. There were still things to sell and people to buy them, and so life proceeded as normal.

What lies had Migdon spun during the hours of travel with their host? And more importantly, just how was Migdon planning on getting him out of this coffin, now that they were in a town? He couldn't just climb out and walk away—that was the sort of thing that would set any town talking for months, and he was pretty sure it didn't fall into Migdon's category of things that were so ridiculously visible they became invisible.

He could feel the panic welling up inside his chest and instinctively lifted his arm to cover his mouth. His knuckles thumped the lid, and his elbow stuck against the side. It was too tight . . . too tight. And for a runner who'd spent three years ducking in and out of chimneys, through cracks between buildings, and under floorboards, that was saying a lot. Squeezing his eyes shut tight, every muscle and sense stretched to its utmost, he fought the panic. One push—that was all it would take. Migdon hadn't nailed the lid shut—*remember*—he'd left it cracked to allow air to seep through.

The cart sagged beneath the weight of someone climbing up into the back. He heard the scraping and thumping of boxes and crates being shuffled around and unloaded, then the clink of coins penetrated the wood slats, followed by Migdon's gruff voice.

"Best be off then."

The cart jolted forward with the coffin still in the back. Ky held in the panic until the noises of the town faded behind them, then slammed his hands up against the lid and shoved it aside. He half sat up, gulping in mouthfuls of crisp evening air and peered over the edge of the coffin. The cart stood alone in the middle of a deserted track that ran through moss green hills. A few sheep dotted the hillside to his left, but there was no sign of anyone else in sight.

"What do you think you're doing, bucko?"

Ky lurched up to his hands and knees and almost fell when his half-asleep limbs gave way beneath him. He caught himself on the edge of the coffin and struggled around to face the front of the cart as it came to a halt. Migdon slouched on the driver's seat with the reins in his hands and an indignant expression on his face. There was no sign of the old man.

"We aren't free and clear yet. Get back in the coffin—you could spoil everything."

"Afraid not, *bucko*." Ky glared back. "How 'bout you tell me what you're doing instead."

Migdon tugged at his earlobe with a grimy hand. "*Then* will you get back in the coffin?"

"No."

"Shame—and here I thought you were showing real style, bucko." Migdon swung around and rested his feet on the edge of the coffin. "Folk are mighty suspicious right now—and who can blame them? What with marauding soldiers marching about killing civilians as they go, and the fighting bands getting in the way and killing more by way of accident, not to mention the looters that follow to prey upon innocent folk. It stands to reason that a man's far more likely to offer a ride to a fellow grieving the death of his son than to two drifters, *especially* in the Soudlands. Common sense—trust me, bucko."

"Like the old man trusted you before you stole his cart?"

"Me steal?" The dwarf spread his hands wide. "Never. Bought it from him—paid him handsomely too, I might add. Simply convinced him that a dozen *dicus* would be far more useful to him than a cart and nag that either the Khelari or one of the fighting bands are sure to commandeer any day."

"You *convinced* him?"

Migdon snorted. "Give me six hours, bucko, and I could convince any man of anything. Silvertongue, that's what they call me. Has just the right sort of ring to it too, if you ask me."

"Who calls you?"

"*They.*" He faced forward again and picked up the reins. "Now would you get back in the coffin? Best sort of disguise there is. Though we really ought to do something more to make you look the part—you know, just in case folk get suspicious and insist on inspecting the body."

"Afraid not." Ky tugged the lid of the coffin into place and hammered it shut with his fist, then clambered up into the driver's seat beside Migdon.

The dwarf looked aghast. "What *are* you doing?"

Ky grinned but it quickly turned to a grimace as he stretched first his arms and shoulders and then his legs. "Six hours, huh? Well, okay then, that's what you've got. Six hours to convince me and my aching body to get back in the coffin, or we start doing things *my* way."

"Oh, bucko." A slow smirk spread across the dwarf's craggy face. "You shouldn't have done that. Silvertongue *never* loses."

• • •

The coffin lid slammed shut in Ky's face, binding him once again in the stale, crushing blackness. He gagged at the stench. Migdon had insisted on treating the wood with every foul and disgusting thing known to man or dwarf—to make it more realistic, the dwarf insisted.

More likely payback for holding out so long.

"Told you, didn't I, bucko?" The dwarf's chuckle was muffled by the boards. "Silvertongue never loses."

Trapped like this, he had no way to escape listening to the dwarf's gloating, but at least he didn't have to see the triumphant expression on his face anymore. Migdon's six hours had come and gone plenty of times since the challenge, so by Ky's way of thinking, he had more than won. Of course the dwarf insisted that falling asleep in the first six hours negated the rest.

"There's a whole lot of six hours in two weeks. Bet's still mine—just saying."

"Sure, bucko, if it makes you feel better."

Migdon snapped the reins, and the cart started off again down the track toward the Khelari blockade guarding the bridge on the southern border of the Westmark. Ky lay as stiff as the boards beneath his back, reviewing every inch of their plan as each rotation of the wheels drew them closer to the dark soldiers, closer to discovery and death. Should they have simply abandoned the nag and slipped past on foot? The question gnawed at him. Oddly enough, it was Migdon who'd suggested it, back when they first heard rumor of the blockade and the young able-bodied folk disappearing when they tried to cross. Taken by the dark soldiers, no doubt, like the folk of Kerby, like Dizzier.

Taken to slave camps, or so the soldier Hendryk had said. Ky's chest tightened when he thought of their fate, but he wasn't willing to give up their cart and nag so easily. She might be long in the tooth, shaggier than a Midlands sheep, and no more than a step or two shy of what some might consider skeletal, but she set a fair pace and covered far more ground in a day than he could have done on foot.

And he'd been gone far too long already.

As they neared the blockade, he strained his neck to peer through the peek hole he'd insisted Migdon bore through the wood, but all he could see was a tiny strip of green hillside. They followed a hybrid plan this time—part his, part Migdon's. There'd be no wailing or sobbing, nothing to draw too much attention. Just a grief-stricken dwarf on a cart with his son in a coffin in the back.

Ky counted the minutes as they waited their turn in line. He could feel his limbs slowly going to sleep and wiggled his fingers and toes to try and keep the circulation flowing. The loaded pouch of his sling pressed into his side. Should they be discovered, he'd need to be able to move—and fast.

"State your name and business, dwarf."

Through the peep hole, Ky could see little of the guard save the dark color of his armor. In the end, that was all that mattered, wasn't it? He wore the dark armor, so he was an enemy. What else needed to be said?

"Name's Listarchus—Hipicarious Listarchus. Just trying to bring my son home, sir."

"That him back there?"

"Yes, sir. My son, Buck—"

"Reckon you won't mind us taking a look then." The guard's voice was stiffer than a zoar tree and had less feeling than cold steel. "There've been all sorts of *nasty* people about lately, trying to slip all manner of trickery past my nose."

For the first time, Ky felt a smidgeon of fear. This was no backward recruit, fresh to duty and authority, stuck on a dead-end assignment guarding some nameless bridge on some nameless road. He spoke like a man mighty used to sniffing out trouble.

"But I've no doubt a fine, upstanding dwarf like yourself wouldn't dream of trying anything untoward like smuggling weapons in that coffin, now would you? Hoy, soldier, remove the lid."

"Yes, sir." Reluctant footsteps shuffled toward the back of the cart, and a gauntleted hand settled with a *thunk* on the coffin.

"You can't do that." Migdon's voice assumed the shrill qualities of a wailing night moth. His voice was louder now—loud enough to reach the others waiting their turn in line. "It's my son, you see. Died of the white fever, he did. You can't open the coffin, sir, else you'll risk spreading the disease to everyone standing here."

A ripple of fearful murmuring, so heavy Ky could practically feel as well as hear it, spread through everyone within reach of the cart. They had good reason to fear—once the white fever seized the lungs, it killed with fierce efficiency.

But the guard wasn't cowed so easily. "I'd sooner spread disease than weapons into the hands of malcontents, dwarf. Remove the lid, soldier, that's an order. Shield your face with your cape if you must."

Ky pressed his back against the boards beneath and sucked in one last breath as the lid scraped back and a chill breeze flooded the coffin. He fought to keep from shivering. Morning light seeped through his shuttered eyes until he could practically see the veins in his eyelids and the rosy hue of blood tinting his skin.

"Just the body, sir. Don't see no sign of weapons." A hard object prodded Ky in the side. "Seems a bit tall for a dwarf young-un—beardling, I think they call them, isn't that right?"

"He's a half-dwarf," Migdon growled.

"Any case, he's a goner, sir. No doubt about that. Delian's fist, what a stench!"

"Signs of white fever?"

"His face is white, sir, and there's specks of blood on his collar."

"That'll do, soldier. Remove the coffin—you there, help him."

Migdon started to protest, but the soldier spoke over him. "I'm afraid that if your son truly perished of the white fever as you say, his body should be burned immediately. Not carted through the Westmark so it can spread the full contagion every step of the way. Without the coffin, you won't be needing that cart and nag anymore, either. And as a good, honest citizen of this grand country, I am certain you intend to turn it over to the Takhran's mighty forces to aid them in battle."

The dwarf did not reply.

Ky felt as if the white fever truly had sucked the life from his lungs. Somehow, this had all gone horribly wrong. He eased his hand an inch to the right and felt for the straps of his sling but didn't launch into the attack. Not yet.

Migdon had been so certain his "silver tongue" could talk them out of anything, and Ky still hoped it would work. He wanted to pass through the blockade and be forgotten immediately afterwards. There was nothing so memorable as a fever-ridden corpse suddenly coming to life.

"Don't touch the—" Migdon broke off in a fit of coughing and wheezing that sounded as if his lungs might burst from his throat any second. "It's dangerous, I tell you. I scarce touched the lad when I put him in there, and look at me now!"

Panicked footsteps shuffled back, cursing broke out, and a voice from the back of the line begged the guard to "Just let 'em pass!"

"Now, bucko, now!"

Ky jumped to his feet and swung his loaded sling full force into the face of the soldier who'd been instructed to remove the coffin. It clanged harmlessly off his visor, but the soldier stumbled back. Migdon cracked the reins and the nag took off at a reeling trot, clipping the guard with her shoulder as she went past. The sudden motion caught Ky by surprise, and he grabbed Migdon's shoulder to keep from falling.

The blockade consisted of two wagons with chocked wheels angled parallel to one another across the bridge, so that in order to pass, you had to weave around and in between them. It would be tight for the cart to pass at a trot.

"Migdon, it's—"

"Leave it to me, bucko."

Ky spun around and braced his back against Migdon's. The guard had managed to stumble back to his feet and stood on the threshold of the bridge, shouting instructions to his little troop. A perfect target. Ky lobbed off a sling-bullet that slammed into the back of his helmet and knocked him flat on his face.

"Hold on, bucko!"

Instead of swerving to make the turn between the wagons, Migdon drove straight into the second wagon, effectively blocking the path for any who might try to follow. The nag went down, tangled in the wheels and her traces.

The impact flung Ky from his feet, but he scrambled up again in time to catch the knapsack Migdon tossed him. The dwarf dug his own massive knapsack out from beneath the driver's seat and slung it on his back. An arrow struck the side and pierced halfway through, but it didn't seem to slow Migdon down. He launched over the side of the cart and raced through the gap between the wagons.

Ky sent another iron sling-bullet zinging into the bunch of Khelari racing toward them, then scampered along the edge of the cart, leapt over the struggling nag into the back of the blockade wagon, and swung over the other side onto the bridge. He took off at Migdon's heels, dodging and weaving in an effort to avoid the arrows that skipped past their heads and glanced off the stones around their feet. Once past the bridge, they abandoned the track and took to the hills, scrambling up gradual inclines and picking up speed on the way down into vales thick with dragon's tongue and tangleroot vines.

The arrows stopped after they crested the first hill, but they still kept running for what felt like a mile before Migdon stopped dead in his tracks and hunched over with his hands on his knees, blowing like a horse after a long gallop. Bowed beneath his massive knapsack, the dwarf reminded Ky of the big turtles he'd often seen trundling along the banks of the Adayn.

Ky glanced back the way they'd come. It was easy to see. Their path slashed through the tall grasses like a main thoroughfare through the city. "They're not chasing us?"

"Think, bucko. Put that noggin of yours to use." Migdon tapped his forehead with one finger. "What did you see at the blockade?"

Ky rolled his eyes. "You can't exactly see much when you're in a coffin."

"Cheeky fellow, that's what you are. Not afraid to speak your mind—I like that about you. Here's what I saw: only about a dozen soldiers and two wagons—two cart horses, neither hitched up. That tells me that the Khelari forces are stretched a mite thin, this quarter leastways. There's a limit to their manpower and resources, same as with any other army. When push comes to shove, what are we but a dwarf and a boy who pulled something new and slipped past their net? They've got bigger fish to catch."

As the logic of the dwarf's words sank in, Ky allowed himself to breathe fully for the first time since climbing back into the coffin. He slid his knapsack off and dropped to the ground, careful to avoid sitting in a patch of sticky, wet dragon's tongue. "Next time we do the whole thing my way."

"It was *your* way that got us in trouble this time, bucko." Migdon eased the knapsack from his shoulders and set it down with a crash. From one of the side pockets, he pulled a handful of seeds and popped them in his mouth one at a time, unshelling them with his tongue and spitting the shells out between his teeth.

"Thought you said your "silver tongue" could talk its way out of anything."

"Said if I had six *hours*. Don't know about you, but I didn't care to spend another five minutes with that lot let alone another couple of hours." He nodded sagely and spat a shell at a tangleroot vine inches from Ky's foot. The vine's tendrils instantly curled around the shell. "No, our problem was that we stood out because we didn't stand out enough."

"What? That doesn't make any sense."

"Sure it does. We stood out because we *looked* like we were trying to be sneaky. Like we were trying to fit in with the crowd but didn't quite succeed. Now, if you'd just followed my suggestion—"

"Oh the one where we were supposed to stagger up to the blockade, hacking and coughing, with our faces painted white and blood dribbling from our lips? We would have been shot and our bodies burned long before we reached the bridge."

"Well, you know what they say, 'It's the best laid plans that rise from the grave to bite you'—or something to that effect. I forget the exact quote." The dwarf popped another seed in his mouth and shoved back to his feet, eyeing the massive knapsack with a rueful expression on his face. "They also say the foolish man packs from a desire for comfort, the clever man from the knowledge of roads traveled, and the wise man from the anticipation of roads to come. Guess I just have a bigger imagination than most."

15

Ky planted one foot and instantly plunged into murky water that lapped at his thighs. Migdon's hooting laughter brought heat surging to the back of his neck and the tips of his wind-chilled ears. He struggled back to what appeared to be moss-covered dry land, only to have the earth sink beneath his hands when he tried to push himself up and out.

He splashed down again and sank to his waist.

"Got yourself in a spot of trouble, eh bucko?" Migdon rocked back on his heels and squinted to survey the surrounding moorland. As if he hadn't a care in the world. "That's the problem with the Westmark, you know. Full of peat bogs, hidden pools, and this infernal marsh grass—you never see it until you're caught."

Ky glared at the dwarf. He lunged for the bank, landing with the upper half of his body flat on at least partially dry ground. The edge sank beneath his weight and cold water crept up his shirt. By the time it reached his ribs, he was shivering. But he hung on, and between digging his elbows in and kicking his heels like a frog in a wallow, he managed to crawl clear of the muck and roll over on his back.

Migdon stooped over him, jaw jutting in a frown. "You could've just asked for help."

Ky spat out a mouthful of mud and stayed where he was, gazing up at the ice blue sky of mid-morning. The high, keening cries of marsh birds sounded in all directions. A gust of wind rattled the frostbitten grasses that pricked the back of his head. It'd been ten days by his count since the coffin escapade at the bridge, and still he and Migdon were tramping across the Westmark.

If it hadn't been for the rising and setting sun, he would have worried they were going in circles. Round and round. Trapped forever on the Westmark until one or both of them plunged into a bog and drowned. But Tauros was his constant, a fixed guiding point, and with every step, he felt as if he were finally getting closer to home.

Closer to *them*.

"You planning on napping there all day, bucko? Cause this pack is getting mighty heavy, and I want to know if I should set it down or keep it on."

Ky sat up and slapped the ground beside him.

"Fine." Migdon dropped his pack, sank down, and groaned as he stretched his legs out. "Reckon we're due for a rest anyway. This walking—it gets to you after a while."

Ky just grunted and dug through his soaked knapsack, wringing out what could be wrung and rubbing the rest dry with the help of his mostly dry collar. Something moved on the back of his neck, and he slapped at it. Something wet splatted across his palm and trickled down his neck. He pulled his hand away and curled a lip in disgust at the large, white, grub-like creature smeared across his palm. Red blood oozed from its crushed belly.

"What is it?"

Migdon hocked a wad of spit and sent it flying into the bog. "Blodknockers. Nasty little bloodsuckers. Live in nests in the marsh grasses around the bogs. Best be sure you haven't more than the one on you. You know what they say, 'Where there's one, there's many.'"

Ky scrubbed his hand on the ground. "You're joking, right?"

"Me joke? Never." The dwarf squinted an eye at him. "Seriously though, check for more. They have a nasty little bite that will put a man to sleep. One bite won't do it. But they tend to swarm their victims and suck them dry."

His skin crawled at the dwarf's words. He jumped to his feet and slapped at his arms and legs until he was there weren't any more blodknockers on him. For all he knew, it could just be one of Migdon's jokes. But better safe than sorry. By the time he was done, Migdon had sprawled out with his head propped on his knapsack.

"You done dancing around, bucko?"

"Yeah." Ky retrieved his supplies and his knapsack and set it all down again a safe distance away from the bog and whatever nasty critters might live inside it. He sat with his elbows on his knees. But the rush of adrenaline still pumping through him made any thought of rest impossible. His mind wandered back to the Underground, to Meli and Paddy and Cade.

"You ever think about home, Mig?"

"Home, sure." The dwarf cracked his knuckles one by one. "Mostly though I think about how good it feels to get away. Oh, it's a grand place, I'll grant you that. But living in the Caran's stronghold can get a mite stuffy. Too many fierce Adulnae shoving about as if they own the place and those pretentious Xanthen making up excuses for them—that's our fighters and scholars, two more revered positions in the mountains. Me, I like to do things my own way on my own time, see?"

"Aren't you a messenger?" In Ky's experience, messengers were the lowest of the low, kept running at the beck and call of pretty much everybody else. Didn't leave you with much of your own time.

"Sure, messenger. Scout. Information gatherer. Official ambassadorial-go-between. You name it, I've done it. More than once I've saved their hides with a timely piece of information, so they've learned to value my work even if they don't understand the skill behind it."

Suppressing a shiver, Ky tossed his supplies back in his knapsack and slung it over his shoulder before rising. With this breeze and so little residual warmth left in the frozen ground, sitting in wet clothes was about as much fun as matching Cade in the Ring. "We should get moving."

Migdon slowly rolled his head back to look at Ky, but gave no sign that he intended to rise. "Now, don't get me wrong. It's not *all* bad in the Whyndburg Mountains. I've never met any folk more loyal to each other and their way of life or more determined to stand against the Takhran. The rest of Leira will give way eventually, you can bet your britches on that, but when it's all said and done and the dust of battle clears, the Whyndburg Mountains will still exist as their own sovereign kingdom, I'd stake my life on it."

Ky stamped his feet on the ground to bring feeling back into his numb toes.

"Manners, bucko. What's the hurry? You so impatient to be rid of my company?"

"I'm ready to be home."

The dwarf rolled his eyes. "Well, lucky for you, bucko my boyo, we're almost there. You hear that low rumbling? That's the River Adayn. One more crossing and we'll be in the Nordlands only a mile or so from your city."

What? So close?

Ky hauled the dwarf to his feet. "You should have told me." He grasped Migdon's pack in both hands and practically flung it at him before starting off in the direction of the river.

"Easy there, bucko." Grumbling, the dwarf adjusted the straps of his pack, hefting its sagging weight higher on his shoulders. "Too much of a hurry, and I'll think you don't like me. Besides that river crossing isn't going to be easy. Word is the Westmark Bridge was destroyed in a flood a couple of months back."

"Yeah …" The memory gave him pause. He couldn't help thinking about Birdie and Hawkness and hoping that, wherever they were, they were all right. "We might have had something to do with that." He ducked his head to avoid Migdon's squint-eyed stare. Spilling secrets, foolish really. A good runner never offered information that wasn't needed.

He really was getting out of practice.

"Then"—the dwarf drew the word out until it carried the weight of two or three words and the implications of a dozen others—"you'll know how fierce the River Adayn can be. I don't know about you, but I'm not much of a swimmer."

Ky just marched away, keeping his tongue locked firmly between his teeth where it couldn't get him into any more trouble. Swimming wasn't his strong point either, but what was one more river crossing when he was so close to the Underground?

So close to home.

• • •

Fifty yards had never seemed so far.

On the top of the westward bank of the River Adayn, Ky crouched behind the prickly concealment of a snaggletooth bush, careful to avoid losing his balance and creating a disturbance that might attract the attention of the dark soldiers below. Through the red-barbed branches, he could see the stone walls of Kerby just visible over the opposite bank. Near but still unattainable. Directly in his path, the river boiled in its course, cutting him off from the mile-long run home. A pair of broken pilings on both banks were all that remained of the Westmark Bridge. In its place, the Khelari had rigged some sort of ferry system, with a barge that crawled back and forth across the river, while armed guards stood stiffly at attention on both banks.

His destination was the line of supply wagons waiting to cross.

Migdon heaved a sigh and spat out a seed shell. "You sure this is what you want to do, bucko? If you hiked another two days northwards, you could cross over Saldan's Ford—less likely to find a passel of Khelari waiting for you on the other side. It'd extend your trip some, but you'd have a better guarantee of not dying."

"Can't wait two days. I got to do this now." *I promised.* Ky nodded his thanks to the dwarf. "So long, Mig. Been nice knowing you." Ky crept forward, knapsack tucked under one arm to keep it from bouncing on his back, and ducked around the side of the snaggletooth bush.

One of the secrets to invisibility was planning your route beforehand, but not being afraid to improvise. So as Ky slipped down the bank toward the river and the line of waiting carts, he trusted his feet to fall on the patches he had selected—quiet and free of dead leaves or twigs—and kept his eyes fixed on the guards. He ducked behind every available shelter, paused in shadows, and counted the seconds whenever the guards looked his way.

In the city streets, you disappeared by blending into the chaos, by fitting so well into the background that you could be seen and overlooked. But out here on the bank, surrounded by wind and sky and brittle marsh grass, Ky felt exposed. He must not be seen *at all.*

So it was slow and tedious work before he finally reached the last wagon in line and slipped up over the side into the bed.

He hunkered down between a pair of barrels and hitched his knees up to his chest with his knapsack in his lap. Peeking over the rim revealed a dark soldier slumped on the wagon seat with his elbows on his knees and smoke puffing from a pipe between his teeth. It was some time before the wagon clattered onto the barge, rocking the boat with its weight. The ferryman chocked the wheels and exchanged weary conversation with the Khelari as the barge swung out into the current.

For a split second, Ky thought he was back on the slave ship. He could hear the thunder of the waves, smell the stench of the hold, and know the sickening taste of his own fear. Then he blinked, and he was on the barge again. He felt for the pouch of sling-bullets at his belt and squeezed it in his fist. Newbie runners often tried holding their breath when they got in a tight spot, only to wind up giving themselves away once they ran out of air or unable to keep up when it came time to run.

Ky slowed his breath to an even, quiet pace.

The barge thumped against the opposite bank, and moments later, the wagon lurched forward, rattling up and away from the river. Now came the hard part: disembarking without being seen. He had no desire to ride the wagon all the way to where the troops were camped to blockade the city. But he had to stay on long enough to get beyond sight of the guards posted at the river.

Ky waited until the wagon had crested the first hill and begun the descent, then eased up and over the back and dropped. As he fell, his knapsack caught on the tailgate and jerked him against the wagon with a thud. The wagon jolted on. His feet skimmed the ground and sharp stalks clawed at his legs. He struggled to work the strap free.

With a ripping sound, it tore loose, and he fell flat on his face in the grass. He waited to rise until the wagon sounds faded to a distant creaking, then shot to his feet, hugged his torn knapsack under one arm, and raced across the flat ground toward the city.

Only a few months ago, he'd made this same run bursting to tell Cade the news about the discovery the Khelari had made. That run had started it all—all the fighting and dying and hardship he had endured over the past months. It had resulted in the theft of the sword, in Rab's death and Dizzier's capture, in the attack on the Underground and Ky's own need to leave to draw the Khelari away. When you boiled it all down, he was even responsible for everything that had happened in the city since—the Takhran's embargo, the blockades, even the slow death by starvation that faced all the citizens now.

Somehow he would find a way to fix it. To fix all of it. And there would be no more skulking and hiding. No more counting his breaths and keeping to the shadows.

Just this one last run, and it would all be over.

He rounded the next rise and stopped dead in his tracks. A Khelari patrol, ten strong, marched in a brisk circuit around the city, not fifteen yards from where he stood. Beyond them, spaced at narrow intervals around the city, were dozens of watch-fires ringed about by Khelari scouts. He *must* be slipping. Of course the city would be under close guard. He should have expected it.

For a breath, he hesitated, unable to stifle the traitorous hammering of his heart and unsure if he should stay still or drop into the grass or race back the way he had come.

Then it was too late.

The shout of discovery assailed his ears, and before he could run or draw his sling, the patrol was upon him, ten tall soldiers crowding around from all sides with their weapons drawn. On reflex, Ky hugged his knapsack to his chest.

"What you got in there, boy?" A soldier snatched the knapsack from his hand and dumped the contents on the ground. The silver bar emblazoned on his breastplate proclaimed some sort of rank, though from the way the other soldiers acted, like a pack, it likely wasn't much more than a step above their own.

"Another runaway, eh?" A heavy hand cuffed the back of his head. "That it, boy, you trying to escape the blockade?"

"No, I wasn't—" Ky stammered, but another soldier spoke over him.

"How'd he get through the watch-fires?"

The heavy handed soldier gave him a shake. "Fool lookouts guzzling brew and huddling around the fires instead of attending to their duties, that's how."

"No, no, that's not it." Ky lifted his hands slowly, palms outward. Last thing he needed was one of them getting twitchy and deciding to run him through. "I'm trying to get *into* the city, not escape it."

The soldier spun him around and studied him beneath bunched eyebrows. He had a craggy sort of face, with more lines and wrinkles than a hallorm tree, and his shaggy beard was turning gray. "Get *into* the city? Delian's fist, what kind of fool talk is that? It's a death-trap."

Ky fumbled for a reply. His knees felt weak as the reality of his situation barreled into him like a pouncing lion. After years on the run, he had actually been taken by the dark soldiers. He would wind up like Dizzier, dragged off to Dacheren or one of the Takhran's other slave camps, which was horrifying enough in and of itself, but the fact that it had happened when he was so close to returning to the Underground only made it worse.

Migdon's harsh chuckle hammered in the back of his skull. "*We stood out because we didn't stand out enough.*"

Fine then. His way had failed. What could it hurt to try Migdon's way for once?

He dropped to his knees and clasped both hands over his head, letting a thin wail escape from his lips. The sound was enough to make him cringe, which only helped the image he was trying to portray. "Please, kind sirs!" *Thick—too thick.* "I just want to get home to my family in the city. Been staying with my uncle—he's a cattle herder up on the Westmark—since summer time. Didn't know about no war or no blockade." He blinked rapidly as he spoke, trying to project an air of innocent dim-wittedness while spouting the first things that popped into his head. "Wasn't trying to sneak through. Didn't know there was any need to sneak. Just want to see my mam and papa and my little sisters . . . all three of them. They've been missing me, you see. Crying at night, my mam says. They want me to come home."

Goodness, he sounded like he was seven.

The graying soldier gripped him by the elbow and hauled him to his feet. Ky flinched from his touch, but the soldier just brushed off his jacket and spoke in a gruff voice. "Get a grip on yourself, boy. There's no getting into the city now. The Takhran's spoken against it, and his word is law. Look, you just head back to that uncle of yours in the Westmark and stay with him. No need to come back here until this is all over, you hear?"

"Not possible." The ranking soldier kicked at Ky's supplies with a muddy boot. The expression of distaste on his jowled face just about begged to be rearranged by a well-aimed sling-bullet. "Only a fool would believe his tale. Even his garb betrays him—unless Westmark cattle farmers have begun donning desert leathers. No, he was spotted sneaking supplies to the city in direct defiance of the Takhran's orders. You know what is required."

Two soldiers seized Ky's arms. He struggled against their grip, but it was like trying to shove a stone wall. They held him fast, and he didn't need to feign desperation now.

"Please . . . my family! I promised—*promised*—to come back."

"And so you shall." The false note of kindness in the ranking soldier's voice raked Ky's nerves on end. "So you shall."

"Sir, the boy is clearly troubled in the mind. I don't think—"

"That's right. Thinking is my job." The ranking soldier shoved the graying soldier aside. "Yours is obeying orders, Doblin. Orders." He spun back to the soldiers flanking Ky. "Escort him to the city. Who are we to keep the poor boy from his family?"

Chuckling their approval, the two soldiers dragged Ky toward the watch-fires and the gates of the city, and he gave no thought to resistance as the others closed around him. Though his sling was still bound about his waist, they had taken his precious pouch of sling-bullets when they stole his knapsack. He had no food, no supplies, and no weapons, but he was almost home.

No doubt the soldiers meant it a death sentence, but he saw only the chance to fulfill his promise, to return to those who needed him.

To him, it was a mercy.

16

The gates of the city slammed shut behind Ky. He skidded to a stop on his hands and knees with the harsh laughter of the soldiers ringing in his ears. Painfully, he picked himself up from the ground. The taste of smoke was thick on the air. Rubbish cluttered the main thoroughfare that twisted away before his feet, deeper into the city toward the market place.

He spun to face the gate, wiping blood from his scraped palms on his thighs. On the outside, the Khelari had removed a dozen sets of wooden blocks and chains before they were able to open the gate to thrust him through. The wood on the inside was scored with axe and chisel marks where the iron bars and slots that once enabled the gate to be barred from within had been removed, leaving the citizens of Kerby prisoners in their own city, forever at the mercy of the soldiers.

No lookouts paced the wall-top, but then what good could lookouts do when the city had already fallen? Still, it reeked of wrongness that they should abandon their one defense. From the look of it, bad things had taken hold of the city—and the Khelari were just the beginning.

He broke into a jog, passing row after row of shuttered houses and ravaged shops as he followed the scent of smoke to the market. Chill air bit at his throat and dead leaves blew across his bare feet. From time to time, he caught glimpses of armed men skulking down back alleys, hoods pulled over their heads, faces streaked with ash. It didn't take a runner to guess their purpose. Soon after, distant shouts fell on his ears, followed by the clatter of weapons and of destruction. It all felt strangely unreal, as though he wandered in a fevered dream.

In the center of the silent market square, flames raged at a misshapen pile, belching black smoke into the air. A group of men with hoods over their heads, gloves on their hands, and scarves wound around their noses and mouths fed the flames with corpses piled high in a barrow.

The sight brought Ky to his knees behind the broken shell of the old fishmonger's stall. Hands moving of their own accord, he tugged his collar up to cover the lower half of his face and a breathless prayer slipped past his lips.

Oh Embran . . . not here . . .

Only one death called for an ashen grave. Only one death left its mark on the passing in a mask of pasty white skin, blue-tinged lips, and blood-flecked mouths. Only one death struck such fear in those who remained.

The white fever had come to Kerby.

It had come and the dark soldiers had left them to rot in it. Probably brought it too. Smuggled ill captives in through the gate or dumped fever-ridden corpses over the wall. It was just the sort of devilish weapon they would devise.

Ky lurched to his feet and dashed across the square to the abandoned market stall that concealed one of the secret entrances to the Underground. Even at a run, he moved as silently as possible, and if the burners saw him, they gave no sign. He ducked beneath the stall, threw open the trapdoor, and dropped inside, scarce bothering to make sure it had closed before taking off at a run, down the tunnel.

With each frantic step, terror pounded within him demanding more. More speed. More strength. More endurance. If he had returned to the Underground too late . . . The thought hovered beside him, a thing of nightmare that teetered on the border between dream and reality. Just when his strides began to falter, the thought gave him new strength and new fear, and he raced on, following a path that had become as familiar to him as the feel of his sling in hand. He should be getting close now, just a little bit farther.

At full speed, he rammed into something solid and fell backwards to the ground. Groaning, he rolled over onto his hands and knees, head hanging down, pounding. He felt his way forward until his hands struck earth. Hard, packed earth.

A dead end.

"No!" The cry burst from him and he rammed his fists into the wall. The passage had been open when he left. Why was it closed off now? Had Cade done it to avoid discovery . . . or had the Khelari buried the Underground?

In either case, the way was shut.

But somehow the ability to simply give up no longer resided in him. Whether it had been beaten from him by the fists of the pirates, or sliced from him by the chill of a knife's edge against his skin, or bled from him by the miles he had tramped since leaving the desert, it was gone.

He staggered to his feet and began clawing at the wall with his bare hands, pausing now and again to thump at the wall with his fists and call out for the runners. If anyone still lived in the Underground, they must hear him, recognize his voice, and let him in. How long he'd been hammering and digging and calling, he didn't know, but when at last he paused for breath with a clump of packed earth in either hand, there was something scraping on the other side of the wall.

Then a muffled voice spoke, and he couldn't recall ever hearing a sweeter sound. "Oi, laddy-boyo, can you hear me?"

Ky fell against the wall and pressed his sweat-soaked cheek to the clawed up earth. "Paddy . . . is that you?"

"Shure an' shake me if I'm wrong an' it isn't Ky himself returned at last. Hold yourself easy there, laddy-boyo. We'll get a hole cleared in a jiffy so you can enter."

Paddy's definition of a jiffy must have been somewhat different than Ky's. At any rate, it felt much longer as he paced back and forth, clenching and unclenching his fists, listening to the rhythmic *clunk-scritch* of shovels and pick-axes within the cavern. Finally the nose of a pick-axe broke through the earth at the top of the wall, sending rock-hard clumps skittering down around Ky's toes. Fire-glow filtered through the opening, and in another jiffy, the runners enlarged it enough that Ky could crawl through.

He emerged in a shower of loose dirt to see a familiar grimy face smiling down at him beneath a shock of red hair, then Paddy seized his hand in a firm grip and hauled him to his feet.

"Shure an' it brightens the world t' see your filthy mug again, friend."

Ky clapped Paddy on the back and found that he could scarce speak, his throat felt so thick. A tattered blouse draped Paddy's thin frame like a sail slack in the wind, and behind the smile, hollows lurked in his cheeks and behind his eyes. Ky might have endured weeks in the hold of a pirate ship, but the Underground looked to have fared little better.

"Meli . . . Aliyah . . . the others, are they well?"

"Well enough—"

But Ky didn't give him time to finish. He brushed past into the heart of the Underground. His gaze roved over the cavern, barely taking in the sealed tunnels, the weak fire sputtering over a bed of damp peat clumps, and the diminished number of runners clustered around the central fire ring. Right now, there was just one thing he was looking for.

"Ky!" Meli's shout reached his ears a split second before she threw her arms around his waist. Gently—oh so gently—he patted her hair. She tilted her head back, wisps of brown hair hanging in a tangled mess over her face. But he could see her eyes—huge they seemed, as big as the sea, and ringed with the shadows of hardship. A tear ran down her cheek and left a damp spot on Ky's fringed jacket.

"I knowed you'd come back," she exulted. "I just knowed it."

"Promised, didn't I?" And in the face of such unwavering trust, Ky wondered how he ever could have doubted it. He lifted his face to the rest of the runners slowly climbing to their feet and approaching with surprised and hopeful expressions on their faces.

Meli pulled him into the middle of the crowd and they closed around him, clapping him on the back, gripping his hand, and punching him in the arm with the fierce camaraderie he'd missed. But there was a sort of desperation to their affection. Runners who'd scarce noticed him in Dizzier's shadow, now laughed and elbowed his ribs and called for stories about where he'd been and how he got into the city.

But Ky had heard enough hollow laughs to recognize one, and he'd grinned too many forced grins not to notice the taut expressions beneath the smiles on every face. They looked almost as battered as he'd felt during his time in captivity—battered but still standing, when standing was triumph enough.

He stood in a sea of familiar faces, but it was the faces that were missing that he noticed most. Over Meli's head, he met Paddy's gaze. "Cade . . . where's Cade?"

Hacking coughs rebounded from the store-room walls, paired with the groan and rattle of the hard-won breaths of the fever stricken. Ky stood in the entry, fringed collar pulled up over his mouth and nose, breathing in the stale stench of sweat and animal hide as he surveyed the rows of occupied bedrolls. Nearly a dozen runners lay there, ashen-faced in the light of a single torch.

"The first fell sick almost a week ago," Paddy muttered behind his sleeve, forehead scrunched with a grim expression that looked utterly out of place on his normally cheerful face. "I'm surprised it took so long. S'pose we've been protected down here. We shunted our supplies out to the armory and turned the store-room into an infirmary of sorts." He gestured toward a girl kneeling beside a pallet, scarf bound around her head and mouth, brown hair hanging in a braid over one shoulder. "Jena's been caring for 'em."

"And Cade?" The words seemed to stick in his throat.

"Must've been one of the first, but he didn't let on 'til yesterday morning." Paddy's nod directed Ky's focus toward the near left corner of the cave where Cade's dark hair and tall frame were easily distinguishable on a too-short pallet. Aliyah sat by his side, crutch propped against the wall, mopping his forehead with a damp rag. Sweat streaked his face, and he clutched a white-knuckled hand to his chest. His eyes flickered behind sealed lids, and a grimace wrenched his face into a terrible expression.

Cade wasn't one to show an ounce of weakness. Not to Ky leastways. Probably not to anyone, except maybe Dizzier. The sight left Ky desperate for the chance to sink a slingstone into a Khelari, if only to prove that he was not helpless. He wanted a physical enemy. Someone he could meet in pitched battle and grind into the dust.

If even Cade could be brought low by this thing, what chance did the rest of them have?

"Aliyah hasn't left his side since he was taken sick. Not that I blame her. We buried Neil yesterday." Paddy's voice grew even fainter than before. "Two others the day before. Behind one of the sealed tunnels." He turned away from the store-room, drifting more than walking over to the stack of barrels that had once served as the armory, and from the look of things, now housed their remaining food supplies.

"It began not long after you left." Paddy halted before an open barrel, and Ky joined him there, shoulder to shoulder, hands resting on the iron rim, gazing into the pitifully empty depths. A sack of dried beans. Shriveled chunks of cheese. A handful of apples. And loaves of bread with crusts that looked even harder than the sling-bullets Migdon had given him.

Little enough to feed over thirty runners.

"A swarm of ravens broke o'er the city that mornin', and the dark soldiers descended on their heels like hounds loosed for blood. They tore through the city, raidin' shops, tearin' into houses, overturnin' carts, stealin' what food there was and smashin' any they couldn't carry. But they didn't kill . . . no, *they* didn't kill."

In Paddy's tight-lipped expression and haunted eyes, Ky read the rest of the tale. For the past five years, the dark soldiers had controlled the city and destroyed any shreds of its former government. Now left to their own devices, the citizens must have dissolved into a panic like none other, more so once their fate and the impossibility of escape became clear. He thought he knew the answer, but couldn't help asking anyway. "Anyone get out?"

"Shure tried—some sneakin', others fightin'. They learned soon enough that even when you're caught—and you *are* caught—there's no relief in death. The dark soldiers just beat you up and toss you back in here to rot."

"I heard fighting on my way in."

Paddy grimaced. "That would be Nikuto and his men. Things were bad enough, then he came along and promised to feed anyone who would swear allegiance to him. Folks started flockin' to his banner, and he set 'em to terrorizin' their neighbors and stealin' whatever they could get their hands on."

Ky toed an empty crate onto its side and sat with his elbows propped on his knees. From this position, he could see a cluster of runners shoveling earth to seal the passage he had entered through. "What about the tunnels?"

Paddy straightened at the question. "Cade ordered all but one of 'em closed off soon as we spotted the army. Feared they'd try to dig us out—too much work, if you ask me. Guess they thought so too. Better to let us starve. Though in faith, we've fared better than most above since we already *had* a goodly bit of food stored up, and Nikuto and his men don't know we're down here."

The emphasis on *had* was faint, but it was there. Paddy didn't need to say more. The truth was evident in the barrels and crates before him. Whatever supplies they once had were fast running out, and there was no hope of harvesting any more from the city.

Between sickness and starvation, the Underground was doomed.

"Still—" Paddy shrugged, and a hint of levity crept back into his voice "—we can outlast the rest of the city. Mayhap the dark soldiers will grow weary of the wait and wander back to whatever new dark purposes their dark master has for 'em, eh?" He kicked his heel against the barrel. "Best chance we've got."

"Chance? There's no chance in waiting."

"Really and what did you have in mind, *master* runner?"

Ky scuffed a toe across the floor, tracing a wide-armed V in the dirt—the hawk, chosen for the great outlaw Hawkness as the Underground's sign, to symbolize the will to fight for freedom. It represented everything the Underground stood for.

But sometimes the hawk was forced to *flight* for freedom too.

His gaze wandered to the one remaining tunnel. "Leaving, Paddy . . . leaving's the only chance we got."

"For the last time, I tell you Cade won't like it." In the narrow expanse of the passage, Paddy's voice rebounded from the walls, punctuating each word with added emphasis, and filling Ky's ears with a dozen nagging voices speaking as one to persuade him to give up and turn back.

He wouldn't mind so much if it *would* be the last time, but he knew Paddy well enough to know that once he had an argument by the throat, he would worry it to death. He'd been vocal enough over the past hour they'd spent wandering in the wake of the sputtering torch in Ky's hand, so much so that Ky finally stopped listening and focused instead on the shaky start of a shaky plan rattling in the back of his mind.

It was a bit like following the patterns of invisibility. He knew the steps were there . . . somewhere . . . but sometimes, you just had to piece it together bit by bit and wait for the dust to clear before it made sense.

The shivering flame painted the bulbous roundness of the tunnel with looming shadows. Ky paused to run his fingers over the walls and found them free of tool marks, bumpy with a natural roughness. According to Cade, most of the tunnels had either been created outright by the outlaws or expanded when they first claimed the Underground as their headquarters, but no man would design a tunnel so full of twists and turns and narrow squeezes.

It was too wild and meandering to be anything but natural.

"Why this tunnel?"

Paddy broke off his argument mid-sentence. "Pardon?"

Not until Paddy answered did Ky realize he'd spoken his question out loud. "Just curious is all. Why close off all the others but leave this one? Don't think I've ever been down it before."

"That's the point, laddy-boyo. Only has a single entrance and exit shaft in a part of town we don't much care to frequent, so it's never been used on a raid. Wasn't ever enough of a crowd to blend into. Works for the occasional pop out and grab, though . . . not that there's much of anythin' to grab at the moment. Cade figured folk were less likely to know about this tunnel 'n any of the others, less likely to give it away if the Khelari or Nikuto started asking questions."

"Huh." Ky shrugged and logged it away. Just another step in the pattern. But he couldn't resist a parting shot. "So, you're saying *Cade* left us an escape route?"

"No, I'm sayin' he didn't want us buried down here." Paddy's grip on his sleeve snapped him to a halt just before the next bend in the tunnel. "Haven't you been listenin' to me? Cade wouldn't want us to just give up on the Underground. This cavern—it's our home. This city—it's ours. We can't just leave."

Ky plucked Paddy's hand from his arm. "Cade's sick—"

"So you think you should take his place?" Paddy's voice dropped into a dangerous growl. "In faith, Ky, I don't know what to make of you. Do you think you can just waltz in here after being gone for months and expect to take charge just because Cade is down? Given up on him already, have you? Maybe we should summon the burners to take him away."

"I didn't—"

"Do you think we've been sittin' around twiddlin' our thumbs waitin' for the great Ky to come back and tell us all what to do?" He shoved past Ky, pushing him against the wall, and strode down the passage. "It's like I don't know you at all."

For a moment, Ky was so stunned he just stood there, back to the wall, listening to the fading slap of Paddy's bare feet. Anger was one thing he was accustomed to. Life with Dizzier had always been an outburst waiting to happen. But Ky never would have expected such ferocity from Paddy. Looked like he wasn't the only one who had changed over the past months.

Straightening his jacket, he broke into a jog and caught Paddy just around the bend. The redhead stood with one heel propped against the wall, hands stuffed in the pockets of his coat. Torchlight captured the furrow between his brows and the forward set of his jaw.

Ky eased against the wall at his side. "Cade's going to get better." Anything else was unthinkable. "I'm not trying to take his place."

Silence stretched between them, then Paddy finally grunted. "Just who do you imagine has been keeping things running around here?"

The answer should have been obvious sooner. Sure there were older and bigger boys and girls, but Paddy had been a member of the Underground longer than most, and in Cade's eyes, experience counted for far more than age or size.

"Paddy ..." Ky swallowed hard. "All I want is to make sure we survive, and right now, that means leaving this cursed city."

"So sure of yourself, are you?"

"Yes, I am." And for once, Ky knew he actually believed it. That knowledge enabled him to stand straight, look Paddy in the eye, and hold his gaze. This was the best course of action . . . the *only* course of action . . . and he had to believe it could work, that there actually was a way to survive the city's doom.

"Fine." Paddy broke eye contact first. "But I'll lead."

He plucked the torch from Ky's hand without a word and started off. It wasn't long before a breath of deeper air stirred across Ky's cheek and the entrance shaft appeared above, iron rungs set into the wall to his right. He scaled the ladder and eased the trapdoor open just enough to peek out into the dull gray of evening.

No one in sight.

He slid the trapdoor another couple of inches until he was able to twist his head to see in all directions. The entrance was hidden beneath a set of wooden steps at the base of a brick mansion—and *what* a mansion! Small wonder the Underground avoided this place. No chance rags would blend in here. This was the rich corner of town, where fine gentlemen once strolled along in feathered caps and fur lined cloaks, and jeweled ladies, clad in gowns with enough fabric to sail a ship, promenaded at their sides—Ky wasn't entirely sure what *promenaded* meant, but Cade had used it once, and it sure seemed fitting to describe whatever it was rich ladies did.

He allowed himself a blink across the wide cobblestone street, taking in the imposing row of columned mansions on either side, the fireless lamp posts spaced at regular intervals like so many sentries on patrol, and the piles of refuse and rubble accumulating at the base of stone steps. Even here, they had begun to feel the effects of the blockade and Nikuto's mob.

"You see? No way out here." Paddy grunted when Ky dropped back into the tunnel. "Lot of good their riches have done them. They're just as bad off as we are and no closer to getting past the Khelari watch-fires."

Ky nodded toward the tunnel curling away before them. "Anyone ever follow it all the way to see where it goes?"

"O' course. Doesn't go much of anywhere. Ends in a cave-in not too far down the line."

Ky shrugged. "Can't hurt to take a look." He started down the passage again, counting his steps now to keep track of the time and distance, trying to visualize where each turn of the tunnel took him in relation to the city above. It was something he knew instinctively could be important to a plan—once he had one—even though he couldn't yet say exactly how or why.

At nine hundred and eighty one steps, he caught sight of the cave-in ahead. The passageway abruptly disappeared in a mound of earth and rock that blanketed ten feet of the floor before rising to meet the sagging ceiling overhead. At one thousand and five steps, he picked his way across the rubble strewn floor, balancing with both hands outstretched, trying not to cringe when rocks shifted beneath his feet. Halfway up, he gave up any pretense of dignity, dropped to his knees, and crawled the rest of the way.

"Careful!" Paddy barked. "Take it easy, laddy-boyo, 'less you want to be buried too."

Ky's head brushed the ceiling, and he instinctively ducked, shivering as dirt slithered down his collar. There was no seam between earth and roof, no crack or breath of air to point to a continuation of the passage beyond. So this was it. A wasted trip and a pointless argument.

There was no way out, not through the city and not beneath it.

Or was there?

Pawing at the rubble cleared a wallow the size of a lion's head in short order. He seized a handful of earth and shifted it through his fingers. The outer layer was loose—easy digging material. No telling about the interior layers or how deep the cave-in extended, but it was a start, and right now, that was enough.

Back on solid ground, he extended his handful of dirt toward Paddy. "How far do you reckon we are from the wall?"

"City wall? I dunno. Don't imagine anyone does."

"Well, you've got a good head for figures. If anyone can figure it out, you can. We'll need tools, too—lots of them—and runners willing to work." He released his fingers and let the clump of dirt spill around his toes. "We've got digging to do."

17

Birdie held Artair's sword to her chest as she slipped through the low doorway of the donkey shed and let the door swing shut behind her. Even with the door closed, there was more than enough afternoon light seeping through gaps in the wood and holes in the roof thatching to see her surroundings. The donkey's stall was empty—knowing Balaam, he was probably out grazing—but the ramshackle hayloft over the far half of the shed sagged beneath the weight of the griffin. And he was the one she had come to see.

The griffin crouched cat-like, neck cocked, wings folded over his back, peering at something below the loft. Birdie followed his gaze. A spear whipped past her face and stuck in the wall to her left. She stumbled back until her heels struck the door, and she half drew Artair's sword, expecting an attack.

But Sym came into view, moving slowly, purposefully, a spear in each hand.

Her eyes were closed.

Sym stamped her feet—one, two—then lunged. Stabbed one spear forward and then the other. Stood erect and leapt to the side, braids flying about her face. Did a quarter turn, then stamped her feet and lunged again. Four times in total, until she had faced each point of the compass.

She pulled back from the lunge, struck downward with one hand and thrust upward with the other, whirled away and brought both spears flying around to strike with the points behind her and the ends forward. Crouching, she shuffled forward then back, thumping her heels against the ground so it provided a sort of rhythm to her movement, keeping one spear in guard position and one ready to throw.

With a yell, she dashed forward, striking in the air, blocking, and spinning back around. Birdie watched in amazement. Sym moved with the speed, agility, and fluidity of a cat. One moment, she gave the appearance of one fighting for her life, and the next, that of a dancer, graceful as a wisp of cloud, such as one might see dancing for coin in the village square. But no matter how quickly she brought her spears or body whipping around, she seemed to be in perfect control.

She ended with a quick double step forward then kicked a leg behind her and rotated her body through the air, landing with one knee down, one spear point in the ground, and the other guarding her head.

Gundhrold clacked his beak in appreciation, and the sound recalled Birdie's purpose to her mind. She ventured away from the entrance. "It looks like a dance."

Sym rose and retrieved the spear she had stuck in the wall. "It is a dance, but it is also useful for training. Some of it can be used in combat. Some is just for show." She sent the spear spinning around her wrist, caught it again and stuck it in her quiver, which was hanging on a peg beside Balaam's stall. "Waste time twirling your spear in battle, and your foe has time to put a blade in your throat. But it builds strength and teaches control, and these are valuable attributes for a warrior." She slung the quiver over her shoulder and turned to leave.

"Wait." Birdie held Artair's sword out in both hands. "Can you show me?"

"My weapon is the spear, little Songkeeper. The sword is a very different weapon." Sym's eyes narrowed, focusing her piercing stare on Birdie. Whatever she saw there, after a moment, she shrugged, hung her quiver back on the hook, and folded her arms across her chest. "Amos or Brog returned from scouting yet?"

Birdie shook her head.

"Then there is time to spare. What training do you have with the sword?"

"Only the little that one of the Adulnae taught me." Thinking of Jirkar and his brother Nisus brought a little smile to her lips. She hoped the Khelari had not yet managed to conquer their homeland too.

"Adulnae?" Sym arched an eyebrow. "Show me."

The Saari warrior vaulted up onto the rail of Balaam's stall, leaving Birdie alone in the middle of the shed, uncertain as to what she should do. Jirkar had taught her several different guard and strike forms, but she had never performed them without someone calling the commands or sparring with her.

She could feel the griffin's gaze resting on her but could not bring herself to meet it. If she did, she knew she would tear the shred of courage fluttering within her and miss out on an opportunity to learn. She seized the sheath and the sword slid free like a knife through butter. The chill of the blade worked its way through her hands and up her arms and settled as burning ice in her shoulders.

She fell into a fighter's stance and loosed a few experimental slashes, then pulled back into a standard guard position. Her slashes were weak, and she knew it.

Off-balanced somehow.

"Picture your opponent," Sym prompted. "Know where you are aiming. Imagine where he will strike and then respond. Simply beating the air will gain you nothing."

Birdie tried to envision an enemy standing before her. Carhartan's stern, weathered face flashed before her eyes, but he was dead. He no longer possessed the power to haunt her dreams. Even her old childhood tormentors, Kurt and Miles, were gone. The Khelari still pursued her, it was true, but they were shadows in dark armor, a faceless enemy no less than their master, the Takhran.

The sword was vibrating in her hands now, and the hum of it seeped beneath her skin, settled in her bones, and grew in volume until it became the melody and her voice awoke in answer. Singing softly to herself, almost beneath her breath, she ran through the guards and blocks that Jirkar had taught her. Slowly at first, then faster, smoother, more instinctively, as the pace of the melody increased and seemed to guide her limbs from one movement to the next.

Not until she came to a breathless halt did she realize her eyes had been closed the entire time. She opened them and nearly dropped the sword in surprise. The blade glowed with a pale shimmering light, like that of the moon. It rippled beneath the surface of the metal, fading now as she gazed upon it.

Trembling, she bent to retrieve the sheath and conceal the sword. Her gaze strayed through the veil of her hair to the hayloft. Gundhrold dipped his head at her, but did not speak.

"Well." Sym dropped from her perch on the stall railing. "That was . . . something . . ." There was a strange look in her eyes, so Birdie couldn't tell if *something* was to be considered good or bad. Sym rummaged in her spear quiver, speaking without turning her head. "You know the correct form. Your Adulnae friend did a fine job of laying the foundation. What you need now is practice and a strong sparring partner to teach you how to avoid taking a hit and how to recover from one. Hawkness would be best."

Quick as an arrow, Sym spun and tossed a broken spear shaft across the shed. Birdie caught it in one hand and rotated her wrist, judging the feel of it. About the same length as Artair's sword, though not so heavy. She backed away and propped Artair's sword beside the door, then found she was strangely loathe to let it leave her hand.

It felt right in her grasp, somehow.

And she felt naked and defenseless without it.

Sym cleared her throat, already standing in a spearman's stance in the center of the shed. Her dark eyes twinkled with a hidden smile. "Since Hawkness is absent, I suppose you'll have to make do with me."

The next hour passed both far quicker and far slower than Birdie could have imagined, and by the end of it, she was sore and winded and only too willing to hand over the broken spear shaft, despite Sym's insistence that she had made good progress. Perhaps she had, if progress consisted of getting knocked on one's face countless times. That was one skill she had mastered.

Birdie retrieved Artair's sword and waited until Sym exited through the low doorway, then squinted up at the griffin in the hayloft. "Shall I come up?"

Without a word, Gundhrold dropped to the floor of the shed. He landed heavily in a flurry of dust, reminding Birdie of the damage done to his wing on the beach outside Bryllhyn, and sat back on his haunches to preen his neck feathers. "Much more comfortable down here, I imagine. The loft is crawling with mice."

Birdie sat down cross-legged with her back to the empty stall and smoothed her crumpled tunic over her legs. Gingerly, she set Artair's sword across her knees. She fiddled with the fringe on her leggings, not sure where to begin on a list of questions that was as long and confused as the road she had traveled since leaving the Sylvan Swan.

The griffin clacked his beak softly. "I have long promised you answers, little Songkeeper, and yet kept you waiting. My knowledge is incomplete, but I will answer as best I can. This I swear." His voice lost its usual rough, rasping edge and became softer, more refined, almost gentle. "There can be no secrets between a Protector and his Songkeeper."

"No secrets." Birdie repeated it in a whisper. What a beautiful world that would make—a world without secrets behind every smile or lies behind every offer of friendship. She trailed a finger across the sword's gold crossguard and pommel. "This was Artair's sword. Did you know him?"

"I met him, but I did not know him well. Your grandmother, Auna, trained under him. He was a good man, and a Songkeeper like none before him." Gundhrold's gaze flickered to the opposite wall, but one glance at his eyes told her that he was seeing something more than gray, splintered wood. "For centuries, my kind have served as Protectors for the Songkeepers and for anyone who showed promise of possessing their abilities—Songlings, we called them. Once we discovered Auna was a Songling, I was assigned to protect her. She was already a mother with two sons when her full gifting came upon her."

Birdie wrapped her fingers around the hilt and tightened her grip until the cold seized the bones in her hand and cooled her heated skin. Her heart was racing. "Do many Songlings become Songkeepers?"

"Nay, little one, only a few. There is generally but one fully-fledged Songkeeper at a time—*generally*, though there have been rare instances of two—and there may be many others who have hints of the gifting. This, I expect, explains what happened with your friend Inali. Sometimes the gifting passes through a family. Other times Songkeepers and Songlings have been completely unrelated. But the new Songkeeper almost always manifests their full gifting before the passing of the previous Songkeeper, leaving them time to be trained."

"But what of me, Gundhrold? I know so little. How can I become the Songkeeper?"

A strange hissing sound came from the griffin's throat. It took Birdie a moment to recognize it as laughter. "You do not need to *become* the Songkeeper. You already are. As for training, I will do what I can, and Hawkness as well, but the best way to master any skill is through practice."

"But Amos glares at me if I so much as utter a single note. He is afraid that my singing will summon the Khelari. Is that even possible?"

"Hawkness is afraid of many things, and most rightly so. It is possible, perhaps. I cannot say for certain." The griffin rose and stretched, forelegs low to the ground, back arching behind him. It was such a cat-like action that it looked terribly out of place on his enormous, winged form. "Know this though, little Songkeeper, there are others with powers in this world, who are sworn to the Takhran's service. It is his hand that bestows their powers, his hand that maneuvers them like playthings. They are called the Shantren . . . and they are dangerous. It is wise to be wary. We must be on guard at all times."

In the middle of the shed, Gundhrold crouched, obviously gathering momentum for a leap back into the hayloft. Birdie didn't try to stop him. She had more questions, dozens of them, and she suspected she always would, but there was only one thing that truly mattered right now.

Somehow she found herself muttering words she never meant to admit out loud. "I don't know how to do this . . . any of it."

The griffin's gaze slammed into her. "You have a gift that no one else can even fathom. Emhran, the Master Singer Himself, speaks to you through the Song." There was awe and wonder in his voice. "You must *listen*, little one."

With a grunt, he launched up into the hayloft. The whole structure shook, showering flecks of hay into Birdie's hair. Motionless, she sat, clutching the sword, if only to have something solid to hold onto in a world that seemed all too fragile, watching dust motes swirl in the beams of light that pierced the cracks in the walls.

Listen, little one.

Inali was propped up in his bedroll beside the hearth when Birdie eased open the door of Brog's hovel. She paused with one foot on the threshold, still warmed enough by her practice with Sym to withstand a few more moments out in the chill wind. Fresh blood stained the bandage that covered Inali's shoulder and bound his arm to his chest, but the color seemed to be returning to his face at last. It was the first time she had seen him looking truly awake and alert since he had been injured.

He had his head tilted back to watch Sym as she stirred something in a pot over the fire. "You stayed." His voice was weak, but there was also a sense of vulnerability in his tone that made Birdie pause a moment more before entering. "Even though I dragged you into this. That must mean something."

Sym ladled a bowl of soup, plunked in a spoon, and offered it to him.

He took her hand instead. "Since when does the huntress Sym Yandel play nursemaid to a wounded warrior?"

"Since when is Dah Inali considered a warrior?" The words sounded harsh, but even from the doorway, Birdie could see the twinkle in Sym's eyes. It made her uncomfortable, as though she strayed upon a scene she was not meant to see.

"One of the Sigzal tribe taken down by a single fighter? The mahtems would never believe it." Sym pulled free and pressed the bowl of soup into Inali's hand. "Eat and regain your strength, and perhaps then you can regain your honor as well."

Inali obediently picked up the spoon. "Still, you could have gone back."

The expression on his face was hopeful, expectant, but Sym just turned back to her cooking, humming tunelessly to herself. Birdie slipped inside, let the door slam shut behind her, and made a show of stamping her feet off. She still tracked muddy prints to the table, though she doubted Brog would care. Gently, she set Artair's sword down and then dropped into a chair, stretching her legs out before her with a heavy sigh.

Sym passed her a bowl of soup. "Any sign of our scouts returning?"

Birdie shook her head and gulped down steaming mouthfuls of soup, wincing when it burned her tongue. Both sparring with Sym and her conversation with Gundhrold had left her hungry enough that she didn't care. Inali was only half done with his bowl when she went back for seconds.

He motioned with his bowl. "I cannot eat another bite. No offense meant to the cook."

"Maybe not." Sym breezed past with a pail of water and plunked it down on the hearth to heat for washing dishes. "But offense is taken all the same."

Inali gestured again with his bowl, trying to catch Sym's eye and failing. His face assumed the miserable expression of an abandoned puppy until Birdie took pity on him and retrieved his bowl. It seemed a shame to waste good soup, so she dumped the leftovers back in the pot when Sym wasn't looking and slipped the bowl into the wash pail. She started back to the table with her refilled bowl, but Inali's voice stopped her before she could reclaim her seat.

"My satchel. I . . . I need it." He seemed anxious, running a hand through his knotted hair until the beads rattled and clacked against one another. "Could you get it for me?"

With a sigh, Birdie left her soup bowl steaming on the table and ventured into the cluttered mess Brog called his home. She found Inali's satchel buried beneath the haphazard pile of their belongings and tugged it free by the strap. It was heavier than she had expected. She nearly ran into Sym and quickly sidestepped so the Saari warrior wouldn't drop her stack of clean bowls. The strap caught on a chair and ripped, spilling the contents of the satchel over her feet.

"Sigurd's mane!" Inali's cry tore her shocked gaze to him—he was trying to rise—and then back to the jumble of parchments, charcoal sticks, quills, and ink bottles scattered across the floor. Sym's stern voice rang out, ordering Inali to lie back, and his own rose in argument.

"I'll take care of it." Cheeks burning at her own carelessness, Birdie scrambled on hands and knees to collect Inali's belongings: a spare fringed jacket, drawing supplies, the black tube and darts he had used to stun Sym—a spear pipe, she thought it was called. One drawing caught her eye when she picked it up, and she couldn't keep her hands from trembling. It was the charcoal image of a serrated mountain peak with an enormous fortress built into its base, and a vast city spreading out across the plain in front.

Serrin Vroi.

Birdie shoved it out of sight in the satchel and reached for the last item, a balled up scrap of cloth. It came unrolled in her hand, revealing an enormous crystal, larger than the pommel of Artair's sword. Firelight shot through the crystal, casting golden rays across the floor and painting her hands crimson.

"The Star of the Desert?" Sym tore the crystal from her hand with the speed of a striking hawk, eyes burning with wrath intense enough to kindle a blaze. Brandishing the crystal like a weapon, she spun to face Inali. "How came you by this?"

Her voice was quiet—dangerously so.

"It . . . I . . ." The blood had fled from Inali's face. Birdie half feared he would collapse. But he shook himself and thrust his chin in the air with the manner of a princeling challenged by a lesser. "What business is it of yours? It should be mine by rights."

"This is the *Matlal's* stone. It is an heirloom of the desert. How is it yours? You were never to be the Matlal."

"No, but I was to be Mahtem of the Sigzal tribe!" Inali shouted. He slammed his good fist down on the hearth and leaned forward, muscles strained and tendons standing out like cords along his neck. "I was the eldest son of my father. The inheritance should have been mine! But what better dowry to offer the Matlal than the Sigzal tribe? Itera and Quahtli took everything from me. They owe me this, at the very least." He sank back against the hearth. "It is a poor price for a birthright."

Sym did not respond immediately. She stood with her jaw clenched and her brows lowered, gazing at the crystal in her hand. Birdie carefully placed Inali's repacked satchel on the table. Matters of desert rule and Saari custom were beyond the range of her knowledge. She had seen the crystal set in Matlal Quahtli's throne and could only guess at its worth, but Sym's expression told her all she needed to know about the severity of Inali's crime.

"I do not understand you, Inali." Sym closed both fists around the Star of the Desert. "Even after helping Hawkness and the Songkeeper escape, you could have returned to the desert in time. But for this, you will be branded a traitor . . . *I* will be branded a traitor with you." Her voice shook. "Were it not for the Khelari amassing on the border, the Matlal would have already hunted you down." She bent, plucked the scrap of cloth from the ground, and covered the crystal. "You are but a foolish boy."

"Aye, foolish an' twice accursed."

Birdie spun around at Amos's voice. His broad form filled the doorway, forcing Brog to stoop behind him to peer between his shoulder and the doorframe. Judging from the thunderous look on the peddler's face, he had overhead Inali's confession.

Or at least enough to be truly riled.

"Ye've been lyin' t' us about yer purpose, lad." Amos stormed into the room and towered over Inali. "If ye know aught at all o'

Hawkness, then ye know I'm not a man ye want t' deceive. Why are ye really here?"

"You know why I'm here." Inali jerked from Amos to Sym to Brog and finally settled on Birdie. "I haven't deceived you. I swear!"

The desperation in his eyes begged her to believe him.

At her side, the peddler whistled a breath between his lips, considering, then seized Inali's good arm and dragged him to his feet. Inali screamed and doubled over, curling in around his injured side. But Amos just started toward the door, hauling the stumbling Saari behind him.

"Beware the stitches!"

"Easy, Amos, don't hurt the boy."

Brog's rumbled words jolted Birdie to action. "Amos!" She darted forward and grabbed his arm. He looked straight at her, but she wasn't sure that he really saw her. His breathing came hard and fast, muscles taut, face redder than his wild shock of hair. "Please, he's been injured. Wounded trying to save me. I think we can trust him."

"Bilges, Birdie, I won't hurt the lad." Amos sounded offended at the suggestion. "I'll *even* thank him for savin' ye, but there's questions that've needed answerin' since first we visited the Hollow Cave. Now that young Inali"—he shook the cringing Saari warrior, eliciting another groan—"has the use o' his tongue an' his wits again, he's got some explainin' t' do." He slung Inali's good arm around his shoulder and hefted him half off his feet, then nodded at Brog. "The door, if ye don't mind. We'll be in the donkey shed. Don't disturb us."

The tavern keeper slung the door shut behind Amos, settled the bolt in place, and turned around with arms crossed over his barrel chest. "It's, uh, best to do what he says when he gets like that." He rocked back and forth on his heels a moment, muttering to himself, then shuffled to the table and eagerly accepted a bowl of soup from Sym.

Birdie slipped over to the door. She didn't dare follow, not when Amos was in a fury like this, but she could listen. If she held her breath, she could hear Inali on the other side, insisting that he had nothing else to explain.

"Look, lad." Amos cut him off. "Ye can't lie t' me. I've been t' Serrin Vroi. I've wandered the paths beneath Mount Eiphyr. I've stood in the Pit. An' if ye were lyin' about seekin' Tal Ethel or about what you mean t' do, I'll know. Ye're goin' t' tell me everythin'."

The peddler's footsteps stomped away.

Amos spun the dirk through his fingers, sitting lengthwise along the top rail of Balaam's stall with one leg dangling, the other propped up. He brought the dirk down with a *thunk* into the rail. Tugged it loose and flipped it again, waiting until the shed door clattered shut behind Sym and Brog as they helped Inali back to his bedroll and the warmth of the hearth.

The interrogation, such as it was, hadn't taken long. All that bluster and shouting had been more for intimidation than aught else. True, he had been honestly riled at the lad's deception. It rankled him. In the old days, a runt like Inali would never have managed to slip anything past Hawkness. He must be slipping.

But runt or not, the lad had stuck to his story with a tenacity Amos hadn't expected.

"Lad's got guts." Amos released the dirk, caught it backhanded, and stabbed the rail again. "Hides it well though." He tipped his head up to look at Gundhrold.

The griffin was perched in the hayloft with his neck craned over the edge, which meant Amos had to look straight up at his murderous sharp beak. Not the most comfortable position to be in, but for a man who had stared upon death itself in the face of an old friend, it made little difference.

"Do you believe he was telling the truth?"

"Aye." Amos whipped his dirk free. "He was tellin' the truth." A man did not simply dream up horrors like those in the Pit unless he had seen them with his own two eyes.

A pause. "Do you trust him?"

That was the question of the hour. "Do I trust anyone?" He chuckled, though it sounded grim even to his own ears. One dark night long ago had taught him all he need ever know about the foolishness of trusting anyone.

He could still hear the screams.

"I don't doubt that he intends t' help us enter Serrin Vroi in search o' this Tal Ethel place, nor that he cares about helpin' the wee lass. He spoke true about that."

"Indeed." The griffin dipped his head, a quick, bird-like movement. "I thought so also. The truth of a man may be seen in his eyes."

"However …" Amos tossed the dirk up, end over end, slapped it in mid-air with his right hand, and caught it by the tip with his left. He sheathed it and swung down from the rail. "I don't doubt that young Inali has an agenda all his own too." He paused in the doorway to straighten his overcoat and flip the collar up to guard his neck. "Best we keep an eye on him."

18

After three days of back-breaking work, digging was starting to lose its appeal. Ky pushed his shovel into the dirt, careful not to exert too much pressure on the cracked handle, and swiped the sweat from his brow with his elbow. His damp jacket clung to his back, and the chill was slowly seeping beneath his skin. He worked from the top of the pile with others below clearing away the earth he dislodged. Another heave, another tug, another twinge of sore muscles, and he dumped another shovelful into the waiting wheelbarrow, topping it off, and Syd—Paddy's assigned little brother—trundled it away.

Right about now, he'd seriously consider trading his right arm for some of Hawkness's ryree powder. If anything could make clearing this passage a cinch, it was that. Of course, there was no guarantee it wouldn't also bring the ceiling down on his head.

"Oi, Ky." Paddy's shout offered a welcome distraction from the continuous rhythm of bending and lifting. With a grunt, Ky straightened and turned. The red-head stood below, arms crossed over his chest, something bundled under one elbow. He jerked his chin. "Somethin' for y' to see."

It was the first time they'd spoken in three days . . . might even be the first time they'd seen each other since Ky threw himself into digging and Paddy took charge of the street project. Trailing the shovel behind, Ky skidded down the pile past five runners working at various heights with shovels and pick-axes. Three days of careful digging and shoring up behind had cleared another twenty feet of what *seemed* to be a continuing passage—progress that was both encouraging and disheartening at the same time.

Twenty feet done.

No telling how many left to go.

But the runners had greeted his half-formed plan with astonishing enthusiasm, throwing themselves completely into the work. In a way, it spoke more of their desperation than anything else. Some dug, others carted dirt back through the cavern to reinforce the seals over the other tunnels, while still others slipped into the city above as singles or pairs and paced out the streets between them and the wall.

All things considered, Ky reckoned it a mighty fine operation.

One Cade could have been proud of masterminding.

At the base of the wall, clear of the line of traffic, Paddy squatted and unfolded a scrap of cloth peppered with a tangled mess of gridlines, squiggles, and all manner of scribbles and mathematical equations, the like of which Ky couldn't hope to interpret. Fingers splayed, he smoothed the edges with a meticulous care that spoke of pride and accomplishment.

"Runners finished pacin' out the streets today, and I've mapped out this quadrant of the city and the tunnel beneath. It's not perfect, but it's accurate enough. I don't think you'll like what we found though."

Was that a touch of satisfaction in his voice?

An unspoken *I told you so*?

Ky crossed his arms. "Go ahead."

"Don't bother yourself with the calculations"—this in an offhand way; Paddy knew well enough that Ky had no head for figures—"but near as I can figure it, your cave-in is still a good hundred yards from the wall, while the watch-fires are located another forty yards out and the patrols cover a goodly distance beyond that." Paddy rocked back on his heels. "In three days, you've cleared what—ten feet?"

"Twenty."

"Fine, twenty. S'posin' the tunnel is blocked for a good distance . . . s'posin' there is no more tunnel and that cave-in is actually the end . . . s'posin' there is a tunnel and it winds on for miles and miles and doesn't come up anywhere . . . or comes up in the middle of the bloomin' Khelari army—"

"I get it," Ky gritted the words between his teeth. "You've made your point."

"Well what then? This"—Paddy gestured at the diggers—"is useless."

Ky shoved to his feet and clutched the haft of his shovel, ignoring the sting of raw blisters against rough wood. "No, this is hope. You have any plan, any ideas at all, other than slowly starving and waiting for the dark soldiers to get bored and move on? You know well enough that's not their way and sitting's not ours."

A dry chuckle sounded beside him. "No, Ky, you never were able to sit still for long."

Ky tightened his grip on the shovel. A heavy feeling settled like lead in the pit of his stomach. He slowly turned around. Cade stood with one forearm propped against the wall, breathing heavily. His face looked thin, almost skeletal, and dark shadows smudged his cheeks and the hollows around his eyes. But his skin was no longer the ghostly white of the soon-to-be dead, and his voice carried the same strength and command it had on the day the Khelari attacked the Underground.

"Cade, you're up—"

"Don't sound so shocked. I'm not dead yet." He coughed into the crook of his arm, but it was a short, dry cough. Nothing like the desperate hacking of three days ago. His eyes flickered over Ky, calculating and judging him lacking. As always. "What of Hawkness? Did you run off and leave him too? Running away seems to be your specialty."

And Ky had no answer. After everything he had faced, Cade could still silence him with a word, make him feel like he was nothing with a look. He'd been so focused on keeping his promise to Meli that he hadn't spared a thought for how Cade would welcome his return.

But if anyone had a long memory it was Cade.

Ky should have known it would take more than a few months for Cade to forget what had happened to Dizzier or who was responsible for the Khelari discovering the Underground.

"And what is all this?" Cade turned a circle with his hands spread wide then moved toward the digging, forcing Ky to fall into place behind. "Digging your way out, are you? Like rats in a hole."

By now, all activity in the tunnel had ceased, and Cade's voice grew to fill the silence. He always had been good at speech-making and crowd-wielding. The runners hearkened to his words like starving men begging for bread.

"Running isn't the Underground way. Out on the streets, it may be every man for himself because that's what we have to do to survive, but not here—not in our stronghold. Here we stand and fight together. Here we are free. We cannot run away and leave our home behind!"

To Ky's astonishment, a murmur of approval ran through the runners. Some dropped their tools with a clatter. One even cheered outright.

Ky grabbed Cade's arm. "This isn't our home anymore. It's a tomb."

"Maybe not *your* home anymore, but we fought hard to keep it, and we won't abandon it now." With a careless sweep of his arm, Cade knocked him aside. The blood pounded so hot in his ears it almost drowned out the rest of Cade's speech. "Put aside your shovels and pick-axes. We have better work to do—work that will fill our food barrels and enable us to stand and fight for what is ours!"

The Underground had little. So much had been taken from them during the rule of the dark soldiers. But they had each other, and they had their pride. And somehow, Cade had managed to summon both to his side.

Ky watched as the runners shouldered their tools, turned away from the digging, and began to stream back toward the cavern. Biting his lip, he clenched his fists around the haft of his shovel, almost welcoming the sting of raw flesh, and marched in the opposite direction.

Toward the cave-in.

Halfway up, he planted the shovel. It looked a bit like a battle flag, wobbling there with its haft cracked above the blade. Arms crossed, he spun to face Cade.

"Staying here is madness." He hammered every ounce of force into his voice that he could, and it got the runners' attention. The retreat halted, and one by one, they began to turn. "If starvation doesn't get us first, the white fever will. Leaving is our only hope. We're close—I know it, but I need your help."

No one moved.

Amidst the dense silence, Ky slowly made his way down the pile to stand before Cade and looked up into the older boy's face. He pitched his voice to reach Cade alone. "Please, you must know this is best."

The old mask had fallen over Cade's features, hard as stone and impenetrable as steel. He gave no indication that he'd heard Ky. "We'll settle this matter as we always have."

The Ring . . . he means in the Ring.

The thought wasn't as frightening as it used to be. For half a second, Ky actually wanted to face Cade. He wasn't the same desperate-to-please runner, struggling to find a place, who had been beaten soundly again and again. It was beyond time to show it and knock Cade down a peg or two. But out of the corner of his eye, he caught sight of the tremor that seized Cade's hands. The shallowness of the older boy's breath struck a nerve. Just the day before, he'd been lying on what could have been his death bed.

It wasn't right.

Ky turned back to the cave-in. "I don't want to fight you."

"That's unfortunate," Cade rasped. "The challenge has already been made."

The hair on his neck rose in anticipation of an attack, but before he could move, a fist slammed into his side, doubling him over just in time for a punch to land below his right eye. He staggered back, head hanging, gasping for breath, but Cade had him by the hair.

Two more blinding, earth-shattering punches landed before he managed to pull himself together enough to draw his fists up to block. He dropped into a crouch and then pushed up with the force of his legs, slamming the fork of one hand up against Cade's forearm, breaking the grip on his hair and tearing out what felt like a sizeable chunk in the process.

The sting steadied him.

He lashed out with his free hand, landing a blow that glanced off Cade's ribs. Jarred the bones all the way up his arm too. Cade backed away, stumbling a little, granting Ky a moment to huddle over his knees, fighting to regain his breath.

The unreasoning panic brought on by the suddenness of the attack was wearing off, leaving pain raw and saw-edged in its wake. His mind fell into the rapid-fire pattern of vague thoughts and images unleashed by adrenaline: Runners crowding around. Tunnel walls pressing in. No room to maneuver. Tools—weapons—scattered just beyond reach.

Then his vision narrowed, and he could see nothing but Cade.

He charged forward and managed to get off a quick *left—right* before another thunderous blow to the head set him reeling. Only a step, then the older boy seized his arm with both hands and twisted, and somewhere within a voice whispered that there were advantages to having long arms in a hand-to-hand fight like this, and Dizzier's voice called him *Shorty*, and a third voice shouted for the others to shut up and focus . . .

Focus!

Pain shot up into his shoulder and neck, and he found himself on the ground, gazing blearily up into Cade's furious face. Grunting, Cade seized the front of his jacket. He scrambled to gain mastery of his feet and propelled himself up with the strength of his legs. The top of his head connected with something hard—there was a wet crack and a cry of pain—and Cade flung him backward.

He slammed into a wheelbarrow with a force that snapped his neck forward and bashed all the air from his lungs. Old boards creaked and groaned, and the wheelbarrow collapsed, tumbling him head over heels. He landed, flat on his stomach, in a pile of earth and rocks and shattered wood.

A foot pressed into his back, keeping him from rising.

But there was no fight left in him.

Only pain and anger and humiliation so strong it was sickening.

"This is our home." Cade ground out between his teeth. His voice was thick and slurred with pain—from the sound of it, Ky had broken his nose—but there was a fire and passion in every word that could not fail to sway the runners. "We will not abandon it.

Follow me, and I will see that we live in safety and security once more. Here, where we belong. Paddy, organize raiding parties—five strong each—all armed. Open up three of the main passages. If any supplies remain in the city, we'll find them. It's time we stopped hiding."

The pressure lifted from Ky's back, and he gasped in a mouthful of air but did not try to rise. Feet shuffled past as the runners left their tools behind and filed back toward the cavern. Silence fell and still he lay, mouth clogged with dirt and sickness and blood. At last, his ears pricked to the release of a heavy breath, hesitant footsteps, then the rustle of clothing as someone knelt beside his head. He didn't bother opening his eyes. No need to see who it was. He knew well enough.

Paddy sighed. "Oi, laddy-boyo, I don't know but what it wouldn't have been better if you hadn't returned."

Bile rose in his throat as he pushed to his hands and knees, but he did not look up. He couldn't. The room swayed too much to lift his head. He forced his swollen lips to give voice to the suspicion that had been growing in his mind since Cade first appeared. "It was you, wasn't it? You told him to come."

Paddy's silence was answer enough.

When Ky finally peeled his eyes open, Paddy was gone.

Two days passed before Ky summoned the courage to drag himself back to digging in the tunnel. He worked alone at the top of the mound, torches in brackets on the walls, breath hissing through his teeth with each painful shovel load that he cast behind. He dug and dug and dug, hardly knowing why he bothered anymore.

Working for the sake of working.

Working because there was nothing else to do.

The runners had jumped at Cade's plan with even greater zeal than they had his. Each day the raiding parties streamed back into the cavern, more often with wounds than with food and always with tales of run-ins and near escapes from Nikuto's men.

And still he dug, frustration seeping from his body with each drop of sweat.

Over and over, he reminded himself that he hadn't done any of this because he wanted to be in charge—right? He'd never cared about that sort of thing. It just grated that the runners could so easily turn their backs on him. Maybe Paddy was right. Maybe it would have been better to have stayed in the desert with Birdie and Hawkness to fight against the dark soldiers.

Maybe there he could have accomplished something.

Aside from alienating his friends and failing to save them from certain death—he'd managed to accomplish that without even trying. *Way to go, Shorty.*

Halfway through his second day of digging, he sensed movement behind him. The stinging taste of fear flooded his throat. He couldn't take another beating from Cade . . . not yet. He tensed for the attack, but no attack came. Just the *scrape-thunk* of another shovel biting into the dirt. He spun around, shovel clenched in both hands like a club, only to snag his ankle on a loose rock and land on his backside with his shovel across his lap, staring into the wide eyes of a small, round-faced boy.

"Syd?" Ky released the breath he'd sucked in. "What're you doing here?" He figured it best *not* to mention how close he'd come to bashing the boy's skull in.

Syd just blinked and went back to shoveling, pale blond hair falling over his eyes as he worked. He moved slowly, methodically, without any enthusiasm or vigor. Without any emotion at all. It was like watching a statue come to life.

For some reason, the boy's silence irked Ky. He brushed himself off and stomped back to the top of the mound. "You know Cade doesn't want you here, right? Better run on back to the cavern with the rest of his lackeys. That's where Paddy is, isn't it?"

No reply.

Ky heaved a sigh and dug in again. Maybe this was Paddy's attempt at an apology—he didn't have the guts to stand up to Cade, so he sent his little brother to help instead. Didn't really matter in the end. If the boy was determined to help, he wasn't about to stop him.

It didn't take long to get a good rhythm going. He chunked dirt behind, and Syd shunted it to the sides of the tunnel. Less effective than carting it back to the cavern, but what else could a fellow do with only two pairs of hands?

A giggle brought him up sharp, balancing a load in the shovel.

Make that *three* pairs of hands.

He couldn't imagine a less Syd-like sound. A second later, Meli threw her arms around his waist, dumping his shovel load over his feet. She grinned up at him, nose wrinkling beneath twinkling eyes, and then launched into work, carting rocks away.

Ky gave a wry smile. It wasn't the help he'd hoped for, but it was enough. He slammed his shovel back into the mound and fell to his knees as the earth gave way beneath the tool. His frantic grasp just kept the shovel from sliding out of reach through the two-foot-wide opening that appeared between the roof of the tunnel and the pile of rubble beneath. Beyond, all was blackness.

He calmed his thundering heart. It could be nothing . . . it probably *was* nothing. Still, he reached an impatient hand back to gesture for light. "Syd! Torch . . . I need a torch."

The boy could move surprisingly fast when the situation demanded. Within seconds, Syd pressed the rough handle of a torch into his hand, and Ky thrust it into the opening, drawing his shovel out at the same time. The flames darted at the earth above and on either side. Ky inched forward, pressed flat, feet and elbows propelling him forward, every bit of him painfully aware of the nearness of a ceiling that had already collapsed once.

Another shove with his toes, and both the torch and his arm extended over a drop. From this angle, it was hard to see anything. The light was too close, too blinding. He released his fingers and the torch fell, and in its flaming wake, he saw the walls and roof of a tunnel extending as far as he could see.

Then the light snuffed out.

But it couldn't erase what he had seen: Hope—uncertain, that was true—but hope nonetheless. As he wriggled back out of the hole, a hand gripped his elbow and helped him rise. He looked down into Syd's pale face, which looked more pale and round and anxious than ever in the merciless light of the torches on the walls, and he read the question in his eyes. Some folks thought Syd was stupid because he moved so slow and didn't speak. Dizzier had always beat up on him because of it. But there was no mistaking the intelligence behind that concerned expression.

"I saw it—the end of the cave-in." Ky grinned at the boy. "We made it through." He chuckled at the sheer impossibility of it. Then his gaze fell on the hole he had just crawled through, and he grew serious again. "Now look, it's not the end yet, not by a longshot, so you can't go telling anybody. We need to know where it goes first."

Both Syd and Meli nodded, solemn as karnoth birds. Such strange little confidants. Ky swiped a dirt encrusted hand across his dirt encrusted forehead. "Right, well then, we need to fetch a rope and extra torches, and then we've got some exploring to do."

Meli's chin thudded against Ky's shoulder as he loped toward the cavern with her on his back. Wispy strands of her hair clung to his neck. Poor girl was completely tuckered out, and he couldn't blame her. After two days of exploring, even his legs trembled with weariness, and his clothes were so drenched with mud and sweat, he couldn't keep his teeth from chattering with the cold.

Syd clumped along at his heels, weighed down by an armload of tools. The boy was stronger than he looked and plenty useful. Maybe Paddy had done him a good turn after all.

But it was time for him to do another.

Ky slowed as he entered the cavern and made for the central fire ring where Cade and Paddy sat side by side on a pair of crates. Gloom darkened the snippets of conversation he overheard as he picked his way through runners lounging on bedrolls or huddled in clumps tending weapons. Most of the raiding parties had returned, and from the look of things, it had been a poor harvest.

"Curse that Nikuto!"

A group of five burst through one of the re-opened tunnels and brushed past on their way to dump a meagre offering into the supply barrels—two loaves of hardtack and a small sack of beans.

"Doesn't matter where we go, his men are there first. How is that even possible?"

Their frustration sparked a twinge of satisfaction in Ky. It was petty, and he knew it, but it sure would be nice if the others began to realize that Cade wasn't the only one with answers . . . and even when he had answers, they weren't always right. He hefted Meli's sleeping form higher on his back, motioned for Syd to hang back, and halted behind Cade and Paddy.

". . . an' that makes another four taken sick today and three more wounded on raids," Paddy muttered. Something inside Ky churned at the sight of Paddy in Dizzier's place as Cade's right hand man. Just another wrong thing in a world where everything had gone wrong. "Slack an' her party haven't come back yet, but the supplies are all but gone. Nikuto has bled the city dry, and we'll be lucky to send out three full teams tomorrow. Look, I know how you must feel, but shouldn't we—"

"We'll manage." Cade slapped his palms against his knees and shoved to his feet. His voice was clipped and harder than steel, but there was a raw edge to it that Ky hadn't heard before. "We always have."

The older boy strode off toward the supply barrels, and Paddy slumped with his head in his hands. He didn't even look up when Ky sidled into Cade's seat and perched on the edge of the crate.

"Oi, Paddy." The words came out in a whisper scarce louder than the silence that followed. Meli still clung to his neck, and the heat of her forehead against his skin mingled with the damp sweat of his run through the tunnels made him a little dizzy. "I need your help."

"I don't know how much clearer I can be, friend." Paddy lifted his red-rimmed eyes. "I can't help you go against Cade. Not now—*especially* not now."

His voice rose at the end, and Ky could feel the focus of the other runners shifting to them.

"Listen . . . listen . . . there's a way through the tunnel. I just need your help—the calculations, the map—to figure out if it can get us beyond the watch-posts."

Paddy started to rise, but Ky caught him by the arm.

"You have to help. Please."

"Still here, Ky?" Cade appeared beside Paddy, arms folded over his chest. Anger glinted in eyes that were swollen and masked with dark purple, and his nose had a new twist in it. But somehow his injuries only served to make him look dangerous, not weak. "Thought you'd have run off by now."

"Believe it or not, I'm just trying to help."

"Did it ever occur to you that we don't *need* your help?" Cade's voice took on the deadly quiet tone that Ky had grown to fear far more than he had ever feared Dizzier's blustering. "You know we wouldn't be in this mess if you and Dizzier hadn't muffed your last run."

"No." Ky pushed to his feet, gripping Meli tight against his back. Somehow, she was still asleep. "We wouldn't be in this mess if you hadn't insisted on stealing from the dark soldiers. Your raid got Rab slain, Dizzier captured, and almost killed Aliyah!" He was venturing into dangerous waters now, and he knew it, but somehow he couldn't turn back. "Now you want us to wait around until the white fever takes us all?"

Cade seized him by the front of his jacket and shoved him back a step. His knees knocked into the crate behind, and he hugged Meli's legs against his sides to keep her from falling. It was only Cade's grip that kept him from losing his balance. White showed in Cade's wide eyes, stark against the surrounding bruising, and for the first time, Ky realized that the older boy was afraid. "Don't talk to *me* of dying."

By now, a crowd of runners had gathered around. Ky could feel them pressing in on all sides, eager for the prospect of another fight, and he would give it to them. He couldn't lose face before Cade again, not if he ever hoped to bring the runners around to his way of seeing things. This wasn't how or where he'd hoped to do it, but it had to be done.

Taking a deep breath, he squared his shoulders. "I challenge you to face me in the Ring."

"What?" Cade released him.

An echo of the question rippled through the gathered runners. Instead of answering, Ky side-stepped the crate and gently eased Meli from his back onto an abandoned bedroll. She mumbled something in her sleep and curled into a ball, but did not wake.

Slowly, ever so slowly, he stood and turned, hands knotted behind his back. "I challenge you to the Ring. Tomorrow. Will you face me?"

For a moment, Cade just stood there, and Ky couldn't help thinking that a fellow's time would have been better spent trying to decipher Langorian than reading the expression on his face. Then he nodded sharply and spoke without turning his head. "Paddy, fetch him a weapon. Why wait until tomorrow? We'll settle this. Now."

"Shure, shure. Would you like the Ring set up too?"

"No need. This won't take long."

At Cade's barked order, the runners scurried out of the way, clearing a circle and giving him room to draw his sword and launch into a series of experimental swings. There was no denying the power and control behind each movement. Despite his illness, Cade's skills certainly hadn't deteriorated since Ky had been gone. His, on the other hand, were more than rusty. He hadn't picked up a sword since the battle outside of Bryllhyn.

His fingers ached to unleash his sling and "settle" the matter in his own way. Cade wouldn't look half so fierce and intimidating when a slingstone knocked him onto his backside and left him drooling in the dust.

"You're insane, laddy-boyo. I hope you know what you're doing." Paddy pressed the hilt of a harvested sword into Ky's outstretched hand and clapped him on the shoulder. Just like old times. His voice dropped to a whisper. "It's Aliyah, Ky. She's been taken sick. Bad."

Ky's heart sank at the news, and with it, his anger toward Cade.

"You get it, don't you?" Paddy's brows pinched together. "Why I can't go against him. He's counting on me."

"Sure, I get it."

Somewhat.

But it wasn't going to stop him from doing what he had to do. Hefting the sword, he moved into the circle, forcing a spring into steps that felt weighted down by bog mud. He didn't wait for the attack—that was something the old Ky would have done—no, he charged in from the right with a battle cry. If he was going to have any chance at winning this fight, it could only come from throwing all of Cade's expectations to the winds, and that meant fighting in ways he never had before.

Cade easily knocked his first stroke aside, but Ky kept at it, hammering away with all the speed and force he could muster. He beat past the older boy's guard and opened a cut on his shoulder, and for just a second, there was a flicker of surprise in Cade's eyes, a hint of hesitation in his guard, and the slightest misstep in his footwork.

Then it was gone.

The tip of Cade's sword slipped Ky's defenses and nicked his shoulder. The Saari jacket was thick, and the hide absorbed most of the blow, but blood still trailed down his arm. The barest hint of a smile twisted Cade's lips, and he transformed into the "whirling dervish of death." Or so Paddy called it—Cade's favorite attack form. It was the sort of thing that was fun to joke about until a fellow faced it in battle. Then it was just plain terrifying.

Ky deflected a thrust and hammered the pommel of his sword against Cade's extended thigh, summoning a curse from the older boy's lips. A minute later a similar blow left a hitch in his stride.

Shoulder for shoulder.

Thigh for thigh.

Payback.

He staggered under the realization. Cade was imitating his moves, countering each landing blow with an exact copy two or three or four strokes later, all the while attacking with a speed and force and precision that left Ky reeling.

Everything about this fight felt wrong. Cade was holding back. His borrowed sword was too clunky. Compared to the perfect balance of Artair's sword, it felt like a misshapen cudgel. His head pounded with each throbbing beat of his heart. They were both fighting more or less injured, but Ky had spent the past several days pushing his body past the limits as he scoured the tunnels for a way of escape. Exhaustion clung to him like a cloud, fogging his mind, dulling his reactions, slowing his thoughts.

He forced himself to breathe. The sheer skill required for Cade's strategy was mind-bending—skill that should have disarmed him within minutes. This plan of attack was showy and time consuming, but it wouldn't be instantly obvious to the runners watching, so it wasn't meant for them. No, it was meant to convince Ky once and for all that he could not win.

So why even try?

Wrapped in his thoughts, he glimpsed the trajectory of Cade's blade out of the corner of his eye and instinctively fell into a high guard position. He barely caught the descending blade in an awkward block over his head and instantly knew he'd made a mistake. The move was so fast and powerful, he hardly saw the flash of steel before the flat of Cade's sword slammed into the backs of his knees, sweeping his legs out from beneath him.

He cracked his head against the cavern floor, and darkness and light flashed across his vision. Blinded, he rolled up onto one hand and knee, bringing his sword around to ward off attack. Cade's boot connected with his wrist, bringing a grunt of pain to his lips, and sending the clunky sword flying across the room.

Blinking to clear his vision, he tried to rise, but his body betrayed him.

He fell back with a groan.

"I didn't mind your leaving, Ky. After everything that happened, it was the only good thing you could do, and I understood that." Cade's harsh whisper came close to his ear. "But you should have stayed gone."

The older boy shoved to his feet and strode away, but there was no cheering from the runners this time. No glorying in Cade's victory or reveling in Ky's defeat. In a way, that was a sort of victory in and of itself. A small one, to be sure, but right now, Ky would claim any ounce of victory he could get.

Cade was halfway across the room by the time Ky managed to lurch to his feet. Head spinning, he yanked the sling from his waist, snatched a rock from the cavern floor, and relying on feel rather than sight, sent it zinging against the blade in Cade's hand.

He spat out a mouthful of blood and forced himself to stand straight. "The fight's not over."

19

"We're done." Cade wheeled around. He held his sword low, but the tip was still raised enough to be menacing. "I beat you, Ky."

"Not yet you haven't." Ky squeezed his eyes shut until the pounding in his head receded, then worked his sling back around his waist like a belt. "I challenge you to fight again."

A tug on his elbow brought him swinging around with fists raised. Syd let out a little squeak, shoved the clunky sword at him, and then swiftly backed away. Ky managed a curt nod of thanks, then gripping the unwieldy weapon in both hands, advanced slowly into the circle—slowly, because if he tried to move any faster, he was liable to fall on his face.

"It won't ever be over, Cade. You're going to have to fight me again, and sure, you might beat me again, but I won't run and you can't keep me down." He halted before his legs gave way, set the sword point down, and leaned on the hilt. "I won't give up. I can't."

Cade was already moving toward him with determined steps, blade poised for the thrust, the anger seared across his face threatening a fight that was bound to be short, painful, and all too decisive.

There could be no reasoning with him now.

Ky shrugged, forcing his voice to remain casual and unconcerned. "But where's fighting going to get us? Nowhere, that's where." He deliberately turned his back to address the Underground instead. "That's why I'm going over Cade's head to you. To let *you* decide for yourselves.

"You see, I found a way out of the city." His voice could never fill the cavern half so well as Cade's, but if there was one thing that could sway the runners now it was a tangible hope of escape. "Now, Cade says we shouldn't even think about leaving, that this—the Underground—is our home."

With a sweep of his arm, he directed their gaze to the cavern with its walls of scored stone, floor worn smooth by the passage of their feet, and a roof that crouched to shelter them like the protective arms of the mothers they had lost.

"But I say that this isn't the Underground. We are the Underground. You . . . me . . . all of your brothers, sisters, friends. This cavern is nothing more than a hole in the ground. We make it something more. No matter where we are, so long as we survive and stick together, the Underground is not lost."

Might not have been near as fancy or fiery a lecture as Cade could have come up with, but it was the most impassioned speech Ky had ever made, and the runners had listened—really listened. He could just about see the debate raging on every face, the scales tilting back and forth, though which way they would tip was still anybody's guess.

Shouting broke out down one of the tunnels. Four runners dashed into the cavern supporting a fifth with blood streaming from his head. They collapsed beside the entrance, and a tall girl with long blonde hair split into a pair of thick braids separated from the bunch and raced to meet Cade.

It was Slack and her crew, returned from the raid.

"They're coming!" Slack gestured wildly with a red-stained hatchet, bearing down so fast it looked like she was planning on knocking Cade off his feet. "We need to barricade the entrance. Hole up. Get ready to fight."

"Settle down, Slack." Cade sheathed his sword and raised both hands—whether to break her flight or ward her off, Ky couldn't say. "Who's coming? What's this all about?"

"Nikuto's men, hard on our heels."

Cade cursed and started toward the armory, shouting directions for the runners to arm themselves. Ky stumbled after with Paddy at his side and Slack pursuing, still explaining.

"We had a bit of a scuffle up top. Nothing serious, you know, not 'til one of 'em grabbed at little Rayne. I might've got a little mad at that. In fact, I reckon there's some as might say I expressed my opinion a mite too violently."

"You killed someone?" Paddy demanded.

"No . . . maybe . . . I don't know. All of a sudden, there was a dozen of them bearing down upon us. We had no choice but to run. Thought we were in the clear, but they spotted us right as we ducked in the tunnel."

She kept talking but Ky was only half listening now. He tucked the clunky sword under one arm, shoved through the scramble around the armory, and seized two pouches of stones. If a fight was coming, it would be sling-work for him. He'd had his fill of the sword. Out of the corner of his eye, he saw Cade slide a small leather pouch into his vest, then grab a bow and quiver and start toward the tunnel, calling over his shoulder, "How long we got?"

"Ten minutes? Still daylight up top and they got no torches, so they're coming in blind. Slow as mud tortoises and twice as loud."

At the tunnel entrance, Cade squatted with his back to the wall and dropped the quiver at his feet, bow lying at the ready over his knees. His head sagged. Gone was the stiff posture, firm jaw, and clipped voice of the Underground leader. He looked suddenly old, war weary. "Ky, you win. Get them out of here."

The order was so unexpected, it took Ky aback. "Uh . . . right. Paddy, can you take front to navigate?" He spun to find Syd and almost tripped over him, and just managed to steady both himself and the boy as he returned the sword. "Paddy, have Syd show you the way. I've got the infirmary."

Paddy nodded and sprang into action. "Quick now, grab your supplies, bedrolls, torches, and any belongin's or weapons you can carry and hightail it after me!"

The barked orders set the runners scrambling around the cavern at double-quick time, with a semblance of order and purpose that Ky could only have hoped for. Slack's team, minus the bleeding boy, gathered at the tunnel entrance behind Cade, ready to hold off Nikuto's men until the Underground was clear.

Ky grabbed a handful of runners in passing and hurried them to the make-shift infirmary. Jena started to her feet when they busted in and tried to head them off, but the runners fanned out as soon as they entered, and Ky dashed her objections aside. The runners were protected only by turned up collars and scarves pulled over their mouths, but they still dove into the work without a hint of hesitation, bundling up bedrolls, hefting those too weak to walk, and offering a shoulder to those who could stumble along with a little help.

Their courage was shaming.

Ky found Aliyah in the far corner and caught her up in his arms, crutch and all. Her skin burned beneath the thin material of her dress, and a cough rattled in her throat. Hugging her to his chest, he set off at a shambling run, back through the cavern, then down the tunnel toward the cave-in.

More than two thirds of the runners had already disappeared through the little opening. Ky handed Aliyah off and cast about for Paddy, spying his lanky form at last in the center of the chaos at the top of the pile, helping each runner through and chucking their belongings to the other side.

"Oi, Paddy! I'm headed back to help Cade. Take the lead." He waited just long enough to see Paddy wave the scrap of cloth tucked in his sleeve—the map—then he turned and dashed away, pulling his sling from his waist as he ran.

The whistle and snap of a bowstring greeted him when he reached the cavern, then Cade's voice, strong and commanding. "*That* my friends, was a warning shot. There are plenty more where that one came from."

Cautiously, Ky peeked around the corner. Cade, Slack, and her team still knelt before the tunnel entrance, arrows nocked and pointed into the dark beyond. The rest of the cavern was clear. He slipped across the intervening space and squatted beside Cade, hastily loading his sling.

"Another five minutes and we'll be good."

Cade's head jerked in acknowledgement. "Leave us be," he shouted down the tunnel, "and you won't be harmed."

Coarse laughter rang out in answer. "Harmed by who? A bunch of wet-nosed boys and girls what stumbled in over their heads, started robbing my marks, and causing ruckus in *my* territory? Now see here, *that* I might have overlooked. No one ever said Nikuto got worked up into a dither over naught." The voice dropped to a growl. "But when a crazed witch hacks one of my men with a hatchet, I'm liable to grow a mite irritated. No, boy, you leave us enter, and mebbe you lot won't be harmed."

A rare grin flashed across Cade's face. "Did you hear that, Slack? He called you a witch."

"Called you a boy." She smacked the flat of her bloodied hatchet on her palm. It was such a casual and pitiless gesture, Ky wondered if she hadn't killed Nikuto's man outright. "Reckon we should enlighten him?"

"Shh!" Ky motioned for silence. Something rustled down the tunnel, stealthy footsteps inched nearer, and he thought he could hear the irregular breathing of men trying—and failing—to be quiet. Threats hadn't worked so well. Maybe this was one time where Migdon's bold-as-brass approach would be best. At least buy them some more time. "I'm warning you." He raised his voice, threw in a few wet, strangled coughs for effect. Didn't sound half bad either—or rather, sounded horrible, and so, realistic. "We have the white fever here. Real bad. You come in here, you'll catch it too."

For a moment, all was quiet.

Ky met Cade's skeptical look and shrugged.

The voice grunted. "Good try, boy. But Nikuto knows a trick when he hears it. Get 'em!"

Nikuto's shout was drowned out by the rush of feet. Ky let fly his sling and was rewarded by a cry. Five bowstrings cracked and arrows zipped down the passage. Ky reloaded and slung again and again, keeping up a constant stream of flying stones, while the others waited with arrows nocked. Arrows could not be wasted on blind shots, especially when there was no return fire, and after that initial volley, no cries.

Ky was reaching for another stone when Cade seized his forearm. "To the tunnel. We've held them off long enough."

Silent as ghosts, they rose, and keeping to the wall, made their way around the cavern to the exit tunnel. Ky hung back to the last. He couldn't help glancing over his shoulder at the cavern that had been his home for the past three years—the tunnels, the armory, the Ring where Cade had defeated him so many times, and the central fire where they all gathered at the end of a day to share the day's misadventures.

His gaze hovered over the fire-ring. There was something lying beside it. It took a second for what he'd seen to register: the filthy sole of a little foot beneath the hem of a tattered dress and a crown of wispy brown hair.

He stopped cold. "Meli."

Then turned and sprinted across the cavern.

Some part of him saw Slack grab for his arm and miss. Some part of him was aware of a dozen burly, hooded figures leaping into the cavern, armed with cudgels and axes and honed butcher's knives. Some part of him heard Cade shout, "Fire!" and felt the arrows winging past and knew that he was an inch away from being killed.

But such sensations seemed distant, almost dreamlike.

Until he slammed to his knees beside the fire-ring and caught a glimpse of Meli's ash white face. *No . . . no.* He shoved down the panic, scooped her up in his arms, sling still dangling from one hand, and turned to run.

"Better drop that sling, boy." A massive man towered over him, a hammer in each hand, dark hair hanging like a mass of tangleroot vines about his coarse, scarred face. A purple welt had formed over his right eye—looked like at least one slingstone had hit home—and didn't seem to have improved his temper any. "And go easy with it. Nikuto knows a trick or two."

Ky's tongue felt thick and swollen in his mouth. He shifted Meli's limp form to get a better grip, and her head tipped back.

"Delian's fist!" Nikuto retreated a step. "What—" But he never got the chance to finish. An arrow lodged in his upper arm, spurting blood across his yellowed shirt sleeves.

Ky dodged past his reach and ran full tilt toward the exit tunnel where Cade was already nocking another arrow to his bow.

"Go, go, go!" Cade shoved him into the tunnel. "The others went ahead."

By the time they reached the cave-in, Ky's breath was coming in hard gasps. Sweat stuck his jacket to his chest. He could feel the heat of Meli's fever through the thick animal hide. It was like holding a burning log in his arms.

Slack waited for them by the opening. Behind, Nikuto's men crashed and bumped down the narrow tunnel. It was only a matter of time before they caught up, and a little squeeze through the cave-in opening was unlikely to stop them.

"Torch!" Cade yelled. "Grab the torch."

Ky spun to look for it, but Slack was already on the move. She snatched a torch from its wall bracket, charged back up the pile, and ducked through the opening. Thighs burning, Ky staggered to the top, handed Meli's limp form to Slack, and then crawled through on hands and knees with Cade grasping at his heels.

"I told the others to go and not look back," Slack said.

"Good." It came out more as a gasp than a word. Ky scrambled to Meli's side, cradled her in his arms, and lurched to his feet. Something crunched overhead, and flecks of dirt spattered his neck. Instinctively, he ducked over Meli then peered around his hunched shoulder.

Grinning raggedly, Cade pulled his sword from where he'd stabbed it into the roof of the tunnel. From inside his vest, he produced a small leather pouch that he stuffed in the crack, leaving a thin strand of tarred string hanging loose.

"Is that—"

"Ryree powder? Indeed it is." Cade motioned to Slack. "Care to do the honors?"

She whooped. "'Deed I do!"

Ky started down, setting his weight firmly on his heels to keep from losing his balance. His mind flashed back to the last battle of the Underground when Hawkness's packets of ryree powder brought the roof down on their enemies. If this was more of the same stuff, he wanted Meli well clear of it.

But he hadn't made it far before Cade and Slack gripped both his elbows from behind and rushed him off the pile of rubble and then down the passage at a frantic run. A rumble grew behind, like the growl of an awakened animal, and the earth trembled beneath his feet. Heat blasted the back of his neck and heels. He hunched over Meli, protecting her with his body, shoulder to shoulder with Cade and Slack on either side. They crouched down, steadying him and one another.

Then it was done.

Dust and ash clogged the passage. No sounds of pursuit disturbed the heavy silence, though whether that meant the opening had been sealed or Nikuto and his men consumed by the fire, Ky didn't want to know. He pushed to his feet, legs quivering. He wanted no more deaths on his conscience.

Cade and Slack were already up and brushing themselves off, breathless and chuckling with the casual bravery of those accustomed to danger. Ky shuffled Meli around until her weight rested against his chest, and started off down the passage, following a course his legs had trodden many times over the past several days. He waited until he was sure his voice was steady, then demanded, "Where in all the Nordlands did you lay your hands on ryree powder?"

"Thought you might appreciate that." Cade's long strides brought him up alongside. "Reckon it could have come in handy with your little digging project, eh?" The light tone bled from his voice. "Don't think I've forgotten about what happened. It will be dealt with."

Ky swallowed the lump in his throat, but his voice still cracked. "I'd say my *little digging project* turned out for the best."

Cade just grunted and readjusted the bow and quiver strapped to his back. But he didn't deny it either, and that had to count for something, right? That was the thing with Cade, though—a fellow could drive himself to distraction and get no closer to guessing what he was thinking.

It was a good five minutes before Cade continued. "Right before you lot left, Hawkness told me about one more tunnel he and his old band had rigged to blow—suggested we bring it down too, lay low for a while. I swiped a packet or two before we set it off. Figured it might be useful."

"Whopping good you did too." Slack broke in. "Else we'd still have that filthy Nikuto and his men on our heels."

"Indeed . . . and whose fault would that be?"

Slack's chuckle died, and for a while, there was no sound but the soft slap of their feet, the rattle of weaponry, and Meli's broken breaths. Twice Ky felt Cade's eyes flicker to him and knew that his steps had slowed. Now that the rush of battle had faded, exhaustion and pain hammered into him with the relentless force of the River Adayn.

"Here." Cade stopped finally and held out his arms. "Let me."

Ky held Meli tighter and trudged past. "I can make it."

Time was difficult to measure in the darkness of the tunnel, so he fell back on counting his steps. At one thousand and fifty-five steps, he heard whispering and coughing up ahead. A moment later, they rounded a bend in the tunnel and stumbled upon the Underground runners crowded in a circular space where the tunnel split and ran off in five different directions. Most of the runners sprawled in clumps on the ground, eyes glazed with exhaustion.

But Paddy drifted between the five tunnels, muttering to himself, with Syd at his heels and the scrap of cloth in his hand. He glanced up at their approach. "Took you long enough to catch up. I take it we no longer have crazed madmen on our tail?"

"No, now what's the hold up?" Cade demanded.

Paddy flapped the scrap of cloth. "Syd doesn't know the way. *I* don't know the way. For Mindolyn's sake, Ky, please tell me *you* know which way to go."

Gray tinged the edges of Ky's vision. He stumbled back until he felt the coolness of the wall behind and slid down it until Meli lay in his lap. "Why did you think I need you here?"

He could practically feel the heat of Cade's glare boring into the side of his head for a full minute before the older boy spoke. "I'll take rear-guard. Let me know when you figure it out."

"Shure, shure. No worries. I've got it. It's all grand . . . just grand." Paddy turned back to his scrap of cloth and flung a hand in the air. "Nobody speak. Nobody move. I need to focus. This might take a while."

Ky drifted in and out of sleep. Every time his eyes flickered open, it was to the same sight: Paddy huddled over his map, torchlight painting his cheekbones with a ghoulish glow, and Syd standing over him, still clutching the clunky sword Ky had given him, an expression of the fiercest determination on his round face.

Then somebody was shaking his shoulder, and he startled awake, looking up into Slack's wild eyes. She had her chin turned to the side and her collar clutched up over her nose, so her voice came out muffled. "Up and at 'em. We're moving out."

He realized then that he was still cradling Meli's fevered form in his arms—had been holding her for hours—and he hadn't once thought of his own protection. Too late now. He was as good as doomed. They all were.

Using the wall for leverage, he pushed up to his feet. The runners were already moving out, following the glimmer of Paddy's torch down one of the tunnels. Cade paced alongside Paddy at the front of the column, and Slack maneuvered her way up to his side. Ky settled into the back of the line, moving with slow, shuffling steps behind the sick and their keepers. Now that they were moving in the right direction, Cade was welcome to lead.

He was more than content to follow.

20

Given the number of things that had gone wrong over the past few days—let alone the past few months—Ky almost didn't dare believe the whispers trickling down the line. *We're free . . . the tunnel's ending . . . there's a way out!* But for the first time in hours, the sluggish mass of runners came to a halt, and he just stood there, swaying on his feet as though his body hadn't yet grasped the fact that he'd stopped moving.

Someone tugged his elbow. He looked down into Syd's wide eyes, and the boy jerked his chin at the head of the line. So he was being summoned then? Big boss Cade finally admitting he needed a little help? Not likely—that wasn't Cade's way.

He was too tired to care.

Syd pointed a stubby finger at Meli and shook his head solemnly.

"Fine." Stifling a sigh, Ky lowered her to the ground. "But you get to stay with her." He hesitated before leaving. The way she was lying on the cold earth with her head crooked to one side and her neck bent—it couldn't be comfortable. He shrugged out of his fringed animal hide jacket and balled it beneath her head.

Bare-chested and shivering, he jogged through the line of runners to where Cade, Paddy, and Slack crouched before an opening. It was little more than a hole in the ground, overgrown by tentacles of tangleroot vine. A dying torch sputtered dull red in Paddy's hand—bright enough to see the opening, but faint enough that Ky could also glimpse specks of starlight beyond.

"Did we make it?"

"Shure. Maybe." Paddy shrugged. "I think?"

"Quiet." Cade's harsh whisper echoed off the tunnel walls. "Scouting mission. Us three. Slack stays behind to guard the others."

Slack snorted. "Uh, no can do, chief. Paddy stays behind. Slack goes."

"Don't press your luck, Slack. I still give the orders around here. Can't risk you getting "just a little mad" and attacking anyone, now can we?" Cade squeezed through the hole, then stuck his head back in. "Ky, Paddy—take ten minutes and loop around. Meet back here. Slack, you keep everyone inside and quiet until we get back. Just have to make sure we're beyond the patrols."

"Fine, but I'm not happy about it."

Ky slipped through after Paddy, leaving Slack muttering to herself. The frostbitten tangleroot vines left icy trails across his back, and he shivered when the crisp night air hit his skin. He emerged in a narrow hollow, slick with mud and loose, smooth stones and clogged with thickets of heather and weeping thrassle. Looked like it might have been a streambed at one point in time, though the stream was obviously long gone.

With numbed hands, he rubbed his arms, trying to keep his teeth from chattering.

"Where's your shirt?" Cade gripped his elbow, but he shrugged free.

"Don't need it."

Ordinarily that kind of response would have triggered a clout from Dizzier and a challenge from Cade, but the older boy just growled something beneath his breath, yanked the cloak from his own shoulders, and shoved it into Ky's hands.

"Put it on, and be quiet. Don't blow this mission."

Ky stood there dumbfounded until the older boy melted into the darkness, then he fumbled with stiff fingers to fasten the cloak around his neck.

Paddy clucked his tongue, but it was a *kind* sort of clucking. The ragging of a friend. Ky hadn't realized how much he'd missed it. "You're a fool, you know that, Ky?"

"'Course I know it. Doesn't stop you from reminding me."

"Shure and I'm only tryin' to—"

In a blur of movement, Cade was back at their side, muffling Paddy's voice with one hand and shoving Ky to the ground with the other. "I *said* be silent. We're yards away from their bloody camp."

He jerked his head for them to follow, then led the way up the side of the hollow and out onto the moorland beyond. After a minute or two of creeping, they crouched behind a weeping thrassle bush on the northern edge of the Khelari encampment. A basin sprawled between them and the ring of hills surrounding Kerby. It was filled with the hulking shapes of countless tents silhouetted against the lights of a hundred campfires.

The camp was quiet, but it was a wakeful quietness, like a hound snoozing on his master's threshold. No telling when it might spring to its feet, barking fit to raise the dead.

Ky glanced at Cade. "Patrols?"

"Doubtless. Probably not so alert on this side of the camp though. Who's going to attack? These are the Nordlands—there isn't a village outside the Takhran's control for miles. Gives us an advantage." Cade pointed his chin to the left, where a couple dozen of the Khelari's oversized supply wagons were circled, horses bedded down in the middle, drivers snoring on their benches. "Think the cursed soldiers will miss one?"

Ky didn't trust himself to speak right away. His body trembled. He hugged the borrowed cloak to his chest, though whether he was shaking from cold or rage, he couldn't tell. "You want to rob the dark soldiers . . . again?" His voice sounded strangled.

"No, I'd rather kill them all. But robbing them will have to do."

"Because that worked out so *well* the last time."

Paddy's groan confirmed his suspicion that he'd gone too far.

He forged bravely ahead, feeling more the fool than the hero. "What about all the runners waiting back there in the hollow? Are you going to forget about them just to spite the Khelari?"

Cade seized his shoulders. "Enough." His voice was deadly quiet. "No more second guessing my commands and challenging me in front of the others. This has to stop. I've led the Underground for years and we've managed just fine—*better* than fine. I happen to know a thing or two about providing for *my* runners."

"Uh, lads." Paddy coughed into his elbow. "Must we discuss this *here*?"

Cade removed one hand from Ky's shoulder just long enough to prod him in the chest with a stiff finger. "It was *your* half-baked idea to leave Kerby behind. Now what? You have a plan for where we should go and how to get there? Or do you intend to walk thirty runners across the Nordlands in search of refuge with barely enough supplies to last another four days and half our number falling to the white fever already? How far do you think we would get? These are the things a *leader* has to think about, Ky." He released his grip so suddenly that Ky wound up sitting on the ground. "So stop whining and *think*."

Thinking sure could get a fellow in a lot of trouble. Almost as much as opening his big gabber and sticking his muddy foot in it. *Well done, Ky. Well done.* Ky squatted beside the front wheel of the northernmost wagon, peeking through the spokes at Cade and Paddy's crouching forms and the horses grazing beyond. The shaggy beasts seemed alert and aware of their presence, but not overly bothered by it.

It eased Ky's mind a bit.

Ever since the whole incident with the orange cat, and the way Birdie and that Carhartan fellow both talked to it and acted like it could talk back, Ky hadn't viewed critters the same way. For all he knew, they could *all* be spies, and none of the common folk would be any the wiser.

Sling in hand, he inched to his feet. The horses were Cade and Paddy's concern. His task was dealing with the driver. He scrambled up and over the side of the wagon, landing in a crouch behind the driver's seat. The man didn't so much as stir. It was but the work of a moment to wind his sling around the man's neck and tighten his grip. The driver's eyes flashed open and his body bucked, once, twice, then he relaxed, unconscious.

At Ky's all-clear sign, Cade and Paddy approached, each leading a shaggy-coated monster of a horse, and backed them into place alongside the wagon tongue. While they harnessed, Ky stuffed his sling through his belt and muscled the driver's limp form over the side of the wagon. The man landed with a thump that made Ky wince. But none of the other drivers stirred, and the hound dog of a camp snoozed on. Every now and then, a soldier appeared as a dark splotch against the firelight, drifting between the tents, just long enough for the camp to rustle, scratch at its fleas, and turn over in its sleep.

Ky leaned over the front of the wagon and almost got a mouthful of swishing horse tail. "You almost done?"

"Getting there." Cade wrestled a heavy collar up around the right horse's neck. "Keep an eye out for patrols. If we're spotted now, we're sunk."

Yeah, and the rest of the runners with us.

Ky folded a stone into the pouch of his sling and trailed the strands through his fingers. Beside the nearest group of tents, a stake crowned with a blazing torch was set in the ground. Shadows lumped at the base of the stake. He strained his eyes to pierce the night and could have sworn he saw the shadows move.

Not shadows then.

A person?

Or one of the Takhran's strange creature spies?

He slipped over the side of the wagon and clapped Paddy's shoulder in passing. "Something to check on. Be right back."

Paddy nodded. "Still got to grab two more horses, but hurry."

From cover to cover, he crept across the intervening space, ready at a moment's notice to send a stone flying from his sling, until he stood beneath the circle of torchlight, staring at the wreck and ruin of a dwarf.

His wrists and ankles were bound to the stake with his arms stretched above his head. Had he been standing, his head probably would have been even with Ky's shoulder, but he sagged in his restraints, knees buckled, head lolling forward like the laden pouch of Ky's sling. Blood and muck matted his curly hair and beard, stained the front of his filthy robe, and formed a crusted border around numerous rents in the fabric. Ky held his breath against the stench of filth and rot.

The dwarf sucked in a ragged breath through snarled whiskers. His chin tilted up, and for just a second, Ky caught a glimpse of the flash of his eyes. "Something wrong, bucko?" The dwarf broke into a wet chuckle. His voice was weak, but there was no mistaking it. "Or didn't your mam teach you staring was downright rude?"

"Migdon?" Ky knelt in front of him. "I thought you'd gone north?"

The dwarf's eyes focused on his, and a scowl deepened the creases around his eyes. "Didn't make it. Dark soldiers extended a *forceful* invite to come back to camp." He tilted his head to one side and spat out a glob of blood. "Hospitality stinks. Mighty kind of you to launch a rescue operation though."

"Don't mention it." Ky was already at work on his bonds, stiff fingers clawing at stiffer knots. "Any guards around?"

"Nope. Reckon I wore 'em out. Won't be long before they're back at it though. They never leave me for more than an hour at a time."

The ropes came free and the dwarf crumpled. Ky caught him before he hit the earth, but the weight almost knocked him flat. Migdon was surprisingly dense for his size. Hugging Migdon's arm around his shoulder, Ky hauled them both upright and started back toward the circle of wagons.

"Not far to go . . . we borrowed a wagon and team . . . riding out in style."

The dwarf jerked to a stop. "My knapsack. We'll need it." He set his feet, resisting Ky's effort to drag him forward. "Can't leave without it."

Ky didn't bother wasting time arguing. Weeks of traveling with the dwarf had taught him that much. A glance revealed the oversized monstrosity perched on a stump not far away. He unceremoniously released the dwarf, heard him hit the ground, raced to the knapsack, and hefted it over one shoulder.

Weighed almost as much as Migdon.

Scads of fun.

Back at Migdon's side, he dragged him to his feet. "Get up!"

"Hoi, what's goin' on out 'ere?" A soldier stumbled, blinking, out of the nearest tent. He was clad in a tunic and leggings. No armor. "What the—"

Sidestepping away from Migdon, Ky launched a stone that slammed into the soldier's disheveled mess of hair. The man swayed on his feet and stumbled back. Ky was already reaching for another stone when Migdon collapsed —or dove, or rammed, he couldn't tell which—into the soldier. Both went down in a heap.

"Mig!"

The dwarf righted himself before Ky could reach him, reeling to his feet like a drunken sailor. "It's done," he rasped, wiping his hands on his robe, leaving smears of something dark that glistened in the light of the moon.

Ky's gaze trailed to the blade protruding from the soldier's throat. "You killed him."

More a statement than a question.

"Fool tried to pull his dagger on me. I pulled first." Migdon swiped a forearm across his chin, leaving a smear of blood. Could have been his . . . could have been the soldier's. He toed the body, forcing it to flop on its back, unseeing eyes staring straight up at the night sky.

Ky swallowed and turned away. It was the eyes that made them human. Faceless soldiers in dark armor were one thing, but up close, you had to face the fact that they were as human as you. In the end, what made them any different from folk like Nikuto and his men?

It was easier to think of them as monsters.

"Give me a hand, will you?" Migdon's words slurred, and Ky could imagine the pain he had suffered at the hands of the Khelari. "Let's get out of here before the whole camp wakes up."

Migdon flung an arm over Ky's shoulder, and he muscled onward, staggering beneath the combined weight of the dwarf and his enormous knapsack. He'd heard dwarves were stout creatures who could tramp all day carrying twice their own weight without even getting winded. Wished he could do the same.

Just when he thought he couldn't go any farther, he heard the faint creak of wheels and the wagon pulled up directly in his path. Paddy was at his side in an instant, lifting the knapsack from his shoulders while he helped Migdon up into the high wagon bed.

"In faith, laddy-boyo!" Paddy tossed the knapsack up and clambered in after. "Weighs almost a ton! What's in there, a bloody suit of armor?"

Coughing weakly, Migdon tugged the knapsack into his lap and sprawled back with his head propped against the side of the wagon. "Among other things." He patted it down, peeking inside the dozens of pockets and pouches. "Good . . . good. All here. Those cursed Khelari dogs kept it sitting just out of my reach to taunt me, kept asking questions and pawing their grubby hands through it."

"Who is that?" Cade scowled from the driver's seat. "And what is he doing on my wagon?"

"Tell you later." Ky stationed himself on the camp side of the wagon, scanning for any sign of discovery. Sometimes explaining wasn't worth the trouble. "We need to get out of here fast."

To his surprise, Cade let the matter drop. Just clucked to the four horses and started them back toward the hollow. The wagon was surprisingly quiet—wheels must have been oiled recently—and even the soft jingling of the harnesses was faint enough that Ky could hear the rustle of wings passing close by his head. Instinct kicked in before his brain had even registered the sound. He slipped a stone into his sling, spun twice, and released toward the noise.

He heard the *thunk* when it hit.

The bird screeched, fluttering its wings in panic.

A glancing blow . . .

Before he could reload, another snap rang out, and a stone buzzed past his ear. Something cracked. The wings fell silent. Mindolyn's pale light glinted off the bird's oiled black feathers as it fell to earth.

A raven.

One of the Takhran's spies.

He glanced back at Migdon who was still lying propped against the side of the wagon. The dwarf stretched his sling and let it snap back with a grin—though his face was so swollen it looked more like a grimace. A prone shot like that was nothing to snort at, and he well knew it.

"Sling-bullets, bucko my boyo, can't beat 'em." Migdon groped inside his knapsack and produced a jar. "Here. You might want to spread this behind the wagon, a handful at a time, until we're well clear of this place."

"Give it to me." Paddy heaved a sigh. "I can do it, so long as you don't mind tellin' me what exactly I'm doin'."

"One spy down. You can bet your britches more will follow. That's ground havva leaves in there. Works wonders keeping hounds off the scent. They can't bear the reek of it." Migdon chuckled and winced. "Personally, I think it's rather nice. Minty."

"Right. Minty." Paddy shuffled to the back of the wagon, giving Ky an elaborate shrug and wink as he passed.

Minutes later, there was still no sign of pursuit. The wagon came to an abrupt stop on the edge of the hollow, and Cade jumped down. "Paddy, with me. Ky, mind the horses. We'll be back in a moment."

The two boys disappeared into the hollow, leaving the seat to Ky. He picked up the reins and held them loosely in his hands, elbows resting on his knees, more to have something to do than from fear the horses would try to wander away. They seemed perfectly content to stand and doze in their traces, waiting for Cade to return.

"Care to tell me why we've halted, bucko?"

"There's a few more of us." Ky kept his tone short, his words clipped, hoping it would discourage the dwarf from talking. Sometimes there just wasn't much to say.

"Care to tell me where we're headed then?"

He let the silence drag for a second, as he rubbed the reins between his thumb and forefinger, breathing in the musty scent of leather and neatsfoot oil. "Away."

"Look, bucko," Migdon drawled. "Is this about that soldier? Because I *had* to knock him off. Couldn't have him setting the whole army on us. It was the reasonable thing to do. End of tale. No need to get weepy over it." He sighed. "Trust me, you don't last long in a job like mine unless you're willing to do the things nobody else wants to."

The dwarf's assumption irked Ky and set his temper spoiling for a fight. Seemed like Migdon was ragging on him for being weak. But that wasn't the problem. If Migdon hadn't been so quick with his knife, another of Ky's slingstones would have done the trick. He'd knocked more than one Khelari flat.

No, the soldier's death didn't bother him.

And somehow that fact stuck in his craw more than anything else.

"Take my advice, bucko, and let it be. You got to learn to act for the good of all. I got my people to protect same as you got yours." Migdon dug around in his knapsack again, pulled out a vial, and chugged it down. "Bleh, stuff tastes like bog water. It's this herbal concoction a friend of mine whipped up. Fights wound rot and infection. Good ol' Tymon …" The dwarf rattled on, but Ky no longer heard what he was saying. His attention had been claimed by the approach of soft footsteps and hushed voices.

The Underground runners.

It took all of five minutes to get everyone loaded up and jammed together like fish in a barrel. Oversized as the wagon was, it still wasn't built to hold thirty runners comfortably, but if there was one thing the runners were used to, it was dealing with cramped quarters. They packed in so tight there was scarce room to breathe. A couple of the more reckless even opted to sit on the raised sides of the wagon with their legs dangling out and arms hooked together to keep from falling.

Ky relinquished the driver's seat to Cade and climbed into the back to take Meli in his lap, while Paddy perched on the tailboard, dropping handfuls of Migdon's ground havva leaves to hide their scent. Of course, it made sense that *someone* should share the driver's seat, but when Slack swung up beside Cade, Ky couldn't help the twinge of frustration in his belly. Frustration that only grew once they were well beyond the Khelari camp and Slack and Cade started whispering and laughing together.

Wasn't it *her* fault Nikuto's men had stormed the Underground? By rights, Cade should be furious at her. Instead, he shrugged it off like it was nothing, all the while tearing into Ky for his mistakes—past, present, *and* imagined.

"*Life ain't fair, Shorty.*" Dizzier's voice drawled in the back of his head. "*And that's the plain truth of it. Sooner you learn that, the better.*"

Ky wormed back into his fringed jacket—thankfully, Paddy had thought to grab it when he pulled Meli out of the hollow—and tossed Cade's cloak back to him. He let his head sag against the side of the wagon, and his eyes slid shut. But no matter how exhausted he was, there was no chance of sleep, what with the jolting of the wagon and the fevered moans of the sick. Not to mention the way his thoughts raced round and round like a petra caged in the market.

Cade's words repeated in his head. "*You have a plan for where we should go?*"

No, he didn't have a plan, and he bet Cade didn't have one either. Even now, they must be traveling blind, driven only by a desire to get as far from the dark soldiers as they could. But what then? Where could they go, with the Nordlands fallen to the Khelari and all routes south blocked by the dark soldiers?

"Bucko!" Across the wagon, Migdon struggled to rise, but the runners were packed so tight around him, it would have been impossible even if he did have the strength. "You didn't tell me you lot had the white fever." He practically spat that last bit out, like it was a curse.

Ky couldn't really blame him. The white fever *was* a sort of death sentence. He glanced at Meli's pale face and sweat soaked brow. "We're all doomed anyway."

"Blazes, boy," Migdon spat. "I can't go marching back to my homeland bearing the contagion of fever with me. The Xanthen will deny me entry, insist that I be quarantined, stick me in some forgotten outpost until I'm dead or they're sure it's safe—and right they should! It would have been better to leave me with the Khelari."

Another time, Ky might have felt more sympathy. Now he just gritted his teeth. "Hey, if you prefer the "hospitality" of the Khelari, you're more 'n welcome to march back and let them have you. See how long you last while they're trying to pry the secrets of the mountains out of you."

The dwarf grumbled something, but Ky just eased back and closed his eyes. Somehow, though, he couldn't get the dwarf's words out of his mind. "The Xanthen . . . didn't you say they were some sort of scholars or something?"

A grunt was all he got in answer, but it was enough to set his mind whirling. Scholars, soldiers—the Whyndburg Mountains had it all. It wasn't such a stretch to imagine they might have healers as well—maybe even medicines that could halt the tide of the white fever.

He sat up straight, jostling the runners next to him. What better place to hide the runners than the far north of Leira, in the one kingdom that Migdon claimed had a chance of withstanding the dark soldiers? "You know." He licked his cracked lips. "I'm no great hand at calculations, but the way I figure it, you owe me for that rescue."

The dwarf glared. "Oh, that is *rich*, bucko. Don't you know they say that when a fellow puts you in greater danger than he rescued you from, all debts are canceled?"

Ky squinted an incredulous eye at the dwarf.

"No? Well, I'm pretty sure they say that. Somewhere. In fact, I'm almost positive."

"I've never heard it." Ky scooted forward through the runners to Migdon's side, lugging Meli along with him. He lowered his voice so only the dwarf could hear. "Look, we need a place to go. You could do with a ride north. What do you say we make a deal?"

"Are you out of your mind? I'd be branded a traitor to my kind for guiding a wagonload of fever-ridden corpses into the mountains. And that's what you lot would be by the time we arrived! You said it yourself, you're all doomed anyway."

"Then you're doomed with us." Inwardly, Ky was screaming for the dwarf to help, but somehow he managed to keep his voice even.

Deadly even, almost. Cade would have been proud. "Unless you have another handy vial of something in that knapsack of yours that'll keep you from getting sick."

Migdon's silence confirmed his wild hopes.

"You do . . . you have something. Give it to me, Mig. Please . . . I'm begging you."

"Not with me, I don't." The dwarf muttered something beneath his breath. "Look, in the mountains, my people have discovered an herb that *sometimes* helps, but it's very rare. Not the sort of thing they hand out to strangers."

"Then we'll make friends." Ky settled Meli more comfortably in his arms, peeling sweat slicked strands of her hair from his neck. "We'll have to."

"You don't make friends with people who show up unannounced on your doorstep, in wartime, with a deadly plague. It just isn't done. No . . . no . . . no, absolutely not."

Funny how *no* sure sounded a whole lot like *maybe* to Ky.

He grinned with a confidence he sure didn't feel. "Give me six hours. I'll convince you."

Tauros hovered directly overhead by the time Cade pulled the wagon to a halt beneath a copse of slick-gum trees and allowed the runners to disembark. It had been a long night and morning of zig-zagging across the golden dunes of the Nordlands, and the horses were due for a rest. Otherwise, Ky had no doubt Cade would have just kept going, driven by the same desperate need for action that he felt pulsing inside of him.

Cade declared it too risky for a fire, so they all huddled beneath the shelter of the wagon and munched on scraps of coarse bread and dried meat while Jena tended the sick. Even at noon, the sun's rays provided only that pale sort of winter heat that never penetrates the bones, leaving Ky grateful to have his jacket back.

Slack pulled first watch, and Ky second. But it felt as though he had just drifted off to sleep when she shook him awake. "Hoy-up, Ky, your turn for watch."

Dragging his eyes open landed his gaze on the blade of Slack's hatchet, less than a foot away, newly sharpened. She spat on the blade, rubbed it on her trousers, and held it up to catch the glint of the sun. Cocking her head, she evaluated the new edge. "Mind if I steal your spot? I'm bushed."

Ky grunted and pushed up onto his hands and knees. His joints were stiff enough that they could have been carved from zoar wood. "Sure. I generally make it a point not to refuse anyone with a weapon in my face."

Her low chuckle followed him out from under the wagon. He circled the copse a few times, idly swinging his sling to flick at frosted grass heads, then plopped down with his back to the left front wheel, elbows propped up on his knees. Within minutes, he was fighting to keep his eyes open, lulled by the *shooshing* of the wind through the grass.

"Wakey, wakey, bucko my boyo."

Ky jolted upright, already spinning his sling, but Migdon's chuckle brought him to like a dunk in the river. The dwarf squatted at his side, splitting seeds against his teeth and sending the shells flying a good fifteen feet before they landed. He had one elbow propped against the wagon wheel for support, the other juggling a small pouch.

"Sleeping on guard duty, eh? Pretty sure there's a death penalty for that in the Adulnae cohorts." He sent a shell flying just over Ky's head. "Good thing they don't let outsiders join"

Ky scrubbed the sleep from his eyes. "Wouldn't want to join if I could."

"Well, good, there's hope for you yet." The dwarf dropped the pouch in Ky's lap. It tipped over, spilling out a handful of sling-bullets. "Because I hear there's also a hefty penalty for misuse of ammunition—such as, oh I don't know, handing it over to the Khelari without first lodging it in their filthy skulls." He clucked his tongue and wagged a finger in Ky's face. "Don't lose these. This is my *extra* extra pouch, so I won't have any more for you until we reach the mountains and whatever forsaken outpost the Xanthen decide to throw us in."

"Wait . . . does that mean ..."

Migdon nodded. "Mad as it sounds, I'm in. Guess my tutoring's finally starting to pay off, that or it's coming back to bite me. They might have to start calling *you* Silvertongue too."

"Not a title I want." A sudden thought struck him. "But if you want to keep yours, you're going to have to prove yourself." Ky nodded toward where Cade slept propped in a sitting position against a tree, sword drawn across his knees. "I know him. He's already got some insane plan brewing. He'll insist that we form some sort of outlaw band and live out here in the wild, like Hawkness before Drengreth. But that's pure madness in the middle of winter with half our number sick already, and we need that medicine. You've got to convince him that the Whyndburg Mountains are the place to go."

"Convince fearless leader yonder?" Migdon cracked his knuckles. "Oh-ho, no worries, bucko. You see, selling an idea is all about figuring out what the other fellow wants and offering what you want in such a way he feels like it was his idea all along. Your buddy Cade there, what does he want more than anything?"

Power . . . authority . . . dominance. Ky shook the thoughts away. Cade had good intentions, even if they didn't always see eye to eye. "I don't know. He formed the Underground so we could survive. Maybe to keep his runners safe?"

"You're not thinking, bucko. That's what you want most, probably what you think a leader should want most too, but it's not what he wants *most.*" A fierce gleam lit the dwarf's eyes. "Leave it to me. I'll have him in three hours . . . or less."

PART FOUR

21

It was the keening of rock gulls that drew Birdie to the rail as the single-masted cog rounded the headland and drifted into Rolis Bay, but it was her first glimpse of the serrated peak of Mount Eiphyr dead ahead that kept her there. She shivered at the sight, but told herself it was only the chill of dawn awakening over the water and pulled the scratchy woolen cloak tighter around her shoulders—a gift from Brog.

Somehow, he had managed to scrounge up enough woolen cloaks for the lot of them from his "less than savory Soudlander friends" to conceal their "outlandish desert garb from unfriendly eyes." At least, that was how he had put it.

"Well, lass, here we are." Amos's low voice just reached her ears. He stood at the rudder, deftly steering the ship with his head thrown back and the wind ruffling his flaming hair. It was easy to forget that the peddler had been a Waveryder and an outlaw—and who knew what else—in his younger days, but she was glad for his presence on deck now that the end was in sight.

Amos radiated strength.

And just as one drew near to a fire to draw heat from the flames, she sought Amos's strength whenever hers was lacking.

The others slumbered still in the narrow crawl space below. It was a good thing that Amos had insisted Balaam remain in the Soudlands with Brog. Between the griffin and four humans, space below deck was limited. The donkey hadn't put up much of an argument either, though he had certainly made a good show of it for Amos. Birdie alone knew his relief at being allowed to remain in the safety of his stall.

"What d' ye think o' Serrin Vroi?"

Birdie followed the slope of the mountain to the enormous walled fortress built into its side, then let her gaze roam across the city that wrapped around its base and sprawled over the foothills, and finally down to the harbor. It looked exactly as she had envisioned it in the Hollow Cave. Though a bit brighter and less terrifying cast in the pale gold of dawn.

"It's not as frightening as I expected ..."

Brave words. Horribly untrue.

"Indeed?" Amos sounded a bit taken aback by her answer. "Well, I daresay ye'll find it looks far less pleasant the farther we venture in."

The tall tales travelers had whispered by the common room fire always made Serrin Vroi sound like some sort of a dead city, painting a picture so grim and dark that it could only be populated by ghosts and monsters. But from what Birdie could see of the wharf as they drew nearer, it didn't look all that different from the other sea ports she had seen during their month long journey beating up alongside the western coast of Leira.

At such an early hour, the place was hardly bustling, but there was a steady stream of people out and about. Ordinary people going about ordinary lives. Both ghosts and monsters seemed to be in short supply.

She joked as much to Amos.

He said nothing, but the grim, almost haunted, expression on his face made her wonder if ghosts might not be too far from the truth. A minute later, the cog bumped to a stop alongside the wharf, and Sym appeared at the rail beside Birdie.

Amos lashed the cog into place, shrugged out of his heavy overcoat and threw it over the rudder along with his feathered cap. "Security's generally fairly lax along the wharf, but I've got to settle matters with the dock master and see about borrowin' a cart so the old catbird can enter the city proper without alertin' every blaggardly Khelari in the place."

"Be careful, Hawkness," Sym said. "You do have the Takhran's price on your head."

"Aye." Amos threw on a woolen cloak and belted it around his body, then bound a headscarf over his forehead and hair. Now he truly looked a Waveryder. Birdie had no doubt he'd melt seamlessly into the crowd of sailors. "We were fools t' come here at all, but it can't be helped now. Be back in a bit. Stay put 'til I am."

He dropped over the side, and Birdie watched him assume a very convincing limp as he made his way up the quay to a heavily whiskered barrel of a man seated beneath an awning, hand over a coin pouch, and then disappear into the sea of buildings beyond.

"Fishing and trading vessels mostly." Sym observed, pulling Birdie's focus from the quay to the ramshackle shipping filling the harbor. "Tauros smiles upon us. The Takhran's armies may have the best of it on land, but we can thank our stars he has no fleet to speak of."

Along the far northern curve of the wharf, a series of sleek ships with iron prongs at the prow rested at anchor. The sight brought a tremor back to Birdie's hands and the tang of fear, sweat, and sickness below deck to her nostrils. She hugged the rail to steady herself. "Langorians . . . here?"

It took Sym a moment to locate the ships, but once she did her dark eyes took on an even darker aspect. She spat over the rail and muttered something in the desert tongue. "It does not surprise me, little Songkeeper. Would that I could sink a spear into all of their throats. The slavers and the Takhran are almost worthy of one another."

Without another word, she turned and slipped below deck, but Birdie couldn't take her eyes off the ships. Were there poor souls chained and despairing in the darkness of their holds even now? Or had they already been given in tribute to the Takhran for his slave camps, as Carhartan and Rhudashka had hinted months ago on the beach at Bryllhyn? The ships were too far away for her to truly hear snatches of the captives' melodies, but she imagined she could hear them even so, their voices blending into a slow, sad humming that hung over her as the hours slipped past and Tauros drifted across the sky.

Night had fallen before Amos returned with a cart drawn by a pair of shaggy Westmark oxen. Rather than sinking into slumber, the wharf seemed to come to life at the setting of the sun. Firepots blazed from iron poles at intervals along the quay and beside the doors of the buildings beyond. Tipsy sailors and peasants, bellowing merchants and vendors, and stern-voiced Khelari all contributing to the hubbub.

Somehow Gundhrold managed to disembark and conceal his bulk beneath the canvas covering of the cart without drawing any attention. The griffin moved with a stealth Birdie would never have thought possible for a creature his size. Amos insisted she ride inside as well, so she squeezed between the griffin's right wing—which had finally begun to heal after a month of inactivity since leaving the Soudlands—and the side of the cart and tried not to breathe in the stifling mustiness of his feathers and coat.

They rattled off. Peeking through the gap between the canvas and the cart revealed Amos and Sym walking on either side to guide the oxen, while Inali slumped on the raised seat, still weak enough to warrant a ride. Birdie caught little more than glimpses of the city as they went. Once beyond the realm of wharfside taverns and curio shops, the streets widened, bordered by tall, respectable houses. But only a few twists and turns later, the streets narrowed again, storied buildings overshadowing the road until the peaked roofs were nearly touching.

Birdie's ears hummed with the nervous throbbing of her pulse. The streets were full of the noise of passing people, hundreds of footsteps and conversations creating a cacophony of sound the like of which she had never heard.

Compared to Hardale, Kerby seemed large.

But Kerby couldn't hold a candle to the vastness that was Serrin Vroi.

The cart took a sharp turn to the right, and the dark melody hit her so suddenly she gasped. A cluster of dark soldiers stood within the gateway of a high wall. Amos exchanged a word or two of bland pleasantries, and they let the cart pass unhindered, but it was a full minute before Birdie managed to breathe again.

Once she did, she realized that the thrumming that had been growing in her ears wasn't just the pulse of her hammering heart. It was the muted sound of voices—*many* voices—singing.

"We've just entered Serrin Vroi proper."

She started at the griffin's harsh whisper in her ear and pulled back from the gap long enough to glance at his stern face and fierce golden eyes and that sharp beak so close within the confines of the cart. "Then . . . what was that back there?"

"Just the outskirts. We entered the true city once we passed beneath the wall. Here the Takhran's hand is felt much more heavily."

She felt the truth of his words within her as she turned back. The city noise was overpowering in and of itself, but now she could hear the layer of music lurking beneath each and every voice. Generally, what she heard seemed to be limited by distance, barriers to sound like walls and enclosed spaces, and her own attention.

But now, the broken five-noted melodies swept over her, like the River Adayn at flood. So much hurt and sorrow expressed in musical form. Oh, there was joy too, and peace, but both seemed small and utterly insignificant in comparison. Engulfed by the tide of despair. Tainted by the strains of the discordant melody. And beneath it all, the ponderous, deep humming of a sad, old song. The noise swallowed her, stopping up her ears, squeezing her throat, and filling her lungs until she felt herself drowning in it.

Gundhrold's wingtip brushed her cheek. "Peace, little one. Focus on my voice. Do not try to listen to it all at once."

Shivering, she closed her eyes, shoved her palms against her eyelids, and strained her ears until she could pick out the griffin's familiar soaring melody. The voice arced and wheeled and raced higher and higher into the great blue expanse above, lifting her soul with it. The pressure in her ears faded into the background.

"It worked," she whispered.

"Of course, little one." The griffin dipped his head. "This is a burden you cannot take upon yourself. The Songkeeper is not meant to right all the pains and sorrows of this world."

She released her hold on his voice and turned her focus to Amos next, honing in on his melody sung in a baritone that somehow managed to drag with melancholy and yet have a spring to its step at the same time. From there, she selected strangers at random in the crowd, plucking at each melody as one might a harp string. An old man on crutches, a child in rags with sad eyes, an auburn-haired woman in a blue robe.

The woman met her gaze.

At least, it seemed like she did, though there was no way she could have seen Birdie beneath the covering of the cart. But knowing that did nothing to dispel the certainty that the woman's eyes were nevertheless fixed upon her.

Stranger still, the woman had no melody.

None that she could hear, no matter how much she tried to focus or strain her ears. There was nothing beyond the roar of the crowd and the broken songs of a thousand hearts. Then the woman too was gone, faded into the night like a ghost.

It seemed an age had passed when the cart at last came to a stop long enough for a door to creak open, then rolled forward one more time before coming to a final halt. The peddler's heavy footsteps approached, then a corner of the canvas jerked back to reveal his grim face.

"Bail out. Stairs in the back corner lead t' a pair o' rooms. Ye lot can wait for me there. Got t' return the cart before it's missed."

He waited while they disembarked, then backed the oxen and cart out, allowing Birdie to get a glimpse of their new lodgings. It was a stable of sorts, judging from the musty straw underfoot, and the bits and pieces of mildewed leather harnesses dangling from hooks on the sagging rough plank walls. A firepot hissed and guttered beside a rickety spiral staircase in the far left corner.

Sym swung the door shut and bolted it in place, then tugged the cloak from her shoulders, bundled it over one arm, and adjusted the spear quiver strapped to her back. "Come. Best we move upstairs. Better vantage point there in case we were followed." She offered Inali her shoulder, but he mumbled a refusal and pushed on up the stairs, leaning heavily on the banister. The treads creaked and groaned at every step. Shaking her head, Sym followed.

The griffin cocked his head at the rickety staircase and motioned for Birdie to pass him. "I think I had best come last."

Scarce a quarter of an hour into Amos's trip to return the cart, winter broke loose upon the city. The snow fell in delicate gasps at first but quickly whipped up into the sort of storm that leaves one blinded and winded. By the time he abandoned the cart a street or two from where he'd picked it up, he was chilled to the core and bone weary.

The return trip took even longer. He progressed by back ways and side alleys, doubling back and cutting left and right to avoid pursuit, but marched right past the safe house he'd procured—not that much was safe in this cursed city, but it beat camping in the middle of the streets with three of the Takhran's most wanted—before realizing it and retracing his steps.

Amos stomped up the stairs and burst into the front room where his companions were seated on a set of wobbly-legged chairs around an even more wobbly-legged table topped by a sputtering candle. The griffin stood sentry at the shuttered window. Four pairs of eyes shifted to him. He could feel the tension in the air, prickling against his skin like the precursor to a storm.

"You look a mess," Inali observed. He alone seemed relaxed, or perhaps merely indifferent, slumped in his chair, head tipped back, good hand fiddling with a piece of charcoal and a scrap of parchment.

Amos held his tongue until he had shucked off his snow-soaked cloak and head scarf and retrieved his overcoat and feathered cap from the pile of belongings at the top of the staircase. Blowing on his hands, he eased into the lone remaining chair between Birdie and Inali and fought against its treacherous wobble. He released a blunt laugh. "That storm—who'd have thought it? Here we are, sitting pretty at the bitter end o' a fairly mild winter, Spring Turning scarce a week hence, and Fallandine refuses t' go quietly—curse her icy breath!"

No one smiled.

"What took so long, Amos?" Birdie's head sagged against his shoulder. "You were gone for hours."

Was that what this was about? And here Amos had thought something had gone seriously wrong. Their concern was touching, if wholly unnecessary. "Ye lot could have slept. No cause for alarm. I had a long way t' go, an' I had t' be careful an' make sure I wasn't followed. No chancin' it in this city, not if we hope t' survive."

"And how exactly do we plan to do that, Hawkness?" Sym's shrewd expression met his over the quivering candle flame. She was well trained, that one—positioned strategically with one eye to the stairs and the other to the window, quiver leaning casually against one knee so the spears were practically in hand. She would be an asset to this mission.

"I agree," Gundhrold said. "It is past time we discussed our plans."

The griffin, on the other hand, would not.

Merely having him in the city was a liability Amos should never have risked. The last of the griffins, known to have been in the company of the Songkeeper. If he were spotted, it would not take the Takhran long to put two and two together.

Amos had been hoping for a bit of grub and maybe a few hours of shuteye before delving into the messy process of hashing out the who's, what's, and how-to's of the plan. But mayhap it *was* best to get it out of the way now in the wee hours of morning, then sleep the rest of the day away and head out scouting come nightfall.

He took a deep breath. "First off, Gundhrold, ye can't come in with us, ye know that right?" The griffin's beak parted, but Amos forged ahead before he could speak. "No room for argument. Any plan we dream up t' get inside that fortress will be a thousand times more dangerous if we have t' sneak ye in too. I've no doubt that ye would give yer life t' save the lass, but can ye stay behind for her?"

A murderous glare was the only answer he received.

It would have to suffice.

"Right." Amos shoved to his feet and scattered the dust on the tabletop with a sweep of his hand. "Charcoal, if ye please, lad." Before Inali could object, he seized it and began sketching out a rough approximation of the city of Serrin Vroi, explaining as he went. "It's been thirty years since last I set foot in this city, but near as I can recall, the main layout hasn't changed much. We can fill in details later after we've done a bit o' reconnoitering. This here's the outer wall o' Serrin Vroi where we entered this evenin', and this is the main road leadin' through the Silent Fountains t' the—"

"That's wrong." Inali muttered.

"Since when did ye become the resident expert on Serrin Vroi?" Amos cleared his throat with a tad more emphasis than was really necessary and went back to sketching. "*As I was sayin'*, this road leads through the Silent Fountains t' the main gate o' the Takhran's fortress, and beyond it, the Keep and Mount Eiphyr—"

"It is wrong, I tell you." Standing now, Inali swept his hands over the tabletop, erasing Amos's crude map with swift, jerky movements, almost like a puppet on a string. "It is *all* wrong. The proportions are just not right. You crammed the area within the outer wall into a circle half its size. Your main road runs straight like a spear, but it should meander like the River Adayn. And I am not sure what *that* is, but it is certainly not Mount Eiphyr."

Bilgewater! Amos bit his lip before he could release the thunderous word. "Fine." He dropped the charcoal. "Ye think ye can do better. I'd like t' see ye try." He plopped into the chair and started to tip it back to set his feet on the table, but thought better when the legs threatened to give way.

Inali set to work at a feverish pace, scattering a web of lines across the tabletop. His eyes were bright and practically glowed in the candlelight. It was the first *real* sign of life he had shown since his injury, and Amos's anger faded a mite at the transformation. Weeks of fever and pain had drained the strength from Inali's limbs and left hollows beneath his eyes that made him appear more corpse than man. Even now, Sym insisted he keep his left arm bound to his chest until the bone, muscle, and sinew had time to knit together again. Whether they did or nor, Amos doubted the lad would ever regain the full use of his arm.

"Mount Eiphyr's the goal, isn't it, Amos?" Birdie spoke beside him, though her voice was so soft he almost didn't hear it over the clamor of his own thoughts. The lass slouched with her chin and forearms resting on the table, dark hair spilling like a loosed fireflower over her shoulders and back. "Or beneath it, rather?"

"Aye, that's the goal."

"So we just need to find a way in . . . Inali knows where to go and what to do after that. How did you manage it last time, Amos?"

Amos winced. He'd been expecting the question—really he had. Given the mad endeavor they'd embarked upon, such questions were unavoidable. But if the lass only knew what she was asking . . .

"Bit o' a lark, really." He forced a note of humor into his voice. To his own ears, it sounded almost as painful as it felt, and from the looks he was getting, no one else was buying it. "The casualties weren't only on our side in the slaughter at Drengreth. We felled a few Khelari before the end. Once Artair was captured, I borrowed a suit o' armor an' marched in as one o' their own. Straight through the main gate, past the barracks, into the Keep, and down the secret passages until I reached the depths beneath Mount Eiphyr."

"Sounds simple enough." But there was no expression in Sym's tone and still less in her face to enable him to judge what she was thinking. The cliffs of Nar-Kog were easier to read than she.

"Anythin' but." Amos dropped the light tone. "Sure I survived, but that way's not likely t' work again, an' it's too blatherin' risky. No, we'll just have t' come up with somethin' else."

"As you wish." Inali straightened from his work and flicked an unsteady hand at the tabletop. "Behold *something else*, as requested, Hawkness."

Amos shoved to his feet, and resting both fists on the table, cast an appraising eye over Inali's attempt to "do better." It *was* good work, he had to admit that. The lad had skill. Somehow, in a matter of minutes, he had managed to translate the key elements of the vast city of Serrin Vroi into simple blocks and lines that matched Amos's somewhat hazy recollection of the city, even improved on it a bit.

"Well, lad, I'm impressed, an' not afraid t' admit it." After all, no one had ever claimed that Amos McElhenny didn't give credit where credit was due . . . given grudgingly, sometimes, but given nonetheless.

The lad's good shoulder lifted in a shrug. "You might say I have a gift."

Amos bent closer to inspect the layout of the Takhran's fortress. Whether by design or a slip of the hand, Inali's charcoal had darkened a circle on the seaward side where the outer wall of the fortress struck the base of the mountain and began to climb. "That right there, what is it?"

"Our way in." A rare smile flashed across the lad's face. "It's a secret way, not much traveled. Less direct than marching through the front gate, I'll grant you, but we run less risk of drawing unwanted attention."

"There are no *secret* ways into the heart o' Serrin Vroi."

Inali sank back into his seat, removed his spectacles, and buffed the lenses against his sling. "So says the great Hawkness . . . so it must be. But if I recall correctly, it has been some thirty odd years since you were last here. You claim to have plumbed the depths below Mount Eiphyr, but do you honestly believe you know all the secrets held in the darkness?"

"O' course not. No man does."

"Then hear me out . . . or rather, let me show you."

Amos bent over the lad until their faces were separated by a mere foot. "If this way o' yours is so secret, then how d' ye know about it?"

"You forget, Hawkness, I've been here before too." The lad met his gaze, unblinking. No man could fake the glint of raw fear that Amos saw lurking behind the lad's eyes. He knew it too well. He felt it crawling in his own. It was a shadow cast by the Pit, by horrors no man could ever *unsee.* At length, Inali glanced away and settled the spectacles on the bridge of his nose. "Shall we go tonight then?"

Amos pulled back. "No, lad, I'm afraid ye're stayin' right here." The lad's eyes were sincere, but Oran's eyes had been sincere too. Before he turned traitor. Before he became Carhartan. "If it's a trap—an' I won't lie, I half believe it is—I don't want ye along t' set it off. Ye tell me where t' go, an' Sym an' I will scout it out. Ye stay back here, relax, let that shoulder heal, let Birdie and Gundhrold keep an eye on ye like a good lad."

"What must I do to earn your trust?" Inali set his jaw, but there was a quiver in his voice that almost made Amos feel sorry for him.

"I was almost killed for the little Songkeeper."

"He's right, Amos. I would have been dead if not for him. Surely we can trust him."

Amos stood and stretched, basking in the relief as the tension in his shoulders and back slowly released. However nonsensical his suspicions might seem, they felt right, and safe was a thousand times better than dead. "Sorry, lass. I'm afraid trust isn't one o' my strengths. Now, I propose a wee bit o' shuteye. We've work t' do tonight."

22

"We should have burned the bodies," Cade said in a soft voice. He stooped and scattered a handful of dirt over the small mound of earth that now served as a final resting place for Jena and three other Underground runners who had fallen in the night to the white fever.

Ky nodded mutely, stabbed his shovel into the frost hardened ground and leaned against the haft, staring dry-eyed at the mound. He had shed too many tears in the month they had traveled since bidding Kerby farewell, as the white fever burned through the Underground like a lion on the rampage, and their numbers dwindled from thirty to nineteen.

Some it had taken quickly, like a lightning strike come and gone in a breath, and he discovered why the fever incited such terror. Some recovered after a matter of days, as Cade had, and now his sister Aliyah. But others lingered in pain and weakness, slowly reduced to shadows of their former selves, clinging to life with a tenuous grip.

Meli among them.

"We should have burned them." Clasping his hands behind his back, Cade stood and took a deep breath. "But I could not bring myself to do it."

In silence, he turned and strode back to the cart, and Ky followed him. Moments later, they were under way again, rolling deeper beneath the shadow of the Whyndburg Mountains, all steep angles, blued ridges, and peaks capped with gleaming snow. They were only in the foothills now, but would venture into the mountains themselves before nightfall.

So close now, so close to achieving their goal, to finding safety and aid for the sick. Every passing moment fueled Ky's desire for action. If he could have lashed the horses to greater speed without fear of the wagon breaking apart, he would have wielded the whip until his arm ached. If adding his strength to that of the horses could have gained any ground, he would have set his own chest to the traces and hauled with all his might.

Anything would be better than sitting, waiting.

When he could no longer stand the bone-jarring *clump thump* of the wheels rattling the teeth in his head, or the *skritching* of a pin working its way loose, or the dull, listless expressions of his companions, he turned to the dwarf.

"How much farther?"

Migdon sighed a world-weary sigh. "Anyone ever tell you that you're more persistent than a petra digging for beetles? Knowing how much farther would be dependent on me knowing exactly where we're going, which I don't. We're less than a week's travel from the Caran's stronghold—though I don't expect us to get that far—and already deep in the area under the protection of the Adulnae, so in case you were having second thoughts, it's too late to turn back now. In fact"—Migdon cast a squint-eyed glance over his shoulder—"I'll bet you a dicus for a dagger we're being watched right now."

Ky's hand strayed to his sling of its own accord as he scanned the snow encrusted countryside. "What do you mean we won't make it that far?"

The dwarf fixed him with a chilling glare. "We'll all be dead of course."

"What?"

Migdon roared with laughter and clapped him on the back. "Try not to look so glum, bucko! I'm expecting an old acquaintance, that's all. Ran into a patrol yesterday when I was out scouting ahead. Sent word to arrange a meeting. If we're going to make this mad scheme work, it's going to take some mighty delicate handling. You better hope old Silvertongue hasn't lost his charm."

Ky hoped it all right.

Hoped it fervently throughout the day whenever he caught sight of his grimy hands, still caked with dirt from the grave he had dug, and he prayed he would have to dig no more. He hoped it throughout the night too, while Meli alternately shivered and burned in her sleep. And he hoped it again, when Tauros rose at last and the wagon jolted forward, bathed in the sickly light of a winter's dawn. Midafternoon, as the wagon crested an arm of the nearest mountain and started down the other side, Migdon's whisper at last fell on his ear.

"Show time, bucko ..."

"Ambush!" Braids flying, Slack shot to her feet, and brandished her hatchet. "Weapons out! Look lively. We're under attack."

Ky scrambled to his feet and balanced precariously on the jolting wagon bed, clinging to the seat back in front of him. Framed by four sets of bobbing horse ears, a company of dwarves stood in rigid battle formation halfway up the opposite hillside. Armed with dual swords strapped to their backs and crossbows in hand, the dwarves wore helmets plumed with sea-green feathers and bronze breastplates emblazoned with designs that shimmered many colors in the sunlight. They looked altogether fierce and terrible . . . and deadly.

Just the sort who might set the Khelari running with their tails between their legs.

In the shallow valley between the two hills, Cade brought the wagon to a stop, horses stamping and snorting in their traces. Without a word, he snatched the hatchet from Slack's hand and stowed it in his own belt. Migdon disembarked and landed with a grunt. "Wait here for now, and try to keep Miss Blood-and-Guts here quiet, or we will have trouble. When I signal, Cade, you and Bucko here can come." He flicked a dismissive hand at Slack as he marched away. "*She* can stay behind."

Two dwarves separated from the others and descended to meet him. Scouting out easy marks in the city square had taught Ky a thing or two about how to judge the measure of a man in a glance or two, but *one* was enough to see that these two were not the sort a fellow wanted to mess with.

He could only hope Silvertongue was up to the challenge.

With the sudden silence left by the stilled wagon wheels, the rustle of anxious conversation rose up around him on all sides. On the raised front seat, Slack argued with Cade, bartering to get her hatchet back. From what he could hear, things weren't looking too positive on that front—and he'd sleep all the easier because of it.

The talking rubbed him raw. It was just *noise* all of it. Pointless noise. His limbs ached for action. He slipped over the side of the wagon and paced alongside. A moment later, measured footsteps heralded Cade's approach from his left, then Paddy's on his right.

"Would you just look at their armor?" Paddy whistled softly. "Must be worth a pretty bit."

"Worth more than coin," Cade said. "Armor like that would more than level the field of contest against the Khelari. Just think—no more dodging arrows in shirtsleeves and leather vests. You'd appreciate that, wouldn't you, Ky?" The older boy cuffed his shoulder hard enough to jar his teeth. "Safety above everything else, right?"

The words stung like a blow to the face.

But Ky knew more than a little about blows to the face, so he just shrugged Cade's words aside as if they weren't worth crediting with an answer, and watched as the three dwarves halted a short distance from one another and each thumped a fist to the side of his head.

The two strangers were a touch shorter than Migdon, but both so alike, they had to be related. They shared the same short, curly, dark hair and cropped beards, and Ky would have had a hard time telling them apart if they hadn't been garbed differently. One wore bronze armor like the dwarves still lined up in battle array, but his helmet had a taller, thicker plume and a fur-trimmed cape trailed behind him, so he clearly possessed some sort of higher military rank. The other was clad in a simple, loose-fitting robe with a wide sash draped over one shoulder and a bronze torc around his neck.

Migdon's voice suddenly rose in anger, but he was too far away for Ky to distinguish the words. All three of the dwarves gestured emphatically, hands stabbing the air with as much force as a Saari spear strike. Even without being able to hear the actual words, the gist of it wasn't too hard to imagine.

For once, Silvertongue didn't seem to be getting his way.

"Just think of it." Cade folded his arms across his chest, surveying the shallow valley as if he was seeing a very different scene than the one unfolding before them. "Fighting alongside real warriors for a change. The dark soldiers won't stand a chance. Finally, we'll be free of them."

So *that* was what Silvertongue had promised Cade to get him here. Honestly, Ky felt a bit the dunce for not guessing it sooner. Too consumed by his dreams of shelter and a healer. Too ready for the fighting to be over.

By the time Migdon finally gestured for them to approach, Ky was sure he'd sprouted a beard of his own. At least earned a few gray hairs or worn the soles of his feet down to nothing with all his pacing.

"First things first." Migdon assumed a wide stance and set both fists on his hips. "Introductions. Meet Chancellor Nisus Plexipus Molineous Creegnan of the Xanthen, and his brother, Commander Jirkar Mundi—"

"Jirkar will do." The armored dwarf grinned, smile lines splaying from his eyes. "Best we keep this moving along, don't you think?"

Ky couldn't have agreed more. In any case, he wasn't sure his head could have wrapped itself around another string of names like the first. He had once heard it said that dwarf names were longer than a dwarf was tall. Hadn't really believed it before.

"If anything is precious now, it is time." The other dwarf, Chancellor Nisus-something-or-other, ran a pensive hand through his beard. Even up close, the only real difference Ky could make out between the two was that Nisus had reddish streaks in his hair and beard, and a sharper look to his features than Jirkar. "Your message could not have come at a less opportune time, Migdon. You do realize we are on the verge of battling these cursed Khelari for our homeland? Their army has been amassing to the southeast of the Caran's stronghold for months now."

Jirkar nodded. "It's a wonder you didn't run into their scouts—they've been ranging all along the southern border of the mountains."

"So tell me"—Nisus's eyes flickered from Ky to Cade and back again—"with the Takhran's might bearing down and war breaking loose upon us, why should *we* help *you*? Why expend valuable remedies and risk exposing our soldiers to the white fever for a wagonload of waifs? Silvertongue said you could be quite persuasive."

And now the dwarf's gaze rested on Ky alone.

His mouth went dry, and he fumbled for an answer—any answer—to give. But all the arguments he'd deployed against Migdon seemed weak and threadbare before Nisus's calculating stare. The seconds slipped past, and he was still no closer to a response.

Time was running out for Meli and so many of the others. Without help, they were all of them doomed. But it had been foolish to imagine the dwarves would risk their own to help strangers. And if there truly was a Master Singer somewhere, weaving the course of the world in song, he couldn't care much about the fate of a bunch of thieving orphans. No, if help was going to come, it would be won by the sweat of their own brows and the force of their own wit.

Ky took a breath to speak, still not entirely sure what was going to come out of his mouth, and at the same time, felt a brush on his sleeve as Cade shouldered past. "Those *waifs* are the Underground of Kerby and—"

"No matter what you call yourself, your people are just children, not even beardlings."

"Hardly that." Cade tilted his chin back, pride lacing his voice. "For five years, we've stood against the dark soldiers when no one else in our city would dare. You will not find us lacking in courage or skill. We ask only the chance to fight the dark soldiers when they come. If you help us, we will help you."

"I'm sorry, truly," Jirkar said and actually sounded like he meant it. "The risk is too great. I cannot endanger my cohort, or the lives that would be in peril should my company be weakened by fever." He executed a sharp turn, cloak flapping, and strode away.

"My brother can be a bit blunt-headed." Nisus spoke in the dry sort of tone one would use to make observations about the weather. "Once he's seized upon a notion, he drives after it with all the force and precision of a battering ram. But for once, he is right. We cannot help you." The dwarf spread his arms in a shrug, then clasped his hands before him and started after Jirkar.

Ky's voice failed him but he finally managed to croak out a desperate plea. "Migdon, *do* something!"

"Sorry, bucko. Got nothing." Migdon puffed his cheeks out and released a heavy puff of air that steamed before his face. "Pity too. Silvertongue's never failed before. It's a dark blot on my otherwise shining record. I've got a reputation to consider, you know."

Ky opened his mouth to protest, but once again, Cade beat him to it.

"Hold! A word, if you please." Both Nisus and Jirkar paused, and Cade advanced toward them, one hand resting casually on the hilt of his sword. Ever commanding. Ever collected. Ky envied him that. "I don't think you understand. I'm Cade Peregrine . . . of Kerby."

"We know who you are."

"No, I don't think you do, but I know a lot about you. Nisus and Jirkar. Names like those aren't easy to forget. You remember Lucas Peregrine, the swordsmith? He was my father."

Both dwarves started at that, and a little of the color leeched from their skin until it was almost the same dull gray as the winter sky.

Cade flung an arm around Ky's shoulder, and he flinched from the touch. "And Ky here is a friend of Hawkness. If you knew my father, I guess that means you must have known Hawkness too. So no, we're not just some strangers asking for aid. You should think of it as helping an old friend."

Jirkar and Nisus pulled to the side and muttered together for a moment. Ky only caught snatches of the conversation. "Well, that changes things ..." "Lucas's son ..." and "Siranos would be best."

Then Nisus stepped forward, arms spread in a placating gesture. "Perhaps we can help one another after all. There is a fortress on the northern side of the—"

"What of a healer?" Ky burst out. The fortress could wait. There were more important things to be dealt with first. "Migdon said you had medicines for the white fever?"

"Yes, you shall have your remedies." The dwarf inclined his head with the air of a longsuffering martyr. "As I was saying, the fortress of Siranos is on the northern side of the range, far enough away for there to be little threat of an attack, so I will leave a few soldiers and there will be little risk of them contracting the fever. It is little more than a pair of towers, and somewhat rough, so …"

Ky didn't hear any more. Others could worry about the details. For him, it was enough that Meli would soon be well, sheltered from the cold, and safe from fear of attack.

What more could a fellow ask for?

23

The floorboards creaked beneath her feet, and Birdie winced, casting an anxious glance over her shoulder. Gundhrold sat before the shuttered window, keeping a "weather eye out," as Amos put it, but his ears did not so much as twitch at her movement. She slipped into the second room, hugging Artair's sword to her chest, and eased the door shut behind her. That should buy her a few minutes of quiet before the griffin realized she had gone.

Within, Inali sat on a bedroll with his back to the wall, strands of dark hair falling across his face, eyes lowered to a thin strip of parchment in his lap where the first lines of a picture were just beginning to take shape. Old blood still stained the bandage on his left shoulder, and a thin strip of cloth bound his arm against his chest.

"Have they gone out?" He spoke without lifting his gaze.

Even the softness of his voice was enough to make Birdie glance back over her shoulder toward the closed door, though there was no way the griffin could have heard it. Nor was there anything to conceal. She was doing nothing wrong. Amos might not trust Inali completely, but then he never trusted anyone. Since what had happened with George, she might have had a little trouble trusting too, had it not been for the blow Inali had taken in her stead.

"Sym and Amos?" She fiddled with the sword in her hands. It was probably foolish to carry it around so, but she was hesitant to set it aside. After scouting all night, Amos and Sym had returned with the first glimmer of dawn to catch a few hours of sleep and had only just gone out again to watch the movements of the Khelari while they could blend in with a crowd. "Yes, they've gone."

Inali just grunted and went back to work. With deliberate care, he brought the piece of charcoal in his good hand down across the parchment with short, stiff strokes. Birdie lowered herself beside him, but he gave no further acknowledgement of her presence, and now that she was here, she wasn't sure how to begin what she wanted to say. So for the moment, they sat in silence, while he drew, and she fingered the pommel of Artair's sword.

In the end, he spoke first.

"What is it like, little Songkeeper, to hear the desperate voices of all around you singing the forgotten notes of a dying song?" He blinked up at her, then directed his attention back to the parchment and the face forming beneath his hand. "To listen to the music of the heart and see into the depths of men's souls?" His soft voice took on a hypnotic cadence, and Birdie felt herself drawn forward to catch each word. "It is frightening, is it not? Overwhelming. You stand on the brink of the gap between mankind and something so vast and unfathomable, you cannot even begin to imagine. Surely you feel it—feel your own smallness and insignificance before it."

"*It*?"

A pair of shadowed eyes stared up from the parchment. As she watched, Inali darkened the corners and edges, but used the tip of his finger to brush a clear strip of white through the center—a reflection of light. "*It*. The power. It does not care about *you*. You will discover that."

He fell silent then, devoting his attention to the work of his hand. This was not the conversation Birdie had anticipated, but he had asked questions and supplied the answers. That in itself told Birdie more than she would ever have gathered the courage to ask on her own.

"You heard them too—the half songs—didn't you?"

A tightening of his hand on the charcoal was the only sign that she was on the right track. Sweeping lines of dark hair appeared on the parchment, blowing every which way about the face as if caught in the grip of a fierce breeze.

She forged ahead. "Do you still hear them?" Only because she was watching so closely was she able to see the almost imperceptible shake of his head. "What *happened*?" The words fell from her lips on a breath of fear, spoken half to herself and half to him.

She did not expect a reply.

With thin lines, he shadowed the face, forming the nose, highlighting the cheek bones, and coloring lips that were half opened in an expression that lingered somewhere between horror and wonder. It was some time before he finally relaxed his hand, set the charcoal aside, and lifted the parchment to survey his handiwork.

A chill settled over Birdie. She had caught glimpses of her face before—once in the watering trough in the Sylvan Swan's stable after she had given it a good scrubbing, another time in the birch-shaded pool beside the road to Hardale. There was no doubt that the face on the parchment resembled her own, but there were slight differences. It was older than the face she remembered, older than she could look now. Stunning in a way one was not likely to forget. But there was something about the eyes that captivated her, caused her to reach out her hand and trace the line of one arching brow.

Such strength there, such confidence.

This was not the face of one with fear caged in her chest.

Inali lowered the parchment. "I was to be a Songkeeper, and then I was not, and the melody was gone. As the eldest son of my father, I was to have become Mahtem of the Sigzal tribe, and then I was not, for my sister was promised to the Matlal and given my birthright for her dowry. Now, I who was to be Mahtem am but *Dah* Inali, a lesser son." He sighed and tucked the parchment into his satchel. "Things come and things go. Such is life, is it not, little Songkeeper?"

Such is life.

The unsettled feeling inspired by the thought brought Birdie to her feet, no longer able to sit still with so much stirring inside. Clutching Artair's sword, she drifted toward the door, but troubled thoughts could not be so easily evaded. Once Inali had been well on his way to being the Songkeeper. Everyone would have heralded him as such, just as they had Birdie, and counted on him to stand against the Takhran. To save them. Just as they hoped in her.

Yet their hope in Inali had failed them.

Who was say that she was not just another Songling? Not just another "look-alike?" That in the end, she would not fail them too and be left to eke out her days in silence, her hopes ended, the melody gone. For as long as she could remember, the music had been there. She had not always understood—still did not completely comprehend it all—but she couldn't imagine life without hearing the five notes sung by those surrounding her and constantly searching . . . searching . . . searching for another chance to hear the full, glorious melody.

Inali sat now with his eyes closed and his head tipped back, to all appearances asleep. But his tense posture gave him away.

"What of the melody, Inali?" Birdie's voice sounded soft and scared, mouse-like. She forced herself to speak louder, stronger. "Did you ever hear the full melody?"

Without opening his eyes, he shook his head.

She drifted to the door. With her hand on the latch, it finally struck her. Hard enough that she almost dropped Artair's sword and it took every ounce of self-control not to wheel around and stare at Inali in shock. The room was silent.

Completely silent.

Inali had no song.

Birdie slumped in one of the rickety chairs in the front room, watching fat dollops of wax roll down the candle stub and plop into a widening pool on the tabletop. The griffin still stood guard by the window, and might as well have been carved from stone for all that he had moved since she had gone to speak to Inali.

She had strained her ears to the utmost and heard nothing. Not a scrap of melody. Not even one of the five notes. Just like the woman she had seen on the way into the city. She cast her mind back, trying to recall if there had ever been anything but silence from Inali, but she had never been alone with him before. There had always been others around, enough other voices singing, or enough impending danger, that she just hadn't noticed.

The melody was gone . . .

Inali's words filled her with a shudder that she couldn't shake. She ran a pensive hand over the clothbound length of Artair's sword lying across her knees and longed to unleash it. Longed to relive those short, glorious moments in Brog's donkey shed, when it had seemed as if she and the blade were one. Longed for action, for simplicity.

Since arriving in Serrin Vroi, Amos insisted that she keep the blade concealed. Regardless of its worth as a weapon prized by the Takhran, the white gold of the hilt could be enough to tempt even an honest man to thievery.

So he claimed, at least.

But Birdie wondered if he wasn't merely afraid that her song and the blade and the strange connection between the two might somehow reveal itself in a way that would get her captured. Maybe he was right. Even now, she could feel the melody humming deep within the sword, syncing with the Song pulsing through her veins, and amplifying the soft strains of the griffin's voice across the room. She had found that the more time she spent with someone, the easier it was to mute their song, but the sword seemed to be making that difficult, and in turn, making it difficult to focus on anything else.

It stirred her blood to action. Less than a week in their safe house, and Birdie was already beginning to feel like it was a cage. It was time to meet the Takhran on his own ground and earn the answers and freedom she desired. Time to discover her abilities. Time to prove, once and for all, that she would not wind up like Inali.

She shoved her chair back. "I'm going below, Gundhrold."

The griffin twisted his neck almost all the way around to look at her, and his huge, golden eyes fell on her with such intensity that it seemed he could read all the fears and doubts and confusion roiling within her. "Be careful, little one."

Birdie felt his eyes following her until she closed the door and tramped down the groaning staircase into the stable. Musty straw crunched beneath her feet, and she breathed deeply of the crisp scent of fresh snow that had drifted in around the door frame and lay in patches on the ground. She halted in the middle of the room, and after removing the scabbard but leaving the cloth wrappings that bound the blade, took up a neutral guard position.

Humming softly with the blade, she ran through the basic moves, sweeping fluidly from one to the next. The Song welled up and swept over her so completely that she had little thought for anything but the music and the blade and the rhythm they shared. Only once she came to a final stop in a forward lunge, did the other sounds she had heard register: the creak of a loose board, the rustle of stealthy feet in the straw, panting breath …

She spun around.

There was no one there. But she couldn't shake the unmistakable feeling that she was being watched. Taking deep, steady breaths, she sought to quiet her pounding heart so she could listen. Soft at first, but growing louder, she heard the discordant melody sung in a voice that sounded like cart wheels over gravel.

Behind her …

A flash of movement caught the corner of her eye. On instinct, she sprang to the side and lashed out with the sword. A yelp, and her attacker retreated and dropped into a crouch, panting. One of the Takhran's hounds. Saliva dripped from its bared teeth, and its milky white eyes made Birdie shudder. There was *hunger* in its gaze.

With a wordless growl, it lunged at her.

Birdie slashed at its corded chest, felt her sword tip pierce flesh. The hound checked itself and tumbled head over tail. But it was up again and on her, faster than she could recover from her strike. She found herself scrambling backwards, barely able to keep the sword between herself and the snarling beast.

Her heels thudded against the wall.

She opened her mouth to call for Gundhrold, but the dark melody pressed in about her and seemed to drain the life from her lungs. The hound hunkered low, just beyond reach of her blade, muscles coiled to spring. She forced her gaze up, past the beast's quivering form, spiked collar, and savage grin, and into its eyes.

Those horrible, dead-looking eyes.

It was like peering into a wall of fog—peering and drowning in it. The Song came to her then, in a whisper, and she clutched at it as if at a life line. The white fog shifted, and somehow she could see thoughts like shapes within: utter hopelessness, fear, hatred, and a longing so deep and vast it was like a yawning pit consuming the beast from the inside out.

The sword hummed in her hands, vibrations working their way up her arms, bringing with them a cold that seeped through the wrappings. A flicker of light, visible through the gaps between the strands of cloth, drew her gaze down the blade.

It was glowing.

Gently now, the Song sprang to her tongue, and she gave it voice. At the first tremulous notes, the hound's eyes met hers. She sensed its fury and the raw hate broiling within. But there was something else too . . . something more like panic …

The hound lunged, and she thrust the blade to meet it, slicing through the spiked collar and piercing his chest. Her elbows bent before the impact. Teeth grazed her shin. She braced against the wall as the beast scrabbled to gain ground. A breath . . . two . . . With a ragged moan, the hound backed away, shaking its head and pawing at its ears, leaving its shorn collar in the straw at her feet.

A glint of red caught her eye. Wrapped in the remains of the mangled collar, lay a single red crystal, just like the one Carhartan had worn. George too. Birdie tightened her grip on the sword. It seemed she would not have to hunt down all of the answers she desired.

At least one had come to her.

The beast's growl claimed her attention, a low rumbling deep in its throat that gradually took on words. "Who are you, little one?" He had a voice like a rockslide, but even so, there was no mistaking the hint of begrudging respect in his tone.

"I think you know who I am." Somehow, she kept her voice steady.

"The little Songkeeper." A snarl curled the hound's lip. "So the rumors spoke true. I did not believe them."

"You know me, but I still don't know you." She eased forward, trying to back him into the corner. The hound instantly fell into a crouch, fur bristling, muscles quivering. "I won't hurt you." She glanced from the tip of her sword poking through its crimson stained covering to the steady stream of blood running down the hound's right foreleg. "Not if I don't have to."

"I could slay you in an instant," he rasped. "Your neck would snap like a twig in my jaws. Better to kill me now and be done with it. There is no telling what I might do. I belong to the Takhran."

"Maybe you *don't* know who I am. I am not so easy to kill as you might think." Bold words considering how the fear raged and tore at its bonds within her chest, threatening at any moment to break loose. Careful to keep her sword trained on him, she tilted only her chin in the direction of the crimson jewel. "What is that? The jewel in your collar. I've seen it before."

The hound's gaze flickered down to the collar, and his breath hitched in surprise. He took a wary step forward, snuffling the ground, shoulders bristling. "It is my talav. My bloodstone." He fell silent. Some of the savagery eased from his face, and he sank back on his haunches. "You . . . you freed me from—"

He broke off, ears cocked toward the door. Before Birdie could react, he was off in a single bound, racing toward the left wall of the stable and out through a narrow gap where several boards had snapped at the base.

Gone.

The sword slipped from her shaking fingers. For a moment, she could not move, overwhelmed with the horror of what had just happened. She had just been discovered by one of the Takhran's hounds, admitted to being the Songkeeper, wounded the beast, and then, like a complete ninny-hammered fool, allowed him to escape.

If he had gone to fetch the Khelari …

Boots stamped outside the stable door, jerking Birdie into action. She seized the sword and raced toward the staircase, her only thought to rouse Gundhrold without shouting and alerting their enemies, in case they hadn't yet been discovered. It was a slim hope. But instead of the furious shouts of Khelari, Amos's brusque voice and Sym's low murmur fell on her ears, bringing her to a stop with her foot on the bottom step.

A scuffling sound drew her back to the gap in time to see the hound's head reappear. "You may call me Renegade. Be wary little Songkeeper. You are in grave danger. We will meet again." Then with a curl of his lip that might have been a smile—if it had not revealed so many fearsome teeth—he was gone.

Leaving Birdie alone with a bloodstained sword in her hands.

The stable door swung inward, letting Sym and Amos in with a blast of swirling snow and cold air. Puffing steam, the peddler hastened to shut and bar the door, then twisted around and shook the snow from his shoulders.

"Quick, lass. Round up the others. We've got trouble."

24

Trapped in fevered sleep, Meli's eyelids fluttered, lashes dark against the ashen pallor of her skin. Ky sat on an overturned crate at her side, aching head cradled in his cold numbed hands. In the fireplace, a sputtering fire competed against three windows to heat the drafty barracks hall they had converted into a sick chamber. The rest of the sick lay on straw pallets all around him, but he had eyes only for Meli. She had become such a frail thing, like a leaf that the wind could seize and toss away at will.

It had taken three days of rough traveling, through a country no less formidable and fierce than its inhabitants, to reach the fortress of Siranos. Three days since Chancellor Nisus had sent for the promised remedy. Ky could only hope it would arrive soon …

And that *soon* would be soon enough.

The clashing of weapons and barked commands drifted in from the courtyard. Never one to let the snow settle beneath his feet, Cade had reinstituted weapons practice and battle drills for all who were well enough to stand. No doubt trying to impress their hosts enough to let the runners join the coming battle.

"Come away, laddy-boyo." Paddy's voice came from behind. "You've been sittin' here for hours. A moment's rest will do no harm."

Ky shook his head and spared a glance at Paddy hovering over him, freckled face etched with concern. "I can't leave her."

"I'll stay." Paddy's hands settled beneath his elbows, guiding him to his feet and across the chamber to the door, and Ky went unresisting. But rest was the farthest thing from his mind. The sounds of battle had set his own hand itching for action.

He emerged into the pale light of day, blinking until his vision cleared enough for him to see the circular courtyard and the stone buildings built in a ring along the outer wall. The fortress of Siranos consisted of two circular keeps built on twin bluffs overlooking a narrow, shallow pass, connected by an arched bridge that ran from wall-top to wall-top. At the base of the bluffs, a low breastwork guarded the entrance to the pass. A company of dwarves manned the north tower and the breastwork, leaving the south tower to the Underground.

Far above, the shrill calls of seabirds served as a reminder of the nearness of the north coast of Leira. Siranos guarded the one entrance from the ocean into the mountains. The rest of the coastline rose from the water in a row of impassable cliffs, or so Commander Jirkar had said, but just beyond sight of the fortress, the pass spread its arms around a slender inlet of the sea.

Grouped in pairs and threes across the snow heaped courtyard, the runners sparred with blunted training weapons that Cade must have "borrowed" from the keep's armory. As Ky wove his way through dozens of mock battles, he caught a glimpse of Cade instructing Slack on sword and buckler techniques. Her eyes gleamed with a fiendish delight over the rim of her buckler, and her harsh barking laugher rang out after each stroke.

Ky hurried past, unwinding his sling from his waist as he went. Only Cade could fall for a girl so completely *bonkers*. He halted on the far side of the courtyard in front of a trio of snow-capped straw dummies that must have been set up for archery practice, but would work well enough for the sling too. His fingers shook a little as he dug in his pouch for a sling-bullet and even more when he loosed the first round. The sling-bullet zipped past the target's left ear and cracked off the wall behind.

Clamping his teeth together, Ky slung once . . . twice . . . more. The first shot struck the second dummy in the forehead. But the third overshot to the right by at least three inches. Ky paused to rub the haze from his eyes and knead his aching temples. Maybe Paddy was right.

Maybe he was worn out.

Head hanging, he jogged over to the target and stooped to retrieve his spent sling-bullets. A sword landed flat-side down, inches from his fingers. Crisp footsteps marched toward him, and he knew who it was without having to look.

Payback.

"Oi, Cade." He pocketed the sling-bullets, forced a stiff smile to his cold chapped lips, and rose. "Raided the armory, I see."

The Underground leader's eyes glinted dangerously. Slack stood at his elbow, flushed and grinning, buckler hugged to her chest, sword hand empty. It must be her blade at his feet.

"Pick it up, Ky," Cade said. "There are things between us, unsettled things. It's time to finish what we began in the Underground. Show these youngsters what real fighting looks like." He jerked his chin back over his shoulder, and Ky saw that the runners had abandoned their practice and were gathering around.

To witness his humiliation again.

Legs strangely unsteady, he bent, settled his hand around the grip, and hefted the blade. For half a second, he glared down the blunted length toward Cade, and he couldn't deny being tempted. If he could beat Cade once—just *once*—surely that wasn't too much to ask?

But more than anything else, he was weary of it all.

Weary of the games. Of the posturing. Of the need to keep face or die trying.

A flick of his wrist deposited the sword at Cade's feet. "I'm not going to fight you again. It's over and done with. I got us out. You led us here. We both just want what's best for the Underground. Besides"—he lifted his dangling sling—"this is my weapon." He turned and strode back toward the sickroom.

Slack snorted. "'Course it is." Already halfway across the courtyard, Ky could hear her well enough to know that she meant him to. "You stand at a distance and pelt your opponent with rocks. A blade? Now, that's a *man's* weapon. Only a coward would use a sling."

Mockery, Ky could take. Hard knocks, those he was accustomed to. But being outright called a coward, now that was too much. He didn't give himself time to think, to breathe, to cool down. Driven by the force of his fury, he spun around and launched three slingstones at top speed at the closest dummy. The straw head burst, showering Slack with golden flecks.

Before she could recover, he broke into a run, released another two shots on the move that cracked against the stone building. The sound drew her attention. He threw himself into a roll and came up on his feet, mere inches away, with his loaded sling back and ready to strike.

"A coward's weapon, you say?"

She met his glare, eyes bristling with anger . . . and a touch of fear.

Did she expect him to actually attack?

His arm lowered of its own accord, and his wrath fizzled out like a torch snuffed in water. Black specks danced before his eyes. For a moment, his vision spun. He was no bully. Slow clapping broke out behind, and an appreciative whistle brought him reeling to his senses. He pulled away and stumbled back a step before his vision cleared and he could see the dwarf, Jirkar, standing by the Keep's gate.

"Bravo, little master." Chuckling, the dwarf shook his head. "If you can all handle yourselves half so well, I imagine any dwarf would be glad to have you fighting alongside when the Khelari come."

Not exactly what he'd intended to prove …

Cade spun his practice sword through the air and easily caught it again by the hilt. "Put us to the test. You won't be disappointed."

"I imagine not." The dwarf smiled and held out an oilcloth bound package. "But your sick must be tended first. I will not risk my soldiers. A few drops thrice a day should do the trick. With Nisus's compliments."

Ky stumbled forward and snatched the package before the dwarf could change his mind or something bad could happen. Something bad always seemed to happen just when things started going right. Cade's shouts chased him across the courtyard, but he wasn't stopping for any man, Underground leader or not. Clutching the precious bundle to his chest, he burst through the door into the sick chamber, startling Paddy from his borrowed seat. On his knees beside Meli's pallet, he tore the wrapping off the package, revealing several brown glass vials.

"Is that ..."

"Yeah." He yanked the stopper from the first vial and managed to will his hand steady long enough to place a few drops in her mouth. Having his head down set his skull throbbing as if he'd been punched in the temple. Shadows lurked at the edge of his vision.

The room turned cold.

"Ky?" Paddy's voice seemed to come from a great distance. "You're white as a ghost."

"What?" He shook his head, trying to clear the jumbled thoughts from his mind. For a moment, everything grayed. He heard a thump and the clinking of glass against stone. A sharp exclamation from Paddy.

Suddenly, he realized that he was no longer kneeling, but slumped with his back to the wall and his chin drooped to his chest. "It's fine . . . I'm fine ..." He struggled to rise, but his head spun, and he couldn't breathe. Why couldn't he breathe?

Paddy's hands settled on his shoulders, holding him down. "Stay. I'm goin' for Cade."

"No ..." He managed to croak. "Not Cade ..."

But Paddy was already gone.

25

The bloodstained wrappings of Artair's blade held Amos's focus as he paced a circle around the table where Birdie, Inali, and Sym were seated, tossing his dirk from hand to hand with each step. He could not look away, not even when he had to weave wide around the griffin's tawny bulk to avoid stepping on his feather-tufted tail.

Hound's blood . . .

But it could so easily have been her own.

Who could've dreamed that guarding the wee lass could be so boggswoggling hard on the nerves? By Turning, if she had but called for help, instead of trying to fend the beastie off all by herself. Now the monster had escaped, and there was no telling what terrors might rain down on their heads.

It was a sheer pity she hadn't killed it with the first stroke.

"Please, Amos." Birdie sounded weary. "I don't think he means to turn us in. He outright warned me I was in danger."

A low growl rumbled in Gundhrold's throat, and his voice exploded with the burst of a thunderclap. "The assurances of a traitor are worthless, little Songkeeper."

Amos caught himself nodding along with the griffin, until he studied Birdie's face. Solemn, she looked. Hard, almost. But beneath he knew her strength was brittle, like ice formed on rigging, bound to snap at the first stiff gust of wind.

He shrugged. "Och, what's one more danger in a city full o' 'em? An' the city *is* full o' 'em, make no doubt about that. I fear . . . I fear our presence here was known even before the beastie made his escape." With that admission, it seemed the last of his restless energy drained away. He rested both fists against the table—careful not to smudge Inali's map—and let the rickety legs sag in support of his weight. "Sym an' I've been watchin' the Khelari all week. It's been silent—almost too silent—until today. Now, all o' a sudden, the streets are full o' hounds and the sky is teemin' with ravens. Soldiers are on the lookout everywhere, stirred up like a blatherin' slickjaw nest."

Sym glanced up from directing Inali on the placement of troops on his charcoal map and took up the story in her pleasantly hoarse voice. "On our way back, we nearly ran into a full company that had been dispatched to reinforce the guards along the outer wall. Word is they've shut all the gates too."

Gundhrold's ears perked at that. "Including the main entrance to his fortress?"

"All of them. This city is nailed down tighter than a keg." Sym rocked back in her chair and stuck her booted feet up on the edge of the table. "If the Takhran knows we are here, he does not want us leaving."

It seemed a mighty small *if* to Amos. What but the presence of the Songkeeper in his city would stir the Takhran to employ such measures? From any other ruler, it would be considered standard precaution when at war. But from one who took such pride in his strength that he had boasted often and loudly that a closed gate was a sign of weakness?

For him, it was a sign of weakness indeed.

"I don't understand," Birdie said. "If it wasn't the hound, how were we discovered?"

"Aye, it does lead one t' wonder . . ." Almost unconsciously, Amos let his gaze stray to Inali, only to be met head on. The lad seemed to have paused mid-stroke, hand hovering over the table, charcoal piece gripped between his fingers, knotted strands of hair falling over his forehead so only his spectacles and eyes were visible—wide, innocent, reproachful eyes. Inali's mouth worked into a frown, but he said nothing.

Bilgewater.

It wasn't anything personal. Inali seemed a fine enough lad, in his own way. But if nigh six decades on this wretched earth had taught Amos anything, it was that the suspicious survived.

The trusting were killed.

Gundhrold hefted himself to his feet and eyed the shuttered window. "Perhaps it is not such a wonder after all . . . or perhaps wonder is not the right word. Terror might be more apt." He twisted around to face them, and his expression was one that Amos knew only too well. "I have seen a ghost."

"A ghost?" Sym repeated.

"Perhaps not a ghost per se—"

"We've not the time for word games. Just what are ye babblin' about? Spit it out!"

"That is just it, I am afraid, I cannot simply *spit it out*." The griffin lashed his tail, the tuft of feathers at the end thrumming through the air. "I saw one who should be dead. In your fanciful human reasoning, I believe that would make her a ghost."

"Who in bilges are ye talkin' about?"

"Someone I knew long ago. But it defies reason. I saw her wounded . . . saw her fall to flame and venom. She *was* slain. And yet I also saw her with my own two eyes in the streets below only this morning."

"Who, Gundhrold?"

The lass's plea worked where Amos's demand had not. "A Songling named Zahar. Long ago, her brother Rav was determined to prove her the next Songkeeper. He brought her before the council of griffins, but when it was determined that she was a Songling and nothing more, he grew angry. Violent. Demanded the Protectors recognize her in Auna's stead. We turned him out. Believed it ended."

"But it wasn't?"

"No, little one." With a sigh that seemed to drain all the ferocity from his voice, the griffin's gaze drooped. "A year later, he returned and begged the Protectors for one more chance to prove his sister's abilities against Auna's. Under the guise of a meeting, he lured us into a trap where he unleashed monsters upon us. Foul beasts I can only assume came from the Takhran's Pit. With flame and poisoned fang, they attacked, and it was all I could do to get Auna to safety Far too many of my brothers and sisters fell behind. But as we fled, I saw her. Zahar. Standing on the brink of the fight. Then she plunged in after her brother only to fall at the feet of one of the beasts. Dead. I am convinced of it."

"An' yet ye claim she's bloody well walkin' about the city now?"

"There is worse still. The woman I saw this morning wore the talav. I fear that somehow, by some cursed magic, Zahar survived and has become one of the Shantren, and if that is true, then we are indeed in grave danger."

The lass opened her mouth, but Amos forestalled further questions with an upraised hand. "Hold a moment an' let the griffin explain. Who or what are the Shantren? I've never heard tell o' 'em."

"Indeed?" The griffin looked surprised. "Suffice it to say, they are a blight in the heart of Leira. Commoners and Songlings alike who have been recruited by the Takhran to become a part of his elite forces. He gifts them with abilities. Dangerous abilities. It may be that she . . . or they . . . are to blame for our discovery."

"The hound wore the talav." Birdie spoke up. "George and Carhartan too."

"This is grand. Just grand." Amos took a deep breath and forced it out between his teeth. This madcap mission seemed to be falling apart at the seams. They had scarce begun, but they were already beaten. The others might not like it, but if anyone was going to make the hard decision, it would have to be him. Sometimes, one had to simply cut one's losses, turn tail and run, and hope for the best.

"Well, my friends, there's only one thing for it. We have t' leave immediately."

To say the outcry was greater than Amos had anticipated would have been an understatement. Sym pulled her feet from the table's edge, grounding her chair with a thud, and glowered at him as she produced a whetstone from a pouch in her quiver and began sharpening her spear points one by one. Inali sank back in his seat, cradling his wounded arm, with the melancholy air of a dejected pup. Even

Gundhrold managed to convey the proper amount of feather-ruffled dismay without looking aught less than dignified.

But it was Birdie's response that set his brain fumbling to recall the arguments that had seemed so conclusive only moments before. She just sat there, face devoid of any emotion, but she could not conceal the hurt in her eyes.

Not from him.

Amos balked before the pressure of so many reproachful glances and blustered for a response. At the very least, he had thought Gundhrold would be on his side. The old catbird was practically rabid about protecting the Songkeeper. "Look, it's leave or be captured, an' I daresay we all agree the second one is not an option."

"Well, when you put it that way . . . but perhaps those aren't the *only* options." Sym observed drily, pausing her sharpening long enough to inspect the angle of a blade. "This heightened security could work to our advantage. After all, if the Khelari are watching for us to *leave* the city, then they won't be paying near as much attention to anyone slipping farther behind their lines. It's the last thing he'll expect."

Inali slid the spectacles from his nose and polished the lenses on his knees, blinking owlishly. "The little Songkeeper has the Takhran running scared. For once, the battle threatens his own turf—putting him on the offensive, reacting to our moves, rather than controlling the field—and he is afraid."

"Indeed." Gundhrold nodded sagely. Somehow the catbird made everything he did appear wise. It was no wonder everyone listened to him. "What is more, his fear lends credence to this wild mission of ours. The Songkeeper must pose a viable threat, else our presence would not worry him so."

"Ye read too much into it! Mayhap he just means t' catch us this time."

"Hawkness." Gundhrold's voice assumed a placating tone as he drifted around the table to stand beak to nose with Amos. The griffin's wing settled on his shoulder, and Amos turned a cold glare upon it, but his scowl had never been enough to dissuade the catbird. "I understand your desire to protect the Songkeeper, but you cannot deny the importance of this mission, whispered in the Songkeeper's ear in the Hollow Cave by Emhran himself."

"Don't patronize me, griffin." Muttered words, imbued with every ounce of the anger he'd bottled up inside. He shoved the griffin's wing away. "Ye know I don't care much for any o' that. I've gone along with this *madness* so far, but I'm done. We're finished here."

Breaking free of the griffin's stare, he marched to their collection of belongings piled just inside the door and shrugged into his damp overcoat. He kept his chin tucked to avoid meeting Birdie's eyes, but he couldn't evade the griffin's voice.

"The decision is not yours to make, Hawkness. It is the Songkeeper's."

A twinge seized the muscles in Amos's chest, as though an arrow had pierced his lungs, leaving him gaping and breathless. He would not have expected this from Gundhrold, pitting the lass—*his* lass—against him. What could she choose but to stay and carry out this absurd mission, only to get herself caught or killed . . . or worse?

Would he, the great Amos McElhenny, who legend claimed had never turned his back on a fight, simply walk away? The legends never got it right. He had walked away before. Away from Artair . . . from Kerby …

He could do it again.

"What say you, little Songkeeper." Inali's soft voice broke the silence, sending a shiver marching down Amos's spine. "Shall we flee . . . or fight?"

Amos's hand found the hilt of his dirk, and he wrapped his fingers around the hawk's head, tightening his grip until the curved beak bit into his palm. The lass's answer came at last, in a voice both soft and sad as a distant shoreline and strong as the ocean's pull.

"We fight."

"So be it." The words fell with the weight of an oath. "But we do it on my terms."

"Terms?" Gundhrold's eyes flashed. "Really, Hawkness, this is too—"

"We do it today. We go in through Inali's secret passage. Sym an' I have been watchin' it off an' on for the past week now, an' I believe 'tis our best bet."

The griffin dipped his head in acknowledgement. "Fair enough. Now—"

"That's not it. Not all o' us are goin'. Ye've got t' stay behind. The streets are full o' spies and those cursed Shantren, not t' mention the Khelari. It'll be risky enough for us t' sneak through, without tryin' t' smuggle the last griffin in all o' Leira along with us too."

"Surely . . . there must be another way."

So old feather-bag didn't much like when the tables were turned on him. Amos could sympathize. Up until now, this whole wretched mission had been a series of compromises, one after the other. He'd given in, allowed himself to be wheedled, pressured, forced against his better judgement. No more.

"There is no other way. Ye claim this mission is important. Protectin' the Songkeeper is no less so, an' I won't risk her safety by havin' ye along. Come now, is it so painful t' admit that I'm right?"

There was a long pause, then Gundhrold stiffly admitted. "Every man has his day."

"Well, t'day's mine." Amos propped one booted foot on the wobbly chair he'd vacated earlier and rested his forearm on his knee. "We do this my way, or not at all."

A heavy tread sounded behind her, but Birdie did not lift her head. She sat on the top step of the staircase, Artair's sword resting in her lap, the blade wrapped in fresh strips of cloth and sheathed in its scabbard. She recognized the voice in his melody even before Amos spoke.

"Why, lass? Why risk it all? Why become *this*?"

The why of anything was always important, but that didn't mean it was always simple. She had only just finished puzzling it out in her own mind. Or nearly finished, rather. It was too complex to explain. If the peddler did not understand now, then he never would.

How could *Hawkness* ever grasp what it meant to be told you were worthless, only to discover that both a gift and a curse had been thrust upon you? To know that your only value rested in a power you did not understand, could not control, were not sure really belonged to you? To know that the only one who held the answers to your family's fate had vowed to destroy you and sent soldiers to hunt you down?

No, such things could not be explained.

Her hands were trembling again. The awareness drifted to the forefront of her mind, and she glanced down at them, willing them to be still. So small they seemed beside Artair's sword and the weight of the responsibility that rested on her shoulders.

Therein lay her answer.

"Because I must."

The staircase creaked and groaned as Amos plopped at her side and heaved a deep sigh. "Ye know, lass, Gundhrold an' the others, they'll talk largely o' destiny an' purpose an' how Emhran's singing wove the way o' the world, an' mayhap what they say is true. Sometimes it does feel like there's a path laid before yer feet an' there's naught t' do but follow it. But right now, as far as I'm concerned, it's all a boatload o' hogwash. All I want is for ye t' be safe an' happy. So I'll ask ye now an' never again, is *this* what ye want?"

Want? No, this was what she *needed*.

She leveraged up to her feet with the aid of the sword and straightened the red tunic and fringed leather breeches she had borrowed from the Saari—threadbare now and weather worn, as she was beginning to feel.

The peddler's eyes drilled into her, and she knew he would not be satisfied until he had received an answer.

"It's who I am, Amos."

26

The first notion that crossed Ky's mind as his eyes blinked open and his vision began to clear, was that he was parched and his head throbbed like he had taken a sling-bullet to the base of his skull. His throat felt drier than the Vituain Desert after a sandstorm. With a groan, he tried to sit up, but his body refused to cooperate.

"Easy there, laddy-boyo."

The second notion was that Paddy seemed to have grown three heads. It took Ky a good moment of blinking and staring and blinking again at his friend's freckled face, to realize that the second and third heads belonged to Meli and Syd.

"Hey," he mumbled. He tried to lift a hand in greeting, but Meli had latched onto his arm. "How long have I been out?"

"Two—three days, mayhap? Whew, laddy-boyo, you gave us quite the scare. Didn't he, Syd?" Paddy elbowed the boy, eliciting a solemn nod. He swung back to Ky. "It's good to see you awake again. You're the last of 'em, you know. The last taken sick. It's a bit of a wonder, really."

Ky just grunted and let his head fall back to the straw pallet. *The last taken sick*. That was one distinction he was happy to have, so long as it meant the Underground was safe.

"*That* would be thanks to me, bucko my boyo." Migdon shuffled into view on his left, face drawn in a scowl as usual, but with a smile showing behind his eyes. "Don't you go giving credit where credit's not due. You can't imagine the number of favors I had to call in—even promise—in order to get you lot that precious remedy. You're welcome, by the way. Pretty sure this makes us even though, so don't go expecting anything else."

"Sure, Mig." Ky had to force his mouth to form the words. Even grinning left him strangely drained. "We're even."

"Good . . . because I hate being beholden to anyone. Makes me feel so terribly low."

"Don't care much for it myself." Cade sauntered into the room. "But even the best of us find ourselves in debt on occasion." He dismissed Paddy and the young ones with a jerk of his head, seized the overturned crate Ky had been using as a chair before he fell sick, and dragged it to his side. Maybe it was the fever, maybe it was just Ky's throbbing headache, but the scraping of the wood against the stone floor seemed to drag on and on, the sound grating against his already raw nerves. He gritted his teeth against the pain flaring behind his eyes.

Cade sat on the crate, one ankle propped on his knee, clad in a bronze breastplate and pauldrons over chainmail—similar in craftsmanship to the armor Jirkar and the other dwarves had worn. He gave a tightlipped smile that didn't quite reach his eyes. "And I do owe you, Ky, though you didn't hear it from me. Encouraging us to leave the Underground and come here was the right thing to do, and you stuck to it and made it happen. That counts for something. Just mind you don't defy me again."

Ky just blinked. Of all the ways he had imagined this sort of conversation playing out, Cade expressing gratitude for his actions in Kerby hadn't made the list. Every instinct told him that this had to be a trick of some kind. Cade wasn't the sort to admit to being in the wrong.

Not unless he was working up to something big.

"The Underground was a good start. We survived, saved a few people, hopefully gave the Khelari a few sleepless nights. Maybe even irritated the Takhran. But I wasn't thinking big enough, Ky. *We* weren't thinking big enough."

And there it was, that magic word—*big.*

Ky glanced at Migdon, but the dwarf refused to look at him. "What do you mean to do?"

"Do?" Cade spread his arms wide, and the smile on his face struck Ky as both genuine and deadly. "Anything . . . and everything. Migdon's been telling me all about the offensives these Adulnae have planned for the Khelari. The dark armors don't stand a chance. I mean to see to it." Some of the levity bled from his face and tone. "You know, Ky, I could do with a new right hand man. Paddy might be a hard worker, but that's all he is—a worker. He's no Dizzier. He doesn't think outside the box. He doesn't *make* things happen. I need you."

Steal Paddy's place? Wasn't it bad enough that his friend *thought* he had come to do just that? No, he'd sooner be thrown to the hounds. He started to object, but Cade stood abruptly to his feet and toed the crate back into the center of the room.

"Think it over. We've got work to do." There was a jaunty spring to Cade's step as he strode away, and once the door shut behind him, Ky could hear him whistling out in the courtyard.

Of all the raw breaks …

For the first time in five years, they were free of the Khelari, set up in a decent place, with a real roof over their head. Now, Cade wanted to throw it all away and chase after the dark soldiers again.

"Easy there, bucko." Migdon broke in. "A sour face like that is liable to stick with you."

"What did you tell him, Mig? What did you promise?"

"Nothing much. Only a firsthand look at the biggest battle of our time . . . providing the Khelari attack here. Which, according to all the brilliant Xanthen strategists, they won't, and that's good, because we haven't got more than a token force. Only thing this place is good for is warding off an invasion from the coast, and if there's one thing the Takhran's probably kicking himself about right now, it's not investing in building a navy years ago. We're too far north to be of any strategic value in an attack from the south and that's where the Khelari have been amassing their forces." He blew a heavy sigh through his lips. "Never fear, bucko, *your* people are safe."

The dwarf fell silent then, and Ky was only too grateful for the chance to wrap his aching head around his chaotic thoughts. He could still hear the fevered excitement in Cade's voice. He had fought and bled and braved Cade's wrath time and again to get the Underground here. He'd thought he was bringing them to safety.

But now that Cade was all-fired excited about it, he couldn't help having his doubts. The Underground leader would not be content to sit in safety when there was any chance—no matter how slim—of striking back at the dark soldiers.

Even if it meant wading into a war zone.

Snow gusted and whipped in Birdie's face, driving the bitter chill through the weave of her clothes and into her bones. She hugged the woolen cloak about her shoulders and kept the hood pulled low over her forehead as they emerged from the tangle of streets to peer around the corner of a building at the deep fosse gaping before the outer wall of the Takhran's fortress. Night had fallen, and firepots burned on the ramparts, glinting off armor and weapons.

Birdie touched Amos's shoulder. "Sentries ..."

"Aye lass, stay low an' they won't see us." Squatting, he shuffled back from the corner and gestured for them to gather around. Frosted breath puffed from his mouth with each word. "Inali's secret way is concealed in the boulders heaped at the base o' the mountain, just the other side o' the fosse. We'll go two at a time—Inali an' Birdie first, Sym an' I will cover. Stick t' the shadows. Be silent . . . an' Emhran help us."

His eyes fell on her at that last bit, but since he'd spoken in a whisper, Birdie couldn't tell if that was a trace of irony she detected in his tone or not. Either way, it seemed a good enough watchword. After all, she'd embarked on this mission at the Master Singer's behest, hadn't she?

She repeated the phrase silently as she followed Inali in spurts of movement to the edge off the fosse, down the side, and through knee deep snow at the bottom. It was impossible to move silently, but the keening wind helped cover any noise they made, and no alarm had sounded by the time they reached the boulders and ducked through a crack in the earth.

Birdie found herself standing in a darkness unlike anything she had ever encountered before. It was so thick and oppressive, she could practically feel it crawling across her skin. They were protected from the wind and the snow, but the air had a sense of stale chillness to it—the chill of a place that is never truly warm.

"We will wait for Hawkness before lighting the torch."

Inali spoke in a whisper, but his voice still sent faint echoes running ahead of them. Standing there, shivering and blind, straining her ears for any sign that Amos and Sym had been discovered, Birdie was once again struck by the void caused by his lack of song. It prompted her to speak, to be bolder than she normally dared.

"Why did you fail, Inali?"

His sharply intaken breath revealed just how much of a blow it was. "Because . . . I was not to be the Songkeeper. I was bound to fail. Fated. But you are, little one. You are not like me."

Measured footsteps sounded behind, and both Amos and Sym's songs heralded their approach. A moment later, the peddler squeezed through the crack and paused just long enough to catch his breath before speaking. "Right, let's move. We've a long night ahead o' us, an' lots o' ground t' cover." The clack of flint and steel rang out and a moment later, a spark leapt to a torch in Amos's hand, casting shadows across the rock surrounding them and revealing a narrow tunnel winding away before their feet. "Ye know where t' go, Inali?"

"I could not forget if I tried." A twinge of bitterness filled Inali's voice. "But the little Songkeeper can walk beside me to set your mind at rest and help me if I err. I walk by memory alone, but she will be able to follow the melody to its source."

Amos offered the torch, but would not release it until Inali met his gaze. "I may not be familiar with this path, Inali, but I know the dangers o' these tunnels. Beware if any harm comes t' the lass—"

"I know. You will hold me personally responsible. Believe me, I have no desire to add to my bloodguilt." Grasping the torch in one hand, he swept a courtly bow in Birdie's direction and motioned her forward.

Summoning all her courage, she turned her back on the entrance and walked on at his side, painfully aware that each step took her deeper into the tangled paths below Mount Eiphyr.

27

Long after the rest of the Underground was asleep, the uneasy feeling in the pit of his stomach drove Ky from his pallet and out onto the snow crusted battlements of the keep. The crisp night air blew soothing breaths across his aching forehead. He broke into a jog, running twice around the walkway before finally coming to a stop in the middle of the bridge that spanned the gap between the twin keeps.

He bent over, pulling long, clean breaths into his winded lungs, enjoying the burst of energy and adrenaline flowing through his veins, driving the restlessness away. Maybe he had just been lying abed too long. Being laid up for any amount of time never had sat well with him.

"Oi, Ky." Paddy crested the bridge, puffing beneath the weight of a bronze breastplate and chainmail tunic. He leaned against the ramparts beside Ky and tipped his head back, causing his plumed helmet to wobble. "You looked like you were about to run away. What's got you so stirred up? Ready to be shed o' this place already?"

Ky glanced at him out of the corner of his eye. To all appearances, it was a friendly enough question, but something about it struck him as sour. "I don't run away, Paddy. You know that."

"Shure, I know it. Reckon Cade knows it now too." Paddy squinted and bobbed his head back and forth with a grimace. "I might've just happened to overhear what Cade said to you t'other day, about you bein' his right hand man." He huffed a laugh. "Here I am, followin' orders like a good little lad—never defied him once—and he picks you to *make things happen*."

"Paddy, I—"

"No need to explain." Paddy blew on his hands and rubbed them together. "Reckon you were always just better at that sort of thing than me."

"Nah, I'm not, an' I'm not goin' to do it, either." Just saying the words out loud helped him to reason it out in his own mind. "Cade an' I, we just can't see eye to eye. Look, I wanted to get the Underground to safety, an' we've done that. Now, I reckon it's time for . . . something else. Don't really know what yet though."

Ky emphasized his words with a shrug and rested his elbows against the battlement, looking out over the shallow pass almost thirty feet below. From here, the sliver of moon provided light enough for a good view of the white stone road that ran from the Caran's stronghold to the coast through the pass beneath the bridge. It also glinted off the armor of dwarf sentries patrolling the ramparts of the north keep and along the earthen breastwork that carved across the road to provide advance defenses for Siranos.

All still. All quiet.

Ky cast a sideways glance at Paddy. "So what's with the get up?"

Paddy struck a warrior's pose. "Dandy, isn't it?" His face scrunched in a grin, and he tugged the wobbling helmet from his head and shook it in Ky's face. "Save your laughter, laddy-boyo. Accordin' to Cade, this might just save your life, and on sentry duty, no less. I swear, he thinks we're his own min-i-ature army." He plunked the helmet down on the edge of the battlement.

Ky grinned. "Now who's never defied Cade?"

"I know." A crease formed between his eyes. "I feel such a *rebel*."

Something whizzed through the air, struck the helmet with a metallic clang, and sent it flying from the battlement to bounce on the stones at their feet. Instantly, Ky flung himself down with his back to the battlement and hastily worked the sling from around his waist. Paddy dropped beside him, looking as startled as Ky felt.

"'Twas an arrow . . . I saw it when it struck."

Sling loaded, Ky pushed up into a crouch and peered over at the silent battlements of the north keep. He couldn't see the dwarf sentries anymore, didn't hear any shouts of alarm, either.

"That could've been my head!"

"Paddy, shh!" He eased around the edge of one of the battlements. Where before, he had seen only the white road stretching away into the moonlight, he now saw a dark mass of armored men pouring up over the breastwork into the roadway and drawing up in rank and file. An arrow zipped past his face and skipped off the opposite battlement.

He ducked beside Paddy. "Bad news. Dark soldiers are here."

"I thought this was the one place in *all* of Leira they weren't likely to come to."

"Yeah, well, guess nobody told them that. Takhran must've gotten himself a fleet somewhere. They're coming from the coast, they've already taken the breastwork, an' they've got archers posted, pickin' off anythin' that moves."

"Right." Paddy blew a sharp breath through pursed lips. "Right. Guess we'd better spread the word then."

"But quietly. The more of us we can get in position before *they* know the game's up, the better. I'll take the dwarves. You rouse Cade. See if you can't put together a warm Underground welcome for 'em."

"Shure thing. Watch yourself."

With a rattle of armor, Paddy was off and away. Ky just hoped he would keep his head down. Bent almost double, Ky ran up and over the crest of the bridge, swung over the battlement onto the wall-top of the north keep and nearly stumbled over a body.

He steadied himself with a hand against the battlement and picked his way past another body beside the steps leading down into the courtyard. He paused before the door most likely to lead into the commanding officer's quarters, then eased it open and slipped within. A sputtering fire provided just enough light to see by. On a straw pallet beside the hearth, an old dwarf sprawled beneath a mound of blankets, snoring loud enough that Ky could have slammed the door without being heard.

He tapped the dwarf's shoulder and jumped back as he roared awake, reaching for the mace propped beside his pallet. Curly gray hair and a beard the color and texture of an unshorn sheep stuck out in all directions around a face that most closely resembled a battering ram.

"Khelari, sir, we're under attack." Ky threw in the dwarvish version of a salute for good measure, hoping to avoid the lengthy explanation of who he was and what he was doing here. Given the way the old fellow was staring about with those rheumy eyes of his, he would probably be none the wiser.

"Khelari, you say? Here?" The old dwarf didn't wait for more than that. Shedding blankets, he stumbled to the door, flung it open, and bellowed for his troops. "To the parapets! We're under attack!"

The echoes of his voice had scarce died away, when the Keep exploded with noise. Bells clanged, followed by the thud of rushing feet and clattering armor as dwarves burst from the barracks and raced to the parapets. A moment later came the zip and crackle of arrows spattering the courtyard and the shouts of the wounded.

And there went the element of surprise …

"Don't dally, beardling. Hand me my mace."

Stunned into obedience, Ky caught up the weapon and passed it to him. Already fully clad and armored, the old dwarf paused only to grab a plumed helmet from a stand beside the door and then marched out into the courtyard, muttering.

"More trouble to take this stuff off than leave it on, at my age. Always be prepared, that's what they say, right, beardling?" He must have figured out Ky wasn't at his side when he didn't get an answer, because a moment later, he was back and gripping Ky's arm. "What'd I tell you about dallying? To the parapets, beardling, to the parapets!"

"Yessir!" Ky saluted and broke free, racing ahead of the old dwarf. For all his intensity, the fellow didn't move very fast.

Up on the walkway, he dodged through the commotion of dwarves running hither and thither, manning all sorts of strange contraptions mounted on the keep walls—crossbows that fired a rapid round of bolts quicker than an archer could draw and fire, miniature sling catapults that launched pouchfuls of fist sized stones at the enemy clogging the roadway—all with deadly effect. Again and again, groups of Khelari with long scaling ladders were repulsed before they could even draw near the base of the bluff beneath the keep. But all too often, Khelari arrows rained death down upon the parapets as well and left Ky wishing he had one of those dwarf-made breastplates and chainmail shirts.

He might've even settled for a plumed helmet.

After one such volley, Ky found a protected perch where the bridge met the keep and took his time singling out the Khelari archers and picking them off. Sling-bullets to the noggin might not be fatal if the targets were wearing helmets, but getting knocked around sure wouldn't improve their aim any.

And Ky was counting on that.

Migdon hadn't been joking when he'd said that this was only a token force of Adulnae. There were barely enough of them to defend the parapets, and most looked to be at least as old as the commander Ky had woken, if not older.

He glanced over at the south keep, where from the sound of things, the Underground runners kept up a steady stream of arrows and stones flying from behind the battlements. Hopefully Cade and Paddy had thought to get the little ones safely hidden away before launching their defense. At least the Khelari were concentrating their attack on the north keep, pulling the heavy fire of the defenders toward the front …

Away from the pass.

A tap on the shoulder brought him spinning around, loaded sling ready.

"Easy, bucko my boyo. Little jumpy, eh?" Migdon scowled at him. "Dark armors are bunching by the breastwork, look like they're fixing to make a concentrated rush through the pass. My guess is they hope to break through and not bother with conquering Siranos."

Ky snapped off another shot. "So, you got a plan?"

"'Course. We've been letting them draw our fire forward. By now, they probably think they've got us duped. We let them rush into the pass, wait until they're sitting nice and pretty beneath us, and rain fire down on their heads." He tilted his head to indicate a pair of steaming buckets beside his feet and tossed a pair of thick leather gloves at Ky. "Boiling pitch and flaming arrows should just about do the trick, don't you think?"

Working with Migdon and a dozen dwarves, Ky ran buckets of boiling pitch out onto the center of the bridge and placed them beside dozens of murder holes that had been concealed by the snow at the base of the battlements. The holes were small enough that a fellow couldn't fall through, but he might twist an ankle if he wasn't paying attention.

By the time they finished, the snow beneath the buckets of pitch had melted, leaving them sitting in pools of water, and the Khelari were already on the move. Through a gap in the battlements, Ky watched as the dark-armored soldiers bore down upon them, the noise of their charge covered by the ongoing attack on the north keep.

"Almost here," he warned.

"Patience, bucko."

The archers fell into position, crouching with arrows on the string, firepots at their feet. Fifty feet out now, then twenty, then ten.

"Now!" Migdon's voice rang out.

Ky seized a bucket and carefully upended it over the murder hole, while dwarves all along the line did the same. Hissing pitch sloshed out around the edges, narrowly missing his feet. Shouts and cries rang out below, broken a moment later by the snap and whine of arrows and then the roar of flames. He poured out a second and third bucket and was reaching for a fourth, but Migdon stopped him, a note of satisfaction in his voice.

"Save it. They're on the run."

Peeling the gloves from his hands, Ky peered over the battlement into a blazing inferno. Horrible screams rose from the pass, and he could just make out dark shapes writhing in the flames. The rest of the Khelari scattered up the roadway, back toward the earthen breastwork, stragglers batting at flames that had latched onto articles of pitch covered clothing.

Bile rose in his throat at the sight, and he touched his forehead to the cool stone. He couldn't imagine a more horrible way to die. It had the intended effect though. Within the hour, the Khelari called off the attack and retreated behind the earthen breastwork as the first glimmers of dawn broke over the eastern horizon. Ky sank down with his back to the battlement, stretching his legs out across the bridge, and wrapped his sling around his waist. His pouch hung limp from his belt, sling-bullets long since spent.

Lodged in the skulls of many a Khelari, as Migdon would have it. Hopefully that would be enough to earn him a new supply from the Adulnae armory, but now didn't seem like the right time to ask. The dwarf paced back and forth, hands clasped behind his back, skirting Ky's legs at each pass without so much as a glance.

"How in blazes did those cursed Khelari dogs get here?" The old commander puffed out into the middle of the bridge and halted in Migdon's path. Glaring did nothing to reduce his resemblance to a battering ram. Ky thought it almost heightened it. "And how was it our top scout had no notion they were coming? If it hadn't been for beardling here"—he jerked his head toward Ky—"we would have been taken by surprise."

"Beardling?" Migdon snorted. "You two have met?"

"Briefly." Ky pushed up to his feet, grateful for an excuse to stretch his limbs after a night spent ducking behind cover, and nodded at the old dwarf. "We skipped the introductions."

"In that case, this is my uncle, Commander Thallus Liturgis Xyamphene Noonan." Migdon turned back to the blustering dwarf. "And tramping across the entire country of Leira isn't a pleasure stroll. I can only cover so much ground in each trip. Near as I can figure it, the Takhran must have made a deal with the Langorians. We know he didn't build a fleet himself, and they were already supplying him with a tribute of slaves. Makes proper sense."

"We did it!" Cade pushed up the slope of the bridge from the south keep, Paddy at his heels, both elated and grinning. From the looks of the empty quiver strapped to his back, he'd spent every last arrow on the attackers. "We held them off."

"For the time being," Migdon grunted. "But they'll be back."

"Then we'll send them running again with their tails between their legs." Cade grounded his bow with a thump that drew all eyes to him. "I've been waiting years for the chance to strike a blow against them that will be remembered. I'm not about to lose heart."

"Huh." Commander Thallus set his hands on his hips and eyed Cade up and down, blinking his watery eyes. "Who is this young upstart? I like him."

Migdon shook his head. "Too many of them, too few of us. You know what they say, 'The only shame in being outmatched is in being too afraid to admit it.' We'll hold out as long as we may, but we should send word to the Caran and warn him that a second force will be coming down from the north once Siranos falls . . . and it will fall."

"To your negativity, maybe, nephew. Who do you propose takes the message?'

But Migdon was already walking away, waving a jaunty farewell. "See you lot in a week or so. With any luck, we'll all still be alive."

His words sapped the last traces of victory from the air. With the fading of his footsteps, the group dispersed. Cade and Commander Thallus split off to visit the armory and restock, but Ky set his steps toward the south keep, moving at a determined pace that worked the crick from his back and the tightness from his legs. He could always resupply later. For now, he wanted to check on the runners and make sure that Meli and Syd had come safely through the night.

Paddy caught up and spun around to face him, walking backward alongside. "I know that look, laddy-boyo, an' it doesn't bode well for Cade's little army." He flung up both hands, forcing Ky to a halt. "What're you thinking?"

"I don't know." Ky gnawed at his lip. A fight to the inevitable but glorious death in the defense of their homeland was well and good for the dwarves—Cade too, if that was his choice—but what about the young ones who had no choice in the matter? "I think it's time we figured a way out."

28

How long they had been marching through the tunnels, Birdie could not say. It might have been hours. It might have been days. She was just grateful Inali knew the way. Already the tunnel had split and converged and become a dozen different tunnels half a dozen times. A weariness deeper than exhaustion and murkier than despair settled over her. She stumbled more than once, and it was all she could do to set one foot in front of the other.

Inali glanced down at her, torchlight glinting off his spectacles and highlighting the concern in his eyes. He leaned close to whisper in her ear. "You feel it, little Songkeeper?"

She nodded but could not speak. With each step, she felt more vividly the throbbing pulse of two distinct melodies warring with one another in the depths of the earth. Or was it in the depths of her own heart? The melodies surrounded her, seeming as much a part of her as of her surroundings, as though they would overwhelm her and she would lose herself in that terrifying, rushing tide.

Behind, Amos and Sym maintained a stolid silence, marching with weapons in hand, ready to spring into battle if aught went wrong. Birdie reached for the grip of Artair's sword, belted at her waist. Beneath the cloth, she felt the coolness of the blade. Somehow that icy touch helped clear her mind and relieve the pressure in her ears.

"Stop!" Inali hissed. He seized her arm, preventing her from taking another step. "Do you hear that?" He tapped his foot on the ground, producing a hollow thump. The earth seemed to shiver beneath Birdie's feet. "It's a false floor. Very thin. Could collapse beneath us. We have to spread out. Let me go first and Birdie next. Hawkness, you should be last."

"Aye, but be careful." Amos ran his hand through his hair, making it stand up about his head like a loaded fireflower. "Bilgewater! What

I wouldn't give for a bit o' rope."

Arms spread out, Inali took slow, shuffling steps that sounded as if he were walking on a drum. After he had gone about fifteen feet, he beckoned for Birdie to follow. She crept after him. Another ten feet beyond, he came to a stop and thumped his foot on the ground. "Solid here."

She hurried across the last bit, only too anxious to have solid earth beneath her feet again, and then glanced back. Sym was half-way across, spears rattling in the quiver on her back as she moved with the same, light graceful step she had used in the spear dance, while Amos fidgeted with his dirk on the far side.

An ominous crack sounded out.

"Sym, hurry!" Inali shouted, but his voice was swallowed by a deep rumble, and the section of false floor disappeared, taking Sym with it, leaving only a gaping hole behind.

Dust clogged the air. The torch sputtered in Inali's hands. Birdie's ears rang with the distant echo of falling rocks. She stumbled to the edge, only to be thrust aside by Inali as he dropped to his knees and held the torch out over the hole. "No . . . no . . . Sym!"

"I can see her," Amos's voice rang out. Birdie could just make out his form, vague and shadowy in the haze of dust that the torch could not penetrate, as he knelt beside the hole. "Only about fifteen feet down or so. The floor looks t' have collapsed into another tunnel. She's . . . she's not movin'."

Inali groaned and staggered to his feet, blinking behind his spectacles as he surveyed the tunnel. "We . . . we . . . need to . . . head on. They'll have heard the noise. This place will be swarming in minutes."

Birdie blocked his path. "I thought you said this was a secret passage."

"Yes, secret. Hidden, little used, but that doesn't mean nobody else knows about it. And there are worse things in the tunnels below than Khelari." He seized her wrist and tried to drag her after him, but she twisted away and ran back to the edge. "I must get you out of here."

"Not without Amos!"

"Hawkness, *please,*" Inali pleaded. "Tell her to leave. There's no time for anything else. You said yourself that her safety was of the utmost importance. Believe me, if I could stay here with Sym I would, but I must get Birdie out of here before it's too late."

"He's right, lass." Amos's voice sounded cold and hard as flint. "I can't get t' ye across this mess, but I just might be able t' get down t' help Sym, an' I have t' try that. It's best ye go on without me."

"No, Amos, no!"

Inali's good arm settled around her shoulders, wrenching her away from the edge and down the passage. She fought against him, but his grip only tightened, keeping her pinned against his side so she could not reach her sword hilt.

"Hawkness!" Inali called over his shoulder, grunting with the strain of holding her back. "Once you get Sym, stick to the right hand passages. That should lead you back to us."

"I'll catch up . . . keep her safe, lad."

Those words, spoken in a quiet, sad sort of voice so unlike Amos's usual hearty bluster struck Birdie to the core. It was all she could do to keep the tears that welled in her eyes from spilling down her cheeks. Unresisting now, she followed Inali through the maze of passages, moving at a half jog up and down steep paths that left her breathless and Inali clutching his wounded shoulder, until they struck a wider passage with smooth walls and flagstone paving. Inali stopped finally in front of an arched doorway covered by a dark hanging, swept the hanging aside with the elbow of his torch hand, and motioned for her to enter.

"We're here, little Songkeeper."

Birdie stepped from the dark of the passage into a cavernous room lit by countless blazing firepots. It had a high vaulted ceiling and massive arches and columns carved from living rock. Dark blue and silver draperies with a single crimson teardrop emblazoned in the middle hung from the ceiling at intervals, bound in such a way that they twisted and curled like waterfalls in solid form.

In the center of the room stood a ring of figures clad in blue and silver robes. A low chanting filled the air, like the distant rumble of thunder before the advance of a storm. It stole the air from Birdie's lungs and seized her limbs with an icy grip.

This . . . this was wrong.

Her hand went to her sword hilt, but she did not draw it yet, just backed toward the door. Only to bump into Inali. She twisted to the side, out of his reach. "What is this?" A glance over her shoulder revealed that the robed figures had broken from their ring and were moving toward her. "Where are we?"

The Saari warrior just stared at her with an eerily calm expression on his face, eyes half concealed behind his spectacles, half concealed behind a glassy mask all their own. "I should think that would be apparent by now, little Songkeeper. These are the Shantren." With his good hand, he fished in his collar and pulled out the gold chain and clay bead he always wore. He crushed it into a puff of dust between his fingers, revealing a crimson teardrop jewel.

The talav.

"*We* are the Shantren."

Already Amos could hear the baying of hounds in the distance and the clatter of swiftly approaching iron shod feet. Khelari, as luck would have it. Far better than monsters. Muttering a prayer for their luck to hold, he dropped into the hole where the false floor had caved in, managing by some miracle—or rather, a marvelous display of skill, as he preferred to think it—to land clear of the debris and scramble to Sym's side.

She moaned and stirred before he even reached her, but it was only with his help that she managed to sit. Judging from the hand she pressed to her side and the taut expression on her face, she had broken at least a rib or two. A cut on her forehead dripped blood into her eyes, giving her a wild, almost savage look.

"Easy there, lass, put yer arm around my shoulder." Hefting her weight, he helped her stand and then hastily collected the spears that had tumbled from her quiver in her fall. "Best we were movin'."

But the boggswoggling lass resisted his tug, even though she swayed on her feet and looked about ready to fall over. "Inali . . . Birdie . . . where are they?"

"Gone ahead, an' we're tryin' t' catch up, just by a slightly different route."

"Do you know where to go?"

"Aye." He stumbled over the rubble, turned back to help her cross, then set his shoulder beneath hers. "Inali said t' stick t' the right, so"—he ducked down the first right-hand passage he saw—"we'll stick t' the right."

It was far from easy going. Even though he was practically carrying Sym, Amos kept to a jog down the steep corridors and around narrow bends, spurred on as much by the sounds of pursuit that seemed to be coming from all sides now, as by the thought of his lass here below Mount Eiphyr without him. But there was a sense of wrongness to their route that gnawed at him, though he couldn't have said whether it came from his own heightened sense of alertness or some hazy recollection from his previous journey through the tunnels.

After a good hour of running, he puffed to a stop in front of the next fork in the tunnel and set his back to the wall to keep from falling over. His legs quivered and specks of light darted across his vision. Sym started to gasp a question, but he flung up a hand and managed to silence her before she could distract him from listening . . . and sniffing.

Bilges, what a stench!

Ash, rotten eggs, and stale meat—the place reeked of it. And it wasn't the first time he had smelled it either. Cold sweat trailed down his back. He shoved away from the wall. "We need t' go—"

Something moved within the right-hand tunnel. Something *large.* He heard the rasp of clawed feet against rock, the scrape of a hefty bulk against the sides of the tunnel, and the shriek of an indrawn, heated breath.

All this, his mind registered in an instant.

"Down, Sym! Down!"

He yanked her to the ground and dragged her away from the tunnel, shielding her body with his. Just in time. A spout of flame shot out, singing the back of his head. The heat sizzled on down his back, but he rolled away, putting out the sparks, and back up to his feet, dirk in hand.

For once, it seemed a worthless weapon.

Out of the tunnel came a beast of nightmare. To be sure, it had stalked his dreams since that fateful night when he first braved the horrors of the tunnels, but night terrors were nothing compared to seeing such a monster again in the flesh. Three heads joined at the shoulders above a massive muscled chest. In the middle, it had the head of a lion, flanked by the head of a long-horned goat on one side and a fanged serpent on the other. Hunched back with knobs of spine jutting like blades. Long, strong forelimbs. Short, squat hindlimbs. Body covered in patches of scales, hide, and tufts of fur.

The goat head bleated.

Amos would have died before admitting that the bleat of a goat could sound menacing, but the utter wrongness of the sound from such a beast made his hackles rise. Cursing their luck, he carefully maneuvered in front of Sym, giving her time to regain her breath and her feet. "Get up. Slowly. Walk t' the end o' the tunnel. Then run an' don't look back."

"Sigurd's mane!" Her hissed oath echoed from the walls. "What do you take me for?"

"Bilges! Just do what I say."

The beast's eyes settled on him. All six of them. And he didn't need a Songkeeper's abilities to know the creature's blind, rabid, unreasoning hate. Fire smoldered in the lion's throat, and black venom oozed from the serpent's fangs to sizzle against the tunnel floor.

Right. Avoid the fire. Don't get bitten. Steer clear of the horns.

Simple.

Chin lowered, he stalked toward the monster on stiff legs. "Aye, beastie, over here. That's it. Look at me, ye foul, putrid, malodorous spawn o' the Pit—"

With a roar and a burst of flame, the beast sprang at him. He dove sideways, narrowly missing the sweep of the goat's horns, slammed into the tunnel wall, and stumbled to regain his balance. There was a lot of power in those squat hind legs. Like springs. Probably the goat in it.

He'd have to keep that in mind.

The beast checked itself and spun around. A risked glance over Amos's shoulder confirmed that Sym was up, but *not* running for her life as instructed. Fool girl even had a spear in her hand.

"Hawkness!"

Her shout brought him reeling around just in time to dodge a snap of the lion's massive jaws. Bloody monster was fast. He slashed away the serpent's head and swung out of reach of the lion, but the goat rammed into his side. His feet left the earth, and he crashed onto his back beneath the beast's feet. The breath burst from his lungs in a groan.

Scrabbling claws tore at his legs and the rock beneath. He jerked out of the way as the serpent's fangs came down only inches from his throat. With a yell, he brought his dirk around with all the force he could muster and hacked through the serpent's neck. The severed head landed, mouth gaping, eyes glazing over, on his chest, and he wrenched away from the venom leaking from the fangs.

On hands and knees, he scrambled away from the beast. But not fast enough. It pounced on him, knocked him flat. His chin slammed against the ground, rattling all the bones in his head. The dirk flew from his hand. With a swipe of a clawed paw, the monster rolled him over on his back so that he stared straight up into the yawning gulf of the lion's blazing throat and read his death in its eyes.

Claws sank like barbed knives into his flesh. The beast's weight settled on his chest until he felt sure his ribs would crack beneath its bulk. Lungs heaving for air, body seizing against the pain, Amos managed to work one arm loose and reached out as far as he could, fingers groping for his dirk.

Gray tinged the edge of his vision.

Distantly, he heard a Saari battle cry, and out of the corner of one eye, he saw Sym leap into the fray. Her spear thrust clattered off the goat's horns. It batted her aside with a twist of its head. She landed hard.

No dirk met his searching fingers.

No trace of metal. Not even a bloody rock to bludgeon the beast to death.

Naught but a scaled head.

Without a breath for thought, Amos seized it, ignoring the burn of venom across his fingertips, and drove the serpent's fangs into the lion's neck. The beast roared and flames curled from its mouth but sputtered out before reaching Amos's face. He shut his eyes against the blast of heat.

A sickening *thunk*.

Then another. The beast's body shuddered, swayed, and collapsed on top of him. Amos just lay there, groaning, almost smothered beneath the weight. Then a hand seized his wrist and hauled him backwards, and that awoke the fight in him again. He shoved and kicked until he was free, then collapsed with his back to the wall.

Sym leaned over, clutching a hand to her side and breathing in short, pained gasps. Two of her spears protruded from the three-headed beast's side, driven in nearly half their length. Took quite a bit of force to do that.

Amos squinted up at her. "Worried about me, eh?"

She glared at him. Only a moment's glance, then her eyes flickered back to the beast and the tunnels. There was the slightest hint of frenzy in her voice when she spoke. "We should be moving. There may be more—"

"Oh there's more all right, but not here." Amos gritted his teeth as he did a mental survey of his injuries. Nothing life threatening or even incapacitating. But that didn't mean it didn't bloody well hurt. "Not here, or we'd be dead already. Sit an' rest a moment. Ye'll need it."

She nodded her chin toward the monster. "What was that?"

"A chimera is—I think—its proper name. Boggswogglin' nasty is what I call it."

"We have legends about such beasts in the desert."

"Legends." Amos swiped the back of his hand across his mouth and chin and brought it up to survey the blood. "Ye know, just once, I'd like a *good*, happy legend t' turn out t' be true. Why does it always have t' be the foul ones?"

Sym chuckled. "Don't know if I'd call you *foul*, Hawkness."

"Oh, so ye believe the legends then? 'bout time, if I do say so."

She snorted at that, but there was a hint of laughter in it. That was good, that was. Because worse horrors were yet to come. False bravery would prove just that—false. But if a man or woman could look death in the face and march boldly to meet it with a grin on his or her lips, well, that was the only true defense a mind had against complete and total despair.

With a groan, he shoved up to his feet and skirted the beast's carcass in search of his dirk. He found it lodged beneath the goat's head. With a toe, he nudged the head aside and then reached down and scooped up his dirk.

"Well, then, shall we be off?"

Before Sym could reply, three soldiers in dark armor and a hound burst from the right-hand tunnel.

29

"Inali, you must tell me why." Birdie clung to the rusted bars of her cell, hands torn from pulling on the rough metal. Blood seeped from a hound bite on her leg and trickled down the leather fringe of her leggings to leave a trail of crimson drops that glistened in the light of the firepot on the opposite wall. "Why do this?"

The Saari warrior just ducked his head and continued pacing outside her cell. It stood in a row of honeycomb shaped chambers carved from the rock and concealed by heavy draperies from the Hall of the Shantren, the cavernous room where Inali had led her to her capture.

Her head throbbed with the constant pulse of the discordant melody that emanated from this place, and every muscle in her body strained with the longing to fight . . . or die fighting.

Flight had done her no good.

At Inali's declaration, she had bolted. But mere seconds had passed before a dozen hounds tore at her heels. One sank its teeth into her right leg and brought her down. Another crouched with its jaws poised over her throat. Within moments, her hands were bound and her sword belt torn away. Surrounded by robed figures, she was hustled past a fountain swirling with dark red liquid and the ring of stone benches surrounding it, to this cell, leaving her well and truly caught in the heart of the Takhran's fortress.

In the place of her nightmares.

The horror of it lodged in her chest, and she let her forehead sag against the bars. Better that she had gone down fighting. "Why would you betray us? I need to know."

"You need know nothing." Inali whirled to face her, dusky braids flying about his face in a clatter of clacking beads. "But by Sigurd's mane, you *should* be thanking me. I am helping you."

Helping?

Bitterness welled in her throat at the notion, and she longed to scream and rail at him for the coward and liar and traitor that he was. But somehow, she managed to restrain her tongue and let him speak unhindered.

"Tell me." Inali snarled, face inches from the bars. "Did *It* spring to your rescue? I warned you. *It* is content to use you and abandon you, but there are greater things here than your Song, little Songkeeper." The wrath eased from his face, replaced by an intense fervor that was no less unsettling. "I saw it in your eyes when I first met you. I knew that you, like me, felt it—the lack of control, the agony of being bound by something greater than yourself, of being used, of being little more than a tool. Believe me, little one, I brought you here so you could be *free*."

Everything within her burned to shout at him, spit in his face, and demand to be released, or at least granted a sword so she could die fighting. But she had come seeking answers too, hadn't she? And Inali, it seemed, was willing to speak.

So she would let him.

"This is freedom?" She dipped her head to the walls of her cell and the bars across the front. "Or will I be free once I take the talav and become one of you?"

"You speak as though it were an evil thing." Inali hooked a finger through the chain about his neck so the jewel dangled close beside her face. "But it is beautiful. Powerful. Strong. Gifted by the Takhran with abilities to bestow upon the wearer. How could such a gift be evil?"

"What sort of abilities?"

"Wondrous gifts! Similar to those of the Songkeepers. But we Shantren are not left idle and drifting, waiting upon the whim of the Song. The talav bestows power *and* control." Inali's eagerness grew as he spoke. "Some are gifted to speak with mute beasts, others with strength in battle, disguise, powers of healing. The cat that Carhartan sent to spy upon you, he was a mimic, gifted to speak and sing in ways you would trust. I am able to see things and fashion them, a gift of the hands, and to fashion things as I *would* see them."

He broke off and rummaged in his satchel, then pulled out the drawing she had seen him working on and held it up to the bars. "Do you not see, little Songkeeper? In the Shantren, all of us are made strong in ourselves. Fear is a thing of the past."

In any other place, the promise of strength would have been tempting. A chance to be free of the fear that hammered in her chest, to set her own course and have the power to pursue it—for Inali to offer such a thing, it was as if he had laid bare her very soul. But here in this cell, in the grip of her enemies, his words simply served as confirmation that he was a liar, a manipulator, and a traitor.

"What of your melody, Inali? You don't have one. Is that a *gift* too?" Her words seemed to catch him off guard, but he gave no answer, and she couldn't bear meeting his eyes any longer. She slid to the ground to relieve the weight from her injured leg. "And what of Sym?"

He pulled back. "That . . . that was not supposed to happen. It was to have been Hawkness who fell, not Sym. I would never have hurt her."

"Yet you, my dear Dah Inali, were incapable of handling her." The quiet voice came from the shadows that lurked beyond the reach of the flickering light. At the sound, Inali instantly fell to one knee, injured arm clasped to his chest. Birdie rose to a crouch and pressed her face against the bars, but could see no sign of the speaker. "Sym Yandel would have seen through you in a moment. Far better to ensure she was out of the way than jeopardize your mission."

"My lord ..." Inali's face had gone pale, and his voice sounded strained. "That was not part of our deal. The raven . . . it brought word . . . you *promised*."

"I recall your promise as well." There was no mistaking the threat in the weighted inflection of the stranger's voice. Out of the shadows he came, a tall man clad in a rich blue robe with a dark silver coat fitted to his frame over chainmail so fine it seemed less armor and more ornament. He bore no weapon, but there was something about him that turned Birdie's blood cold, brought her scrambling to her feet, and whispered *dangerous* in her ear.

The stranger towered over Inali. "Or have you forgotten?"

Gritting his teeth, Inali patted the satchel at his side. "No, my lord, I have not forgotten. It is here, as I promised, and I have brought you the little Songkeeper as well." A hint of eagerness crept back into his tone. "Please, my lord, tell her, as you told me, what the talav can do for her. How it can set her free, bring her strength she has never imagined."

The stranger's gaze lifted, and pale blue eyes beneath dark brows locked on Birdie's. Hair the color of Vituain desert sand swept back from his forehead and fell in waves to his shoulders. A wide silver collar draped over his chest, inlaid with dozens of red crystals like those worn by the Shantren, and in the wake of his voice, a deep note hung in the air. So deep, she could scarce tell if it *was* a note or merely the throb of a tremendous pressure. It slammed into her, and it was all she could do to keep from sinking to her knees beneath the force.

She tightened her grip on the bars in a vain attempt to still the trembling of her hands, not yet ready to believe what her hammering heart had already acknowledged.

That *this* was the Takhran.

He halted before her cell, so close she had to tip her head back to look up into his face, and cocked his chin to one side, considering her. "The talav can do nothing for this one, young Inali. I have far better plans for her."

"Better plans? But my lord—"

Without breaking eye contact, the Takhran lifted his voice, cutting Inali's remonstrance short. "Come, Zahar. What think you of our little Songkeeper?"

Both the name and the whisper of a soft step drew Birdie's eyes from the Takhran to the woman who entered, robed in the blue of the Shantren, with hair like autumn leaves that hung in long, silver-banded braids to her waist. A red crystal dangled from a chain about her neck. Save for the dark hollows beneath her eyes and cheekbones, neither age nor worry had yet lined her forehead or marred her skin. Regal, she seemed, even more so than Sa Itera.

Inali shuffled aside to yield her passage. Shoulders hunched, hands clasped before him, almost cringing—he looked more a slave than a desert prince.

Was this the *freedom* of the Shantren?

"What say you?" The Takhran summoned the woman to Birdie's cell with an almost imperceptible gesture of his hand. "Is this child the Songkeeper of legend?"

"Surely my lord knows better than I." Her voice was lower, rougher than Birdie expected.

"Indeed."

The Takhran's quiet, flat tone allowed no room for argument or deflection. With an inclination of her head, Zahar turned to Birdie. Hers was an edged gaze that made Birdie feel as though her flesh would be sliced away, layer by layer, until nothing remained, and even her hidden thoughts had been revealed to this woman who had been a Songling. This woman Gundhrold had known.

It brought heat to her cheeks and sparked anger in her chest. Setting her teeth, she matched the woman's stare and somehow felt that she could see her more clearly. Although no emotion marred the stone-like stillness of Zahar's face, still there was something about her that struck Birdie as brittle and frail. Like the petals of a sundrop sapped by winter's frost.

A single note of pity swept through her, but she dashed it aside.

Zahar's head jerked up. "It is as you say, my lord. She is the one."

"Yes, yes." Inali broke in. "I swear to you, by Sigurd's mane, she *is* the Songkeeper. She is strong, but with the talav, she could be so much more." He ventured nearer until he stood between the Takhran and Zahar, but his good hand trembled as he removed his spectacles and wiped the lenses on his vest. "She is lost, afraid, confused—as I was. Please, my lord, can you not aid her as you aided me?"

"Enough, Inali." Birdie forced the words between her teeth. "I do not want your help."

Her defiance went unnoticed.

Inali alone gave any indication that he had even heard her. Not one word had either Zahar or the Takhran spoken to her directly. After all this time, all this talk about her importance as the Songkeeper, perhaps she should have realized. *She* as a person, didn't matter at all. To them, she was just a thing, to be done away with or used at will.

"Would you welcome such blood within the ranks of the Shantren, Zahar?"

Again, the woman's scrutiny sliced through Birdie. "Welcome it, aye, but such talk is worthless. She will not bend. Her mind is set."

The Takhran nodded once, then turned swiftly on his heel and strode away.

"But my lord!" Inali chased after him. "Is not the choosing what you promise us all? Freedom to decide, control of our lives. Should she not have the choice, my lord?"

The Takhran paused midstride and his shoulders settled as with a long exhaled breath, but he did not turn. "He speaks true, little Songkeeper. There is much the Shantren offers. Much you have yet to learn. Do not let the ill-conceived prejudices of a few alter the course of your life."

"I …" Birdie took a deep breath. Her gaze darted from the Takhran to Inali's hopeful face stained red in the light of the guttering firepot. "I won't join you."

It was madness to consider otherwise.

"She will not yield." The stone of Zahar's mask cracked at last, but Birdie saw only disgust. "There is weakness in her, yes, but there is also stubbornness. Unthinking, unreasoning stubbornness, like her father and grandmother before her. She will not break."

A tremor ran through her at those words.

"Spoken true, perhaps, but *break* is such a harsh term." A half turn from the Takhran granted a glimpse of his face and the hint of a thin-lipped smile. "We will seek to *enlighten* her. Should she prove as foolish and unyielding as the rest of her line, then she may share their fate."

• • •

The sight of the dead chimera broke the soldiers' rush. A moment's hesitation, no more, but time enough for Amos to ready his stance before they fell upon him, the longer reach of their swords pinning him against the wall and cutting off escape, while the hound tore past toward Sym. Ordinarily, having one's back to the wall was a decent method for holding off multiple opponents, especially when fighting injured. But only if one's weapon had comparable reach.

So Amos did what he did best in such situations.

He leveled the field of contest.

He dropped to one knee and caught the middle soldier's sword-hand, while simultaneously stabbing up beneath the man's breastplate into his gut. A twist of his wrist, as the man crumpled, deposited the sword solidly in his own grip, just in time to stand and turn aside a thrust from the second Khelari.

But evading the thrust required him to sidestep out into the middle of the passage, exposing his back to the third Khelari. He felt the rush of a blade through the air and dodged on instinct a second before pain sliced through his upper arm. A shallow cut—he knew the feeling—but no less painful. Gritting his teeth, he charged at his current opponent, striking hard and fast in an effort to force him around and into his comrade, but a crash, groan, and wet *thunk* sounded behind him in quick succession.

He snatched a glance and saw Sym leaning on her spear over the third Khelari. Teeth flashing, the hound lunged at her, but she smacked it away and gestured for Amos to attend to himself. The glint in her eyes didn't bode well if he argued.

Back to the fight, he turned. The Khelari rushed at him with a yell, but now that it was a one on one bout, Amos managed to cut him down in a furious barrage of strokes. The man dropped to his knees and then crumpled beside the chimera. Amos's borrowed sword fell from his grip to clang against the rock underfoot. Breathing heavily, lip curled in a snarl, he stood amidst the carnage and surveyed the damage.

Bilges.

A chimera, three Khelari, and a hound all slain, and that was all well and good, but now both he and Sym were injured, and there was no way to hide evidence of the fight. Anyone who came along would know intruders had been here, might even be able to wager a guess as to where they were going.

And if not, surely the hounds would pick up their scent.

Though all things considered, the way the soldiers had reacted at the sight of them—not a shout of alarm or surprise—it was like they expected to find someone here. Mayhap it was the tunnel collapse that had given them away. Or mayhap it was something more sinister …

An idea floated through his mind, dredged up from the past. Distasteful as it was, he acted upon it without a second thought, dropping to his knees and removing the armor from the third Khelari—a man close enough to his own size and height—and then hastily buckling it on himself. "Gear up, lass."

Such a disguise wouldn't withstand any sort of a search, especially once the Khelari found the bodies stripped of armor, but if it made the soldiers think twice about trusting their *own* comrades, it could gain them a little time.

Time to find Birdie and break free of this death trap.

Fingers fumbling with the last straps, he pushed up to his feet and tiptoed to the fork in the passage. The baying of hounds and shouts of soldiers relaying messages rebounded from the walls, but if he strained his ears, they seemed to be coming more from the right than from any other direction. It only served to fix more firmly in his mind the notion that they'd been heading toward danger . . . not away from it.

"C'mon." He buckled the soldier's belt around his own waist and sheathed the borrowed sword, then beckoned Sym into the left-hand passage. "Change o' route."

Her dark eyes flickered up at him beneath the shade of the Khelari helm she had pulled over her braids. Somehow she had managed to strap her spear quiver over the bulky armor too. Didn't aid the disguise, but he imagined he would have about as much luck getting her to leave her spears behind as she would have convincing him to set aside his dirk.

"I thought Inali said to stick to the right."

"Aye, he did." A sour taste flooded Amos's mouth. "But it sounds t' me like that's where our pursuers are comin' from, so either yer helpful young friend doesn't know this place so well as he thought, or . . ."

He left the sentence hanging, because anything else was unspeakable, but the fear drove him on at an increasingly faster pace as the passages grew more and more familiar, heedless of all but the need to go on. He had been a fighter for long enough to trust his instincts, and the unsettled feeling that had broiled in his stomach ever since this cursed mission began promised little good for Birdie.

Had he been fool enough to leave her unprotected, as he'd left Artair? Oh Emhran, let it not be true! It was boggswoggling how easily that name he had so often cursed slipped past his lips when the world spun out of his control.

"Hawkness—" Sym called.

He spun around, reaching for both his dirk and sword. But there were no enemies in the passage, only Sym, a good thirty paces behind. She slumped against the wall, head hanging, breath coming in the short, wheezy gasps of someone in pain.

Bilgewater!

Cursing his own forgetfulness, Amos jogged back to her side and hauled her arm over his shoulder. "It's only a wee bit farther . . . we can make it."

"How could you know that?"

"Because I know where he's taken her, an' it's not good." His mouth went dry as he uttered the last words he would have ever hoped to have to utter. "We're goin' t' the Pit."

• • •

Birdie sat on the floor with her back pressed to the wall of her cell, knees drawn up beneath her chin. The bite on her leg had finally stopped bleeding. Congealed blood stuck her leggings to the wound, forming a sort of makeshift bandage. She could feel the dull, throbbing melody pulsing through the stone, and caught the beat of her own heart and breathing gradually aligning with the dreary rhythm as she stared dry-eyed at the iron bars.

The Takhran's words repeated endlessly in her mind, a chilling whisper.

Their fate.

Since leaving the desert, she had given little thought to the family Gundhrold had told her about. Caught up in all the fighting, running, and planning, all her questions about her family had drifted from the forefront of her mind, forgotten in the mad scramble to survive. The grandmother, father, mother, and uncle she had never known, all taken by the Khelari, all stolen from her by the Takhran.

Had any of them ever attempted this mission?

Soft boots scuffed the rock, and Inali stepped into view outside her cell. The stains of travel had been scrubbed from his face and clothes, and over his desert leathers he now wore the blue robe of the Shantren. It draped his narrow frame like a tent. Without a word, he knelt and slipped a piece of parchment through the bars. The scrap uncurled at Birdie's feet, revealing the charcoaled lines of her own face.

But in the sketch, a talav hung around her neck.

"Consider it . . . Birdie."

She tore her gaze from the sketch and slammed both fists against the bars. "I will never yield!" But her voice rang through an empty corridor. Only after she tore the parchment in half, crumpled the pieces, and threw them out into the passage, did she realize that it was the first time Inali had called her something other than *little Songkeeper.*

The hours passed slowly, time crawling inexorably on, while Birdie shivered and dreaded the fate the Takhran planned for her. A lump settled in her throat, so thick she could hardly breathe, choked by fears so great and terrible she didn't dare whisper them to herself, even in the solitude of her cell.

Her mind drifted to her friends and the perils they faced, no less terrifying than her own. Amos and Sym, Ky and his beloved Underground, the griffin. She had flung her arms around Gundhrold's neck when she bid him farewell, as if even then, she had sensed the finality of it, while he whispered words of peace and encouragement in her ear. So confident of the outcome, of who she was and what she would become.

But it was Inali's assurances that had led her here. The false promises of a pawn and a traitor. Even now, his words from the Hollow Cave echoed in her ears, declaring her the Songkeeper who would release Tal Ethel and save Leira from the Takhran's rule. How could she hope to untangle the truth from the lies?

It was true that the Song had rescued her in the past. On the Westmark Bridge, the beach of Bryllhyn, and the deck of the Langorian ship …

If only she could summon it now.

"You must *listen*, little one." The words Gundhrold had spoken in Brog's donkey shed—ages ago, it seemed now—crept to the forefront of her mind. "*Listen.*"

And oh how she listened. Eyes closed, head lifted, breath held. If she could have silenced the traitorous beating of her heart for but a moment, she would have. Then finally she heard it. Soft, gentle, little more than a whisper of hope or a glimmer of starlight in the endless night.

It did not rise in answer to her summons.

"I am the Songkeeper," she whispered, clenching her fists so hard her arms trembled.

Still the bars did not snap, nor did the stones crumble to allow her escape. There was no explosion of strength within her. No force that leveled her enemies. Her straining ear caught only the whisper of the Song, and even that seemed almost drowned by the tendrils of the broken melody creeping through the stones to surround her like an errant mist.

She was a prisoner still.

Abandoned again.

30

"I don't like this. An' I don't mind sayin' so, either."

Ky only half glanced up at Paddy before returning to his work. "Me neither." He trailed the singed end of his stick across the stone in front of him, marking a few more lines into his drawing before frowning and smudging half of them out with the tip of his finger. When it came to slinging, he was your man.

But an artist he was not.

Still, volunteering to serve as lookout had its perks. He'd managed to surprise Cade, skip battle drills run by Slack, and swing a perch in the battlements that granted a bird's eye view of the whole countryside. Of the courtyard where Slack had the runners sweating despite the cold, the north keep walkway where Commander Thallus berated his forces with a voice that rivaled an earthquake, and the too silent earthen breastwork where the Khelari had set up a hasty encampment. Just the sort of view one needed to plan an attack.

Judging by the ravens wheeling overhead, the Khelari thought so too.

"It's too quiet, isn't it?" He squinted against Tauros's noonday rays bouncing off the white road and the snow heaped alongside. "Just doesn't sit right."

"I don't mean the Khelari."

Something about Paddy's voice made Ky sit up straight and focus. The freckles stood out on Paddy's face like a spattering of mud as he darted a glance across the walkway and down into the courtyard. "Goin' behind Cade's back like this . . . it just feels *wrong*."

Was that all?

"We're not going behind Cade's back. Just not telling him yet. With any luck, Migdon will bring help, and all our planning will've been for nothing."

"Luck?" Paddy snorted. "Shure."

Ky couldn't fault his skepticism. The way things had been going, if the Underground had any luck at all, it was bound to be of the bad variety. Still, they had managed to stumble across one or two fortunate breaks along the way. Like Cade hitting it off with Commander Thallus. Somehow, he'd managed to talk the old dwarf into handing over four mounted crossbows *and* sending dwarves to install them at strategic points along the south keep battlements.

Under Cade's direction, no less.

If nothing else, it kept Cade out of their hair and might just give them a bit of an edge when the next attack came.

"What's that?" Paddy gestured at the mess of lines Ky had scrawled on the battlement.

"Battle plan . . . of sorts." Nothing Paddy, the Underground's mapmaker, had been meant to see. He rubbed his hand across the lines, smearing them into a meaningless black smudge. "Just scribbles really. Thinking through what I'd do if I were the Khelari." He dusted his hands on his fringed trousers. "So, did you get it?"

"Shure, I got it." Paddy fished around in his jacket pocket and produced a leather pouch that he carefully deposited in Ky's hand. "Had a grand old time convincin' that commander to part with it too. Care to tell what you need ryree powder for?"

"Well, the way I figure it, the walls are bound to be the weakest part of our defense. Not enough of us to guard every inch, and the gate's inaccessible so long as we hold the pass." He jerked his chin toward the massive wooden gate on the south side of the circular keep. "They'll have to come up over the walls. Once they gain a footing, we'll bail and set off our distraction, leaving us free and clear to walk out the main gate."

"*Walk* out? What sort of distraction were you thinkin'?"

"Couple ryree packets in bonfires spaced out across the ramparts and at the top of both sets of stairs." Might not be quite so brazen as trying to sneak past the Khelari in a coffin, but the plan had a nice, bold Migdon-ish feel to it. Ky figured it would make the dwarf proud. "We can set a fuse, like Hawkness did with the packets in the Underground—two would be best, one for each of the wall-top stairs, so we can light them on our way down. Reckon that'll do the trick."

Paddy pursed his lips and rubbed a hand across his chin. "An' what, you an' I set this up all by our-handsome-selves?"

"Nah, I recruited Meli and Syd too. They've been hunting supplies for me all morning." Paddy elbowed him, but he kept talking. "Don't worry. They won't get in trouble. We'll need to lay the fuses out and build the bonfires beforehand and make sure—what is it?"

"Movement in the Khelari camp."

Ky spun around. Sure enough, dark-armored men milled about in the open in front of the earthen breastwork, slowly forming up in rigid lines. But they didn't move with the purpose and precision of soldiers about to march into battle, or even the frenzied enthusiasm of those about to launch a ferocious assault. A moment later, as if in confirmation of his suspicions, a mounted Khelari rode out in front, holding a white flag aloft.

"Best sound the alarm." Paddy started toward the south end of the bridge.

"I think they mean to talk first."

"Shure, an' they're welcome to, but I mean to cram an arrow down their throats while they're at it. I'll fetch Cade if you'll go get Commander Thingummy."

Ky sprinted to the north end of the bridge and shouted the alarm down into the keep. Back in the middle of the bridge, he waited for the commanders to arrive, while runners and dwarves flocked to the parapets and his sling hand tingled in anticipation. It wasn't long before Cade loped up from his left with Paddy at his heels, and a moment later, Commander Thallus stormed up from his right with a white kerchief already stuck to the top of his mace.

Muttering, he stuck the makeshift flag up over the edge of the battlements and waved it around until the mounted Khelari approached. "Now, look here, beardlings," he raised his voice just enough to carry to both keeps, "we're under a flag of truce, so hold your shooting at least until after I've heard what he has to say."

A good thirty paces out, the Khelari halted and removed his helmet. "I speak for Lord Cedric, Fourth Marshal of the Takhran's—"

"Stop right there!" Thallus slammed his mace against the battlement, cutting off the messenger's speech. "That won't do at all. Fourth Marshal Cedric can speak with us himself, or not at all." Then, out of the corner of his mouth, "Just a warning shot to speed him on his way."

Three arrows zipped down toward the messenger. For warning shots, they sure came close. One glanced off the helmet in the messenger's hand. Without another word, he yanked his steed around and spurred the beast all the way back to the Khelari line.

Paddy met Ky's glance. "Wasn't that a mite risky? Firing under a flag of truce?"

Thallus just chuckled and clapped him on the back, hard enough to make Paddy stumble. "Negotiations, beardling, aren't so much of a delicate art as those stuck up Xanthen chancellors would have you think. It's more a matter of figuring out who's got the bigger sword and the guts to use it."

"Looks like it worked." A hint of admiration filled Cade's voice.

Ky joined him at the battlements. A silver cloaked Khelari rode out from beneath the shadow of the breastwork with six men marching in tight formation behind. They halted farther back than the messenger had, and the officer did not remove his helmet.

"I am Fourth Mar—"

"Don't care who you are, Khelari, so best you just say what you mean to say and be done with it before our arms tire of holding our bowstrings."

"Injure one more of my men and nothing will save you," Marshal Cedric snapped. "This is my offer: surrender immediately, throw down your arms, and abase yourself before the Takhran's mercy. Then and only then will your lives be spared. Unlike your unfortunate comrade."

At a nod from Cedric, the wedge of Khelari split and fanned out, revealing a smaller figure that had been concealed in their midst.

Migdon.

Ky's breath caught in his throat, and he lunged against the battlements, hands already flying to unwind and load his sling. One of the soldiers shoved Migdon forward and then kicked his legs out from under him. With his hands bound behind his back, the dwarf had no way to ease his fall. Somehow, he managed to get his knees under his body and leverage up into a kneeling position. Even at a distance, Ky could see that his face was a mass of bruises and dried blood.

Cedric dismounted, and drawing his sword, paced around Migdon with measured steps. "My hounds caught your friend sneaking around outside your little fortress. Now he swears that he was just out for a morning stroll. Persuasive, too. I might just be inclined to believe him."

Quick as a whip, Cedric spun and sliced his blade across Migdon's throat. The dwarf's head toppled back, bright blood gushing over the front of his tunic, and his body crumpled to the ground at the Khelari's feet.

"No!" Ky rammed a fist against the battlement. Pain shot through his knuckles and into his hand, so strong he almost dropped his sling. But he wanted to punch the battlement again. Pummel the stone, if need be, until his hand shattered or the wave of anger broke.

Whichever happened first.

Cedric wiped his sword and sheathed it with a sigh. "As I was saying, I might have been inclined to believe him"—his voice hardened—"had I not known that all dwarves are inveterate liars. You have two hours to decide your fate. Will you surrender and live? Or fight and die?" He tapped a toe against Migdon's body. "Like him."

"Cursed Khelari dog!" Thallus roared, and his voice cracked. "I don't need two minutes to decide, let alone two hours! Send your worst. We'll not surrender."

"So be it."

As the Marshal mounted and retreated toward the Khelari lines, Thallus wheeled around and marched toward the north tower, heels punching the bridge with a force that rivaled the striking power of a catapult. "Ready yourselves for the attack. It won't be long now." Then quieter, so quiet Ky barely caught it. "I fear I may have doomed us all."

• • •

Doomed or not, Ky didn't plan on leaving the Underground trapped. No sooner had they dispersed, leaving a double watch on the parapets, then he set the team to work preparing for escape. He took upon himself the task of setting up the five ryree-laced bonfires on the walkway. Heavy work that required splitting and hauling wood and soon had him sweating despite the cold. But no matter how hard he toiled away, he couldn't get rid of the lump in his throat or the ache in his chest. Over and over, he saw Migdon's death in his mind's eye.

He saw it all.

Every agonizing detail.

The way Migdon's body slumped and his limbs went slack as the lifeblood gushed from his wound. The arrogant satisfaction on the face of that cursed Khelari marshal. The sling dangling useless from his own hand, too late to save the friend who had given it to him.

That thought fueled his anger and stoked his limbs to action.

But he only just had time to run pitch-covered fuses between the bonfires before the warning bells clanged in the north keep. Dusting his hands on his knees, he stood back to find Cade staring suspiciously at him.

"It's . . . just in case ..."

But Cade didn't press for an explanation, just nodded and waved him on, and he didn't wait to be told twice. Only fools questioned a lucky break. Driven by the frenzied tolling of the bells, he ducked into the barracks, hastily donned a chainmail shirt, and belted a borrowed sword about his waist.

"Look lively, Ky!" Paddy rushed through on his way to the battlements, clutching a lit torch in one hand with half a dozen unlit torches tucked beneath his arm. "They're comin'."

"Right behind you." Ky looped a few extra pouches of sling-bullets and stones through his belt, then halted in the center of the room and cast a final glance around.

The young ones of the Underground were all huddled in the corner by the fireplace—Meli, Syd, and four others—while Aliyah stood armed with a bow and her crutch to guard them. Cade's doing, no doubt. For all his talk of war, he wasn't mad enough to throw his own little sister into the thick of it. Not when she could be talked into protecting the young ones.

Ky adjusted the quiver on Aliyah's back. "Make sure everyone stays in here and keeps their heads down. I'll give the whistle if we need to leave, and then Meli and Syd know what to do, right?" Somehow, he managed to keep his voice light, but when Meli's hopeful eyes met his and an eager expression lit her face, that lump lodged in the back of his throat again.

She took his hand and hugged it.

He patted her on the top of the head, nodded at Syd, and beat a hasty retreat out the door and up the wall-top steps. If anything went wrong—and with such a shaky escape plan, a thousand things could go wrong—it would be his fault. Sure, it was easy to blame Cade's obsession with revenge for throwing them into danger, but Ky was the one who had brought them here.

Oh, he made things happen all right.

Time alone could tell if they were good things, or not.

The roar of the oncoming soldiers filled Ky's ears even before he reached the battlements and paused beside Paddy. The redhead was positioned directly above the barracks and closest to the first fuse, while Ky's station stood across the way, by the second set of steps. He rolled a sling-bullet between his fingers as he cast an appraising eye over their defenses. Commander Thallus had lent a handful of his dwarves to fill the empty sections of the south walkway, but even so, there were too few of them, and the forces in the north keep and along the bridge were already stretched far too thin to spare any more.

Paddy stood with an arrow already on the string, a lit torch propped against the wall at his feet, far enough away that it wouldn't cast light on him now that the sun hovered over the western horizon.

"Shure an' that's a grim sight." He dipped his head to indicate the Khelari.

The broiling throng was almost upon them now, bearing weapons that ranged from hand bows to swords and spears and long, siege ladders. They moved with less discipline than Ky had expected. Looked more like a pack of ravenous hounds thirsting for blood than anything else. From the sound of things, they had already reached the north keep. A minute later, the crossbows mounted on both keeps began to fire.

Paddy spun back to the battlements and sighted down an arrow. "Any hope of escape was a long shot to begin with." His bowstring twanged, and the arrow launched into the mass of Khelari. "Don't forget a torch."

Ky plucked a torch and spare from the pile Paddy had carried up, paused to light one, and then hurried to his station and set the torches on the ground just within reach. Slowly at first, he spun and released his sling, conserving his energy, saving his strength. But the Khelari would not be stopped. They came on again and again, an endless dark tide.

For the first time, Ky understood Cade's need for battle, for success, for revenge. He poured all of his frustration, sorrow, anger, and fear into his slinging, releasing stone upon stone and sling-bullet after sling-bullet. He clamped his teeth on his lip until he tasted the tang of blood on his tongue, and spun his sling until his arm ached.

Arrows sliced all around, clanking and skipping across the stones at his feet. One flew so close to his face that he felt the breath of air as it passed his cheek. The Khelari set ladders, and he threw them down. They slung grapnels, and he cut the ropes. They charged at the wall, and he felled them in their tracks. They reached the top, and he buried his sword in their chests. Thought faded before the intoxicating pulse of adrenaline in his veins. The world blended into a terrifying, thunderous cacophony of motion and sound and death less than a breath away.

Then the fighting lulled, and Ky collapsed against the battlement, breathing hard and stained with blood that was not his own.

His gaze roamed the walkway, settling on Paddy, Cade, Slack, and a dozen other familiar faces, most sporting injuries of some sort.

But somehow, they were alive, and that was enough.

Far too many were not.

His throat swelled at the thought of Migden, and he pushed it from his mind again. Because that was what he had to do to focus, to survive and see the runners safe. He still dared hope they would be able to hold the Khelari off, even though no reinforcements could be expected. If only long enough to buy another day of life. Another moment of hope.

Then wild and desperate, the call came, spreading from dwarf to dwarf and runner to runner, until it made the circuit of Siranos and broke hard upon his ears.

"They've taken the Pass!"

31

Rough hands gripped Birdie's shoulders, hustling her along at such a pace that she had to half jog to keep up with the rapid tramp of the soldiers' feet. Stolid as the mountain itself, the soldiers refused to answer any questions about her destination or the need for haste. The only response they gave was that the Takhran had summoned her.

But that was answer enough.

It was time for his plans, whatever they were, to come to pass.

She took some comfort—faint and grasping though it was—in the fact that her hands were not bound. With fifteen soldiers grouped tightly around her, a veritable wall of armor and steel, there was no need. The Takhran had not even bothered to order her gagged, as though somehow he knew that the Song had not answered her pleas for escape. Or perhaps because he knew that if it did, a gag alone would not hinder it.

Without slackening pace, they followed the web of tunnels down stranger and darker paths than those Inali had led her on. She could not have retraced her steps had she wanted to. Gaping passageways gouged the walls of the tunnels on either side, and terrible unknown spaces loomed in the dark beyond. Sometimes, she caught sight of pale, luminous eyes gazing unblinking after them. At others, she heard the dull rumble of a growl or the rustle and thud of some large form shifting within.

At last, the passage spewed them out into an enormous subterranean room, lit in the center by a single blazing torch on an iron stand. Like a lone star in the night sky, the torch drew Birdie's focus from the encroaching shadows. Flanked by a dozen Khelari, the Takhran was mounted on a massive black steed with the head, beak, and wings of a raven, and the muscled body of a horse, on the far edge of the flickering circle of light. Inali and Zahar stood at his stirrups, one on either side. A great blackness spread before their feet, and Birdie knew instantly what it was. Even in faraway Hardale, she had heard whispers of the Pit. Like a living thing, the vast emptiness drew her forward until she stood, shivering, before the Takhran.

The place reeked of death.

A steady dripping fell on her ears, but she could not look . . . did not dare look.

The Takhran's steed jerked its neck and snorted. Its beak clipped the air only inches from her head. Corded muscles stood out along its chest and deep-cut hindquarters, and an iron collar encircled its neck, visible through the feather-like strands of its mane. The Takhran flicked a hand, and the soldiers spread out along the edge of the Pit, lighting torches in stands at regular intervals, revealing an iron staircase that twisted back and forth down into the cavern. The light petered out before reaching the depths.

But the burning glow stretched above and beyond the Pit, carrying Birdie's gaze with it. The far-flung edges of light revealed the body of a man hanging spread-eagled from a wooden frame. No amount of pride nor hope of dignity could have kept her from gasping at that sight. She stumbled back, straight into the ribs of the Takhran's steed.

The beast twisted its neck around to fix her with a beady eyed stare.

"Behold my banner, little Songkeeper." A tinge of amusement twisted the Takhran's voice, but the look in his eyes spoke of something else, a deep and undying loathing that touched all who bore the Songkeeper name. He dismounted and beckoned to her, and she came, for she had no other choice. Both Inali and Zahar fell into step at her side, and for the first time, she noticed that the Saari warrior carried a long, flat box in his good hand. The Takhran led the way out from beneath the circle of light toward the staircase, and she followed, the heavy hoof-falls of the raven steed at her heels.

At the edge of the Pit, she halted, heart beating with the wild impulse to flee. But she could not get far. Not with so many Khelari.

A furtive survey of the cavern hammered that truth home. Even now, two soldiers detached from the group and moved toward her, as if they sensed her desire to escape and meant to cut her off.

"Wait here." The Takhran seized a torch from one of the soldiers and turned toward the staircase, but instead of falling back as ordered, the soldier dove forward, shoving the Takhran to the edge. A bronze dirk gleamed in his hand.

"Lass, run!"

But Birdie stood still, rooted with shock.

With deceptive ease, the Takhran caught the dirk on his vambrace and turned Amos's stroke aside, forcing him to yield ground. At the same time, the raven steed launched into the air behind Birdie, wings beating with the chaotic force of a desert wind. She dropped to her knees. Just in time, or its hooves would have clipped her head in passing. The beast landed beside the Takhran, forelegs striking Amos in the chest and sending him reeling back a dozen feet.

The peddler regained his balance and cast aside his helmet, revealing a ruddy shock of hair and a face livid with rage, but the Khelari were upon him before he could charge the Takhran again.

"Amos!" Birdie darted forward, but a vice-like grip seized her neck, forcing her to look up into the pale blue eyes of the Takhran. Gone was any vestige of the debonair mask he had assumed in the Hall of the Shantren. A snarl twisted his face, almost animal-like in its ferocity.

He held her gaze, savoring the weight of his words. "Kill them. Kill them both."

"No!" She struggled to free herself, but she might as well have tried to break steel with her bare hands as tear free of his grip. The Takhran dragged her to the edge, snapped his fingers at Inali and Zahar, and then shoved her and the torch into the woman's hands. Before Birdie could rally to the attack, Zahar had started down the iron staircase, and she was forced to march along or be dragged off her feet.

Over her shoulder, Birdie caught a glimpse of Amos battling the Khelari with a sword in one hand and his dirk in the other, a smaller dark-armored figure at his side. The Takhran motioned, and a brazen horn call rang out. Once. Twice. Thrice. Silence fell, broken only by the occasional clash of blades and the grunts of fighting men.

Then the rumbling growl Birdie had heard in the tunnels.

She strained to look back, but they had rounded the first bend in the staircase and the fight no longer waged on the edge of the Pit. Her foot caught on the next step, and she lurched forward. Zahar's grip dug into her arm, yanking her back. "'Ware your step."

The sharp words struck Birdie's ear with more force than Zahar probably intended. More than the warning, she seized upon the idea. As they rounded the second bend, she dropped her shoulder and rammed full force into Zahar's side. The woman hit the low rail with a grunt and pitched forward, instantly releasing her grip on Birdie's arm to steady herself.

The torch dropped from her hand.

Birdie took off at a run, ignoring Inali's shouted warning, leaping down three, four, sometimes five steps at a time, catching herself against the rail, and running again. Her lungs ached by the time she reached the bottom and sprinted out into the Pit, but she only made it a few steps before she came to a shuddering stop.

Zahar's torch lay on the ground a few feet away, still burning faintly, casting a dull red glow over her surroundings, and there at her feet, was a human skull. She tore her gaze from its insane, crooked grin and caught the torch up from the ground. Elevated, the light extended farther. She was surrounded by corpses, most skeletal, a few still clad in decaying shreds of flesh and clothing. They were piled in haphazard heaps along the rocky banks of what looked to have once been a streambed, though the stones were covered with dark flecks and splotches that could only have been dried blood.

Heavy wings beat overhead, drawing her back to the present.

"What think you, little Songkeeper?"

Senses afire with fear and disgust, she craned her neck back and instantly had to duck as the raven steed plunged past and landed a few yards away. Surrounded by the slain, the steed's nature as a carrion beast revealed itself in its snuffling breath, rasping voice, and the taut lines in its outstretched neck. It took a little hop-skip toward the nearest corpse, but a harsh word from the Takhran bade it be still.

Everything within Birdie screamed for her to flee, but she could not hope to outrun the flying steed. Her only hope lay in finding a place to hide . . . or a weapon.

The Takhran turned his gaze upon her, an easy smile playing on his lips. Yet now that she had seen what truly lay beneath his mild mannered façade, no amount of charm could make her forget. "Welcome, little Songkeeper. Meet your kind and your kin. Shall I tell you where your father and mother lie?" He spread his arms wide, disarming. "You must venture farther in for that, though in truth I have almost forgotten …"

He was taunting her.

Birdie gritted her teeth at the thought. There was no way out. If there was, he would never have allowed her to continue to roam free, even with the threat of the raven steed to chase her down if she tried to bolt. But if he wanted her to go farther into the Pit, perhaps the best thing she could do was stand her ground here. Or perhaps that was what he wanted her to think.

Mind games, that's what this was.

Yet what other choice did she have?

Choking down her horror, Birdie set her back toward him and the piles of the slain and strode on into the Pit, following the course of the dry streambed. The sputtering torch cast a feeble glow that lit the next step and revealed nothing beyond. Uneven rocks jarred her ankles. The two warring melodies she had heard on her journey through the tunnels were even louder here, loud enough that a pounding ache battered her temples and almost brought tears to her eyes.

But the ache she could bear.

It was nothing compared to the dull throb of horror brought on by the clang of weapons, thunderous roars, and groans of the injured and dying filtering down from above, where Amos fought. To save her.

Somehow, she would find her way out of this and back to him. The thought strengthened her resolve, and still she walked on and on. Time lost all meaning, measured only by the pause between one stride and the next. Her steady footfalls were broken only by the rustle of her torch, or the crunch of bone or squelch of something slick underfoot. There was no sound from the raven steed, no sign that the Takhran followed.

But she felt his eyes upon her.

Ahead, the streambed narrowed and ended abruptly in a dome of dark rock at the base of the far wall of the Pit. The torch in her hand kept flickering, but the weak light cast myriad reflections on the rock's faceted surface. Birdie passed a hand over the stone. Beyond, held back by some unseen force, a river of music surged and thrashed against its boundaries. She could sense it with just one touch. It swept over her, poured into and through her, flooding her being with a glimpse of something utterly terrifying in its vastness.

She pulled away, gasping for breath.

In one thing, at least, Inali had spoken true, for there could be no mistaking this for anything but the mysterious Tal Ethel, the legendary spring of melody.

A rough patch in the center of the dome caught her eye, and she bent for a closer look. Something wet struck the back of her bowed head and trailed down her neck. Hardly daring to look, yet not daring *not* to look, Birdie tilted her head back.

But her dim torch failed to penetrate the shadows above. Behind her, the sharp *tck tck* of flint and steel rang out. A stolen glance confirmed that Zahar and Inali had overtaken her, though they hung back, just as the Takhran had. For a second, the impulse for flight thudded through her chest. Then the second torch flared, flooding the Pit with orange light and chasing the shadows away from the body of the man on the wooden frame. Blood pooled at the edge of a jagged wound in his throat and fell, one drop at a time, onto the dome of rock. In that sickening cadence, the dark melody burst upon her.

Choking, blinding, smothering.

The dying torch slipped from her hand and scattered burning fragments across the rock beneath her feet. She stumbled away, gasping for breath, one hand scrubbing furiously at her neck to remove the bloodstains. The other, she clenched, willing it to be still.

Her heel struck against something.

A dark shape behind caught the corner of her eye. She froze. The rock beneath her feet was wet, the stale odor of sweat and the rankness of decay drifted through her nostrils, and if she strained her ears, she could hear the whisper of faint breathing. At any moment, she expected to feel the weight of rough hands on her shoulders, dragging her away.

Hooves rang against stone. The Takhran emerged from the shadows a short distance away, an imposing figure atop his massive raven steed. He eased the beast to a halt and sat watching her with amusement evident on his face. Holding the torch aloft, Zahar made her way to stand at his side, followed by Inali. The torch spewed an angry tongue of flame that bathed her face and hands in crimson and unleashed the blaze in her hair.

A gesture from the Takhran bade Birdie look behind.

She released the breath she had drawn into her lungs, slowly turned around, and found herself staring up into the bloodless face of a man.

For a moment, she stood there, mind scrambling to process what it was that she saw. Then the full weight of the sight struck her, and she fell back a step. The rest of the body came into view. It was a dark haired man with the hint of a beard shadowing his jawline, bound to a column of stone that stood level with her head but only reached the man's shoulders. She heard no hint of a melody from him, and his face was ghastly pale, like moonlight on still water. His body sagged against iron restraints that crossed at his chest, hips, and knees. Neck lolled forward, chin resting on his chest, fixed eyes staring out beneath the sweep of his hair.

It was the eyes that gave him away.

Dead, they seemed, and yet somehow *not*. Whatever it was—a flicker of movement, a comprehension hidden deep within the depths—it spoke of life, like the faint breathing she had heard. Weak and passing life, perhaps, but Birdie seized upon the idea. Until she caught sight of the wide red slash beneath his chin.

His throat had been cut.

The scarlet flow drained from the gaping wound with a steady drip, drip, drip, to pool in the rocks beneath their feet, and then trickled down and away into the streambed.

And yet the man still lived.

Struggling to breathe with the horror of it all, she felt rather than saw the Takhran dismount and come to stand beside her. "The choosing, this Dah Inali has asked for you." His mild voice spoke beside her ear. She tried not to flinch from the oppressive weight of his presence, dared not move lest her limbs betray her fear. She meant to show him her strength, not reveal her weakness. "He believes you are ready. But there can be no real choice without truth. So *this*, my dear, is truth."

"Truth?" Her voice broke over the word.

"No secrets. No concealment. No half promises and whispered legends. Nothing but truth, unembellished, in all its gory detail." The savage look mastered his face. Almost a snarl. "There are places in this world where the echoes of the master melody run truer than in others. Yet this is the most powerful of all. Tal Ethel, a place of wonders . . . or of horrors." He seized her hand in his iron grip and pressed her palm against the bound man's chest.

It was cold.

She tried to wrench her hand away, but the Takhran tightened his grip until pain ran up into her shoulder, and she stilled. Her palm resonated with the slow throb of the man's heart. It was irregular, almost musical …

He jerked her away before she could seize the thread of melody and spun her around. "You see it, don't you, little Songkeeper?" He released her and patted her shoulders stiffly, as if trying to erase the memory of his painful grip. "The magic of this place? It keeps him living on in his death . . . it keeps them all."

At a gesture from the Takhran, Zahar advanced past the bound man and swung in a wide arc. The glow from her torch extended beyond and around her, revealing the dome, the end of the Pit, and a semi-circle of a dozen stone columns surrounding them, split in half by the course of the streambed. Bound by iron bands to the columns, the broken forms of men, women, and children. Decaying corpses littered the bank behind.

Birdie's feet carried her forward without her command, bearing her in Zahar's wake along the sweep of the arc, past the dead who were yet living. She had walked through them on her way to the dome without seeing.

Without hearing.

Now, although their melodies were still silent, she could not help but see. The images seared into her memory. An old man with hair and beard the scraggly gray of a hallorm's bark. A small Saari boy in desert leathers, black hair cropped close to his head. A young dwarf woman with smile lines beside her eyes that mocked the terror on her pale, still face.

Twelve in all.

Zahar halted before the last in line. Once he might have been tall, rugged even. But now the bones showed through his emaciated frame, his skin looked like crumpled parchment, and lank, colorless hair fell across his face. The stench of decay clung to him like a cloud, but Zahar did not retreat from it.

Birdie found her voice at last. "What is this?"

"This is power." Zahar answered without turning.

"And power, my dear, comes at a cost." Once more at her side, the Takhran smiled down at her. "It cannot be created. Simply transferred. And that in itself is a strange and wondrous thing. Behold your kin, Songkeepers and Songlings alike. Tal Ethel prolongs their lives for a time, and it is marvelous, but eventually the strength of the melody within them fades and their bodies rot and decay, becoming nothing more than scraps for carrion."

As if to confirm his words, the raven steed appeared to their right, pecking at something at the base of one of the far columns. The Takhran whistled, and the beast jerked away, like a naughty child caught in the act.

Birdie fought the urge to be sick.

"Some last a month. Others a few years. Your lovely parents graced the Pit for a good seven years, though dear Auna only made it a paltry eight months..." The Takhran kept speaking, but his voice faded into the background under the numbing weight of this revelation.

So they were dead then.

Birdie had known it to be true.

"Young Rav here"—the Takhran jerked his chin toward the skeletal figure before Zahar—"has been among us now, what is it, fifteen years?"

"Seventeen." No emotion clouded Zahar's voice.

Still, she did not turn.

"So long?" The Takhran chuckled, and the sound of it was enough to send a shiver through Birdie's bones. "Yet I fear not much longer. Young Rav is nearly finished by the look of it. Only the truly powerful endure long." There was something unnerving in the Takhran's fervent expression as he lifted his face toward the distant cavern ceiling. It was almost gleeful, as if he reveled in this moment. In this display. "You have already seen my greatest victory. Behold my pride and banner, the Songkeeper Artair."

Birdie's eyes flickered to the body hanging over the dome.

"Thirty years and yet the blood still flows. This, little one, is power, and it is mine." His voice fell to a growl. "You have been told that you are powerful, but I say that you have been deceived. You are weak. Limping along on a strength not your own. Unable to control it, incapable of deciding your course, fated to follow the dictates of a Song you do not understand."

Beneath the weight of his eyes, eyes that were somehow old and young at the same time, Birdie felt that he spoke true. What little strength she possessed was not her own. The Song did not answer her call, did not yield to her demands. She had braved the journey to the Pit, drawn by the mysterious voice in the Song, and yet now that she was here, she had no idea what it was that she was meant to do. Somehow, all her plans lay shattered at her feet, and she could do nothing but watch everything spiral out of her control.

While the Song remained silent.

The utter hopelessness of her position threatened to swallow her and the cursed trembling seized her hands. She forced them down to her side, but she knew the Takhran's keen eyes had caught her weakness.

He swept a hand toward the columns. "This is what awaits you."

"But it doesn't have to." Inali spoke for the first time since entering the Pit. He pushed forward, still clutching the long, thin box in his good arm. "This is the choosing. The burden of the Song was thrust upon us, whether we willed it or not. But you can choose the talav. You can choose to be more than your weakness. You can choose freedom . . . or not."

Above, a strangled cry rang out and rebounded from the sides of the Pit, and in its echoes, Birdie heard the notes of the peddler's melody. "Amos?"

"Choose and be done with it!" Zahar snapped.

But the spell of the Takhran's words was already broken. Birdie strained her ears for any sign that harm had come to the peddler, but on the heels of his melody, she caught the first strains of the Song. It did not burst upon her with a flood of strength and power, and yet it was still there, like a gentle hand, beckoning to her.

Waiting.

Waiting for what?

She thrust the melody aside. Gritting her teeth, she turned to face the Takhran. "Choose freedom . . . or choose a living death? That isn't a choice. You claim I am weak. Maybe so. But I am strong enough to know that I don't need to drain the life from others to become what I am. I will not take the talav."

The force of her words tore through the Pit.

Then silence.

32

Sling dangling limp from his hand, Ky slumped against the battlements and watched the Khelari stream into the Pass below like the floodwaters of the Adayn. A chill wind stirred the hair plastered to his scalp and sent a shiver through his body. He didn't have a clear view of the bridge from his position, but the Khelari movements could mean only one thing: the dwarves manning the bridge's defenses must have fallen, and the north keep was too beleaguered to send reinforcements.

They were all of them doomed now, runners and dwarves alike.

Close to a quarter of the Khelari remained behind, mustering for the attack at the feet of the twin bluffs. With a clear path through the Pass, they could now attack from all sides at once. And now that the Pass was lost, there was no way to halt the march against the Caran's fortress, no more purpose in fighting, but to survive.

The blaring of trumpets summoned the Khelari to the next assault, and Commander Thallus's voice rang out in answer from the opposite keep. Gritting his teeth, Ky slung until only a few sling-bullets remained in his pouch and the earth before the keep was littered with the wounded and dying, but the Khelari would not be stopped. Everywhere he turned, ladders thudded against the wall, weapons clashed, and men, dwarves, and runners howled in pain.

If evil had a voice, Ky reckoned it would sound a bit like this.

He flung his weight against the nearest ladder, straining to force it away from the wall. Out of the corner of his eye, he caught a glimpse of a bearded face, then a helmeted forehead slammed into his skull. He staggered back and caught one hand on the battlements. It was the only thing that kept him upright. The Khelari swung over the battlement and strode toward him.

Ky fumbled for his sword.

A thud, the slick crunch of a blade tearing into flesh, and then the weight of the Khelari slammed against his legs, knocking him down.

"You're welcome." Slack set a foot to the man's back and yanked her hatchet free, wisps of hair flung loose from her braid and flying about her face. Warm blood gushed from the man's wound and seeped into the fringe of Ky's trousers.

Cade tugged the corpse off him, hauled him to his feet, and cuffed his shoulder. "Try not to get yourself killed."

Sure trying not to.

Ky took a breath, sending a fresh wave of pain shooting through his throbbing forehead, and turned to face the battlements. "Ready?"

All three of them rushed the ladder, shoved it to one side, and then flung it back from the wall. Shouts and screams rang out below, and they collapsed behind the battlement just before a hail of arrows shot overhead and dropped into the courtyard to splinter and crack on the stones.

A few near misses skipped off the walkway only inches away. Cade seized those within reach, inspected the shafts for cracks, and then stowed them in his quiver. "I take it those burn piles you were setting up earlier mean something."

"Diversion . . . so we can escape."

"Escape?" Slack snorted. "Course *you* would be thinking about that. I don't know why you bother with him, Cade."

Ordinarily, her words would have needled him, but the din of battle seemed to grow louder in his ears, reminding him of what was at stake. He refused to take the bait.

Not this time.

"Cade, you know as well as I do that this fortress is doomed. The Khelari have won already. Holding out here any longer won't do anything but get us all killed. Do you want to condemn Aliyah to death or slavery, or help me get her out?"

The battle raged in Cade's eyes. For a moment, he just crouched there, shaking his sword as if weighing the options in his hand, then he shoved away from the battlements.

"Wait!" Ky caught his arm. Cade swung around, sword raised, and the look in his eyes made Ky release his grip. But he wasn't about to give up. "You can stay and fight. That's your choice. But I *will* get the young ones out. When you hear my signal, clear the walkway, 'cause it'll be going up in flames."

A grapnel clanked against the battlement to Ky's left, calling him back to the fight. He broke away from Cade and swung into action, slashing through the rope, then ducking on instinct as an arrow sliced past his head. When he glanced back, Cade and Slack were in the thick of things near the bridge.

All around the keep, wave after wave of the Khelari reached the top of the walls, only to be forced back or thrown down. The runners kept up a mad dash along the walkway, slicing, hacking, shooting and stabbing. But such ferocity could only last so long. Already, Ky's breath rasped in his lungs. Dots of gray pinpricked his vision. The chainmail felt like a thousand pounds weighing him down as he swung and hammered with a sword that had begun to feel more like a club than a blade.

Just another moment longer …

Just one stroke more …

He muttered the words to himself over and over, as one stroke stretched into a dozen and one moment into a hundred. Act too soon and his plan would fail. The Khelari had to have already established a firm footing on the walkway or his plan to walk out the front gate would have even less chance than a plea for mercy.

All at once, it happened, so quickly Ky almost missed it. It was too easy to focus on his section of the wall and see nothing else. But one moment, the Khelari were fighting tooth and nail to gain a footing anywhere along the walkway. The next, almost twenty Khelari were scattered across the parapet, guarding ladders that shook with the weight of climbers.

In that moment, Ky realized what had changed. Since the fight began, the bells of the north keep had kept up a steady clanging, but now they were silent.

The north keep had fallen.

• • •

Ky forced a shrill whistle through his lips. In the Underground's simpler days of pickpocketing and running raids, it had been Cade's signal to end a mission. All along the walkway, runners started and looked around at the unexpected sound, but Cade had drilled them too well for any to question such a signal now. They broke away from the fight and retreated toward the courtyard.

Still whistling, Ky caught up his torch and raced full speed toward the wall-top steps. A Khelari rose in front of him, and he charged straight at the man without slackening stride, bashed both his sword and torch into the man's midsection, and shoved past. He threw himself to his knees on the middle step and readied the fuse, counting heads as the runners streamed past to gather outside the barracks. Paddy hurried down the opposite steps, dropped into position, and threw a quick *all's good* signal in his direction when Meli and the rest of the young ones emerged.

But Cade . . . there was no sign of Cade.

Or Slack.

Torch hovering over the fuse, Ky scanned the walkway. Side by side, with their backs to the bridge and one of the burn piles, the two battled three Khelari. Behind them, a score of Khelari crested the peak of the bridge while others choked the walkway, cutting them off and fast approaching the steps.

If Ky didn't light the fuse now, it would be too late.

He touched the flame to the string and held it there until it sizzled and caught and raced away toward the ryree-laced burn piles. He broke away, set his fingers to his lips, and whistled as loud and shrill as he could. Up on the walkway, Cade stabbed his opponent, kicked the man off his blade, and spun around. His eyes widened.

"Jump!" Ky shouted. "Jump!"

Cade caught Slack by the hand and threw himself over the edge of the walkway. They landed rolling in a snow heap and staggered upright. Seconds later, Ky's first burn pile exploded, followed a split second later by Paddy's, setting off a chain reaction that turned the walkway into a whirlwind of flying sparks, blazing chunks of pitch covered wood, and jagged bits of stone.

Ky thrust the screams from his mind. The flames would die all too soon. Feet skidding on ice-slick stones, he dashed up to the runners as arrows pelted the courtyard, hugged Meli to his side, shielding her with his body, and sprinted toward the gate.

He set his shoulder beneath the bar and shoved up.

A fiery blast ripped through the door.

33

As the echoes of her voice died away, Birdie drew a deep breath and steeled herself to withstand the wrath to come. Inali would not look her in the eyes, just stared down at his feet over the rims of his spectacles, mumbling beneath his breath. She turned from him in disgust. Whatever weakness resided in her, in this at least, she would be strong.

But the explosion of fury that she expected did not break.

A hint of amusement twisted the Takhran's lips, but he did not speak. Just regarded her with wise, knowing eyes that set fear churning in the pit of her stomach.

"I told you she would not yield." Zahar's deep voice broke the silence. She turned at last from the column where Rav's skeletal form was bound, and in the torchlight, her eyes blazed like embers. "My lord, she has refused the talav. Now honor your word. Release him."

"My dear." A tint of annoyance crept into the Takhran's tone. "You know how I honor my word, but no blade can break the bindings."

"I did not become the leader of your Shantren for naught. Perhaps no blade can break the bindings, but *you* can. You have your replacement. Twelve there are. Twelve there will remain."

"The little Songkeeper has a higher calling. Your brother made his choice. As did you."

"Release him." Zahar took a step forward, anguish shattering the rigid inflection of her voice. Such depth of feeling seemed to contradict everything Birdie had seen from the woman. "Seventeen years we have served you. You swore to uphold your oath."

A knife appeared in the Takhran's hand. "So I did." He weighed the blade in his hand, then slashed it across his open palm, clenched his hand into a fist, and held it over the man's restraints. At the first drop of blood, the iron bands cinched tighter and then snapped open. The man fell against the Takhran, and then crumpled to the ground at his feet, shuddering.

"No!" Zahar's scream startled Birdie.

Until she saw the knife protruding from Rav's thin chest.

Zahar seized her brother's shoulders and cradled his limp head until the shuddering ceased and his body stilled. Only then did she seem to awaken to the world around her again. She raised her face to the Takhran, expression devoid of all emotion and all the more frightening because of it. "You killed him ..."

The Takhran bent and jerked the knife free. "I released him." Dripping blade raised, he twisted around and stared Birdie full in the eye, then dipped his head in salute.

She stumbled back.

Then as if his gaze were the impetus she had needed, she took off at a run, like an arrow from a string. But it was too late. She knew it even as she pushed herself to run harder, heels slamming into the rock with enough force to jar her teeth. She cursed herself for not acting sooner. Caught up in the mystery of the Shantren and the talavs and every puzzling word that fell from the Takhran's mouth, she had missed her chance.

To be free ...

The blow from a wing snapped her from her feet.

She landed hard on her hands and knees, rocks tearing into her palms. Wincing, she twisted over onto her hip and tried to rise, but the raven steed stood over her, hooves penning her in, murderous beak inches from her throat. She could sense its hunger at the scent of blood and closed her hands over the stinging cuts.

"Let her rise."

At the Takhran's voice, the beast pulled back, allowing her to push up to her feet. Its beak clamped around her shoulder, blade like tip piercing the flesh and bringing a cry to her lips.

"Bring her here."

The raven steed spun on skittering hooves and pranced back toward the dome, dragging her with it. The arch of its neck forced her to scramble on tip toe to keep up, pain lancing through her shoulder with each step.

It deposited her at the Takhran's feet.

Before she could catch her breath, he seized her by the arm and slammed her against the dome. The back of her head smashed into the rock and spirals of light shot across her vision. "So good of you to wait for us, my dear." The edge of his blade slid into place against her throat, forcing her neck back so she looked up at him. "The sword and crystal, Dah Inali."

Rolling her eyes down and to the side, Birdie watched Inali remove the Star of the Desert from his satchel and hand it reverently to the Takhran, then kneel and open the flat box he had been carrying. She did not need to see to know what was inside.

Artair's sword.

"Do you know the other name for a talav?" The Takhran pinched the Star of the Desert between two fingers and lifted it to his eye. "A bloodstone. Fascinating, isn't it? With the blood drained from your people, I have built my forces. And it is the magic of this place, this hallowed Tal Ethel, that keeps the blood flowing. Yet by the time they truly die, their melodies have waned such that there is no power left in them. Such a waste. Imagine if all that power could be collected at once, in one *glorious* death."

Her muscles seized at that, but she dared not move with the knife digging into her throat. She could not speak, could not defend herself.

Could not even beg.

"Long have I sought for Artair's sword." The Takhran's eyes gleamed. "And here at the last, you stumble into my hands, the little Songkeeper and the missing Songkeeper's blade in answer to my desires."

"But what is it that you desire, my lord?" Inali sounded genuinely confused. "I have run your errands, done your bidding. I seek only to comprehend your—"

"Be still." The Takhran's voice cut across Inali's. "It is true that the whole world turns upon the notes of the Song, and yet the master melody is not alone. It is fraught with moments of disharmony and discord, a thousand melodies warring with one another to become paramount. In this, my melody has triumphed."

His voice rose in tempo and volume, and the pressure of the blade increased against Birdie's neck as his grip tightened, knuckles standing out rigid and white against his skin. Strangled sobs built in her throat. She gritted her teeth, trying to hold them back.

"You were not *meant* to wear a talav, little one, nor to become one of the twelve. You have a much higher purpose." He leaned in closer, as if to impart a secret. "In this . . . *beautiful* . . . disharmony I have orchestrated, the Songkeeper is slain by the Songkeeper's blade, and in the slaying, the most powerful talav imaginable is created, housed in the greatest crystal in Leira. It is . . . *a pity* . . . that you will not witness its glory."

Something like regret passed across his face.

An instant, then it was gone.

He reached behind. "The sword, Dah Inali."

"But, my lord, you—"

"The *sword*."

Birdie drew a final breath into her lungs and closed her eyes, waiting for the strike to fall. But instead of a blade whistling through the air, Inali's agonized scream rang out, followed by the clatter of metal on stone. Her eyes flew open again.

Inali stumbled into view, clutching a hand to his chest.

"A Songling should know better." Zahar's dull voice drew Birdie's eyes down, to where the woman knelt beside the lifeless form of her brother. "Here of all places, the blade will not suffer an unclean hand."

"Then you must do it." The Takhran's tone allowed for no argument.

"I am less a Songkeeper than the boy . . . but I do not fear pain." Slowly, as if each movement bore the knell of doom, Zahar rose, wound the hem of her robe around her hand, and knelt to retrieve the sword. The hilt sizzled in her grip and steam rose in coils.

But she did not cry out.

Over the Takhran's mail clad shoulder, Birdie met her eyes and recoiled from the hate broiling in their depths. But it was not directed at her. Mouth set in a snarl, Zahar seized the talav around her own neck and slid the sword across the chain, splitting it like a sapling twig. The crystal shattered into a thousand flying shards on the stones at her feet.

The skin on one half of her face shriveled.

It happened in an instant. One moment, Zahar's face was flawless. The next, blackened edges surrounded a raw and blistered center where a waxy thatch of muscle, sinew, and bone was visible. The breath rasped in her throat, and one arm dangled limp at her side, the hand seized into a claw.

Birdie gazed upon the wreck and ruin of the woman and could scarce comprehend it.

"Free …" A harsh sound, halfway between a laugh and a sob burst from Zahar's throat. She swayed and nearly fell, but caught herself with the tip of the sword on the ground, intent upon the Takhran. "You are a liar." She spat the words through ruined lips. "You slew my brother and stole both our lives. But now . . . I am *free*."

Reeling like a drunkard, she lunged at the Takhran.

He shoved Birdie away and turned aside Zahar's strike with a sweep of his knife. Heart hammering, Birdie rolled over the top of the dome, putting it between her and the fight. Had she a weapon, she would have charged into the fray. As it was, there was nothing she could do but watch and wait for an opening. Although Zahar was armed with a sword and the Takhran with naught but a knife, it became clear within moments that she had no chance against him. He fought with a savage ferocity that left her battered and bewildered, and he reveled in his mastery.

With a screech, the raven steed plunged into the fight, wings and forelegs beating the air, and Birdie knew that it was over. Zahar sidestepped a hoof-strike and delivered a heavy blow to its neck, releasing a spray of feathers and blood. But the maneuver brought her within the Takhran's reach. Before she could retreat, he seized her shoulder and dragged her closer.

Onto the knife in his hand.

Zahar's cry echoed through the Pit. Her body convulsed on the Takhran's blade, and he held her there, gazing into her eyes for what seemed an age before flinging her away. She collapsed beside Rav. A crimson stain seeped through her robe and spilled into the empty streambed, pooling around the Takhran's feet.

"I gave you *everything*." He spat the words over her body, then turned with a sweep of his robe and stalked back to the dome, one fist clenched to his forehead.

Birdie seized her chance. Half running, half crawling, she scrambled to Zahar's side. The woman's burned face had gone slack and cold. There was no life left in her limbs. Huddled beside her, Birdie's gaze leapt to the shocked expression on Inali's face, to the raven steed preening the feathers around its wound, and to the Takhran slumped against the dome, scrubbing the blade of his knife on his own robe.

Anger heated her blood to action.

Her hands were steady as she pried Artair's sword from Zahar's grip. The blade had eaten through the cloth Zahar had wrapped around her hand, and frost darkened her skin. Something about this hallowed place seemed to make the sword more potent and deadly than ever.

Gritting her teeth against the cold, Birdie hefted the blade in both hands and rose.

The raven steed screamed at her. Didn't attack. Just stuck out its long neck, revealing the crimson jewel planted in its iron collar, and screeched, as if the sound alone could frighten her off. Her first stroke tore through one wing, severing feathers and cracking the bone. That earned a real scream. Then the beast struck, beak clashing against her blade. A stray hoof caught her in the side, but she dodged in close and slashed the blade across its throat.

Its knees buckled and it fell with a thud.

The Takhran's pale blue eyes flickered up when she was scarce a step away, and surprise, disbelief, and disdain flashed across his features in less than a second. Mouth open in a wordless cry she lunged forward and stabbed the blade deep into his chest.

34

The force of the blast slammed into Ky, flinging him backward. His head smacked the ground, jarring his teeth, and sending waves of pain through his head. The world blurred into flickers of movement and blinding bursts of color, but no sound.

No sound but a high pitched keening in his ears.

Gasping, he rolled up onto his hands and knees, pain stabbing his side, head throbbing. He caught a flash of a dozen Khelari materializing out of the broiling smoke, then a glimpse of Cade leaping to fight them, Paddy at his side, and Syd with a sword in his hands.

But Meli . . . where was Meli?

His search seized on a small form curled in the snow a few yards away. Somehow he managed to force his limbs to move and crawled toward her. Looked to be asleep, her face was so peaceful. He reached for her and paused at the sight of his outstretched arm, gaping at his burned and blistered skin. Swallowing the pain, he hovered over her until he felt a faint breath of air on his cheek.

He shoved his arms beneath her and rocked back, cradling her against his chest, then surged to his feet. Gaze sweeping the courtyard, he staggered forward.

Ash filled the air. Half a dozen bodies lay twisted in the gateway—some Khelari, some from the Underground. Through the gate, he glimpsed the backs of the runners melting into the growing twilight as they raced to freedom and safety. Then the Khelari formed a line before the gate, blocking his only hope of escape.

His knees buckled, but a hand seized his elbow and kept him from falling.

"Oi, Ky, steady."

"Paddy?"

"Shure, who else? You didn't think I was goin' to leave you behind, did you?" Paddy steered him into a jog toward the wall-top steps where the ryree fires were only beginning to die down. Enough confusion reigned in the courtyard with the Underground escape and the onset of night that they made it to the first step before any Khelari started in pursuit. "Let's pick up the pace, shall we?"

Somehow, Ky willed his legs to run, though every step jarred his insides and practically blinded him with pain. Paddy was more than supporting his weight, he was almost carrying him and Meli both, up the wall-top steps through a haze of smoke and rubble.

Shouts behind.

Muted.

Heavy footsteps ahead.

A soldier loomed out of the haze.

Paddy's shove sent Ky staggering against the battlement, only just able to keep from dropping Meli. The staccato clatter of swords matched the uneven thudding of his heart as Paddy and the soldier went at it hammer and tong, but there was nothing he could do. He was unarmed. Sword gone. Strength gone. Sling-bullets all but spent.

Worthless in a fight.

His gaze latched onto one of the Khelari ladders still propped against the battlements, and he lurched toward it. All clear below. Supporting Meli with one arm despite the pain lancing through his ribs, he managed to drag himself up onto the battlements and swing out onto the ladder, giving him a clear view of Paddy's fight.

Sidestepping a thrust, Paddy brought his sword sweeping up under the Khelari's guard. The man stumbled back, clutching his arm to his side, and Paddy followed with his favorite pair of moves, a forward lunge and a slash at the midsection. The Khelari crumpled, and Ky breathed a sigh of relief as Paddy started toward the ladder.

Then everything went wrong. A second Khelari stormed out of the haze.

"Behind you!"

Paddy swung around and just managed to block the first strike. It threw him off balance, and he stepped wide to regain his footing. A mistake. The dark soldier's blade swept around and sliced across the back of his thigh, driving him to the ground with a cry.

Bile burned the back of Ky's throat, and he clutched at the ladder.

A weapon . . . he needed a weapon.

"No, Ky. Get out of here." Paddy struggled to rise and cradle his injured leg at the same time. "Please. For Meli's sake—"

"Stay down, *cur*." The dark soldier set a foot in Paddy's back and shoved him down, grinding his face against the stone. "We'll catch your little friend too, never fear."

"Go!"

Paddy's desperate voice broke Ky from his daze. Half a dozen Khelari raced along the walkway from the right. More from the left. Below, he caught snippets of voices rounding the curve of the keep. And here he was, pinned on a ladder, barely able to stand, let alone walk, with a girl in his arms.

A girl who was counting on him to keep her safe.

He had never felt so hopeless.

Paddy's eyes locked onto his, pleading, and somehow, he found his arms and legs moving without his command, carrying him down the ladder to freedom and safety. With each painful step, he swore that no matter how long it took, he would rescue his friend.

No one was getting left behind.

35

Cold unlike anything Birdie had ever known before seized her hand and radiated up her arm and into her chest, setting every nerve on fire, and drawing a cry of pain to her lips. She pulled the sword from the Takhran's chest and let it fall from her shaking fingers—fingers that were graying at the tips, as if the color had been drained from her skin. As she stared, the color slowly returned, and with it came a tingling rush of pain.

The Takhran reeled back, eyes wide and staring. He stumbled and dropped to his knees, catching himself with both hands in the streambed where Zahar and Rav's blood mingled. Head hanging, he knelt with his breath coming in gasps and blood dripping from his open mouth.

A flash of memory overtook Birdie. For a moment, it seemed as though she saw herself as she had in the Hollow Cave. *Standing in the dark of the Pit. Artair's sword in her hand.*

Bodies all around.

She blinked and emerged into the present, catching Inali staring, eyes bulging behind his spectacles. His horror unsettled her. Whether it was directed at her or the Takhran, she could not say. But it shook her into motion.

Drawn almost against her will, Birdie crouched over Zahar and touched a quivering finger to her neck in search of a pulse, a breath, any sign of life. *There.* A flicker of movement. She yanked the cloak from her shoulders and pressed it against the gaping wound, hoping, as warm blood seeped through and spurted over her fingers, that it would be enough.

Whoever Zahar truly was, whoever she had become, surely she did not deserve to die like this, bleeding out on the floor of the Pit.

Forsaken.

A low chuckle sent a shiver down her spine.

She knew what she would see, even before she turned around. The Takhran no longer knelt in the streambed, but stood with his hands clenched into fists at his sides, blood dripping between his fingers, the wound in his chest gradually sealing before her eyes. The red jewels in his wide silver collar pulsed with the dull blaze of embers.

"You cannot harm me, little Songkeeper. Do your worst! Release Tal Ethel, if you think yourself able. Its power will become mine. Life unending in my grasp. You cannot win."

And Birdie believed him.

Believed him with every ounce of certainty in her heart. This mission was madness. To think that she could stand against the monster who crushed armies and toppled kingdoms, who used people as pawns until they were worn through and then cast them aside to be trampled in the dust, who bled her people dry to siphon their strength and make it his …

What hope had she against such as him?

"Come away, little one." Inali's terrified voice whispered in her ear. "Come away."

"Help me." She strained to lift Zahar's limp form.

It was a foolish burden to take on, perhaps, but everything they had done so far had been foolish, and Birdie could not simply leave her behind. Inali bore the brunt of it, but together they managed to lift the woman. She sagged in their arms, moaning, as they took off toward the iron staircase. Birdie tried not to think about the warm blood running down her shoulder and seeping into her tunic, tried not to wonder if there was any point to any of this anymore, as the Takhran's chuckle chased them across the broken surface of the Pit.

"Run, little Songkeeper, you cannot get far."

And yet he did not follow.

Perhaps her sword strike had done some harm, even if it was merely temporary.

Wings fluttered overhead, and Birdie knew that a raven followed high above, where weapons could not reach. It could alert the soldiers to their coming and bear tidings of their path wherever they went, making escape impossible. But for now, there was nothing to do but run.

Run like cornered beasts, charging blindly at the walls of their trap.

Up the staircase they climbed, lungs heaving, legs burning with the strain of supporting Zahar. At the top, a dark soldier raced toward them, and Birdie reached for her sword, only to recall that it still lay in the empty streambed below.

"This way!" The soldier tossed the helmet aside, revealing Sym's snapping eyes and wild braids. "No time to delay."

"But . . . Amos? Where is he?" Birdie scanned the cavern. Clumps of wounded and dead Khelari littered the ground beside the corpse of a massive, three-headed monster of a beast, but there were countless more soldiers racing toward them, and even more pouring in from the tunnels every second.

Across the Pit, the light of a torch flared on red hair where Amos fought with sword and dirk against three Khelari. He was tiring, Birdie could see that. Strokes coming slower and slower, steps lagging, armor rent and broken. Another moment, and he would be on the retreat. He blocked the next strike, but his foot slipped and his opponent flung him back.

Straight into the path of one of the three-headed monsters.

The warning died on Birdie's tongue as the beast pounced, lion's head seizing Amos in its jaws and shaking him like a leaf. One set of flashing claws tore the breastplate from his chest. Then it flung him down again, the jolt snapping his head back with a force that should have stunned him. It crouched for the kill, but Amos brought a fist up to guard his throat, and the snake's head sank its fangs into his hand instead.

Still he managed to batter his way free and stagger to his feet, assuming the wide-footed stance and belligerent broad-shouldered pose that she knew so well.

Then the goat head rammed its horns into his chest.

Birdie's breath caught in her throat. Her ears burned with the peddler's agonized scream—a scream that she was too far away to have truly heard. She had no power to speak or cry out, nothing but the blinding impulse to move, to go to Amos though a hundred Khelari stood in her path. To save him.

As he had saved her, over and over again.

"We must go, little Songkeeper." Sym seized her shoulders and wrenched her away. "There is nothing you can do. We must leave."

Birdie lashed out blindly, but the Saari warrior held her tight and dragged her after Inali and Zahar. Her vision faded until there was nothing but dull flashes of torchlight, and she heard nothing but the thudding of feet mingling with the hammering of the blood in her ears, and felt nothing but the sickening sensation of movement and of loss.

36

Frantic barking jolted Birdie, drawing her back to herself. They were running along the far edge of the cavern toward a series of tunnels that led back beneath the arms of the mountain, with the raven winging overhead, and the sounds of pursuit close upon their heels.

A hound appeared alongside, and Sym spun to slay the beast, but a familiar rasping voice sounded in Birdie's ear. "Little Songkeeper, I said we would meet again."

"Renegade?" Birdie found her voice again and with it her wits. She caught Sym's arm before the blow could fall. "Wait. He's a friend."

The beast's white eyes glinted up at her. "Follow me." He took off at a bound, and wordlessly, Birdie started after him. They ran at full tilt now, Sym aiding Inali with Zahar, Renegade steering them toward the nearest tunnel. But just before they arrived, a dozen Khelari clattered out and drew up in rigid formation before the opening.

Cursing, the hound skidded to a halt, and Birdie nearly fell over him in her haste. The soldiers advanced toward them, and Sym danced out in front of Inali, a pair of spears whirling in her hands.

"Catch!" She yelled to Birdie.

On reflex, Birdie's hand shot out and caught the spear, but she found she could not move beyond that. She just stood there, clutching the unfamiliar weapon, watching as the soldiers closed in, all grins and brandished weapons and muttered strains of the discordant song. But she was too weary, too soul-sick and broken inside, to even care.

A screech rent the air.

The broken body of a raven landed at Sym's feet. With a roar like that of thunder, in a storm of feathers, beating wings, and flashing claws, Gundhrold bowled into the Khelari, knocking three down at the first pass. He pounced and brought down another two, then Sym leapt to his side, cutting through the Khelari like a scythe through wheat with Renegade at her heels.

In a moment, the dozen Khelari lay expiring on the ground or had fled into the tunnels. Birdie stumbled forward and found herself caught and held beneath the griffin's wing. There was no time to wonder how or why he had come. The cavern was alive with shouts and cries and the clatter of weapons and armor.

A brazen horn call rang out somewhere in the depths of the tunnels before them, and the color faded from Inali's cheeks. "They are calling out the Shantren."

Sym helped him lift Zahar to the griffin's back. "Then we must leave before they regroup."

A wet muzzle pressed into the hollow of Birdie's palm, and she glanced down into the blank eyes of the hound. He nudged her forward, teeth showing in a snarl. "Go, little Songkeeper. You will know the way. I will draw them off your scent. Go and do not stop."

With a grunt, he spun around and took off down one of the side tunnels, baying in a voice that could shatter stone. And in his wake, tendrils of the Song crept up around Birdie. She shrank from the melody that had not answered when she called, but it would not be silenced. It filled her ears with whispers of music and lit the path before her eyes.

What choice did she have but to follow?

With the others at her heels, Birdie chased after the Song into the dark of a tunnel without torches, down through the maze of passages beneath the mountain, and out at last onto a snow covered hillside beneath the light of a waning moon and the morning star.

A distant roll of thunder greeted her, and energy charged air sent tingles spidering across her skin. In the east, three bright stars hovered over the horizon, bearing in their radiating beams of light a three-noted harmony that spoke of warmth and life and growing things. A warm breeze sprang up, ruffling the hair plastered to her neck and leeching the chill from the air. In minutes, the melting snow squelched beneath her feet.

Spring Turning had arrived.

Murmured voices drew her gaze to Sym and Inali as they lifted Zahar from Gundhrold's back and laid her down on a cloak, then worked feverishly to tend her wounds. Birdie hung back, studying the blood staining her upturned hands. They were still now, as if broken at last of the cursed tremors that had plagued her. She should help. After all, it had been her decision to rescue Zahar from the Pit. But no matter the reasoning, she couldn't muster the motivation or stomach for the work or the company. Inali had betrayed her. Zahar was one of the Shantren.

Yet for some reason, *they* had escaped . . .

She felt the griffin's eyes resting on her, and welcomed the distraction from the bitterness of her thoughts. "How did you know to come?

With a rustle of feathers and folding wings, he settled on his haunches beside her and heaved a deep sigh. "The Master Singer does not speak to me in the same way that he speaks to you, little one, nor can I hear the grand, sweeping melody of the Song. Yet I am a Protector. I sensed that you were in danger, and I came. It is as simple as that."

Simple, perhaps, but no easy task.

Zahar moaned and her eyes flickered open, roving in a wild circle before settling at last on the griffin at Birdie's side. Sorrow bloomed in the uninjured half of her face. "So . . ." Her voice was so low that Birdie could scarce hear it. "We meet again."

"You were dead." Never one to mince words, Gundhrold padded over to her, and Birdie followed, reluctant to leave his side. "I saw you fall."

"Fall, yes, to chimera venom and flame." Zahar's eyes misted over. "But not dead. That would have been better by far. I survived . . . and Rav traded his life for my healing. I took the talav, *his* bloodstone, but only once the Takhran swore that he would be released one day." She laughed, a low, choking laugh that brought blood spilling from her lips. "Betrayal. It is his favorite weapon. And yet... he cannot fathom when it is employed against him."

Her eyelids drifted shut.

Birdie seized her hand. "No! What about Tal Ethel? What do you know of the Songkeeper of legend?"

"Only . . ." Zahar's gaze drifted up to Gundhrold. "Only that you . . . must release Tal Ethel . . . our last hope . . . defeat the Takhran." Her face had gone whiter than the melting snow, yet somehow she managed to lift a trembling arm to point at Inali. "You cannot trust . . . one wearing the talav . . . the sword . . . must remove it . . . the sword . . ."

Then her arm went limp and her eyes sank.

And Birdie knew that she was gone.

The griffin's wing settled around her shoulders, and she endured it, though it brought no comfort. She just sat there, listening to the *drip drip* of melting ice mingling with the gasp of breath leaving Zahar's lungs and the echo of the peddler's agonized scream. But it was not sorrow that burned and broiled in her chest . . . it was rage.

Finally, Inali spoke. "I should leave you now."

"Leave us?" Gundhrold surged to his feet, hackles bristling along his neck and back. "So you may return to your master and tell where we have gone?"

Inali's mouth dropped open. "My life is forfeit for what I have done."

The griffin rumbled an assent.

"No, you do not understand. I cannot return." Inali's voice shook. "Death awaits me in Serrin Vroi. You think I betrayed you, but I only meant to aid the little Songkeeper. To offer her the freedom that my master gave me. My intentions were good."

"For your own good, perhaps." The griffin stalked forward, muscles standing out like cords on his chest. "Sheathe your tongue, twice accursed traitor. If you are doomed either way, far better that we end you here and leave your rotting corpse for your master to find. I offer you a swift death. Will the Takhran be so merciful?"

Inali backed away, stumbling over his own feet in his haste. "Wait . . . wait. I *helped* you escape. Betrayed my master for it. Sigurd's mane! Whatever my error, I have atoned for it."

But his words had no effect on the griffin.

It was all spiraling out of control. Birdie had that dizzying sense that the world was crumbling around her, and there was nothing she could do to steady it. In another moment, Inali would flee and Gundhrold would attack, and she couldn't reason out the right or wrong of it. All she knew was that she had seen enough bloodshed and spilled enough of it herself to last many lifetimes. The thought of more sickened her.

Inali broke and ran, and with a grunt, the griffin raced after him. The Saari warrior's legs might not have had the ground-devouring power of the griffin's, but he was spry. At the last moment, he dodged to the side, and Gundhrold skidded past him. But before Inali could disappear over the hillside, something whirled through the air and struck the back of his head. He crumpled facedown in the snow.

Sym materialized out of the predawn gray and bent to retrieve her spear. Holding it in both hands, she stared down at the limp form at her feet, expression unreadable in the dim light.

The griffin halted at her side. "We cannot leave him to wander free."

"No, we cannot." With a determined nod, Sym slid the spear into the quiver on her back. "He must answer to desert justice for his crimes. I will escort him there and leave him to the judgement of the Matlal." Her eyes darted across the hillside. "And the sooner we are gone from this cursed place, the better. What of you, griffin?"

"It is for the Songkeeper to determine my path."

The griffin's quiet words hung on the air, an invitation. But Birdie didn't know what to say. She shrank from his penetrating gaze and let her own fall past Zahar's body to the snow seeping into the thirsty earth beneath her feet. There was no one left. No place to go. Nowhere to turn. She had not a friend left in the wide world save the griffin and . . .

Ky.

• • •

Drooping with pain and an exhaustion so deep it sapped the strength from his limbs, Ky stumbled into the midst of the runners gathered in a hollow not far from Siranos. Meli walked alongside, half leading him, half supporting him, until he dropped with his back to a fallen boulder and let his head sag back against it.

Without a word of welcome or greeting, Slack tossed him a water flask. Her face looked stony and grim in the moonlight. He offered the flask to Meli first, but she pushed it back at him, so he lifted it with trembling hands to his mouth and let the glorious burst of coolness wash over his tongue and down his throat.

He wanted to bathe in it.

Bathe both body and mind and somehow wash the horrors of this night away.

A tug on his sleeve pulled him from his thoughts. Syd crouched at his side and stared solemn eyed up at him, a question marked into his brow. Ky just shook his head, unable to speak for the lump lodged in his throat. A wordless cry burst from the boy's lips, and he rammed a fist against his mouth to hold it in and dropped, shuddering, to the ground.

Ky turned away.

His oath burned within him, and he longed to take off into battle, storm the keep with just his sling and his stones, and rescue Paddy from the Khelari—even if it meant he would be taken instead. But the Underground needed him.

It wasn't safe for them to just *sit* here. He had found them easily enough. How long would it take the cursed hounds? Steeling himself against the pain of his injuries, he pushed to his feet. "Where's Cade?"

Slack tipped her head toward the far side of the hollow where a tall figure sat with his head bowed and his back toward the others. As Ky neared, he could make out the smaller form lying in Cade's lap.

Aliyah.

Words failed him at the sight. Yet another horror to feed the dark pool churning in his chest. Ky eased himself to the ground at

Cade's side, but the older boy never once looked at him, just stared straight ahead, cradling Aliyah's lifeless body in his arms. Her head was tipped back, hair spilling over Cade's knees, eyes gazing unseeing at the stars. The broken stubs of two Khelari shafts protruded from her chest.

"Cade …"

No answer.

Ky cleared his throat and began again, gentling the words as much as possible. "Cade, we need to move. It won't be long before they set the hounds after us."

"Let them come."

"We have to get the Underground to safety firs—"

"Not anymore!" Cade spat out and twisted to face him. For once, the mask of control that usually commanded his features was completely gone. His face was pale and lined with sorrow. "I killed her, Ky." His voice broke. "It's my fault she's dead."

Ky saw the raw anguish in Cade's eyes and glanced down, down at his own burned hand. He couldn't face this now, not with Paddy's capture and Migdon's death hanging so heavy around his shoulders. Because it was *his* fault. Not Cade's. All of this. Beyond the hollow, crickets chirped and glimmer moths buzzed through the air, signs that Winter Turning was indeed over. With each Turning, there was an air of eager expectancy for something new—a change of pace, a new stage in life.

The air reeked of change all right, Ky just doubted its goodness.

When Cade spoke again, his voice had regained its measured strength, though there was still a brittle quality to it. "I'm leaving the Underground. Take them somewhere safe. You'll look after them better than I." His voice fell. "I'm done."

"Where will you go?"

But Ky knew the answer, even as he asked.

Cade's gaze slid forward once more. "I have a score to settle with the Khelari."

37

Sleep did not come to her that night, as it had not come for many nights since she had braved the horrors of the Pit. Birdie sat on the bare hillside with her arms clasped around her knees, watching the slow, flickering dance of the three spring stars above the eastern horizon, while the griffin slumbered but a few feet away, head tucked beneath his wing, and behind her, the sea crashed against the base of the cliff below.

Three weeks had passed since they emerged from the maze of tunnels onto the slope of Mount Eiphyr. Three weeks since Sym and Inali split off on their own. Three weeks of wandering the mountains north of Serrin Vroi, just her and Gundhrold, ever on the lookout for Khelari, hounds, or ravens on their trail.

And yet the three weeks had done nothing to ease the ache inside.

Or the agony.

It burned until Birdie could no longer sit still. It drove her to her feet, past the griffin, and out along the cliff edge. Walking, then running, heedless of peril, until she gasped for breath and came to a stop, gazing out over the tumultuous sea far below, pallid in the moonlight.

"Why?" She forced all her fear, anger, and sorrow into the words. "Why are you silent?"

A gentle breeze toyed with her hair, playful at first, lifting it from her neck and tangling it in knots, then turned to whipping the loose fabric of her tunic. It crescendoed into a gale that howled over the edge of the cliff and lashed the ocean waves below into a boiling frenzy. The cliff shuddered beneath Birdie's feet, and she dropped to her knees, digging her fingers into the trembling earth.

But the Song was silent.

Thunder cracked overhead and a bolt of lightning crashed into the hillside, striking a hallorm tree only a few feet away. Flames sprang up and devoured the leaves and long-fingered branches, belching smoke that settled over Birdie like a cloud, then thunder rolled again, and a drop of moisture hit her bowed neck.

But the Song was silent.

She crawled to the edge of the cliff and sat with her legs dangling over the drop to the sea below, while the clouds above burst and rain broke over the hillside, smothering the flames and washing the stench of smoke away.

"Where are you?" she whispered. "Have you abandoned us?"

The rain slackened then, and even the wind died down until it was nothing more than a whisper trailing through the rocks and spring grasses, but in that whisper, she at last heard the notes of the Song. So soft, they were scarce discernable over the breath of wind.

She held her breath.

The notes crept toward her and around her, visible now, like specks of fire, of light, of power untold. They swept over and through her, gentle but fierce. Tearing but rebuilding anew. Behind them, the vast melody rose in all its glorious splendor to surround her, and she felt herself pulled into the warmth of that embrace.

Listen, little Songkeeper, the voice whispered, *and I will sing you a Song.*

ACKNOWLEDGEMENTS

Writing a novel is a bit like blacksmithing, I think. As a writer, you take an unwieldy lump of an idea and work it into shape. It isn't an easy process, nor a pretty one. There are plenty of sparks along the way, and you might get burned by a molten shard or two. But eventually the novel is hammered out into a blunt and unseemly approximation of what it is meant to be. And then the real work starts. The refining. The hammering. The tempering. Until lo and behold, at the end of the day, a battleworthy novel rests in your hands.

So here you have it, my friends, *Songkeeper*, razor sharp, double edged, and honed for the fight! But (thankfully) I was not left to wordsmith (or stretch metaphors) alone. So to Steve Laube, my publisher and editor, a heartfelt thanks for helping to make my books truly "*shiny*," and also to Amanda Leudeke, my agent, for continuing to believe in my harebrained novel ideas.

To my friends and family, thank you for your support and patience when I disappear into my storyworlds for lengthy periods of times, and for never failing to ask me when the next book is coming out. Your enthusiasm is what gives me the incentive to grit my teeth at the end of a long day and keep typing away.

To Brynne, my absolutely brilliant big sister, thank you for being my go-to design expert and for the dozens of projects you have willingly taken on for me over the past few years as "birthday" and "Christmas" presents. I hope you don't regret giving me such a dangerous gift, because I have *so* taken advantage of it! And a huge thank you goes to you, my readers! Honestly, you folks are amazing. Knowing you are out there makes writing a book both a thousand times more difficult—because I am terrified of letting you down—and a thousand times more rewarding—because I am thrilled to know that you care so deeply about these characters of mine.

Thank you for embarking on this journey with me.

ABOUT THE AUTHOR

Gillian Bronte Adams is a sword-wielding, horse-riding, coffee-loving speculative fiction author from the great state of Texas. A love of epic stories and a desire to present truth in a new way drew her to the realm of fantasy. During the day, she manages the equestrian program at a Christian youth camp. But at night, she kicks off her boots and spurs, pulls out her trusty laptop, and transforms into a novelist.

Visit her web site: www.GillianBronteAdams.com

THE SONGKEEPER CHRONICLES BOOK I
ORPHAN'S
SONG
GILLIAN BRONTE
ADAMS